Dear Reader,

This month I'm delighted to include another book by Kay Gregory, whose first ***Scarlet*** novel, *Marry Me Stranger* was such a hit with you all. You can also enjoy the second book in Liz Fielding's intriguing 'Beaumont Brides' trilogy.' Then we have another romance from talented author Maxine Barry. *Destinies* is a complete novel in itself, but we're sure you'll want to read *Resolutions* next month to find out 'what happens next!' And finally, we're very pleased to bring you another new author – Laura Bradley has produced an exciting and page-turning story.

Do let me know, won't you, what you think of the titles we've chosen for you this month? Do *you* enjoy linked books and books with a touch of mystery or do you like your romance uncluttered by other elements?

By the way, thank you if you've already written to me. I promise I *shall* answer your letter as soon as I can. Your comments will certainly help me plan our list over the coming months.

Till next month,

Sally Cooper

SALLY COOPER,
Editor – ***Scarlet***

About the Author

Kay Gregory was born and educated in England. Shortly after moving to Victoria, Canada, she met her husband in the unromantic setting of a dog club banquet! Since 1961, Kay and her husband have lived in the Vancouver area, and they have two grown sons who frequently return home to commune with the contents of the family fridge!

At various times, Kay has cohabited, more or less willingly, with dogs, hamsters, gerbils, rats and ferrets . . . currently down to one neurotic dog. Over the years, Kay has had more jobs than she can count: everything from packaging paper bags (the bags won and she lost the job!) to running a health food bar, cleaning offices and working as a not-very-efficient secretary.

As the author of twenty plus romance novels, Kay says: 'Writing books is definitely the best job I've ever had and one I don't plan to change. Selling my first long contemporary novel (*Marry Me Stranger*) to ***Scarlet*** was one of the most exciting things that has happened to me.'

KAY GREGORY

THE SHERRABY BRIDES

Enquiries to:
Robinson Publishing Ltd
7 Kensington Church Court
London W8 4SP

First published in the UK by Scarlet, 1997

A copy of the British Library Cataloguing in Publication data is available from the British Library

ISBN 1–85487–713–5

Printed and bound in the EC

10 9 8 7 6 5 4 3 2 1

To MARK, who invented Sherraby and introduced me to Lincolnshire. With love and thanks for a lifetime of friendship.

CHAPTER 1

'Ripper! Rip? What the devil have you eaten this time?'

Shaking his head, Simon bent to pick up a battered red exercise book that lay face-down on the top step in front of Sherraby Manor's solid barrier of a door. He frowned at the book, which was riddled with tooth-marks, and looked around for the owner of the teeth. But Rip had evaporated discreetly into the soft summer air, a talent he frequently employed when it seemed expedient to avoid his master's notice.

Simon shrugged and carried on until he came to a narrower but no less solid door set into the wall on the north side of the sprawling, ivy-covered house. He pushed it open and stepped into an old-fashioned kitchen with an enormous Elizabethan fireplace.

'Mmm. I smell the smell of friendly bread, and it's ambrosia to my nose,' he murmured, sniffing pleasurably as remnants of his classical education returned unexpectedly to inspire him to heights of misquotation. 'Good morning, Mrs Leigh. Bread-baking day, is it?'

'As you very well know, Mr Simon,' replied a thin woman with spiky grey hair who was sitting at the table shelling peas. 'And no, you can't have a slice. It's not done yet.'

Simon grinned. Mrs Leigh still thought of him as the little boy who had hung around her kitchen for years, waiting to scrape bowls, lick spoons and be the first to test sweets as they emerged from the oven. And he had to admit he had always felt more at home here than anywhere else in the house. There was something about the fresh gingham curtains, the antique copper warming pans and even the red, decidedly modern countertops that lent the big room an air of warmth and country comfort which always drew him back.

'I see the Ripper got at the post again,' he remarked, propping himself against the nearest whitewashed wall.

Mrs Leigh shook her head. 'No, he didn't. Not this time. Mr Cousins brought the letters up from the gatehouse. He said he beat that Ripper to it this morning and took them off the postman before they got ate.' She picked up a pea that had escaped on to the table and popped it into her mouth. 'You ought to get one of them wire baskets to put on the door, Mr Simon. That'd stop the little devil from making a meal of your mail.'

'No doubt it would. I *had* hoped to teach him to concentrate his energies on the bills and debit statements. But he's a slow learner.' Simon threw the cook a poker-faced look as he headed out of the kitchen.

'Go on with you.' The lines around Mrs Leigh's mouth cracked into a smile. 'Find a dog who could do that and you'd make a fortune.' She dropped a pea-pod then added with a self-conscious laugh, 'If you wanted to, that is.'

Simon smiled slightly and didn't answer. No, a second fortune wasn't high on his list of priorities.

He left Mrs Leigh to her pea-shelling and made his way along the narrow brick passage that led into the manor's main hall. Portraits of frowning and long-dead Sebastians stared down at him from the walls as he crossed to a delicate Chinese table placed strategically beside the seldom-used door. Ignoring the ancestors, he pulled open the table's Ripper-proof drawer and removed a fat pile of correspondence. No toothmarks on the letters for a change. Good. He tucked the pile under his arm, along with the chewed exercise book, and headed for the stairs up to the gallery and the bedrooms.

With a vague sense of pleasure, he noticed the morning sun had cut a bright swathe of yellow across the thick blue quilt that covered his ancestral four-poster. A good sign. He'd picked the right week to start his holidays. Tossing the mail on top of the quilt, he went to look out of the window.

In the distance, puffy clouds drifted above low, tree-dotted hills. Closer to home, smooth lawns sloped down from a paved terrace to the edge of a jade-green lake, and, as he watched, two ducks waddled to the edge of the water and splashed in.

A peaceful scene. Sherraby at its most seductive and bucolic. Simon frowned, and shook his head with an unexpected twinge of regret.

Six years ago, when he had made the decision to trade in one life of shadows and secrets for another, he hadn't taken the time to think much about what he would be missing. If he had, then maybe he would have taken up a different occupation. One closer to home. As it was, there had been little opportunity to play the country squire these last few years. Until now, when for a week or two at least it seemed safe to leave business in the hands of his more than competent junior partner.

If there were problems, Zack Kent could be trusted to get in touch with him at once.

A small grey squirrel scuttled across the grass as Simon turned reluctantly from the window and began to leaf through his pile of correspondence.

Bills, a couple of invitations to parties featuring very young women and their marriage-minded mothers, a petulant note from Althea, his current and soon-to-be-history girlfriend, requests for donations – and a postcard from his cousin Emma, now basking in the sun somewhere in Greece with her latest conquest. Nothing of vital importance. At least not to him. He read the postcard, smiled at Emma's typically frantic scrawl, and was about to shove the whole lot into a drawer when his eye fell on the mysterious red book.

If it hadn't come with the post, where *had* it come from?

He picked it up. No name on the front. No name on the inside page either. Only a date followed by a page of neat, rather precise handwriting. He tried the last page. It was blank, so he flipped back to where the writing came to an end. Just three and a half sentences dated two days earlier.

'Jamie and I are having a picnic in Sherraby Woods. If only Dan could be with us. Dan as he used to be, not as he was in the end . . .'

The last word trailed off as if the writer's pen had slipped on the paper.

Simon sat down on the bed and leafed through the rest of the book. It seemed to be a diary started just over eight years ago and added to, sporadically, until the present. But there was no name on any of the pages, no address or phone number. Nothing to identify its owner. More out of habit than curiosity, he ran his eye over the first few paragraphs.

He had read another six before he put the diary down.

The writer was a woman, young and filled with vitality. He could tell that much. Intelligent too. It showed in the quality of her writing. She was also very much in love with her husband, whose name was Dan.

Dan? Simon ran a hand round the back of his neck. Was there a Dan living in the village who fitted the description in the diary? Not that he could think of. He read on, skimming the text for information that would help him to identify the writer – who appeared to have an uncommonly happy marriage.

A child was born to the star-kissed couple. His name was Jamie. The marriage was still deliriously happy. Then Dan lost his job. Consternation, but no less love and optimism. The writer was a tenacious woman, intensely loyal and filled with determination that her out-of-work husband would find employment whether he chose to make the effort or not. Simon's eyebrows lifted. This lady was by no means all sugar and spice.

He read that Dan had started to drink. His wife coped with that too. Supported him, tried to keep drink away from him, urged him to get help, and all the time worked to make sure that the child was shielded from any knowledge of his father's excesses. She seemed to have kept the family together by sheer willpower, but it was all too obvious this was a woman who had suffered deeply over a period of some years.

Perhaps the diary had been her escape – her way of coping with stress.

Except for one or two very brief entries like the one about the picnic in the woods, she had stopped writing ten months ago when Dan had suddenly caught pneumonia and died.

No great loss, thought Simon.

At that point it occurred to him that without setting out to, and more or less by accident, he had just read all of some unknown woman's very private diary. Not that she had any reason to be embarrassed by what she'd written – and since he had no idea who she was, there wasn't much he could do about it anyway.

He put the book into a drawer along with the letters and bills, and went downstairs to tell Cousins to saddle Cactus.

Without any real hope, Olivia poked through a layer of last year's rotting leaves between the exposed roots of a battered old oak tree. Nothing there except a few disgruntled beetles. She sat back on her heels and glanced briefly at the whispering summer foliage overhead.

What now? There was nowhere on the carpet of bright green moss at her feet where a flat red book could easily lie concealed. Nor was there any sign that some other visitor had recently disturbed the peace of this secluded woodland glade. Except – hadn't she heard an animal of some sort on the day she and Jamie had their picnic? Yes, a rabbit probably, or perhaps a fox. Or even a dog.

She cast a dubious eye at the mat of tangled greenery on the edge of the clearing. It didn't look all that prickly . . .

Making up her mind, Olivia dropped to her hands and knees, and began to crawl through a thick clump of bracken, groping in the underbrush for anything that wasn't plant or animal life.

She came up with more beetles and something wet and squishy that smelled of mould. She decided not to investigate further.

This was hopeless. Wherever her diary might be, she wasn't going to find it today. She might as well give up, and hope it hadn't fallen into the hands of a bunch of giggling schoolboys. Or their parents.

Moving cautiously, she began to ease her way out of the bracken.

Behind her, a man cleared his throat.

Olivia froze. Fear, unreasoning and instinctive, tightened her muscles and siphoned the breath from her lungs. She was alone in the woods with a man who had appeared out of nowhere. The palms of her hands were clammy with sweat as slowly, very slowly, she backed out of the bushes and turned around.

Boots. Brown, quality leather boots planted next to a small brown and white dog that looked like a cross between a terrier and a used paintbrush. Olivia allowed her gaze to travel upwards over well-used, snugly fitting breeches encasing legs that seemed to go on up forever. She paused when she came to the waist, drawing breath before she carried on over a white, open-necked shirt stretched across a formidable chest, and up to a rugged, deeply tanned face topped by thick bronze-coloured hair. Longish hair, waving just below the neck. She eyed it for quite some time before she dredged up the courage to study the man feature by feature.

Ouch. Classic country beefcake. A tough, self-assured face, with piercing, surprisingly icy blue eyes. A broad forehead, strong cheekbones, slightly cleft chin and full lips over the whitest, straightest teeth she had ever seen. Teeth that were currently parted in a tauntingly provocative smile which would have been heart-stopping if her heart had still been up to being stopped.

'Who are you? What the hell do you think you're doing here?' Olivia demanded, nervousness making her belligerent.

The smile broadened, became positively wolf-like. 'Simon Sebastian. These are my woods. And if you want the truth, I was admiring your bottom. It's a very nice one.'

Olivia discovered she wasn't nervous any more. She was angry, embarrassed and resentful. But definitely not frightened.

'My body parts are none of your business,' she snapped.

'No?' Simon Sebastian shrugged and went to drape himself against the nearest birch tree. 'I was afraid it was too good to be true.'

Olivia glared. 'What was?'

'The perfect end – and I use the word advisedly – to a pleasant walk with the Ripper.'

His voice held no hint of mockery now but she didn't miss the ironic blue glitter in his eyes. Olivia felt her temper flare again at once. 'These may be your woods, Mr Sebastian, and I suppose, technically, I'm trespassing –'

'Technically, I suppose you are. But according to centuries of custom, you do have a right to walk here. And I have no objection to your adding a touch of glamour to my bushes.'

'Glamour?' Olivia stumbled to her feet. 'In faded jeans and my old black sweatshirt? I'm not that easily flattered, Mr –'

'Simon. Forget the mister. No need to stand on ceremony, Ms . . .? He raised an eyebrow in enquiry.

Nice eyebrows, Olivia thought vaguely. Thick and deeply bronzed like his hair.

'Olivia Naismith,' she admitted grudgingly. 'Look, I'm sorry if. . .' She stopped. She had been going to say, 'if I disturbed you.' But Simon Sebastian didn't look remotely disturbed. Lounging against the tree with his arms crossed and the paintbrush sitting docilely at his feet, he was the picture of confidence and ease – lord and master of his domain. Which, of course, was exactly what he was. Not a lord, but certainly landed gentry. If there was such a thing any more.

'What are you sorry for, Olivia Naismith? I haven't seen you in the village before, have I?'

Olivia decided not to answer the first part of his question. 'No. My son and I only moved down from London a month ago. But Mrs Critchley – she's our landlady – said you wouldn't mind us having a picnic on your grounds.'

'I don't mind.' Simon's ice-blue glance scanned the tranquil little glade and came to rest meaningfully on the undisturbed moss at her feet. 'At least I wouldn't if I saw the slightest indication that you were, in fact, having a picnic.'

'Not now. Two days ago.'

'I see. So to what do we owe the honour of your return? Missing the odd crumb or soggy sandwich, are we?'

What Olivia was actually missing was a suitable object to throw. 'I lost something that belonged to me,' she said coldly. 'Jamie's in school, so I came back to see if I could find it.'

She wasn't sure what alerted her to the sudden change in Simon's attitude. It wasn't his face, which remained as bland and unrevealing as ever. Nor did his position change in any way. But she knew she had his total attention.

'Jamie?' he repeated. 'Your son?'

'Yes.'

'I see. And what have you lost, Olivia?'

Why did she sense that he already knew the answer? He couldn't, could he? Unless . . .

'A red exercise book,' she said quickly. 'Have you seen it?'

He didn't answer directly. 'An exercise book? What's so important about an exercise book?'

'I – it's my diary. *Have* you seen it?' She tried to keep calm, to keep any note of panic from her voice.

But there wasn't much point in beating about the bush. If this exasperating man had found her diary, there was every chance he already knew what it was. The thought made Olivia lower her gaze quickly to the moss.

She waited for him to respond. A wood-pigeon cooed somewhere among the trees, a soft sound that usually made her smile.

Today it didn't.

'I may have seen it,' Simon admitted, after what seemed like an aeon. 'Was it full of toothmarks?'

Olivia raised startled eyes to his. 'No! At least – not when I last saw it.'

'Mmm. Doesn't mean much. Not when you factor in the Ripper.'

The Ripper wagged his short, stubby tail.

Olivia swept a wing of dark hair out of her eyes. 'You mean – he ate it?'

'If we're talking about the same red book, he certainly sampled it. But don't worry, he didn't actually digest it.'

Olivia swallowed. 'Have you – have you still got it?' She wasn't sure what she wanted him to answer. Her diary was important to her. It had been ever since she'd begun it as a gloriously happy bride for no other reason than that she loved to write about her life with the endlessly fascinating man who was her husband.

Later, with happiness receding down the grey London streets with frightening and ever-increasing speed, the diary had become therapy, a way of releasing tension on those days when her heart was breaking – breaking even as she continued to present a serene face to the world for the sake of Jamie. After Dan died, and once the first anguished shock had worn off, she hadn't seemed to need the diary as much. Until the day of the picnic.

A picnic in the green Lincolnshire woods had seemed to her the ideal way to celebrate the move from London. In her mind it became the symbol of a new beginning, of a gentler, more peaceful way of life than the one she had endured through the last difficult years of her marriage.

She had brought the diary with her to the woods because she'd wanted to record the beginning of that new life filled with hope. But she had only just started to write when it had begun to rain.

Then Jamie had lost a shoe and cut his foot. He'd started to cry, and in the confusion the diary had somehow been overlooked.

She had come back for it as soon as she could. The rain hadn't lasted, the glade was secluded, and she hadn't anticipated anyone coming upon her property before she did.

But now this large and disturbing man was telling her his dog had sampled it – and apparently found it wanting as a snack. Was she supposed to be grateful for that? And what if he told her he still had it?

Dear heaven. Would that mean he had read it? Read her most private thoughts and all the pain she had poured on to the pages? She couldn't bear that. Couldn't bear him to know how Dan, her beloved Dan, had made her suffer. Because if he knew that, then her innermost being, everything that made her what she was, would lie exposed and vulnerable, not to someone who loved her, which would be bad enough, but to a man she scarely knew. A man she had taken an instant dislike to.

As she watched him now, afraid of what he would say yet needing desperately to know, Simon detached himself from his tree and smiled fleetingly. A cool smile intended to reassure.

She didn't trust it.

'Yes,' he said. 'I still have your book. Come back to the house with me and I'll fetch it.'

She nodded. 'All right. Thank you. I'm sorry if I've caused you any trouble.'

'You haven't. So far. Although I've no doubt you're capable of it.'

Now what did he mean by that? He didn't know anything about her. Unless he *had* read her diary. She moistened her lips, trying to bring herself to the point of asking point-blank. But Simon didn't give her time. Instead he took her arm in a proprietorial fashion, marched her out of the clearing and began to urge her down the path towards the manor. She could just see its chimneys above the trees.

The Ripper scampered ahead of them, carrying what looked like a small, dead tree.

'What brought you to Lincolnshire?' Simon asked, not as though he especially cared, but as if he assumed he had a right to know.

Olivia shrugged, uncomfortably aware of his square-tipped fingers on her arm. Her head only just reached his shoulder, and without trying to he somehow made her feel smaller and more insignificant than she was. She wished the path were wider so he wouldn't have to walk so close beside her.

'I wanted to get Jamie out of London,' she answered. 'He was starting to get involved with the wrong crowd at school, and although he hadn't actually been in any trouble, I could see it coming.' When Simon said nothing, she went on a little defensively, 'I'm a widow. It isn't always easy to keep food on the table and an eye on Jamie at the same time. So when my friend, Sidonie – she worked in the same office I did – told me that her aunt wanted to rent out the top floor of her house in Lincolnshire, I decided to move. Sherraby sounded ideal. A small village in the country, but close enough to Louth so I could work.'

'Yes, if you're lucky enough to find work,' Simon said neutrally.

'I've found it. I do the accounts for a firm of solicitors three mornings a week.'

'And you can live on that?'

He sounded sceptical. Simon Sebastian might be the wealthiest man for miles around, but he seemed to be aware that not everyone in these times was as fortunate. Not, she supposed, that good fortune had much to do with his phenomenal success. He might have inherited his country estate when his brother had died unexpectedly, but the business he owned and ran in London was reputed to be enormously successful in its own right. Olivia hadn't lived for a month in Sherraby without hearing the story of the village's best known yet most mysterious son. At least a dozen times.

'Yes,' she told him. 'I can live on that. By taking on the odd cleaning job as well.'

Simon threw her a look she couldn't interpret and all at once quickened his pace.

'Hey,' she cried. 'I'm not a greyhound. Just because you have legs as long as Nelson's Column –'

He slowed down at once as they came out of the woods and stepped into open fields. At the bottom of the gentle slope in front of them Olivia spotted wrought-iron gates and a brick gatehouse. Beyond the gatehouse, a row of lime trees stood sentinel beside a long, straight driveway leading to the manor's massively imposing front entrance.

'Sorry,' said Simon, sounding more impatient than sorry. He paused for a moment to glance down into her face. 'No, definitely not a greyhound. Maybe a cat, though. You have remarkably catlike black eyes. And that thick, smooth hair looks eminently strokable.'

Was he *trying* to annoy her? His features were utterly deadpan, but she was beginning to get a feeling that what went on under Simon Sebastian's tanned skin had very little to do with the outward manifestation.

'Try it and I'll scream,' she said, equally deadpan.

'Will you?' He raised his eyebrows. 'I wouldn't have thought it. You don't look like a screamer to me.'

'Oh? Does that mean I look like a pushover?'

He laughed, a low, seductive laugh that took her by surprise. 'No, Mrs Naismith. It means I find you – interesting. Not my type. Too damn cheeky. But interesting. For a cat.'

Olivia's mouth fell open, and at the same moment the Ripper dropped his tree and started to bark.

'Not that sort of cat,' Simon told him. 'Quiet, Rip.'

Rip was quiet. Olivia's mouth remained open.

Was Simon Sebastian really that direct? And that impertinent? Or was he, for some devious reason of his own, trying to get her goat? If so, she wasn't about to let him know he had succeeded.

'Keep it up and you may feel my claws,' she replied drily. 'Because I don't find you interesting in the least. Not even for a rat.'

It wasn't entirely true. Simon wasn't her type either. Nobody had been since Dan. But in spite of his impossible effrontery, she had to admit there was something very attractive about that cool, enigmatic smile. And as bodies went, his could rank up there in the top ten. But since Dan's death – long before, really – she had somehow lost interest in bodies. Just as well, probably. There was little time for lust in her busy schedule.

She took a quick step backwards. No doubt this particular body had an ego – which she had just quite brazenly assaulted. She waited, hands in her pockets, wondering how he was going to react.

To her bewilderment, he merely put a finger under her chin, tipped her face up, and said, 'Not bad. Has anyone ever got the better of you, Mrs Naismith?'

Oh, yes. Someone had got the better of her all right. Someone she had loved very much. Which was why she didn't plan to love that way again. She pushed Simon's finger away, disturbingly aware of a sudden point of heat.

'Yes,' she said shortly. 'Someone has.'

Again she sensed a change in Simon's reaction. And again she couldn't pin it down.

'Interesting,' was all he replied, before taking her arm to lead her down the grassy slope to the point where the long sweep of the driveway began.

Olivia gazed at the solid façade of the house that she knew had been lived in by generations of Sebastians reaching back over the centuries. It wasn't huge, as manor houses went. But, standing as it did at the end of the honour guard of limes, and with its mellow orange brick warm and tinted by the sun, it had an air of weathered permanence and tranquillity, of roots stretching back into the past and extending endlessly on into the future.

To Olivia, who had known permanence only in brief snatches, it was the ultimate fantasy come true.

'It's lovely,' she said to Simon. 'You're lucky.'

He glanced at her shrewdly. 'I know.'

'Has it always looked so – so enduring?' Olivia asked, an unconsciously wistful note creeping into her voice.

When Simon answered, she thought she detected a certain speculation in the piercing blue of his eyes. 'Not exactly, no. The brick was added in the 1700s. Before that the walls were mud and wood. The roof was originally thatch, but that went up in smoke – oh, about a hundred years ago, I suppose.'

A hundred years, Olivia thought. And I felt as if I'd lived in the same house for an age when we spent a whole four years in that council house in Harlow. Her gaze went to the narrow, lead-paned windows of the manor, and she remembered the permanently smudged and finger-smeared windows she'd grown up with. Her mother hadn't cared much about sparkle. She had been too busy cleaning other people's houses in order to supplement her father's sporadic income as an encyclopaedia and dictionary salesman.

Simon took Olivia's arm again as they emerged from the avenue of limes. 'This way,' he said, steering her round a corner of the house. 'We generally use one of the side entrances.'

'What, no butler to usher in the master?' Olivia exclaimed, unable to keep the tartness from her voice.

It wasn't that she meant to sound envious. But she found it hard not to feel an unfair resentment towards this man who seemed to have everything, including a double helping of arrogance, while she had to struggle for every penny.

'No,' said Simon, with an acidity he didn't trouble to hide. 'No butler. Sorry to disappoint you, but I manage with Mrs Leigh, who cooks and generally runs the kitchen, and Annie Coote, who handles the housekeeping with help from the village. Oh, and a couple of gardeners, along with John Cousins who doubles as a groom for my horses. He lives in the cottage by the gates. Do they up my status at all?'

Horses. He had horses too. And he actually had the nerve to be sarcastic.

'I didn't mean . . .' Olivia began indignantly. Then she stopped. He was looking at her with a cynical awareness that made her think he knew exactly what had been going through her mind. 'Your staffing arrangements don't interest me, I'm afraid,' she finished grandly.

'No, I can't see why they would,' Simon agreed, as he escorted her in through the side door.

He's laughing at me, Olivia thought bitterly. I know he is. Even though it doesn't show. 'Can I have my diary, please?' she asked.

'All in good time.' He led her through the kitchen, which now showed no signs of life, and along the passage to the hall. 'If you'd like to wait in the drawing room, I'll fetch it.'

Olivia, feeling as if she'd been subtly put in her place, followed him into a long, rectangular room overlooking a rose-bordered terrace. She sat down on the edge of a delicate Hepplewhite chair, but immediately felt restless and stood up again.

A gilt-framed mirror hung on the east wall, and she started to move towards it, then changed her mind because she didn't want Simon to come back and find her checking her appearance.

It shouldn't matter what he found her doing, of course. But somehow it did. In any case she knew exactly what she would see in the glass. A pale, oval face with a strong chin and straight, determined mouth – the whole framed by bobbed, shoulder-length hair that was almost as dark as her eyes. Unless, by chance, she had undergone a startling metamorphosis since last she'd looked. Which didn't seem likely.

Olivia reversed direction and was on her way back to the chair when she discovered Simon was already in the room. He walked quietly for such a big man. She supposed that considering the nature of his occupation, both before and after he had traded in his cloak and dagger for an office, his ability to pounce from behind shouldn't surprise her.

All the same, she jumped.

'Nervous?' asked Simon. 'No need to be. I like my victims willing and preferably warm.'

Why had no one warned her about this man? The village people all said he was charming, amiable and reserved. She hadn't realized they meant about as amiable as a tiger intent on stocking up its larder.

'That's all right, then,' she said quickly. 'Because I'm not willing. Did you find my diary?'

Simon brought his left hand from behind his back. 'Is this it?'

Oliva stared at the chewed corners and purposeful pattern of toothmarks on the book that, at one time, had been her chief link to sanity and normality. 'Yes,' she said, taking it from him. 'I'm afraid it is. Your Ripper has healthy bicuspids.'

Simon nodded. 'I know. I'm sorry. You should see what he did to the Christmas cards last year.'

Olivia didn't much care what the dog had done to the Christmas cards last year. She did care what he'd done to her diary. But she couldn't complain, because she was the one who had left it on Simon's property. Flipping it open, she breathed a small sigh of relief. It was still readable. She raised her head, meaning to thank Simon for his help before beating a grateful and strategic retreat.

But something in his eyes stopped her, and she remembered her earlier suspicions.

'Have you . . .? You haven't . . .?' She took a deep breath and started again. 'Have you read it? My diary, I mean?'

Please God he hadn't. She really *couldn't* bear it if this rich, successful, coolly provoking stranger knew every intimate detail of her disaster of a marriage – knew how her joy and optimism had turned to sorrow, and how, in the end, she hadn't been able to keep Dan from destroying himself.

She stood mutely, clasping her hands at her waist, hoping he wouldn't guess the extent of her anxiety from the livid spots of colour that always appeared on her cheeks when she most wanted to appear calm and collected. Was her fear screaming at him from the painful entreaty in her eyes? Please, God, let it not be . . .

She couldn't bear Simon to see her panic.

He surveyed her from under deceptively sleepy-looking eyelids, taking his time about answering until she was ready to howl with frustration and dread.

'Please – have you?' she whispered. '*Have* you read it?'

Still he didn't answer. Instead he moved across the room to the unlit fireplace and rested an elbow on the carved white mantel. 'It's full of holes,' he observed, eyeing the Ripper's handiwork with disfavour. 'Would it matter if I'd read it?'

'I . . .' Yes, it would matter. But she had no intention of letting him know just how much. Why make herself more vulnerable than she already was? She shrugged, assuming a nonchalance she couldn't feel, and replied obliquely, 'Why should it? *Have* you read it?' Maddeningly, her voice cracked slightly on the 'it'.

Another silence, even longer this time, then Simon said curtly, 'No.'

Olivia released her breath on a long sigh. 'Thank you,' she said. 'Thank you so much.'

She wasn't sure why she was thanking him for not reading something that was none of his business in the first place. But it seemed to be the thing to do. And anyway, she meant it. He could so easily have skimmed it in a moment of idle curiosity. And at one time knowing other people's business had been his job. Presumably it still was, in a different, less life-threatening way.

'Mmm.' His grunt was non-committal. 'Do you want some tea?'

He didn't want her to want tea. She could tell.

'No, thank you,' she said. 'It's kind of you, but I have to be home before Jamie gets out of school.'

Simon nodded. 'Of course. I'll drive you.'

'No, don't bother. It's only a mile or so. I enjoy walking.'

He moved aside to let her pass. 'As you wish.'

Olivia nodded and stepped past him, but as she reached the door he moved in front of her and put an arm across to bar her exit. 'If you decide to picnic in my woods again,' he said softly, 'remember not to leave anything behind. Next time you might not get it back.'

When Olivia started away, unnerved by his closeness, he laughed and removed the arm at once. She hurried into the hall without speaking.

Now what had he meant by that?

So intent was she on trying to fathom Simon's enigmatic words that she didn't realize she had wandered into a cloakroom off the hall until she fell over a pair of green wellingtons.

'Wrong way,' Simon's laconic voice murmured in her ear. A hand grasped her shoulder and swung her pointedly in the direction of the door.

'Oh. Sorry. My mistake.' Olivia, flustered, clasped the diary protectively to her chest and fled down the steps to the accompaniment of a volley of excited barks from the Ripper. Only when she reached the start of the driveway did she slow down and reduce her speed to a brisk trot.

Phew! Olivia wiped her palms on her jeans. There had been a dangerous sort of intimacy in the way Simon had spoken at the end. Yet she didn't really believe he was dangerous. Just exasperating, naturally arrogant and – oh, yes, she might as well admit it – disturbingly attractive.

Funny. She hadn't found anyone attractive since Dan.

She shook her head, dismissing the thought. It didn't matter. She and Jamie would find somewhere else to picnic from now on. And if she happened to run into Simon in the village there would be no need to do more than nod politely. Besides, she'd heard he spent a lot of his time in London and the States.

A comforting thought. Olivia kicked at a clump of dirt beside the road and watched it disintegrate into dust.

CHAPTER 2

He had lied to her. Simon picked up a ruler, laid it back on his well-ordered desk and glared at the vine growing over the trellis that framed his study window.

Damn. He hadn't wanted to lie. Not that he was fundamentally opposed to it; in his line of work he couldn't afford scruples of that sort. But when it came to his personal life he had always made a point of sticking to the truth. Until today. Until Olivia.

He picked up the ruler again and ran it slowly through his fingers. That independent, gutsy young woman had looked so stricken, so unnecessarily frantic at the idea that he might have read her diary that it had seemed pointless to confirm her worst fears. A private person himself, he understood her anxiety to a point.

Lying to her, at the time, had seemed the wisest and kindest thing to do.

He rapped the ruler sharply on the edge of the desk. Of course it had been the right thing to do. Olivia Naismith might have gone off annoyed with him, but at least she hadn't gone devastated by the knowledge that a man she hardly knew was privy to all her personal dreams and demons.

There was no reason she should ever learn the truth. For one thing, he was unlikely to see much of her in the village. He didn't go there often, and when he did he rarely stayed long. The villagers' well-meant interest in his activities was hard to take for any length of time.

The hot summer breeze tapped a branch of the vine against his wide open window. Simon closed his eyes. The incident with the diary wasn't important. He took a deep breath and felt himself relax. Tipping his chair back, he linked his hands behind his head and gazed pensively at the dark beam above his head.

In a way, it was too bad he wouldn't see more of Olivia. Tough, that was what she was, in her self-sufficient, undemonstrative way. Worth sparring with, and definitely amusing to provoke. But, as he had told her, she wasn't his type. Since Sylvia, his preference had been for blue-eyed, etiolated sirens not overburdened with brains – and over whom he was in no danger of losing his head. Althea Carrington-Coates fitted those specifications to a T.

Olivia, on the other hand, was curvaceous, pale but not etiolated, and she had quite as much brain as was good for her – a chauvinistic notion for which he had no doubt she would demand his scalp on a platter if he made the mistake of voicing it in her hearing.

Simon was grinning as he tipped the chair forward and switched on his computer. Just as well he wouldn't be seeing her again any time soon. Althea, of course, would be waiting for him when got back to town, no doubt full of plans for parties and dances, not to mention complaints about his wasting so much time in the country. Simon's grin slipped, then disappeared.

He placed his fingers resolutely on the keyboard. The fact that he was on holiday didn't entitle him to neglect his clients' business.

Ten minutes later, just as he was getting into his stride, a door slammed. He dropped his hands instantly. Slammed doors in this house usually meant only one thing.

Sure enough, almost immediately, a commotion started up down the hall.

'Oh! Oh, Miss Emma! You didn't half give me a fright.' Annie Coote's voice, raised in delighted and ear-splitting astonishment.

'Sorry, Annie.' Another voice, younger and less grating than the housekeeper's. 'There was no one around, so I walked in.'

'Well, of course you did. Mr Simon *will* be surprised. And that pleased to see you.'

Mr Simon, hearing the racket, pulled a cover over his computer and stood up. He wasn't unduly surprised. Nothing Emma did surprised him. As for pleased – that depended on the purpose of her visit.

'Hello, Emma,' he said, strolling into the hall just as Annie bustled off to prepare his cousin's room. 'I thought you were in Greece. What happened this time?'

'Nothing happened.' Emma threw up her arms theatrically. 'That's just the trouble. Ari took me to Skiros and fell asleep.'

'A bonus, I would have thought,' Simon murmured.

'Oh, *Simon.* Don't be such a curmudgeon.' Emma hurled herself across the hall and flung herself into his arms.

Simon patted her smooth blonde head and gently detached her fingers from his neck. 'Emma, don't be such a nitwit. Why did you go with Ari in the first place?'

'I don't know. To have fun, I suppose. He's famous, and funny and – well, handsome in a venerable sort of way. But once we got there, he didn't want to *do* anything. Just stroll around and show me off and have the press take our picture together. Then, once we got back to the villa, he'd order drinks and turn on the TV. He was *boring*, Simon. The most famous actor in Europe, and he was boring.'

Simon hid a smile. 'As your sober older cousin, aren't I supposed to celebrate boring? By the way . . .' He was genuinely sober now. 'Am I safe in assuming he didn't provide you with either an heir to the house of Colfax or a social disease?'

'Oh, Simon. Don't be so –'

'Boring?' Simon suggested.

Emma giggled. 'No. Just – oh, I don't know. Just *you*. Not boring exactly, but – upright. You know. Nice.'

'Thanks,' said Simon. 'Who was it that wrote those lines about damning with faint praise?'

'Shakespeare, I expect. He wrote most of that stuff people are always quoting and can't remember where they heard it.'

'Mmm. You have a point there. Emma, what are you doing here?'

'I couldn't think of anywhere else to go.' She unbuttoned a black cloak with a flaming scarlet lining and swirled it dramatically over her shoulder. 'Ari didn't want me around once the photo opportunities were over. He told me to go home and find someone my own age.'

'I see.' Simon regarded his young cousin's brittle, courageous smile with trepidation. All the usual signs were there. Pale skin stretched across delicate cheekbones, bright smile, over-bright eyes. Emma had made another mistake. Taken up, for the twentieth or thirtieth time, with a man who was totally unsuited to deal with her volatile, impetuous temperament.

Ari was a fading film star with a bank account. Emma was a social butterfly who, at this rate, would never achieve anything that wasn't paid for by a man.

That, at least, was the opinion of most of her relations.

'You didn't think of going home to New York?' he asked, knowing what the answer would be.

'Well, I did,' Emma admitted. 'But I thought I'd see what you were doing first.'

Simon suppressed a sigh. In other words, she had heard he was at Sherraby, and hoped for news of Zack. Even Emma had learned better than to approach his partner directly.

No one in the family ever spoke of it, but all of them were aware that Emma, at the age of sixteen, had formed a passionate attachment to Zack Kent from which, eight years later, she still showed no signs of being cured. Simon often thought the succession of unsuitable escorts she had collected over the years were merely red rags with which to taunt her reluctant bull. Ari was just the latest in a long line.

Zack, nine years older and from a much less privileged background, had never shown the smallest sign of reciprocating Emma's affection.

'Since you asked,' Simon told her, 'I'm trying not to do anything. I'm on holiday.'

'Oh. Who's looking after your office?'

'Who do you think?'

'Zack?'

From the way she said his partner's name, he could tell that nothing had changed there. She was still besotted.

He nodded. 'Of course. And once I get back to London he'll be leaving for the States. We have a couple of new contracts over there.'

'Whereabouts?' Emma asked eagerly. 'Whereabouts in the States?'

Simon hesitated. If he told her Zack was planning to stay on Long Island at her parents' house she would probably fly home like a shot. Which would get her, and whichever undesirable male she picked up next, out of his hair – at least until Zack returned to England. Zack probably wouldn't thank him. He tolerated Emma, but he had never seemed particularly fond of her. On the other hand, Zack was a big boy. He could take care of himself. With luck, he might even take care of Emma.

'New York,' Simon replied, making up his mind. 'He's going to New York. He'll be staying at Oakshades while your parents are away in San Francisco.'

It wasn't that he didn't enjoy Emma's company, he told himself, but when she wasn't involved in one of her ill-fated relationships – and often when she was as well – she had a tendency to get underfoot. Once this holiday was over, he would have neither the time nor the inclination to cope with her disruptions.

'Oh,' Emma said, with a nonchalance that didn't deceive him for a moment. 'That's when I'll be going home as well.'

'I thought it might be. In the meantime, I expect

Annie has made up your room. You'll be staying on until I go back to town, I suppose?'

Emma laughed. 'You suppose right. Mr Cousins is bringing up my bags.'

Oh. That explained why the hall wasn't knee-deep in expensive suitcases, tennis rackets and carrier bags from Harrods and Macy's. Emma had never heard of travelling light.

'I'll see you at dinner, then.' Simon turned to go back into his study.

'Yes, all right. Simon . . .?'

'Mmm?' He stopped.

'Have you heard from Gerald?'

'No. For which small mercy I say a prayer of thanks every morning and evening.'

'Simon! He is your cousin.'

'I know. That's why I'm grateful to the Deity. If I did see him, it would only be because he wanted money.'

'Gerald's not so bad. I mean I know he's a bit –'

'Feckless,' said Simon. 'Irresponsible. A pain in the –'

'Yes, but it's not his fault Aunty Jenny and Uncle Roger let him think he deserved to have anything he wanted the moment he wanted it. Or his fault they died when he was so young.'

'No. But it is his fault he got through a perfectly substantial inheritance and is now attempting – without success, I might add – to go through mine. He hasn't asked you for help, has he?'

'Yes, but Mom and Dad only give me a monthly allowance, and *Fashion Fair* doesn't pay me for my articles at all unless I actually write them.'

'I can't think why,' murmured Simon.

Emma stuck out her tongue. 'Pig,' she said amiably. 'I've been on Skiros, and there wasn't anyone there I could interview. Not about clothes. The point is, I don't have as much as Gerald needs.'

'Needs?'

'Wants, then. Anyway, I don't have enough.'

'I doubt if anybody has.' Simon frowned. Emma's casual attitude to the business of earning a living was a constant source of exasperation. But strictly speaking it had nothing to do with him. 'I wouldn't waste your time worrying about Gerald,' he said. 'Last time I heard, he had another lonely widow in his sights.'

Emma giggled. 'Not just his sights, I'll bet.'

'Behave yourself, young Emma.' Simon gave her a severe look that didn't jibe with the reluctant smile tugging at a corner of his mouth.

Emma giggled again, so he told her he had a report to finish and left her standing in the hall.

Emma could look after herself, at least for the next hour or so. It annoyed him to think that if she would just settle down and concentrate on the fashion interviews and articles she was so good at, she could easily be self-supporting. But she wouldn't make the effort. Too busy driving men crazy, he supposed. If his aunt and uncle had any sense, they'd withdraw that monthly allowance.

Light footsteps sounded across the hall, and Simon glanced back in time to see Emma's slim figure in tight black skirt and boots running up the stairs with the red-lined cloak swinging from her shoulders.

He watched her until she disappeared. An eyeful, was his cousin Emma, with her model's figure, cropped blonde hair, and the emerald eyes he knew owed more to contact lenses than to nature. Definitely an eyeful. And a handful. She seemed to cavort through life dreaming of Zack and refusing to think about the future.

At least she wasn't as bad as Gerald, who was convinced the world owed him a living.

Simon sat down heavily at his desk. With Emma in residence, his country holiday promised to end on a considerably less restful note than he'd had in mind when he'd told a pouting Althea that he needed some time to himself.

Upstairs, in the yellow and white bedroom she always occupied at Sherraby, Emma threw her cloak and bag on to the bed and hurried over to the window.

Nothing had changed. The grass, newly mown and fresh, was as smooth as it had ever been, and the lake as green. She smiled with the relief she always felt on coming back to find this house, this view – everything about Sherraby – exactly the same as it had been when she'd left. Other places, other *people* changed. But not Sherraby. Lovely, predictable Sherraby. Her first and most beloved home. It wasn't that she didn't like Oakshades. But all her life she had shuttled back and forth between two continents according to the dictates of her American father and his latest business ventures. Sherraby, her mother's birthplace and her own, had remained the one constant in her life.

Besides, it was here that she had first met Zack, who was another constant. For all it mattered. For all he cared.

Emma rubbed her eyes and watched the breeze-blown ripples spread across the lake.

She had been standing in exactly this spot the day that Zack, wearing nothing but frayed denim shorts, had emerged from the lake with the water glistening off his dark gypsy skin and his blue-black hair streaming behind him in the wind. She had seen him shake himself like the Ripper, and stand on the grass with his head thrown back and his arms outstretched to the sun. Watching him, for a moment Emma had seen, not a muscular modern man, but some ancient Celtic priest offering up a sacrifice to the gods. She had shivered a little, then pulled up the straps of her white sundress and hurried out of her room and down the stairs.

She reached the terrace at exactly the moment her Celtic priest reached the top of the wide steps leading up from the grass. He paused with his hand on the balustrade.

'Hello,' he said, in a that mellow, bass-baritone voice she had instantly fallen in love with. 'Who are you?'

'I'm Emma Colfax. Simon and Martin's cousin from New York. Who are you?'

'Zack. Zack Kent. I'm a friend of Simon's. We work together.'

'Oh, then you work for the government as well. Simon says it isn't a bit exciting.'

'Simon's right.' Zack's flat, straight mouth closed over long, straight teeth.

Emma sighed. Simon always got all close-mouthed too whenever she asked him about his job. Martin, his older brother, was much more fun. He talked about farming – horses and sheep and tractors, the tenants who lived on the farms – and how to raise pigs.

'Where do you live?' she asked Zack.

'I used to live in Aberdeen. Now I live in London.'

Oh, that explained his voice with its trace of a Scottish lilt. In another time, another century, he really could have been some wild Celtic priest – although now that she saw him close up, he wasn't much taller than she was, and his square jaw and craggy features had more of a warrior's belligerence than the saintliness she expected of a priest.

She wanted to touch that face, to run her fingers through the long, black hair . . .

'Do you want to go swimming again?' she asked, trying to sound casual. 'I could get my bathing suit.' She could do with some cooling off.

Zack shook his head. 'No. I want to lie in the sun and go to sleep.'

'I'll lie with you,' Emma said promptly.

The pupils of Zack's eyes widened, and he said gruffly, 'I wouldn't go around saying things like that, if I were you,' and he turned his back on her and went into the house.

From then on, that had been the pattern of most of their encounters. Zack was polite, as friendly as he needed to be, and reserved. He steadfastly refused to engage in any activity alone with Emma.

After a while Emma wasn't sure if she wanted him because he was a challenge, the only man who routinely turned her down, or because he also just happened to be the most attractive man she had ever met. Either way, she wanted him. And one day, she vowed, she would have him. One day he would wake up and discover what he was missing.

That day, the day she had dreamed of for so long, came the summer she turned nineteen. But it didn't work out the way she hoped.

Martin had died the previous summer, Simon was Lord of the Manor, and Zack had come down from London to discuss going into partnership with his friend.

It had been over a year since Emma had seen Zack, and during that year she had been pursued by enough men of all ages to know that she didn't lack appeal. Zack *couldn't* continue to be oblivious to her charms.

This time he would notice her. This time Zack Kent was not going to be allowed to brush her off.

She waited until a balmy evening late in May. Zack was spending the weekend at Sherraby, and after dinner on the Saturday he told Simon he was going for a walk. Simon, used to his friend's passion for solitude – which Zack explained as the result of growing up in a small stone house with eight siblings – nodded without comment.

Emma made up her mind.

While Simon was immersed in the papers, she pulled on a long, bottle-green cardigan, changed her high heels for sandals, and padded off in Zack's wake. Across the fields, she could just see him disappearing beneath the trees.

The path through the woods was crescent-shaped. That meant that if he didn't turn around, there was only one way he could come out.

Emma took her time walking through the fields, stooping to pick buttercups and daisies and waiting until Zack was likely to be coming round the curve of the crescent before starting down the path into the woods.

Her timing was perfect.

As Zack sauntered round the bend humming something gloomy that might have been Loch Lomond, Emma dropped a handful of buttercups and shoved her hands into the pockets of her cardigan. Then, lowering her head and affecting a sudden interest in her feet, she walked full-tilt into her oblivious victim's chest.

Zack, winded and taken by surprise, but trained to react quickly, automatically grabbed her by the arms. Before Emma knew what had happened to her she was lying flat on her back on a bed of pine needles and dust.

Zack's knee was at her throat.

Emma blinked up at him. Not exactly what she'd had in mind, she decided, gazing into furious dark eyes that looked as though murder was a distinct possibility. Which, come to think of it, and given Zack's background, it might have been if he hadn't been so perfectly in control.

He raised the knee as soon as he saw who she was.

Emma lifted her head. She was still in one piece, albeit a slightly bruised piece – and this was a situation that could very well be exploited.

'Oh. Oh, Zack,' she moaned. 'Please, I didn't mean . . . ouch. My leg. I think it's broken.'

Zack, in one swift movement, was off her and kneeling in the dust. Taking her ankle in his hands he began, very gently, to examine her left leg.

Mmm. He had nice hands. Big and firm and warm. She waited until he had worked them all the way up to her thigh, before saying weakly, 'I think it's my right leg that's broken.'

Zack paused in his ministrations and abruptly sat back on his heels. When he switched his gaze to her face, she squirmed and wouldn't meet his eyes.

'I see,' he said without inflection.

'Aren't you going to check the other one?' Emma asked.

'What for?'

'To see if it's broken.'

'I doubt if I'd find more than a few bruises. Which you richly deserve. What the hell do you think you were doing, walking around as if there wasn't a soul in the world besides yourself?'

Emma, who had been a star turn at drama in school and was currently repeating her successes in college, produced two large and convincing tears which welled up and tumbled down her cheeks.

Zack swore. 'Did I hurt you?' he asked.

Emma sniffed. 'Just a little.' She gave him the smile she had worn as Lady Jane Grey going bravely to the scaffold.

'I'm sorry,' Zack said.

'It's all right. My fault.'

'Yes, it was,' he agreed, standing up. 'Come on. Let's see how well you can stand.' He held out his hand.

Emma took it. 'What about my broken leg?' she asked.

'If you can stand on it, it isn't broken.' He gave her hand a jerk and reluctantly she allowed herself to be hauled to her feet.

'Just as I thought. Nothing broken,' Zack sounded as if he thought a bit of breakage might have done her good.

Emma stumbled and reached for her left knee. 'I think I pulled a muscle,' she said.

'Not likely. You look fine to me. A bit dusty, and your cardigan's covered in needles. But you'll live.'

Emma scowled at him, stumbled again and clutched at his arm.

'Wrong leg,' said Zack, as Emma raised her left foot and winced. 'You broke the other one, remember?'

Damn him. 'Don't you ever laugh?' she snapped.

'When there's something to laugh at. I don't find scheming little girls very funny.'

'I wasn't scheming!' Emma exclaimed. 'And I'll be nineteen next week.'

'Will you? I'd not have guessed it.'

Not even the ghost of a smile – and he was looking at her now as if she were a rather annoying bug that had attached itself to his person and spoiled his walk.

Emma, disappointed, embarrassed and not used to being so summarily rejected, said angrily, 'I'm a woman, Zack Kent. I can prove it.'

'I doubt that, Little Miss Silver Spoon. Why should you bother to grow up when everything you want is handed to you for the price of a smile and a blink of your emerald-green eyes?' He bent towards her. 'They are green this week, aren't they?'

Emma glared, and Zack shrugged and said dismissively, 'Just so you know, a woman is someone like my sister Morag, who raised all eight of us on her own after my mother died. Or my little sister, Catriona, who nurses dying children.' He detached her fingers from his arm, put his hand in the small of her back and urged her ahead of him up the path. 'Go on. It'll be dark soon.'

So it would. The breeze had died down and the woods were quiet now except for the sound of their breathing. The air smelled of earth and the rich scent of summer. And as Emma listened to the silence, what was left of her precarious control snapped.

She'd show him. She'd show the sanctimonious bastard! It wasn't *her* fault that her father had a lot of money and that she hadn't been brought up in a slum.

She stopped in her tracks, swung round, and aimed her closed fist at Zack's nose.

Just for a second, he was taken by surprise. She saw him blink. Then her wrist was grasped in strong, bony fingers. She raised the other fist. He caught that too – and now, at last, Zack was laughing.

'A lady prize-fighter, are you?' he chuckled. 'Who would have thought it? Were you trying to bloody my nose, then, wee Emma?'

'Yes,' said Emma, the anger draining out of her at once in response to his laughter. She smiled self-consciously. 'I was. You spoiled my aim.'

His eyes glittered at her in a way that made her feel hot. 'Do you want to try again?'

'No.' She weighed her chances. What the hell, she had nothing to lose. 'I'd much rather kiss you,' she said.

The glitter in Zack's eyes faded and he let her go at once. 'Oh, no,' he said, shaking his head. 'Oh, no, young Lady Colfax. You'll have to look elsewhere for kisses.'

Emma didn't want to look elsewhere. Zack, in his dark fisherman's pullover and with the evening shadows accentuating the mysterious hollows of his cheeks, was the man she wanted. The only man she had *ever* wanted. And if she didn't make the attempt to get him now, she might never have the courage to try again.

Without giving herself further time to think, Emma took a step forward, wrapped her arms around his waist and pushed her lips against his mouth. Somewhere behind them, a twig snapped.

Zack didn't move, didn't respond, didn't react in any way. Emma dropped her hands below his waist, felt the smooth, solid curve of his rear and shimmied her hips a little as she opened her mouth and extended her tongue. He smelled of bark, and the sweet, piny scent of the woods.

She heard him suck in his breath, felt, rather than heard him release it – and then he was returning her kiss, with a rough competence that would have made her gasp if she'd been able.

She had been kissed before. But this wasn't like those other, experimental kisses. This was the kiss of a man who knew what he was doing and meant to prove it to her. When he had finished, he held her away from him and said, 'Is that what you wanted?'

She didn't answer, and after a while he returned his hand to the small of her back and gave her a quick push along the path.

Emma couldn't look at him. It *had* been what she wanted. And yet it hadn't. Because although Zack had set her blood to boiling and turned her limp with desire, his kiss had been passionless – thorough but uninvolved. Yes, he had finally kissed her. But his kiss held no meaning. His mind had seemed a million miles away.

Zack, without even trying – or perhaps he had been trying – had made her feel young and cheap and foolish. And hopelessly alone.

She made herself stop and face him. 'No,' she said, looping an arm around the trunk of a young birch tree. 'It wasn't what I wanted. I thought it would be. But it wasn't.'

'Thank God for that,' Zack said.

'What do you mean?'

'I'm not blind, girl. My job is to observe, not to ignore. I've seen what you were up to.' He took a step backwards. 'I'm nine years older than you are, or near enough, and believe me, we're about as suited to each other as Red Riding Hood and the wolf. Now . . .' He put his hands in his pockets and smiled at her as if it took an effort. 'Have I succeeded in proving that to you? If I have, perhaps we can finally manage to be friends.'

Emma didn't want to be friends. Zack had humiliated her, quite deliberately, because he wanted to teach her a lesson. She saw that now. But if he thought he'd succeeded, he was wrong. The only lesson Zack Kent had taught her was that if he ever took it into his head to make love to her as if he truly meant it, it would be the closest to heaven she would get. And, oh, it *would* be worth waiting for.

Zack might not believe it, but Emma was better at waiting than he thought.

As it turned out, she had to be – because only three months after their brief encounter in the woods, Zack announced to the world that he was married. To a woman he had met on a train.

CHAPTER 3

'Mum! Mum? Can we go to the fête on Saturday? Please? Chrissy's going. And Roger and Dave and – and *everybody*. Can we go? Can we?' Jamie burst into the small suite beneath the eaves of Mrs Critchley's narrow red brick house like a fair-haired jumping bean with freckles.

'Fête?' Olivia put a handful of receipts back into the folder she'd brought home from the office. 'What fête?'

'*You* know. The one there's notices about in all the shops. And at school, and – Mum, you must have seen them.'

'Oh. Those notices.' Yes, Olivia supposed she had seen them. But she hadn't paid any attention. She had been too busy hustling back and forth between the solicitors in Louth and her various housecleaning jobs. There never seemed much time to stop and stare.

'Where's it being held?' she asked, taking off her reading glasses and setting them down on the rickety wooden table they used for everything from eating, to paying bills, to rolling pastry dough.

'At the manor. You remember. Where we went for the picnic.'

Oh. Yes. She remembered that all right.

It had been almost three weeks since the ill-fated picnic that had resulted in her one and only encounter with Simon Sebastian, Lord and Master of Sherraby. She hadn't seen him since, and had more or less put the incident out of her mind – although twice now she had woken in the middle of the night feeling warm and happy after dreaming she was once again in a man's arms. Not Dan's arms, though. Different arms, whose owner had waving, bronze-coloured hair and eyes that were as blue as the sky in winter.

'Mum? I said *can* we? It's going to be really cosmic.' Jamie's insistent treble brought her back to the matter of the moment, and the fact that if she agreed to take her son to this fête there was a fair chance she would run into Simon. She didn't want to run into Simon. He embarrassed and confused her, and there had been enough confusion in her life.

'All right,' she said reluctantly. 'I suppose we can go.' She wasn't working on Saturday. There was no real reason to deny her son this treat. 'Will – um – will Mr Sebastian be there? Did you happen to hear?'

Jamie looked blank. 'I dunno. Chrissy says there's a fête at the manor every year. Did you know Mr Sebastian was a spy?'

Olivia blinked. 'Well, not exactly a spy, Jamie.'

'Yes, he was. Roger's Dad said so. Except he called it – cleverness or something.'

'Intelligence,' Olivia corrected him. 'Yes, I heard he was once in the special services –'

'Like James Bond,' said Jamie, who had recently seen his first 007 video.

James Bond? Olivia found it hard to envisage Simon, that strikingly large and highly provoking man, as any kind of undercover agent. He just didn't seem to fit the image. But she knew it was true that he had retired from some kind of government intelligence work to form his own enormously successful security consultancy. It was rumoured that Simon Sebastian's firm handled security for several of Britain's most high-powered corporate tycoons, as well as for assorted dignitaries from foreign parts, and including clients in Washington and New York – or so she'd heard.

'I don't know what Mr Sebastian was before,' Olivia said firmly to Jamie. 'Not for sure. So you mustn't go round saying he was a spy. He's a businessman now. Quite an important one.'

'I know.' Jamie said disgustedly. 'That's what Roger's Dad said. I don't get it. Why would he want to do boring old business when he could be something cosmic like a spy?'

'Jamie . . .' Olivia warned.

'OK.' Jamie nodded vigorously. 'I won't say it again. As long as we can go to the fête. There's going to be games and food and toys and you can win all kinds of cosmic stuff.'

Yes, thought Olivia. Provided you can afford to buy tickets. She hoped they wouldn't be expensive. On the other hand, maybe it would rain.

It didn't.

There wasn't a cloud in the sky when she awoke on Saturday morning in the cramped little alcove where she slept so that Jamie could have the only bedroom to himself. By noon the sun was beating down on the roof, shortening her temper and convincing her that if she didn't get out soon she would melt.

By one o'clock, dressed in a red halter and a brief red and white striped skirt, she was on her way to the fête with Jamie, who hopped most of the way like a one-legged grasshopper on stilts. He was still hopping when they reached the manor gates. Just watching him made Olivia feel hot, sticky and in dire need of a long, cool bath.

On her last visit to the manor, the smooth lawns close to the house had been oases of cultivated tranquillity. Today a collection of multi-coloured awnings dotted the grass, while busy organizers scuttled about like worker bees putting last-minute touches to the stalls.

'I want to try those,' said Jamie, pointing to a stall festooned with multi-coloured balloons. 'If I can burst two of them with one dart I get a prize. And can I ride the ponies? And fish for barracudas in the fishpond, and – oh, look, Mum. Roger's mum is making toffee apples.'

'Barracudas?' Olivia repeated dazedly. She put out a hand to hold Jamie back as a quick murmur rippled through the crowd. 'Wait a minute. I think Mr Sebastian is going to open the fête.' To her annoyance, she found herself swallowing.

'Is that him?' Jamie asked, pointing, and not questioning his mother's familiarity with the formidable figure mounting a makeshift platform in the centre of the lawn. A small band shuffled into place behind him and began to strum out-of-tune marching music. 'He doesn't look like a spy,' Jamie grumbled.

Olivia sighed. 'No,' she agreed. 'He doesn't. That's because he isn't one.'

Her son threw her a pitying look. 'Let's get closer,' he urged.

But Olivia hung back, not wanting to be seen. The band screeched into merciful silence.

Simon strode to the front of the platform, raised a hand to still a short burst of clapping, and made a brief opening speech that she guessed he had delivered many times before. The crowd, presumably applauding his brevity, clapped with enthusiasm as he declared the fête open. Immediately afterwards Simon put a hand on the edge of the platform and jumped down to join a slender young woman who had been standing a few feet away on the the grass.

So that was Simon's type, Olivia thought, remembering their conversation of a few weeks ago. Svelte, blonde and expensive. That skimpy white sundress must have cost a fortune.

'*Now* can I burst the balloons?' Jamie cried, tugging impatiently at her hand.

Observing that Simon and the young woman were headed in the opposite direction from the balloons, Olivia acquiesced with alacrity.

Jamie burst five balloons and won a whistle and a plastic stegosaurus. After that he rode the ponies, investigated a stall selling hand-made toys – which he pronounced, 'Non-cosmic,' because they didn't feature batteries or zap bad guys – circled the toffee apples like a buzzard on the make, and ran up to his mother to ask if he could buy a goldfish. Olivia said she would see after tea.

'Tea,' he exclaimed. 'Can I have pop? And crisps and cake and –'

Olivia, who felt she could use a cup of tea, said she supposed he could.

They headed for the tea-tent, but just as they were about to sit down, a plump woman in a flowered overall came puffing up to them. She had a little girl with red pigtails in tow.

'Olivia!' the woman gasped. 'Oh, thank goodness. Would you do me a favour, dear?'

'Of course, if I can.' Olivia smiled.

'Would you mind taking care of the craft stall for me? Just for a couple of minutes. Mary Bacon's girl is handling it for now, but I can't trust her not to put all the customers off.'

'Jamie . . .' Olivia began.

'I'll look after your Jamie for you,' the plump woman said at once. She lowered her behind into a chair. 'But I *must* sit down for a bit, dear. It's my back again. Been acting up something awful lately, it has.'

'Of course I'll do it,' said Olivia. 'Jamie, you won't mind staying with Mrs Downer and Chrissy for a bit, will you?'

Jamie said he wouldn't.

Olivia pushed her way through the crowd until she found the craft stall, which was in the care of a surly-faced teenager with one side of her head shaved bald. When Olivia said she had come to take over, the girl shrugged, lit a cigarette and skulked away without a word.

The next half-hour passed quickly as Olivia did her best to sell a motley pile of hand-made dolls, unseasonal Christmas tree ornaments, pottery, jewellery and lumpy knitted slippers. It wasn't her idea of the ideal way to spend a too-hot summer afternoon, but she liked Gladys Downer and was glad to help because she knew Gladys Downer liked her.

It was too bad Chrissy's father, Harold, didn't feel the same. As far as he was concerned anyone whose family hadn't lived in Sherraby for at least forty years was an outsider to be regarded with suspicion.

When Gladys finally waddled back to take up her position behind the stall, Olivia asked at once, 'Jamie? Is he –?'

'Him and Chrissy are with her dad,' Gladys assured her. 'I think they was going to play bingo.'

'Oh. That's all right, then.' Having ascertained that her friend's back was much better, Olivia made her way directly across the grass to the bingo tent.

Harold Downer was certainly there with Chrissy. But Jamie was nowhere to be seen.

'Little devil ran away on me,' growled Harold. 'Said he was off to find you.'

Olivia started to ask him why he hadn't bothered to go after Jamie, then bit back her indignant reponse. What was the point in recriminations? What she had to do now was find her son. He couldn't have gone far, but it would be easy enough to miss him in this crowd.

Feeling more irritated than anxious, Olivia headed for the platform, long since abandoned by the thirsty band. From there she ought to have a better view of the surrounding gardens.

She had only just reached the top of the makeshift steps when she heard what sounded like cheering from the direction of the lake.

A few seconds later a young woman with a nose the colour of strawberry ice-cream came panting up the slope in a crab-like run. 'What's happened?' Olivia called to her with a sense of foreboding.

'Kid fell in. Mr Simon pulled him out,' the woman puffed.

Olivia felt her knees turn to sponge. In spite of the heat she began to shiver. 'Is – is he –?'

'Kid's fine,' said the woman, wiping the back of her hand across her face. 'I'm off to fetch some towels to dry him off. Mr Simon's in a rare old rage, though. Says the kid's parents ought to be horsewhipped.'

Olivia's knees regained their normal resilience and she began to feel hot instead of cold. Calling out her thanks, she jumped off the platform and ran towards the lake while her informant bustled off into the house.

A little crowd had gathered by the edge of the water. Olivia made herself small and edged her way to the front.

Immediately her fears were confirmed.

Simon Sebastian, wearing saturated white trousers and nothing else, was resting on his heels holding a wet and quivering child between his knees.

'It's OK, young fellow,' he was saying. 'You're all right now. And I wasn't yelling at you. I promise.' He made what Olivia could see was a valiant attempt to control his temper, and added with a smile, 'Now – where's your mother?'

The last words were spoken in a different, much less understanding tone. It was obvious that the child's mother, when she appeared, was in for an unpleasant few minutes.

Olivia stepped forward. 'I'm his mother,' she said.

Simon looked up. She saw first censure, then recognition, then a formidable anger cross his features. Unlike the last time they had met, today he was making no attempt whatsoever to hide his feelings – and his expression did not bode well for the mother of the child he had just rescued from his lake.

'So, Mrs Naismith,' he said. 'We meet again.' His voice was quiet, but his eyes were flashing blue ice as he rose to his feet with Jamie in his arms.

'Yes.' Olivia, still recovering from the terrifying knowledge that she could have lost Jamie, was resentful of Simon's instant condemnation, yet uncomfortably aware of his virile body gleaming wet and golden in the heat of the sun. She heard her words came out strained and uneven. 'Yes. It seems we do. Meet again, I mean. Thank you for rescuing Jamie.' She turned to her son. 'What happened?'

Jamie hung his head in embarrassment. 'Not now, Mum. I'll tell you later.'

'I could hardly have left him there to drown.' Simon put in. He didn't add, *Unlike you, Mrs Naismith*, his tone implied it.

The woman with the ice-cream nose came hurrying up at that moment waving an armful of fluffy white towels. Simon took one. 'Thank you, Annie,' he said, wrapping it snugly around Jamie.

'I'll take him.' Olivia held out her arms. There was

nothing to be gained by reacting to Simon's unspoken disapproval.

She took Jamie, stood him on the grass and removed his dripping wet T-shirt. Then she folded the towel around him again and said, 'I do apologize for the inconvenience. Will it be all right if I return this later?'

'The child or the towel?' asked Simon.

Olivia didn't bother to answer, but instead scooped Jamie into her arms and started to walk up the slope.

'Where do you think you're going?' Simon's voice sliced at her from behind.

She stopped. 'Home.'

'I don't wanna –' began Jamie.

'Don't be ridiculous,' Simon said coldly.

'I'm not being ridiculous –'

'I'm afraid you are, Mrs Naismith. The boy's soaked. It's over a mile to the village. I'll drive you.'

'I don't wanna go home,' wailed Jamie.

'You should have thought of that before starting a brawl on the edge of my lake, young man.' Simon was adamant. 'The fact is, you don't have a choice.'

'There's no need . . .' Olivia began.

'There is a need. Have you no sense of responsibility at all? Do you want the boy to catch a chill on top of almost drowning?'

'Of course not, but –'

Simon stood up. 'Then come into the house while I fetch the car.'

Neptune passing judgement on an escaped mermaid, Olivia thought wildly. Taking an indignant step backwards, she glanced around for a way out of her dilemma. There didn't seem to be one, although a dozen or so pairs of eyes were observing the interchange with interest. And Simon was right, damn him. It didn't make sense to walk home with Jamie in his present saturated state. Especially as she had no spare clothes for him. He would dry off soon enough, of course. There wasn't much likelihood of his catching a chill in this heat. But he'd had a shock, and perhaps it would be best to get him home . . .

'Thank you,' she said coldly. 'It's very kind of you.'

Simon muttered something under his breath and strode ahead of her, leaving her to follow more slowly with Jamie, still wrapped in his towel. It was too hot to walk fast. She could feel the perspiration dripping off her neck. And the delectable sight of Simon's rear in clinging wet trousers didn't help.

'Wait here,' he said when they reached the front hall.

Olivia sat down on a hard Chinese chair and held Jamie firmly on her knee.

'I don't want to go home,' he grumbled. 'I want –'

'Hi, there. Is this the little guy who fell in the lake?' enquired a soft voice with unmistakably transatlantic overtones. 'How's he feeling?'

Olivia looked up to see the young woman she had observed earlier with Simon hurry into the hall with a travelling bag slung over one arm. She had changed from the sundress to casual trousers and a short fitted jacket.

'I'm fine,' Jamie said sulkily. '*Perfeckly* fine.'

'That's good. I'm Emma Colfax. Simon's cousin.'

Cousin. Oh-h. Olivia beamed at her, then wondered if she'd overdone her enthusiasm when Emma Colfax took a quick step backwards.

'Olivia Naismith,' she said crisply, turning the beam down to low. 'From the village.'

Emma nodded. 'Hi. I'm glad the little boy's OK. Listen, I'm sorry, but I have to rush. John Cousins is loading my bags in the car. I'm just on my way back to the States. You haven't seen Simon, have you? I ought to say goodbye.'

'I think he's upstairs . . .'

'He is? OK, I'll find him. 'Bye.'

''Bye.' Olivia watched, blinking, as Emma turned round and hurtled up the stairs.

Less than a minute later she was back, waving and skidding towards the door. 'Mission accomplished,' she called. 'Simon says to tell you he won't be long.'

'Thanks . . .' Olivia began. But Emma was already in the driveway. Olivia gazed after her as the door swung slowly shut. What a frantic sort of person Simon's cousin was. Nice, though. She could like her if she ever had the chance.

'Jamie, how did you manage to fall in the lake?' she asked, putting Emma out of her mind to concentrate on her son, who smelled strongly of swamp. 'You were told to stay with Chrissy's father.'

'I did. But Mr Downer doesn't like me. He told me to keep still and behave. So I ran away. Then Roger said, "Race you to the lake." So I raced him, and I won, but he said I hadn't. Then his dad came up and said it didn't matter, and Roger shoved me and I shoved him back and Mr Sebastian shouted at us to get away from the edge. And – and I fell in. The lake got in my nose, and I was choking.'

Olivia closed her eyes. 'I see. And then –'

'Then Mr Sebastian came. And he made all the water come out of me. And he started saying bad things about – about people who don't watch their kids. But you couldn't watch me, could you? 'Cos you weren't there.'

'Exactly my point,' said a harsh voice from halfway down the stairs.

She looked up. Simon, no longer wet, and, dressed in fawn-coloured shorts and a yellow shirt, was frowning down at her as if she were something unpleasant brought in by the Ripper – who was bustling down the stairs at his master's heels.

Olivia glared at him. She was under no obligation to explain her actions to Simon or anyone else. Except that – well, he *had* pulled Jamie from the lake. She couldn't avoid that unpalatable fact.

'I wasn't there because I was running the craft stall, Mr Sebastian. Mrs Downer needed to sit down. Her husband was watching Jamie, but he ran away.' She spoke curtly, almost rudely. In the wake of Simon's high-handedness, she didn't feel she owed him more than a brief explanation and cool thanks.

'I see.' Simon didn't appear to be impressed.

Olivia stood up. 'I won't take up more of your time –' she began loftily.

'Cut it out, Olivia.' Her name fell quite naturally from his lips as he came the rest of the way down the stairs. 'We've agreed that I'm taking you and Jamie home. If you want to come under your own steam, that's fine with me. If you'd prefer to come kicking and screaming, that suits me too. Now which is it to be?'

Oh, lord. He meant it. She could tell from the coiled tension in his shoulders as he walked purposefully across the hall and paused with his hand on the doorknob.

'Chauvinist,' she muttered.

Simon half turned towards her with a look in his eye that boded her no joy.

'All right. I'm coming,' she said quickly.

Fuming, but unable to do anything about it, she followed Simon and the Ripper out into the sunshine and around to the side of the house. They came to a stop in a cobbled courtyard surrounded on three sides by what was obviously the stables. A separate building that must once have been the coach house was occupied by a maroon-coloured Rolls.

'Wow,' said Jamie, recovering from his sulks. 'That's a Rolls-Royce, isn't it?'

'It is.' Simon smiled at the boy's enthusiasm as he opened the doors and helped Olivia in. Jamie jumped into the back. The Ripper jumped in beside him.

'Cosmic dog, too,' said Jamie. 'What's his name?'

'Ripper. Rip for short.'

'Oh. I never had a dog.'

'Or swimming lessons either,' said Simon, with a hard look at Olivia.

'He was scheduled to have them when we moved,' Olivia said, bristling. Why did she feel so defensive around Simon? He had a most infuriating way of putting her back up. And yet – he was being nice to Jamie, and he hadn't made an issue of the fact that his expensive car was almost certain to end up smelling like a swamp.

His eyes flicked sideways, but he said nothing as he backed the Rolls out into the courtyard. In the end it was Jamie who defused the highly charged atmosphere by asking suddenly, 'Were you really a spy, Mr Sebastian?'

Olivia put a hand over her eyes.

Simon laughed softly. 'I suppose you could call what I used to do spying. I don't do it any more.'

'I know. You do *business*.' Jamie sounded so disgusted that Simon chuckled again.

'It's quite an exciting business sometimes,' he assured the boy.

'Not as exciting as spying,' said Jamie with conviction.

'Oh, I don't know. My old job was often very dull.'

'Was that why you stopped doing it?'

Simon pulled the Rolls on to the road. 'No. I stopped doing it when I inherited Sherraby. The project I'd been working on was finished, and I decided it was time to move on.'

'You don't look like a spy,' Jamie informed him.

'Jamie,' groaned Olivia. 'What did I tell you . . .?'

'It's all right,' Simon said coolly. 'I expect he means I'm too tall to go unnoticed in a crowd.'

And too arrestingly good-looking. And too sexy, Olivia thought.

'You see, sometimes it helps to be noticed,' Simon explained. 'Depending on the kind of job you happen to be on.'

'Oh.' Jamie obviously didn't see. Neither did Olivia really, but she wasn't going to ask for clarification. For one thing, she didn't want Simon to think she cared. For another, she didn't suppose he was at liberty to explain.

Speculation ended at that point, because they were already pulling up at the kerb beside Mrs Critchley's white-painted gate.

'Thank you,' Olivia said, jumping out before Simon could open the door. 'It was very kind of you.'

'You already said that.' He looked up at her through the open window. There was an incendiary little smile on his lips. 'But you can say it again if you like.'

'Can I? Does that mean you've put your temper back on hold,' she asked tartly.

'Better watch yours, Mrs Naismith. It could get you into trouble. However, it's just possible I owe you an apology for taking you to task as I did.'

'Yes?' Olivia waited, pleased. She had finally got through to this overbearing man.

'Cancel the smug smile,' he said dampeningly. 'Because I'm not going to give you one.' He strummed his fingers on the door. 'Unless you consider dinner an apology.'

Olivia's heart leapt into her throat. 'Dinner?'

'Mmm. With me. Tonight.'

'I can't. There's no one to look after Jamie.'

Thank heaven there wasn't. She'd sooner dine with the Big Bad Wolf than with Simon Sebastian. And anyway – why should he *want* to take her to dinner? There was something odd about this invitation. If it was an invitation.

'I'll take care of arrangements for Jamie.' He spoke as if the matter were decided. 'Annie will look after him. She's devoted to children.'

'No! Jamie won't want –'

'I don't mind,' said Jamie, climbing out of the Rolls and coming to stand beside his mother. 'Annie was nice to Roger and me before I fell in the lake.'

Betrayed by her own flesh and blood! Olivia gritted her teeth. 'I'm afraid it's impossible,' she said, trying to keep her voice level. Simon only smiled, and in the end she couldn't stop herself adding, 'It really is impossible, but – well, why did you ask me?'

It *didn't* make sense. Half an hour ago Simon had been behaving as if he considered her an unfit mother. Now he was asking her out.

'Why?' He ran his eyes lazily over her stiff, indignant figure in red stripes. 'I told you the last time we met that I found certain parts of you attractive.'

'They're not available,' she said quickly.

'Maybe not. But everything has its price.'

'*Mr* Sebastian!' Olivia drew herself up to her full five feet seven inches. 'I assure you you couldn't be more mistaken.'

'Oh?' Simon raised his eyebrows. 'I'm not, you know.' He glanced at his watch. 'I'll pick you up at – say seven.'

'No!' Olivia bent down to emphasize her refusal, but at once Simon reached up to wrap a lock of her dark hair around his fingers.

'All right,' he said. 'Seven-thirty. Don't be late.' He released her and reached over to close the passenger door.

Before Olivia could think of a suitably deflating rejoinder, he had switched on the engine and the Rolls was gliding smoothly down the street.

'Mr Sebastian likes you,' said Jamie, who was standing on the hot pavement, saucer-eyed. 'Dave says after his mum went out with Mr Snowdon, they decided they'd better get married. Does that mean –?'

'No,' his mother replied faintly. 'No, Jamie, it doesn't. And I am *not* going out with Mr Sebastian.'

'Oh.' Jamie looked crestfallen. 'I like Mr Sebastian. He was cross when I fell in the lake, but he's got a cosmic car – and a dog. And I don't think he *meant* to be cross.'

'No,' Olivia agreed wearily. 'I don't suppose he did.'

All the same she wasn't going out with Simon. He came from a world she had no part in – and he was also, without a doubt, the most impossibly overbearing man she had ever met.

As well as one of the sexiest, whispered a tiresome voice out of nowhere.

All right, as well as one of the sexiest. It didn't change anything.

She trailed up the stairs to the flat feeling hot, clammy, thoroughly out of sorts, and determined to put Simon out of her mind.

She might have succeeded if Annie Coote hadn't arrived promptly at seven-fifteen, all bouncing and cheerful and ready to take over Jamie.

Well, why not? Olivia thought. All at once her objections seemed unimportant. She didn't have to *like* the man to enjoy being taken out to dinner.

'I'll just be a minute,' she said to Annie, and hurried into the bedroom to change.

Her all-purpose black, she decided, standing glumly in front of the flimsy, khaki-coloured wardrobe. It would just have to do. She pulled out a slim-fitting dress with spaghetti straps and slipped it on before she had a chance to change her mind.

The dress was quite the wrong colour for an evening that promised to continue boiling hot. But it was the only elegant dress she owned. And she was damned if she was going anywhere with that upper-crust powerhouse of a man looking like a refugee from a jumble sale.

She still didn't entirely believe she was actually about to go out with His High and Mightiness. But – she fingered the thin gold band she still wore on her left hand. It had been years since anyone had taken her to dinner. It wouldn't hurt, just this once. And Simon did owe her some kind of apology.

At the edge of her mind a small voice whispered that she was inventing reasons to accept his invitation.

She ignored it.

When Dan had died she had vowed she would never again allow herself to fall for a handsome face and superficial charm. She knew all too well how easy it was for love to turn sour, for something begun in starry-eyed enchantment to end in disappointment and regret. She had been through that hell once already. She refused to go through it again. For that reason alone there could be no danger in accepting Simon's invitation.

Outside in the street, a dog barked. It sounded a bit like the Ripper. Olivia reached for her scent, the very expensive bottle Dan had given her on their first anniversary, and which she had used sparingly and only on special occasions ever since.

There hadn't been many special occasions lately.

Olivia breathed in the delicate fragrance of lilies and thought of Simon's ice-blue eyes and subtle masculinity. She had to admit he frightened her a little, although she knew that to him she was only a passing amusement. What was it he had said? That he liked his victims willing and warm? She had told him she was neither. She couldn't afford to be a victim again.

'Olivia Naismith, this is ridiculous,' she announced to her reflection in the small mirror that always made her face look lop-sided. 'Totally ridiculous. You can't possibly go out with that man.'

'No, of course I can't.' She nodded at the mirror, agreeing with herself, and started to peel off the dress. Lucky there was still time to change her mind . . .

She started, as a sharp knock sounded on the bedroom door.

It was Annie. 'Mr Simon's here, miss,' the young woman announced importantly. 'He says to tell you to get a move on.' She giggled, as if Simon's arrogance was daringly endearing.

Olivia, who didn't find it endearing in the least, realized she had vacillated too long. Escape was out of the question. She was trapped.

With fingers that had suddenly gone clammy, she fastened two minute silver studs in her ears, straightened her shoulders and took several deep breaths. Then she waited five long minutes before walking out to meet Simon in the low-ceilinged room that served as kitchen, sitting-room and playroom.

She smiled at him, her emotions well under control now, and hoped she looked as cucumber-cool as was possible on this hot summer evening.

'You're late,' observed Simon, whose seductive form in grey trousers and lightweight blue blazer was overflowing a small, flowered chair. He inspected her slim figure in fitted black linen with appreciative amusement. 'But worth waiting for. You're the only woman I know who can wear black in the middle of a heatwave and get away with it.'

Olivia smiled politely. If he was going to keep that up, the evening might pass quite pleasantly.

He didn't keep it up, of course. Rather the opposite. But she supposed it could have been worse.

'Your nose is peeling,' Simon remarked as soon as he had her settled in the Rolls. 'With that alabaster skin of yours, you ought to wear sunscreen.'

Phrased differently, it could have been a compliment. Olivia didn't think it was. And she knew her nose was peeling and didn't much want to be reminded of it. 'I thought you were going to apologize,' she said. 'Not make personal remarks about the way I look.'

'Apologize?' Simon spun the Rolls expertly round a corner. 'Because I was sorely tempted to chastise you soundly and toss you into the lake after your son? Yes, it does seem I may have misjudged you there. It was somebody's father I should have thrown in.'

'I don't think it was altogether Harold's fault. Jamie's very quick to seize an opportunity.'

Simon shook his head. 'You're a remarkably charitable woman,' he said drily. 'Provided I'm not the charity, of course. Not many mothers would be as forgiving of the man who had just mislaid their son.'

'I try to give people the benefit of the doubt,' Olivia said pointedly.

Simon's lips twitched. 'And I don't? You're right. I don't. In my profession there isn't a lot of room for indulging in doubts.'

'So you're used to making snap judgements?' Olivia was equally dry. 'But now that you no longer live on a knife-edge, don't you think you could learn to get your facts straight before you start passing judgement? It's called tolerance, I believe.'

Simon changed hands on the wheel. 'I'm damned if I'll tolerate children drowning themselves in my lake. Every year, at least one of them tries it. It was the same in my father's day. And my brother Martin's.'

'Oh?' Olivia was momentarily distracted from her irritation at being patronized. 'Of course. You had a brother.'

'Yes. I had. He was killed six years ago in Scotland. He fell off a horse.' Simon's voice was neutral, as if his brother's death was a matter of indifference.

Olivia was shocked. She understood that his career had made him a master at concealing his emotions, but he was talking about his own flesh and blood . . .

'You obviously miss him,' she remarked with undisguised sarcasm.

Simon's eyes remained on the road, but she didn't miss the quick hardening of his jaw. 'Yes. As a matter of fact I do. Sherraby should have been his. And after that his children's. Not that he had any children. That requires a wife.'

Oh. Perhaps Simon did care after all. 'He wasn't married?' she asked quietly.

'Divorced.' The word was flat, very final. Olivia understood the subject was closed.

'You love Sherraby, don't you?' she said suddenly. Who wouldn't love a home as beautiful as his? Again she felt a wistful kind of – not envy exactly. But an overwhelming longing to put down roots.

'Yes,' Simon answered. 'It seems I do. Far more than I realized when all the responsibility lay with Martin.'

'I think I'd feel the same if Sherraby were mine,' Olivia said.

He sent her a sharp glance, and she shifted to the far edge of her seat.

Soon Simon was turning the car into a narrow lane running beneath a green archway of chestnuts, and when they came out into the sunlight again they were in a large, wooded clearing beside a river. In the centre of the clearing stood an old mill. Its wheel had long since fallen into disuse, but the warm brick walls provoked images of a quieter, more pastoral era when life was shorter and change came slowly. Beside the millpond, rustic tables had been set for a meal.

'We're eating outside?' asked Olivia. She might have known Simon's choice would not be conventional.

'If you like. There's a restaurant inside the mill if you prefer it.'

Olivia shook her head. 'No. It's beautiful here. so peaceful –'

'Until the midges come,' Simon said.

She laughed for the first time since he had arrived to pick her up. 'There's a breeze now. They won't be too bad.'

He shrugged and led her to a table apart from the others set beneath a weeping willow tree.

They sat quietly, sipping wine, gazing into the tranquil depths of the pool, and absorbing the peace of the summer evening.

'"Thro' quiet meadows round the mill
"The sleepy pool above the dam,
"The pool beneath it never still . . ."' Olivia quoted softly. 'It can't have changed a bit since Tennyson's day. This was his country, wasn't it?'

'It was. But in his day you wouldn't have gone to a mill to be served the best French wines. Or the kind of food you won't find in a cottage kitchen.'

His tone was quietly amused. But he was right.

When it came, the meal was superb, the wine dry and delicate. They dawdled over it, and by the time the midges drove them inside for coffee it had grown dark.

Olivia, pleasantly drowsy and full of the kind of food she hadn't tasted in years, found she was having great difficulty remembering that she mustn't allow herself to enjoy Simon's company too much.

Simon Sebastian, with his cool smile and husky bedroom voice, entertaining her with practised ease as he refilled her wine glass and spoke of the countryside he loved, was a very dangerous man. A ruthless man, too, from all accounts. At least in his former life. And he had made no secret of the fact that he wanted more from her than she was willing to give . . .

The thought sent a quick, hot quiver down her spine.

'Have you – have you always lived alone in that big house? Since you inherited it, I mean?' she asked abruptly.

Oh, lord. She hadn't meant to say that. And she had interrupted him just as he was replying to a question she'd asked about how the waterwheel had worked in the days when this was still a working mill. Now he would know she hadn't really been listening.

Simon's eyes narrowed, and he leaned forward with his hands linked on the table. He was studying her features as if he expected them to yield up information.

Olivia smiled brightly, anxious to disguise her inner turmoil. 'Sorry. I didn't mean to interrupt. It just occurred to me that . . .' Her voice trailed off. What had actually occurred to her was that Simon looked incredibly delectable. His burnished head contrasted strikingly with the darkly panelled wall behind him, and the shadows cast by a lantern wove mysterious patterns across his face. Without wanting to, she began to imagine that glorious head resting on a pillow – or perhaps below her on the dark green grass of Sherraby.

Simon smiled slowly, and she was mortified to see that he had caught the drift of her thoughts and found them promising.

'No,' he said, unclasping his hands and leaning back. 'I haven't always lived alone. But apart from Mrs Leigh and Annie, I'm alone now. Why? Were you thinking of offering your – services?' There was a wealth of meaning in the word.

'Oh!' Olivia drew back, but she couldn't tear her gaze from the mouth that had just uttered those unforgivably provocative words. 'No!' she exclaimed. 'No, that's not . . . Listen, it was none of my business. I don't know why I asked.'

She didn't either. Somehow the question had just erupted out of her mouth.

'I see,' Simon murmured. 'But since you did ask, the answer is that my mother lived at Sherraby until she remarried and moved up to Scotland to play golf. That was less than a year ago. So you can forget all those notions about debauchery and orgies by the lake. Mother has strong opinions on the subject of propriety.' He smoothed a hand over his jaw. 'However, as she's not in the picture at the moment, if you'd care to volunteer as my – shall we say companion? I'm considering accepting applications . . .'

Olivia gaped at him, then gave a strangled gasp. Was he serious? For a moment the thought caused an odd prickling at the back of her neck. But when she studied the line of his lips, all curved and seductive and mocking, she knew he was only trying to get under her skin.

'Sorry. Not interested,' she said, attempting to match the careless lightness of his tone. 'I don't do orgies.'

'I thought you mightn't. What *do* you do, Olivia?'

There was an unmistakable suggestion in the question. Studying the crooked slant of his mouth and the meaningful glitter in his eye, Olivia felt an electric curl of heat deep in her abdomen.

She mustn't succumb to it. That way lay further pain and grief.

'Nothing that would interest you,' she said.

He studied her through thick, unexpectedly dark lashes. 'I wouldn't be too sure of that,' he drawled.

In spite of the heat, Olivia found herself shivering.

'You should have brought a wrap,' Simon said, standing up and holding out his hand. 'Time to take you home, Mrs Naismith.'

Olivia stood up. But when she didn't take the proffered hand, Simon smiled with a certain malice, placed it deliberately on her waist and turned her gently in the direction of the door. Only when he was obliged to help her into the Rolls did he remove it.

Although nothing specific had been said to make her nervous, Olivia kept herself pressed against the door of the car on the drive home, as far away from Simon as she could get. And when they pulled up at the kerb she was out and on the pavement even before he had switched off the engine.

'What's your hurry?' he asked, getting out, and taking his time about strolling round to her side of the car. 'I know you can't ask me in. Too much of a crowd. But that doesn't mean we can't say goodnight.'

Olivia backed away hastily. 'Goodnight,' she said. 'Thank you for a – a lovely evening.'

'Spoken like a true Victorian miss. Is that the best you can do?'

'Yes. Yes it is.'

'What are you afraid of, Olivia? Me? I'm really quite harmless.' The smile he gave her was anything but harmless, but to be fair to him, he couldn't know that.

Olivia's stomach rolled over. 'No. No, of course I'm not afraid of you,' she whispered.

'But you don't want to kiss me?'

She moistened her lips, tried to tear her gaze from his mouth and found she couldn't. Oh, yes, she wanted to kiss him. The knowledge hit her like a blow in the face. But she didn't *want* to want to. He was magnetically attractive, terrifyingly seductive – but if she kissed him, or allowed him to kiss her, the whole agonizing business of love might start again. Not, of course, that Simon would want to marry her. But even a temporary attachment could hurt. *Would* hurt. She wasn't the kind of woman who loved lightly. Or even lusted lightly. If she had been, the hell she had lived through with Dan might not have been so bad, might not have left her so determined to shield her heart from further pain . . .

Simon's lips tipped up in a blatantly come-hither smile.

'No,' Olivia gasped, taking another step towards the gate. 'No, I don't want to kiss you.'

His eyes were hooded in the light from the lamp on the corner. 'Don't you?' he said softly. 'You forget, Olivia, I've had too much experience not to recognize lies when I hear them. And liars.'

That did it. Suddenly she wasn't dazed and hesitant any more. She was angry. Furiously angry with this smug, self-assured man who gave away so little of himself, and yet assumed he knew exactly how she felt. And the fact that he was right, that she was indeed lying, didn't do a thing to cool her temper.

'OK, macho man,' she snapped. 'Show me the truth, then. Do you honestly believe no woman can look on your manly visage without wanting to swoon into your arms? Because if you do, you're a bigger rat than I thought.'

'And you're a much prettier little cat,' said Simon. 'What man could resist a challenge like that?'

He stepped forward and took her in his arms.

Heat. A raging, all-encompassing heat that surged through her the moment his fingers touched her bare shoulder. That was her first sensation. It was followed, almost instantly, by panic. She didn't want to feel this way. Not any more. Not with Simon. Only with Dan. And Dan was dead. Which only proved that feelings like this were dangerous, meant to be ruthlessly stamped out.

As Simon's arms held her lightly but inescapably, and his wine-sweet lips moved deliciously over her mouth, Olivia struggled frantically to break free. Free of fear, free of her desperate confusion. But not, in her heart, free of Simon who, responding to her struggles, muttered something she didn't catch and let her go.

'My apologies,' he said, inclining his head. 'Apparently I mistook sheer temper for a challenge I was expected to take up. Goodnight, Olivia.' He turned his back and put one foot on the running board.

Olivia stared at the rigid set of his shoulders, unable to grasp what had happened. Her body was still shuddering with shock. 'No,' she said, as she realized he was about to drive away. 'No, you didn't mistake me.'

She couldn't lie to him, or to herself, after all. All at once there didn't seem much point.

Simon turned slowly and, closing the door of the Rolls deliberately behind him, he leaned against it and folded his arms. 'Is there something wrong, Olivia?' he asked. 'I know I kissed you. But I promise I had no thought of assaulting you – not in full view of Mrs Critchley's cat.' He nodded at a black shape sitting on the gate, watching them with yellow-eyed disdain.

Olivia glanced at the cat, swallowed, and managed a wavering smile. 'I know. It's just that – that I can't – it's too soon –'

'Nearly a year. Do you plan to stay celibate forever?'

She swallowed again, watching the play of muscles across his chest. Then she raised her eyes to the strong column of his throat, and above it to the mouth that seduced her even as it tightened. *Did* she plan to stay celibate forever? Until today, the alternative had scarcely occurred to her. And yet . . .

No! No, she mustn't even think it. Hadn't her life with Dan demonstrated graphically enough that love was precarious at best, downright disastrous at worst? And from some instinct deep within her she knew that for her there could be nothing less than love. Which was why there would be no more kisses.

'Yes,' she said. 'Yes, I do plan to stay – single.'

'I didn't propose marriage, Olivia.' Simon's voice, light and dry as dust, came to her as if from a distance.

'I know. I didn't mean . . .' She took a deep breath, and caught the faint scent of Mrs Critchley's roses.

'I'm sorry if I gave you the impression I was available. Because I'm not.'

'No?' Simon glanced at the hands curled tightly at her sides and said quietly, 'We'll see.'

She waited, tensed for flight, in case he should try again to prove to her just how vulnerable she was. But instead he turned her deliberately around and gave her a gentle shove towards the gate.

'Goodnight, Mrs Naismith,' he said.

'Goodnight,' Olivia replied. She heard the car door slam. 'And – um, thank you.' It wasn't clear in her mind why she was thanking him, but it seemed the right thing to do. Even if he couldn't hear her.

As she drifted up the path to the side door which gave access to her suite, the black cat darted out of nowhere to rub itself up against her leg. She bent to pick it up.

'Are you wishing me luck, Ebony?' she murmured, burying her cheek in the soft fur. 'I hope I'm not going to need it.'

She remembered how she had felt during those electrifying seconds in Simon's arms. If she hadn't fought it, would she have discovered again those feelings she had once shared with Dan? And would she, one day, come to regret this lost opportunity? Maybe. Yes, maybe she would. But still, it was surely for the best. She was content now with the life she had with Jamie. Why leave herself open to further hurt?

No reason at all, she assured herself as she climbed the narrow stairs to her home beneath the eaves. So why did she feel this painful tightness in her chest?

It was dark on the stairs. Out there by the millpond with Simon, everything around her had been green.

Simon slid from the saddle and gave Cactus, his coal-black Arabian with the snow-white feet, a perfunctory pat before handing him over to John Cousins, the gatekeeper who doubled as a groom.

'Nothing like a good gallop for clearing the mind, Mr Simon,' Cousins remarked. 'You look the better for it.'

'I feel the better for it,' replied Simon, who never ceased to be amazed at his staff's ability to discern his frame of mind. If some of the rogues he had come up against in the past had possessed a similar ability, it wasn't likely he would be here now to tell the tale.

As he strode towards the house he heard Cactus whinny softly behind him. He too was good at sensing his master's moods.

Olivia reminded him of Cactus in some ways. Strong, spirited, perceptive. But there the resemblance ended. In spite of her squirming, she had felt most deliciously soft and yielding when he'd held her in his arms.

Simon slashed his whip reflectively at a clump of wild grass. Olivia would also need careful handling, probably some training, and a very light touch on the reins. Or, to put it another way, a way she might find acceptable in this age of masculine sensitivity – if he went ahead with the plan that had begun to germinate in his mind somewhere between the coffee and the kiss, he would have to be subtle as a poker player and considerably more tactful than was his habit.

He bent down to pick up the Ripper, who was scrabbling enthusiastically at his knees.

'What do you think, Rip?' he asked. 'I've coped with tougher assignments in my time. And she's intelligent. It won't take her long to learn the ropes.'

Rip wagged his tail.

'I know,' Simon said. 'I know. Althea Carrington-Coates already knows the ropes. But Althea Carrington-Coates doesn't make me laugh. Althea Carrington-Coates is no fun whatsoever to provoke because she hasn't the wit to know she's being teased – or the gumption to give as good as she gets. Besides, I have very little desire to share a bed with Althea C-C.'

Rip nuzzled his ear.

'You're right,' Simon said. 'I'll take a few more days to think it over. But I'm pretty sure she's the one for the job.' He scratched the squirming little dog under his chin. 'You know something, Rip? If all goes well, that overgrown brat, otherwise known as my Cousin Gerald, may soon find his expectations drastically reduced. And if Emma thinks I ought to feel sorry for him, that's her problem.'

'Rrr,' Rip mumbled agreeably.

'Quite so. Of course Mother will make noises about Althea's superior qualifications, but I think in the end she'll be delighted.'

Rip said, 'Mmph,' and licked the other ear.

Simon smiled. As he walked round to the kitchen he was whistling softly through his teeth.

CHAPTER 4

Zack growled a routine thanks to the shapely customs officer behind the counter at Kennedy Airport, and hoisted the battered hold-all that no degree of affluence could cause him to abandon. Not before the day it actually fell apart.

Morag had bought it for him when he left to take up the scholarship to Cambridge. She had been so proud of him, the first one of the family to vindicate all her years of selfless sacrifice. He recognized now, as he hadn't then, that his sister had given up her youth for the sake of her young brothers and sisters. Their father, never caring much after his overworked wife died of tuberculosis, had brought home a pay cheque until he slipped into the River Don one day and drowned. No one had ever been sure if his death was deliberate. After that everything had fallen to Morag, who sewed, looked after other people's children, stuffed envelopes for mail order houses and did anything she could to hold the family together.

The social workers had kept a close eye on them at first, but they had never been able to fault his sister's care.

The day Zack won the scholarship, Morag had hugged him and said the first thing they must do was buy him smart luggage so that the other scholars would know he came from a nice home. He had never told her that most of the other undergrads came with expensive trunks instead of hold-alls, and weren't interested one way or the other in Zack's luggage.

A tall man with a beard jostled his left elbow. On his right a woman in a yellow sari attempted to juggle two suitcases and two very small, very active children.

Airports. They were the same the world over, he supposed. Noisy, crowded and full of glassy-eyed people intent on their destinations and oblivious to what was going on around them.

'Can I help?' he asked the woman in the sari. But she looked at him with mystified brown eyes and shook her head.

Zack sighed, and set out to capture a taxi. It seemed that nowadays people were either too afraid or too independent to accept help when it was honestly offered. Which reminded him; he should have arranged for some help himself at this juncture, preferably in the shape of one of Matthew Colfax's chauffeur-driven cars. Matthew and his wife, Margaret, were in San Francisco. They had said he could use the house and any transportation he needed. But he had to get there first.

He stepped off the kerb in order to dodge round a stout couple locked in ecstatic reunion, looked up when he thought he heard his name called – and groaned out loud.

'Emma! Bloody hell!' he muttered, as a familiar figure stepped briskly in front of him.

'Yes, it's me,' said Emma, looking cool and glamorous in white shorts, sandals and a cream silk blouse. 'You don't sound very pleased to see me.'

'I'm not.'

'You should be. I've brought a car. It'll take you ages to get a taxi.'

'No, it won't. I have my methods.'

'Well, this time you won't need to use them. I've brought the Porsche.'

'Don't tell me *you're* staying at the house? You're supposed to be in Greece, aren't you? With – who was it this time? Ari Andrakis?'

Emma winced, and he knew he'd hit home. 'Yes, of course I'm staying at the house. It's my home. And as you can see, I'm definitely not in Greece.' She jerked her head. 'Come on. The car's this way.'

Zack fixed his gaze on Emma's trim behind as, unwillingly, he followed her through the jostling throng to the place where she had left the Porsche. She looked good from the rear, Emma did. He'd never thought her pretty – her nose and her chin were too pointed for pretty – but there was no denying her appeal. He swerved round two Japanese businessmen wearing suits and cameras, and reminded himself that it was precisely Emma's nineteen-year-old appeal that had driven him to marry Samantha.

And what a disaster that had been.

Hell! Why hadn't Simon told him Emma would be here? If he'd known, he would have booked a hotel – with bars on the windows and a security guard. Even those would have been no guarantee of keeping the little witch out. He sighed. She was nothing if not resourceful. Unfortunately she was also Emma Colfax, spoiled and privileged daughter of Matthew Colfax, whose financial wizardry had long ago provided his family with a fortune. And, as if that wasn't bad enough, she was Simon's cousin.

It was all very well for his friend and partner to come from a different background. But he'd seen enough of Emma and her ever-growing string of male scalps to know that any attachment he allowed himself to form for her would only lead to further disenchantment and disillusion. For him, and probably for her – which could very well put a strain on his relationship with Simon.

No. Zack raised his head and glared at the hot blue midsummer sky. Delectable as Emma had become since that day five years ago when she had attempted to seduce him in the woods, he was damned if he was throwing away everything he'd worked for, including his peace of mind, for a maddening, dizzy little piece who collected men as if they were trophies to be nailed up on her wall.

All the same, he watched appreciatively as Emma bent over to unlock the Porsche. He might not be willing to be collected, but that didn't mean he couldn't admire the view.

Emma gave the wheel a slight twist and swung the car expertly through the gates of a sprawling white mansion overlooking Long Island Sound. It wasn't Sherraby, but still it was good to be home. Traffic on the drive from the airport had been horrendous, yet the moment she turned into the driveway of Oakshades the world became a gentler, more civilized place. A place of peace where the sound of engines and wheels spinning was replaced by the cries of the gulls and wood ducks who inhabited the rocky shoreline just below the garden.

Beside her Zack was silent, as he had been for most of the tedious drive to the North Shore. He was angry, she supposed. Or at best, displeased to find her in New York. She knew he wasn't indifferent, which was something, because every now and then, when he thought she was concentrating on the road, she had caught him looking at her, appraisingly, as if he was trying to decide how to deal with this unexpected glitch in his arrangements.

Emma didn't like being a glitch.

'You're not staying here by yourself, surely?' he said, breaking silence at last as she pulled the car to a stop on the gravel beneath the branches of a huge oak tree.

Would he rush straight back to the city if she told him she was? 'No, as a matter of fact, I'm not,' she was able to acknowledge honestly. 'Most of the staff are on holiday, but Harvey stayed on to look after the house.'

'And to look after you, I suppose.'

He sounded contemptuous, as if he imagined she was incapable of looking after herself.

'No. Harvey's getting old, Zack. He doesn't do much any more. But he's a great caretaker when my parents go away, and they wouldn't think of asking him to retire. He's been with them for over thirty years.'

'Hm,' Zack grunted non-committally. 'But I suppose he still does your housekeeping. And cooks for you.'

'No, he doesn't.' Emma did her best to hide her irritation. 'There isn't much housekeeping, and we do our own cooking. Well – except when Harvey gets to the kitchen before I do. Then he does it. Like you, he doesn't think I'm capable.'

She had the satisfaction of seeing Zack's head come up sharply.

'And are you?'

'Yes. You needn't worry. I won't let you starve. Zack, are you planning on helping me out of the car? Or are we going to sit here all day?'

Zack muttered something about pampered princesses under his breath.

Emma put a hand over her mouth. Damn. Why had she said that? Zack's dour disapproval must have gotten to her. But she knew her thinly veiled hint that he was lacking in manners would have gotten to him a lot worse – and getting to him wasn't part of her plan.

His lips had gone all flat and hard. 'Deepest apologies, my lady,' he said with exaggerated remorse. 'How could I think of putting you to the trouble of opening your own door?'

Emma started to say she had only been joking, which wasn't entirely true, but Zack was already out and jerking open the door on the driver's side of the car. As she stepped sheepishly on to the gravel, he bowed so low that his head was on a level with her knees.

'Oh, don't be so ridiculous,' she snapped. 'I didn't mean it.'

'Most gracious of your ladyship,' he drawled, with his nose now somewhere in the vicinity of her ankles.

'Zack, do stop it. If you bend any lower, you'll fall over.'

'No, I won't.' He straightened abruptly. 'I'll have you know my body's in verra good shape.'

She eyed him suspiciously. Was he teasing her? He always rolled his R's like that when he wanted to provoke a reaction. But – he never made suggestive remarks, so his reference to the shape of his whipcord body could probably be taken at face value.

She decided to find out.

'Why don't you prove it to me?' She giggled and draped herself seductively over the hood of the Porsche.

Zack's eyes, which had perhaps been laughing at her, immediately turned several shades darker. 'If I do you won't like it,' he growled. 'Behave yourself, Emma.'

Emma sighed and pushed herself upright. There was a lovely, wasted scent of roses mingled with the salt in the air. 'Why are people always telling me to behave myself?' she wondered to no one in particular.

'Probably because you don't.' Zack picked up his hold-all and headed up the broad wooden steps to the porch. 'What happened to Ari Andrakis, then?'

Emma groaned inwardly. She wished Zack hadn't heard about Ari. 'Didn't Simon tell you?' she asked. 'As far as I know, Ari is still on Skiros snoozing his way through re-runs of long-dead dramas in which he starred.'

Zack paused long enough to say over his shoulder, 'I don't believe it. The man must be half-dead himself if even *you* couldn't keep him awake.'

'Thank you,' Emma said drily to his back. 'Was that a compliment?'

'No.' Zack put his hold-all on the top step and reached into his pocket for the key Emma's parents had sent to him via Simon.

He didn't get a chance to use it. Just as he was about to insert it in the lock, the door was swept open from the inside by a beaming, very bent old man with toffee-coloured skin furrowed as deeply as a freshly ploughed field.

'Hello, Harvey,' said Zack. 'It's good to see you again.'

'Good to see you too, Mr Kent. Good to see you,' Harvey bellowed. 'Come in, come in.'

Zack had discovered on his only other visit to Oakshades that Harvey Simpson never said anything once if twice would do.

He stepped into the spacious, cedar-panelled hall with Emma hot on his heels.

'You're in the same room you had last time, Mr Kent,' Harvey told him. 'The same room. At the back looking over the Sound, the –'

'Thank you, Harvey,' Zack said, before the old man could say 'Sound' again. 'I'll find my own way.'

He was halfway up the highly polished stairs that always smelled pleasantly of cedar when he sensed that Emma was behind him.

'I need a shower,' he said, turning to face her. 'And I'll see to my own meals, if you don't mind. There's no need for us to get in each other's way.'

'I've already made supper for you,' Emma said.

She would have. Zack opened his mouth to tell her he didn't want it, but she looked so crestfallen that he couldn't bring himself to do it. 'Well, in that case, then, of course I will eat it,' he said.

Her big eyes brightened. 'It's cold. We can eat whenever you want to.'

Cold? That was something. Even Emma couldn't do much to salad. Except, perhaps, forget to wash the lettuce. He glanced at his watch. 'What about seven o'clock? I should be human by then.'

'Fine,' said Emma, who thought he looked mouthwateringly human as he was in his sports jacket and open-necked shirt – even after six hours on the plane.

She hurried down to the big, airy kitchen with its rows of polished pine cupboards to put the finishing touches to the meal she had spent all day preparing. It was by no means certain that Zack's stomach would prove to be a pipeline to his heart. But it was worth a try.

'We're eating in the dining room?' Zack exclaimed. 'Emma, there's only the two of us.'

Damn. She'd goofed again. She was always forgetting that although Zack could, and did, move comfortably in the most affluent circles, and was as at ease with dukes as he was with their servants or the postman, at heart he was still the boy from the wrong side of the river. The boy who saw virtue in simplicity, and very little in the pretensions of rank, wealth or Norman blood.

Emma hadn't meant to seem pretentious. She had chosen the dining room for its relaxed, gracious atmosphere. Somehow the thought of seducing Zack over the knotty pine kitchen table, or up against the fridge, hadn't appealed to her. But here, in the big, light dining room with its pale gold curtains and her mother's collection of antique bird plates on the walls, she had no difficulty seeing herself in the role of fragile Southern Belle entertaining the mysterious and attractive foreign guest . . .

She might have known Zack would find a way to spoil her dream.

'It's already set in the dining room,' she said sulkily, wishing she had used the blue and white pottery instead of her mother's Crown Derby.

'The dining room it is, then.' Zack's hearty enthusiasm didn't quite ring true.

He knew. Damn him, he had seen at once that she was disappointed and was trying, belatedly, to make it up to her. That was the trouble with Zack. Deep down he was nice. Just when she felt like punching him on the nose, he would smile his rare, killer smile, and once again she would be lost.

Not that she wouldn't have been lost anyway. He looked so – so touchable in his jeans and the blue silk shirt he had probably thrown on without thought. *She* had spent the better part of an hour deciding on her white sundress with the red poppies embroidered round the bodice.

Zack pulled out her chair as if they were dining formally at the Waldorf. Emma sat down self-consciously, and then realized that without thinking she had set his place at the far end of the table. That was where her father always sat.

Zack eyed the long expanse of bare wood, then without a word picked up his place setting and moved it so that he was seated on her left facing the bluffs.

'There,' he said. 'Now I won't have to use a megaphone so you can hear me.'

She made a face. 'I wasn't thinking.'

'No,' Zack agreed gravely, and Emma guessed it was his opinion that she rarely did.

'Would you like to taste the wine?' she asked, hoping it wasn't the wrong thing to say.

Zack nodded and did so, solemnly, but as if he found the whole performance mildly ridiculous. Emma smiled brightly and passed him a basket of crusty rolls. 'How long do you plan to be here?' she asked, hoping he wouldn't guess how much his answer mattered.

'I'm not sure. That depends on the clients.'

'Oh. Who *are* your clients?'

Zack tore off a chunk of roll with maddening concentration before replying patiently, 'Emma, our clients hire us because they know that's a question we won't answer.'

'Yes, of course. What I meant was, what will you actually be *doing*?'

'Whatever I'm paid to do.'

'Yes, I know that. But *what*? Surely you can tell me something.'

Zack eyed her darkly over the top of his wine glass. 'No. I can't. In the past I've advised on company and government security, acted as personal bodyguard to the rich and nervous –'

'Bodyguard!' Emma exclaimed. 'You? But why –?'

'Why not? Because I'm not six foot six, and don't weigh twenty-two stone? Don't worry, I've always been up to it.'

Emma had no doubt he had as, automatically, she began to translate his stones into pounds.

'I didn't mean it that way,' she said, hoping he wasn't insulted. 'Will you be bodyguarding here?'

Zack shrugged. 'Maybe.'

'Zack the clam,' Emma said crossly. 'Is it dangerous, being a bodyguard?' She didn't want Zack to be in danger.

'Not usually.' He buttered another chunk of roll. 'Your salads are very good. What's in them?'

She knew that was all she was going to get out of him on the subject of why he was actually in New York.

All right, if he wanted to change the subject, she'd oblige him. In spades.

For the next ten minutes Emma regaled Zack, in minute detail, with a list of exactly which ingredients had gone into each salad. She waited for his eyes to glaze over, but they didn't. Instead he listened with an appearance of genuine interest, as if he were pleasantly surprised by her knowledge.

He really is a pro, she thought grudgingly. No wonder Samantha divorced him. How could any woman get close to a man like Zack? She chased an elusive slice of green pepper around her plate. If only, just once, he would let his his guard down, let her in behind that unrevealing wall . . .

Without changing tone or expression, she said, '. . . and a pinch of turmeric in the mayonnaise,' and brought her recitation to a close.

Zack nodded and put down his knife and fork.

Emma's eyes narrowed. She wasn't out of ammunition yet. 'Are you still waiting for your divorce to go through?' she asked. If that didn't shake him, nothing would.

Zack placed the knife and fork carefully together. 'Why do you ask?'

All right, so he wasn't shaken. Emma shrugged and gave up. 'I just wondered.'

He picked up a piece of celery and crunched it extra-slowly between his teeth.

'Is that some kind of statement?' Emma asked.

'Statement? No, I don't think so. Should it be?'

'You're crunching that celery as if you'd like it to be me.'

'No. I wouldn't like that.' He continued to crunch. 'As it happens, my divorce became final a month ago.'

'Oh.'

He smiled briefly. 'Don't get any ideas, Emma. I know you're not one to let opportunity knock without opening the door, but just so there's no mistake – I'm not available. Not to you.'

Emma took a sip of her wine. It went down the wrong way, and she choked.

Zack waited until she had recovered and then asked, 'Is something wrong?'

'No,' she spluttered. 'Nothing's wrong. But I hope it won't be too much of a blow to your ego if I tell you that you're not the kind of opportunity I'm looking for.' It wasn't pride speaking. Not altogether. She knew it would do her no good to admit to Zack that she wanted him. Had wanted him with an obsessive, painful hunger that had been eating away at her for nearly eight years. A hunger so deep that often it deprived her of sleep.

'Good.' He nodded and refilled her glass. 'I've never wanted to be an opportunity.'

'It must be a relief,' she said coldly.

'What must?'

'Having it all settled. Your divorce.'

He picked up his glass then put it down without drinking. 'Not really. It's never easy when failure becomes final.'

Emma tried not to gape at him. Was that bitterness she heard in his voice? Regret? Was the clam opening up a crack at last to reveal, not an empty shell, but muscle and nerves that could feel pain? For the first time, Emma thought of Samantha's defection from Zack's point of view.

'Oh, Zack,' she cried, forgetting that he had just mortally insulted her. Impulsively, she reached across the table to touch his hand. 'Did you love her very much, then?' She swallowed. 'Do you – still?'

Zack withdrew his hand and laid it on his thigh. 'No,' he said. 'I don't know that I ever did.'

Emma released the breath she hadn't known she was holding. Had the crack closed again? Or was this the opening she'd been waiting for?

Confused, a little shocked, she asked, 'Why did you marry her, then?'

'She asked me to.'

'But –'

Ignoring her, Zack picked up the wine bottle and raised his eyebrows. Emma shook her head, and he emptied what was left into his glass. She stared at him, momentarily bereft of words, and after a while he shrugged and said, 'I thought I was ready to settle down. Samantha wanted marriage and there seemed no reason for it not to work.'

'No reason! When you married her because she *asked* you to?' Emma knew she was staring at him as if his skin had broken out in green stripes, but she couldn't help herself.

'There were other things,' he said. 'Do you know that in some cultures respect in a marriage is what's important? Besides . . .' he swallowed a mouthful of wine as if he were drinking whisky '. . . I liked the way she looked.'

What man wouldn't? Emma thought. Zack's ex-wife, whom she had met only once, was luscious. No other word could do justice to Samantha Kent's ripe figure and sultry allure – so different from her own understated attributes. Emma had absorbed that unpalatable truth the moment she set eyes on Samantha.

'And you respected her?' she said to Zack, not wanting to dwell on the other woman's looks-to-die-for.

'I did. At first.'

'But not later?'

'No. Not once I found out she had married me to spite her ex-husband.'

Zack spoke matter-of-factly, as if his wife's behaviour was tiresome but not unusual.

'I don't understand. Why should that spite him?' Had she forgotten to clean out her ears?

'I don't know that it did. Sam wasn't thinking clearly at the time. I suppose I was living proof that she didn't need him any longer.'

'But she did? Oh, Zack.'

His smile was caustic. 'Don't worry. My heart wasnae broken.'

Was it capable of being broken? Emma wondered. With Zack it was impossible to tell. And he was doing his Scottish thing again. But at least he was finally talking about his marriage.

She was about to probe further when the dining room door opened and Harvey tottered in with a tray of coffee.

Emma groaned inwardly. What incredibly awful timing. 'Harvey, it smells wonderful,' she said. 'But you needn't have bothered.'

'Maybe not, Miss Emma. But if I hadn't, you'd likely have tried to make it yourself. And you know what happened last time. Last –'

'Harvey, that was ages ago.'

'Not so long. Not so long. Can't have you burning the house down round Mr Kent's ears.'

'It wouldn't be hospitable,' Zack agreed soberly.

Harvey grinned, and Emma glared at both of them. 'You're hopeless,' she said. 'Thank you anyway, Harvey. Zack, shall we drink it on the sundeck? Not that there's much sun at this time of day, but we can smell the sea and listen to the waves.'

'Why not?' Zack said. 'And after that I'm going to bed. It's been a long day.'

That was that Zack's way of saying there would be no further revelations tonight. She thought of him stretched out in all his naked glory in the room right across the hall from her own, and involuntarily let out a sigh.

Zack heard it, and she saw his lips twitch as he picked up the tray and followed her out on to the deck.

'Harvey's never forgotten I once burned out his favourite pot,' she told him as they settled themselves in Cape Cod chairs with primrose yellow cushions. 'But I honestly *can* make coffee.'

'I'm sure you can,' Zack said soothingly.

Emma, feeling patronized, was not soothed.

They drank their coffee in what might have been a companionable silence if she hadn't been so conscious of Zack's closeness, and of the fact that if she moved her hand just a fraction her fingers would connect with his thigh.

As the sun went down and the shadow of the big house stretched across the grass, they listened to the waves swishing over the rocks and watched purple-tinged clouds drift across the sky. When the wind came up and the sky began to darken, Zack said it was time to go in.

Without being asked, he carried the remains of the coffee back into the kitchen, and afterwards Emma followed him upstairs.

When they reached the top he said, 'Goodnight,' politely, and opened the door to his room.

Emma gazed at him with a longing she couldn't hide. He looked so beautiful standing there all dark and intense and desirable. But when she took a step forward, he met her eyes briefly and turned away.

'Zack . . .' She held out her hand.

'No,' he said, and closed the door firmly in her face.

Damn him. He hadn't even known what she'd meant to say. For that matter, neither had she. But it was obvious what he *thought* she'd had in mind.

That, Emma Colfax, is because he's right, she reminded herself as she shut her own door and crossed to the long window looking out over the cliffs. How could he *not* be aware that you want him – have wanted him almost forever?

She opened the window and listened to the familiar wash of the waves and the rustling of the leaves in the trees by the tennis court – all the sounds of the night that had always had the power to calm her spirit. Even as a little girl, whenever she wanted to think clearly she had stood at this window and breathed in the sharp, salty air. And she *must* think clearly now.

Zack was here, within yards of her door. He was unapproachable as ever, but this time, for once, they were not surrounded by a houseful of people. Harvey didn't count. For one thing he slept like a log. For another, he was the only person in the world who thought she was an angel incapable of serious misbehaviour. Burned coffee pots didn't count in his books.

Emma leaned out into the night. Was Zack awake too? No, he'd had a long flight. He was probably sprawled across his bed, fast asleep. She ran her tongue hungrily over her lips. Tomorrow. Tomorrow would be time enough to put her plan into action. He would be here for at least a week, probably longer. And if she, who had attracted the eye of Ari Andrakis, couldn't overcome Zack's resistance in a week, then . . .

Emma left the window and trailed back to her large, lonely bed. If she couldn't overcome his resistance in a week . . . No. That wasn't conceivable. She wanted Zack. He was no longer spoken for. Therefore she would get what she wanted.

An hour later she was still wide awake, staring up into the void where her vaulted wooden ceiling soared beyond the reach of the moonlight.

There had been moonlight that other night, three years ago at Sherraby, when she had lain awake just like this listening to the frogs in the lake and, as usual, fantasizing about Zack, who had arrived unexpectedly to spend the weekend.

He had come without Samantha and without excuses. When he'd found Emma there, just for a moment his dark expression had lightened and he had smiled. Then the shutters had come down again and he turned away and began playing with the Ripper.

Later, as Emma lay restless and unsettled in her bed, a strange, lonely tune had risen above the cacophony of the frogs, and drifted eerily in through her open window. She had listened for a while, puzzled, and then got up.

It wasn't a tune she recognized, yet it was being played on an instrument that ought to be familiar. She frowned. The music was coming from the woods. Sherraby Woods. A long time ago, she had believed those woods to be magic.

Knowing it was probably unwise, but drawn by a magnetism that those who knew her would have labelled plain curiosity, Emma pulled on jeans and a sweatshirt and went outside.

It was a warm night for early June, with little or no

breeze, and as she approached the woods the mournful notes came to her clearly in the stillness.

By the time she reached the edge of the trees, she was almost certain she knew what she would find.

Zack was seated on a mossy stump just inside the woods. She couldn't see the moss, but she knew it was there. The moonlight filtering through the branches lit his face only indistinctly, but as Emma moved closer she saw that he was holding a harmonica.

The tune he was playing was no longer some nameless sadness, but the familiar strains of 'Loch Lomond'.

He turned his head when a twig cracked beneath her feet, but he went on playing until the end.

'*And me and my true love will never meet again on the bonny, bonny banks of Loch Lomond,*' Emma sang softly.

Zack lowered his harmonica. 'You've a bonny voice,' he said.

'I like to sing. Sometimes. When there's something to sing about.'

'You've plenty to sing about,' he replied gruffly.

'Not really. Zack, what are you doing here?'

'What does it look like? I'm playing my harmonica.'

'Yes, but why? Why now, here, in the middle of the night?'

'Maybe I'm the Pied Piper,' he said. '*You* came.'

'Did you want me to come?'

'No.' He spoke with a harshness that made her shrink back. 'I'm married, Emma.'

'I know.' She went to lean against a tree trunk for support, pushing her hands deep into the pockets of her jeans. 'Why isn't Samantha with you?'

He didn't answer right away, but when she repeated the question, he said, 'She wanted the time to herself.'

'Oh.' Emma didn't understand. If *she* had been Samantha she would have wanted to be with Zack. It wasn't as if he was some boisterous extrovert, the kind of man who wore you out. But she couldn't see Zack's face properly and she didn't like to ask if there was something wrong with his marriage. Instead she said, 'Aren't you coming back to the house?'

He stood up then and, to her surprise, took her hand in his and gently kissed her forehead. 'Yes,' he said. 'Yes, wee Emma. I'm coming.'

As they walked side by side through the fields, not touching, Emma said quietly, 'I'm not little, Zack. I'm five foot eight.'

He laughed. 'I didn't mean you were short.'

'I'm not all that young either. I'm twenty-one.'

'I know. And I'm nearly thirty. And married.'

It was the closest Zack had ever come to admitting he was aware of her as a woman.

Three months later he told Simon that he and Samantha were getting a divorce.

Nearly three years later, on another continent, Emma wriggled her shoulders on the pillow and decided it was time to plan their future. Three years was too long. She could wait for what she wanted if she had to, but now the need for waiting was past. She lay there for a few more minutes, settling everything in her mind, then turned on her side and closed her eyes.

Tomorrow night. It shouldn't be difficult. She had played a sleepwalker once in a school play. After that, once she was in his room, things were bound to turn out the way she wanted.

When she finally fell asleep she was smiling.

By the time she got up the following morning, Zack had already left the house. In the afternoon he phoned to say he wouldn't be back for dinner.

It didn't matter. There was no hurry. Emma refused to be daunted.

Midnight came. Zack still wasn't home. Shoulders drooping, she set her alarm, yawned, and went to bed.

At five-thirty the alarm screeched her awake.

'Shut up,' Emma muttered, extracting an arm from beneath the sheet and slamming it off. She turned over and prepared to go back to sleep. But just before her eyes closed she remembered.

Zack. Her perfect plan.

Groggily, and before she could change her mind, she swung her legs on to the plaited rug beside the bed.

The polished floor felt cold beneath her feet as she pattered across to the door, opened it, and peered into the hall. No sign of life. Not that she had thought there would be. Lifting the hem of her white satin night-gown, Emma sped across the few yards separating her room from Zack's and turned the handle on his door.

He didn't stir as she pushed it open. Emma raised her chin, focused her eyes straight ahead and, trying not to feel like Lady Macbeth on the prowl, glided resolutely over to his bed. She could see it quite clearly in the moonlight.

When her knees connected with the softness of a quilt, she saw something else.

Zack hadn't stirred because he wasn't in the bed.

Emma bent over, checked the quilt. It was exactly as he must have left it that morning.

He hadn't come home. It was morning and Zack hadn't come home.

Emma lifted her fists to her mouth, biting her knuckles to stifle a foolish scream.

Had something happened to him? Of course, if he had been anyone but Zack . . .

But he *was* Zack. That was the whole point. And, since Samantha, not so much as a rumour of another woman had reached her ears. A one-night stand then? No, Zack wasn't like that. He was too smart to go in for one-night stands. He had to be.

Which meant that if he wasn't in his bed, something *was* wrong. Something related to that business he and Simon were so proud of? He'd said what he did wasn't usually dangerous, but . . . Oh, why couldn't the two of them have started up a bank? Or an accounting office? Or a department store? Anything – *anything* that would have kept Zack in his bed where he belonged.

She looked around helplessly, seeking inspiration in the shadows. What ought she to do? Of course, it was possible he was perfectly all right and going about his business. But she didn't believe it. If Zack was all right he would have phoned, just as he had earlier when he'd let them know he wouldn't be in for dinner . . .

What was that? Emma lowered her hand and clutched the yoke of her nightgown. Was someone coming? She froze, holding her breath, waiting for the sound of footsteps.

Silence. Then from the far end of the hall, faintly at first but gradually increasing in volume, came the rhythmic sound of . . .

Snoring. Oh, for heaven's sake! Emma let go of her nightgown with a groan. Harvey. He always snored. She gave an exasperated sigh and began to pace back and forth across the floor.

What should she do? The police wouldn't believe anything was unusual. If she told them a healthy young man wasn't in his bed they would laugh at her. There was *nobody* she could turn to. Except . . .

Wait a moment. She stopped pacing abruptly and sat down on the bed.

Simon. There was always Simon. He would know what do do. She glanced at her watch. Wednesday. Ten forty-five in England. He would be in his office.

Almost laughing with relief, Emma sped back to her room, picked up the phone beside her bed and began to dial.

CHAPTER 5

Simon, absorbed in the report he was reading, ignored the phone when it started to ring. Hadn't he told Diane to hold his calls? He threw an irritable glance at the closed door to the outer office. Dammit, his secretary was supposed to be running interference out there.

'Diane!' he shouted. 'Diane, get the damn phone.'

The phone went on ringing, and Simon, with an oath, picked it up.

'Sebastian and Kent,' he said, smoothly suppressing all signs of irritation.

'Simon! Oh, Simon, thank goodness –'

'Emma?'

Now what? She'd only been gone three days. And Zack couldn't have arrived in New York until – he glanced at the calendar on his desk – until Monday. This was Wednesday. Surely his wayward cousin couldn't have manufactured a crisis already. Or could she? Simon sighed. Who was he kidding? Emma could manufacture a crisis out of a paper bag if she put her mind to it.

'Oh, Simon, you've *got* to help,' he heard her wailing. 'I don't know what to do . . .'

'Neither do I, until you tell me what's happened. What have you done?' Simon rolled his black executive chair against the wall and propped his feet on a black metal waste-basket. This call promised to take longer than he'd hoped.

'I haven't done anything. It's Zack,' Emma moaned.

Surprise, surprise. 'What about Zack?' he asked.

'Simon, it's awful. He's disappeared.'

'Nonsense.' He swung his feet to the ground and rolled himself back to the desk. He might have known this was only another of his cousin's idiotic dramas.

'It isn't nonsense,' she insisted. 'He left the house yesterday morning, and now it's morning again and he *still* hasn't come back.'

'Zack's a big boy, Emma. Don't worry about him.'

'But –'

'Listen, if you must know, he called me earlier. He's fine, I promise you.'

'He called *you*?'

Simon picked up a pen and scribbled a note on the abandoned report. Now they were getting somewhere. Emma was indignant instead of in a panic. 'Is there something wrong with that?' he asked mildy. 'I am Zack's partner.'

'Yes, but he's staying *here*. At Oakshades. Why wouldn't he let us know what he's doing?'

Simon looked at his watch. 'Emma, it's not even six o'clock in your part of the world. He's probably under the very reasonable impression that you're asleep. Which you ought to be. Go back to bed, there's a good girl. And try not to drive my partner crazy. I can't afford to lose him.'

'Simon!' Emma's howl of indignation assaulted him over the wires as he replaced the receiver carefully on its cradle.

He raised his eyes to the ceiling. In the same moment, someone sneezed on the other side of the door.

'Diane?' he called. 'Is that you?'

'Yes, it is. I think I'm catching a cold.' A pale, string bean of a woman appeared in the doorway and wilted there looking put-upon.

'Is that why you've stopped answering the phone?' Simon wasn't in a particularly good mood. Zack's call had been satisfactory, as expected, but he had also heard from Gerald, and that was never good news. The call from Emma was typically overwrought, as well as mildly disturbing. He could have stopped her going to New York, but he'd chosen not to as much for his own sake as for hers. Now he wondered if he had done the right thing. He didn't want Zack's ability to get on with the job compromised by the antics of his tiresome young cousin. On the other hand, if his normally level-headed partner *could* be persuaded to take on Emma, it would be the very best thing that could happen to her. Zack, of all people, would cope.

Simon finally took in that Diane was sniffling into a hankie and gazing at him with a look of deep reproach. 'Can't I even go to the ladies?' she asked.

'What? Oh. Yes, provided you don't spend half the day there.'

'I never do! That's not fair, Mr Sebastian.' Diane fled into the outer office, blowing her nose loudly in protest.

Damn. Simon knew it wasn't fair. He also knew he ought to hire more staff. But in the interests of security he and Zack preferred to keep the operation small and low-key, using extra operatives only when they needed them. Most days he took her workload into account when dealing with the mousy but discreet Diane.

He pushed a hand through his hair. This business with Olivia must be getting to him more than he had thought. It would be good to have it settled over the weekend.

Olivia. Simon was half-smiling as he turned back to the report. She wouldn't be easy to convince. He understood that, because he didn't convince easily himself unless it suited him – as it just so happened Olivia Naismith suited him. Althea Carrington-Coates didn't, and she never would, no matter what his mother said. Besides, Althea was scared of him. Olivia wasn't, which meant he must be careful not to count his chickens too soon.

He'd never thought of himself as God's gift to women. Since Sylvia, he had left that sort of arrogance to Gerald. All the same, Olivia wasn't indifferent to him. He'd established that much. And he had a feeling he could deal with most of the arguments she would inevitably bring up. The trick was to keep her off balance – and that was something he was good at.

Simon's half-smile stretched into a grin. He finished scanning the report, scribbled a couple of notes at the bottom, and settled back into his chair to contemplate the weekend ahead.

Yes, on the whole he looked forward to it, as he hadn't looked forward to a weekend in some time.

Olivia was in the bath when the phone rang. Jamie was next door playing with Chrissy, so she was taking advantage of the opportunity to soak away the strains of a day that had been hotter than ever and a lot more exhausting than usual.

She hadn't slept well following her unsettling evening with Simon. It hadn't been easy to forget the hot urgency she had felt in his arms – or the way he had said, 'We'll see,' and then casually dismissed her when she'd assured him she wouldn't be available for the kind of date he seemed to be suggesting. What had he meant by that enigmatic comment? And did she subconsciously *want* him to make her change her mind? She dragged lilac-scented soap across her chest for the fourth time, and gradually became aware that the phone was ringing – had, in fact, been ringing for some time.

Should she ignore it? No, better not. It might be something to do with Jamie.

Grumbling under her breath, Olivia clambered out of the old-fashioned bathtub with the feet, grabbed a towel, and skidded into the sitting room in time to pick up the receiver. There was a click, and the line went dead.

Damn. She glared at the black instrument squatting silently on its small oval table. It reminded her of a misshapen bomb that had failed to explode. She waited for it to ring again. When it didn't, she climbed back into the bath.

Immediately the ringing started over.

This time Olivia leaped out of the bath like a missile heading for the moon, and as she dashed into the sitting room she caught herself muttering a few choice words of the type she had heard Dan use when he couldn't find his hidden supply of whisky. Whoever it was wouldn't have rung again so soon unless it was urgent. It *had* to be about Jamie.

'Olivia?' The voice on the other end was familiar. But it wasn't remotely urgent. Her panic evaporated, turned into irritation.

'Yes? Who is this?'

'Simon. Your favourite rat. Don't tell me you've forgotten already.'

Her traitorous stomach did a loop-the-loop and settled uncomfortably in her ribcage. 'No, I haven't forgotten. No such luck.'

'Hmm. Then maybe we can do something to change your luck. I'll be at Sherraby for the weekend and I want to talk to you. I'll send John Cousins over with Annie tonight around nine-thirty, if that's all right. I would have suggested dinner, but I'm tied up in town at the moment. There's something we have to discuss. As soon as possible.'

'I don't have anything I want to discuss with you.' Olivia knew she sounded more surly than assertive, but that pretty much reflected the way she felt.

'Somebody put gripe-water in your porridge this morning?'

'No.' She took a deep breath. There was no point in being rude to Simon. It wasn't his fault that just the sound of his voice was enough to shatter her hard-won peace of mind. 'No. I'm sorry. It's just that I'm tired. And I don't see that we have anything to talk about.'

'You're mistaken. We have.' When she said nothing, he added, 'It involves Jamie – among other things.'

'What does?'

An impatient sigh hummed down the wires. 'Olivia, I do not propose . . .' He stopped, then continued abruptly, 'At least not over the phone. So if you could just keep your options open and your shirt on until I've spoken to you –'

'It's not on now. My shirt, I mean. I'm dripping all over the floor.'

There was a long pause, and then Simon's choked voice said, 'You mean I got you out of the bath? You're standing there naked?'

'Quite naked,' said Olivia coldly.

'Not even a towel?' His voice wasn't choked now. It was warm, suggestive . . .

'I'm not a sleazy phone service,' she snapped.

'No. Of course not. If you were I wouldn't be calling.' Simon was brisk now. 'Sorry to have caught you at a bad time. I'll send Annie over at nine-thirty, then. To take care of Jamie.'

'No, I –'

But he had already hung up.

Olivia groaned and hurried back to the bathroom to fetch a towel. Damn Simon Sebastian. He was undoubtedly the most infuriating man she had ever met. Also the most autocratic. And why did he feel he had some God-given right to organize her life? She had planned to be in bed by nine-thirty.

She dried herself off, pulled on a skirt and top and went to pick up the phone to tell Simon he'd have to cancel his arrangements.

But when she got through, Annie answered. 'Mr Simon's not home,' the housekeeper explained.

Oh. No, of course he wasn't. What was the matter with her?

'He said I was to be at your place at nine-thirty,'

Annie went on. 'And . . .' She broke off to shout something Olivia didn't catch. When she came back on the line, she said, 'Sorry. That Ripper just ate Mr Simon's *Times*. He'll be fit to be tied, he will.'

'The Ripper?' Olivia asked faintly.

'Huh. Not a chance. Little beast is as slippery as an eel. And Mr Simon won't have him locked up. Says only criminals deserve to live behind bars, and that this is Rip's home.' Annie sighed. 'It has been too, ever since Mr Simon caught some little ruffians throwing stones at Ripper and he brought him home to clean up his cuts. Been here ever since, he has. Thinks Mr Simon's the sun and moon. But he still eats his paper when he can get it.'

So *that* was why Sherraby was guarded by a used paintbrush of a dog instead of by the large and intimidating hound she would have expected of a man as blatantly virile as Simon. It threw a new light on his character. One she hadn't suspected.

She liked a man who was protective of creatures weaker than himself. Maybe, if he wanted to talk to her this evening – well, there was, after all, no real reason not to oblige him. Just this once.

'Can I give him a message?' Annie asked.

'No. No, it's all right. Thank you.' Olivia put down the phone with a feeling that she had somehow been outmanoeuvred.

At nine-thirty precisely, John Cousins arrived with Annie in tow. At nine-forty the Rolls drew up in front of Sherraby Manor.

Simon came down the steps to greet her looking smooth and seductive in a white silk shirt and trousers that sheathed his legs to such elegant perfection that Olivia couldn't quite control a gasp of admiration.

If Simon heard her, he gave no indication. 'Thank you for coming,' he said civilly.

'You didn't give me much choice,' she pointed out.

'I know. But I have no doubt that if you'd put your mind to it you would have found some way to avoid me. I'm glad you chose not to.'

Olivia frowned. He sounded suspiciously conciliatory. And in her experience men only spoke like that when they wanted something.

She said so.

Simon's smile was non-committal. 'You're right, of course. I do want something. Which I hope will be to our mutual advantage.'

Olivia doubted that, but she allowed him to take her arm and steer her up the steps, and from there into the long drawing room where she had waited in such trepidation while he fetched her diary. This time though, she was more curious than anxious as Simon escorted her to a gold brocade love-seat. For a moment she thought he meant to sit next to her, and pushed herself back against the arm. But instead, after going to a mahogany sideboard to pour them each a glass of sherry, he drew up a battered brown corduroy armchair and sank into it like a lion home from the hunt returning to an old and familiar lair.

Olivia crossed her ankles primly and wondered if her red skirt was too short.

'Don't worry,' Simon said, with his annoying habit of seeing right through her. 'I won't pounce. Anyway, Mrs Leigh would probably hear you if you screamed.' He put his head on one side. 'On the other hand, she *is* getting rather deaf.'

'Stop it,' said Olivia. She was in no mood for banter. It was nearly ten o'clock, she was tired and on edge, and she had a busy day planned for tomorrow. 'What do you want to talk about, Simon?'

Simon extended his endless legs and clasped his hands loosely behind his head. The blue eyes that had been studying her with a kind of teasing awareness gradually turned smoky and inscrutable.

'Marriage,' he said.

Olivia blinked, but otherwise she didn't react. It wasn't what she had expected him to say. He hadn't mentioned that he was planning to marry. But with his mother up in Scotland it was probably quite natural for him to think about installing some suitable female at Sherraby to see to the smooth running of the manor. Though why he should discuss his wedding plans with her. . . Olivia allowed her thoughts to follow their own erratic channels. It was easier than trying to analyze her feelings. Less painful, too. Through the open window she heard the frogs begin their nightly chorus from the lake.

'Marriage?' she repeated. 'You're getting married?'

'I hope so.'

A muscle in her lower left eyelid began to flutter. 'Who's the lucky lady?' she asked, smiling brightly and keeping her tone light and unconcerned.

Simon lowered his arms to rest them on the arms of his chair. 'I'm glad you put it that way.'

'What way?'

'You called my intended bride lucky.'

'Figure of speech.' Olivia tossed back her hair. 'Who is she? I suppose I don't know her?'

'Oh, you know her. But maybe not as well as you ought to. Her name's Olivia Naismith.' His eyes weren't smoky now. They were blue spears piercing her defences and, idiotically, making her want to cry. Maybe she *didn't* know herself as well as she thought.

'I suppose you think that's funny,' she said.

'No. I never joke about business.'

'Business? Simon, marriage isn't a business –'

'Ours will be,' he replied, unperturbed. 'Olivia, I've made no secret of the fact that I want you in my bed, from the moment I saw your sexy little backside enticing me from under a bush. But don't get any foolish ideas. This has nothing to do with moonlight and roses and love at first sight. A myth if ever there was one, by the way.'

'Oh.' Olivia wanted to say more. A whole lot more. But she couldn't get the words out.

Simon fixed his gaze on the empty fireplace. 'My partner, Zack, believed all that romantic rubbish,' he murmured, as if he were talking to himself. 'Married a woman he fell for on a train, and within a year his marriage was on the rocks. Within two years his wife had left him.' His fingers began to strum rhythmically on the arm of his chair. 'There was a time when I was equally impressionable. Luckily the lady I set my sights on was a lot more practical than I was.'

Olivia leaned forward, forgetting to worry about the length of her skirt. Simon had spoken drily, without heat, as if he looked on the passionate emotions of the past as mere building blocks to the cold practicality of the present. Except that his fingers were still beating a restless tattoo on the chair. She couldn't see his eyes, but she had no doubt they were as blue and wintry as ever. Was it possible that their very coldness reflected wounds long since healed which had, nonetheless, left hidden scars?

This nonsense about marriage and wanting her in his bed was suddenly almost comprehensible. But surely, in this day and age, men didn't marry for lust. Unless . . .

Oh. Of course. By the very nature of what he was and who he had been in the past, Simon had learned to take an indirect approach. He didn't really want marriage. Not for keeps. What he wanted was a warm body in his bed. She bit her lip, oblivious to the hurt because the hurt inside her was all at once far worse.

'I'm sorry your plans didn't work out with . . .' Olivia paused to brush a hand across her eyes '. . . with –'

'Her name was Sylvia,' Simon said.

'With Sylvia,' she continued, wondering what had happened to cause Simon to speak of his old girlfriend in that tight, contemptuous voice. 'But that's no reason to start talking about business arrangements with me. I take marriage seriously, Simon. To me it's forever, not some phony formality to be gone through before jumping into bed with your latest fancy. Followed, I suppose, by divorce. Is that what you have in mind? I suppose it must be.'

'Must it?' Simon was icily impersonal. 'I was thinking of a genuine formality, as it happens. A binding one. The kind you say you take seriously. I know you don't love me, Olivia.' A smile flicked at the corner of his mouth. 'And I see that as a definite advantage. It's my opinion that a marriage based on mutual convenience stands a much better chance than one based on stardust and dreams.'

Outside, the chorus of frogs was suddenly silent.

Dear lord. He was serious. Olivia felt moisture dampen the palms of her hands. An uncomfortable pressure began to build behind her eyes.

Simon Sebastian was asking her to marry him. Not for love. Not for anything that made any sense. Yet he was looking at her as if he'd suggested a brisk walk in the woods or an energetic game of croquet, and didn't see what the fuss was all about.

Olivia laid her sherry carefully on a small, oval table beside the love-seat, then stood up and moved to the open window. She pressed her knuckles against the sill and stared at the reflection of the room in the glass.

'Why?' she asked.

The frogs started croaking again.

When Simon answered her, his tone was soft, less distant. 'I've already given you one reason.'

Olivia moved her head in negation. 'No. That's not it.'

'Not all of it, I agree. Not even most of it. But it'll do for a start.'

'All right. Go on.'

Simon went on.

'All this – Sherraby – was my brother Martin's up until six years ago. It was my home too, of course, and I suppose I was casually attached to it. But I didn't give it much thought because I knew it would never be mine.'

Olivia, staring into the glass, saw him run a hand across his forehead.

'Oh, it provided me with an income, of course,' he continued, as if he were discussing a cheap, one-room apartment. 'The Sebastians have been luckier than many in that respect. Our ancestors had the widom to diversify their assets – and we still make something from the land. But the actual responsibility was never mine.'

'But now it is.' Olivia watched a moth land lightly on the sill. 'And that makes a difference?'

'Yes, it does.' Simon's voice became as crisp and concise as his words. 'Sherraby's future is secure until the day I die. After that, unless I have issue, it goes to my young cousin, Gerald. In that, according to tradition and the terms of an ancient entailment, I have no choice.'

The moth flew out through the window and Olivia found the courage to turn around. 'Yes, I see. What I don't see is what it has to do with me.'

Simon didn't change his position but there was a tension about him now, a coiled energy, that told her he was about to say something significant. To him anyway.

'I don't want Sherraby to go to Gerald,' he said. 'My cousin is a weak-kneed parasite who spends his life sponging off others. He has a pretty face, and he's had some success charming the ladies. But they always catch on to him in the end. If Gerald owned Sherraby, in a matter of months he'd run it into the ground. Anything worth selling would be sold, what was left would become a weekend refuge for party idiots with no more scruples or brains than a bunch of slugs – or perhaps I should say locusts. Believe me, within a few years Sherraby would be nothing more than a shell. I don't want that to happen.'

'Of course not.' Olivia was genuinely shocked. 'But I still don't see –'

Simon held up his hand. 'You will. The solution, naturally, is for me to produce an heir.' His lips twitched, and she saw the muscles around his jaw start to relax. 'My mother pointed that out to me roughly once an hour during her last visit here. And she has continued to point it out in every letter she's written to me since. Not to mention the phone calls.' He stretched his arms slowly above his head. 'I have agreed with her that the idea isn't without merit. A pleasant task – once I find a suitable woman.'

A suitable woman? No. He didn't mean it. Olivia refused to accept what she was hearing. Simon couldn't think *she* was suitable. And even if he did . . . She put a hand on her chest because her heart had started to beat abnormally fast.

'Yes, I do see that –' she began carefully.

'Good. But in order to produce a legitimate heir, it will be necessary for me to have a legitimate wife. Is that what you were going to say?'

It hadn't been, but Olivia nodded anyway.

'Exactly,' said Simon. 'And that, my dear Mrs Naismith, is where you come in.'

Olivia closed her eyes and waited for the implications of what he had said to sink in.

For some reason that was totally beyond her, Simon Sebastian, with supreme and inexcusable arrogance, had picked her out to be his brood mare. Her bemused gaze came to rest with rapidly increasing fury on the tanned fingers curved around the fragile stem of an old-fashioned crystal sherry glass.

'No,' she said. And then again, 'No. I am not a cow or a horse. I don't breed on demand. And I can't think of one single reason why you imagine I might want to marry you.' Her eyes felt as if they were burning. Her face was beginning to burn too. How *dared* this patronizing, lordly, unfairly attractive man assume that all he had to do was beckon and say, 'I'll have you,' for her to swoon gratefully into his bed and start reproducing?

She glared at Simon. But to her disbelieving rage he was laughing. Actually laughing.

'Definitely not a cow,' he agreed. 'Although I do see a certain similarity to a horse I know. His name is Cactus. As for a reason you might want to marry me – well, one of them we've already discussed. Beyond that, there's the matter of your current circumstances – and Jamie.'

'What's Jamie got to do with it?' Olivia wanted to scream at him, but she knew that wasn't the way to handle a man like Simon, so she spoke quietly. His ridiculous suggestion had to be met with calm, inexorable logic. If only her heart wasn't pounding along like an engine about to come off its tracks. If only she could just cross the room, tweak his aristocratic nose and walk right out of his house and out of his life.

The only problem with that idea was that she found herself unable to move.

Simon put down his glass, tipped his head against the back of the chair and said, as if he hadn't noticed her heightened colour or the fingers clasping and unclasping at her waist, 'You told me yourself you have trouble making ends meet. And that you're concerned about Jamie's future. I can provide him with everything he needs – including a place at a reputable school. He's also something of a handful, I suspect. He needs a father, Olivia. I can be that to him. And you, I think, need a husband. I can be that too.'

His cool blue gaze was not unfriendly, but it made her doubt herself, as if he were telling her to stop reacting like an idiot and see sense.

Olivia lowered her eyes. She had to. She wanted desperately to puncture his self-assurance, to convince him that he couldn't just saunter into her life and take it over because she happened to suit his current needs. But he was right, in a way, about Jamie. He was also deplorably easy to look at, and if she kept on looking she might lose her grasp on reality.

There was no point losing her temper as well.

Simon *was* right about Jamie's needing a father. And in spite of the fact that she hardly knew him, she had a feeling he would fill that role well. He was also right that she worried incessantly about money, about having enough to provide her son with at least the basics of a normal childhood. She was like her mother in that. But her mother's struggles had often ended in defeat.

Olivia didn't mean to be defeated. She meant to raise her child to successful adulthood, and one day, when the time was right, perhaps to own her own accounting firm. That should be enough to fill her days.

Only now, in the present, there was still Jamie. She adjusted the waistband of her skirt. He was the crux of her dilemma. The local school which he attended at present was adequate in most ways. Although when he grew older that might change . . .

Her mind veered in another direction. Simon had said she needed a husband. But she'd had one of those once. She didn't need another. Especially she didn't need another who only wanted her so she could bear his children. Olivia traced a pattern on the carpet with her sandal. On the other hand, provided there was no emotional involvement, was there any reason why a marriage of convenience couldn't work? She would like more children . . .

Also, because she didn't love Simon, he would never hold the power to break her heart.

Olivia lifted her chin a fraction, mainly to give herself confidence that she trusted her own judgement – and from the corner of her eye she saw Simon shift his thighs to a more comfortable position. They were magnificent thighs. She felt her mouth go dry. Oh, yes, his masculine magnetism was undeniable. That part of the deal should be no hardship. But to marry him, to live with him for the rest of her life – to be Lady of the Manor? She, Olivia Naismith, whose upbringing had been anything but genteel . . . How could a marriage between them ever work? Simon was crazy even to suggest it.

'Olivia.' His demanding voice cut into her thoughts.

She raised her eyes, startled out of her reverie. 'Yes?'

'I'm a patient man. Please don't try my patience too far.'

'What?'

'When I ask a question, I expect an answer. Preferably before midnight.'

Oh. He was being sarcastic again. Had she been dreaming that long? Olivia twisted a lock of her hair and answered his question with another.

'Why, Simon? Why, of all the women who might have been glad to marry you, did you pick on me?'

He stood up then, with a grace that was remarkable in such a large man, and moved unhurriedly towards her. 'Not the most fortunate way of putting it,' he murmured. 'I *chose* you, Olivia, because you seem uniquely suited to meet my needs.'

Like a custom-designed overcoat or jacket. Or designer trousers. Her gaze flicked to the smooth cloth flexing over his hips and thighs.

'I don't see it that way,' she said breathlessly, as he came to a halt directly in front of her. 'I'm presentable enough, I suppose. But I come with a child –'

'Precisely. Proof of ability on that score.'

Olivia opened her mouth to tell him what she thought of men who judged women on their looks and reproductive skills. Then remembered that she *had* asked for his reasons. He was only being honest. Brutal, but honest.

'I suppose so,' she said frostily. 'All right, so you fancy me in bed and you know I can have children. The same can be said of a million other women much better suited to run Sherraby than I am. Women who were brought up the way you were, who move in your circles, who speak the way you do –'

'Emma doesn't speak the way I do. But I've never held it against her.'

'Emma is American. That's different.'

'I don't see why. Nor do I judge people by their backgrounds. There's nothing wrong with the way you speak, Olivia. You forget, I spent twelve years away from . . .' He waved vaguely at the room behind him and at the terraces leading to the lake. 'From all this. I know there's a world out there that's never even heard of a silver spoon.'

It was almost a rebuke. As if he was accusing *her* of snobbery. And maybe he was right. Maybe she did have a chip on a shoulder because her childhood had been essentially rootless, whereas his had been ordered and secure.

She swallowed. If only he would move away, she might be able to think clearly. 'Yes,' she said, after a pause. 'I expect you have seen more of the world than

I have. But I still don't see why you picked me. There has to be more to it than my face and my – my fertility.' Maddeningly, her voice cracked on the word.

'Yes. There's more.' He put a hand on her shoulder, and she had to struggle not to flinch away. 'I know that if you agree to marry me, it won't be because of stars in your eyes. You've been married. You know what marriage is about, and you're not likely to go running off to your family – or to another man – every time we have a disagreement –' He smiled slightly. 'Which I suspect we occasionally will.'

'Only occasionally?' Olivia gulped because his thumb was moving closer to her neck. She hesitated, then admitted reluctantly. 'You're right in a way, though. I don't have a family to run to.'

'Don't you?' Simon lifted a lock of her hair and ran it through his fingers.

Because he didn't say, 'That's a bonus,' Olivia felt she had to explain.

'My mother died shortly after I married. My father disappeared years ago and turned up dead in Yorkshire. Ellen, my only sister, moved to Australia with her husband. I miss her terribly, but I can't run to her. And as for another man . . .' She tried to smile, but knew it hadn't worked when she saw Simon's eyebrows go up. 'As for another man, in my experience one man is more than enough.'

Simon's thumb moved to a hollow just below her ear. 'Exactly my point. You're loyal. If you take something on you stay with it. I need a wife, but she has to be a woman I can trust – a woman who will work to make the marriage last and who will give my children a stable and loving home. What I don't need is some sentimental little fool who will expect more from me than I'm able to give her. My work takes up a lot of my time, so I'd expect you to be capable of managing on your own. Which I'm sure you are.'

Olivia felt her temper begin to rise again. 'For all you know, that may be exactly what I am,' she said irritably.

'What? A sentimental fool?' His mouth turned down in disbelief.

'Yes,' she snapped. 'And what about *my* needs? I don't even want to get married.'

'Don't you?' He moved his hand to the back of her neck. 'But I think you do have needs, Olivia? Needs I can satisfy. And you do want security, for Jamie if not for yourself. Is there any reason we can't come to an arrangement that will benefit us both?'

'Would you take your hand off me, please?' Olivia said in a strangled voice.

Simon laughed softly and complied, as if he knew she was incapable of coming to any decision as long as his touch continued to short-circuit her brain.

That was better. She allowed her shoulders to relax. At least she could breathe again, although it didn't seem to help much. Her thoughts were still tumbling around in her head like bewildered atoms. 'I don't know,' she mumbled. 'The whole thing's crazy. Simon, are you sure this isn't your warped idea of a joke?'

'Quite sure. I've been thinking about it for some time. Well . . .' He smoothed a hand over his jaw. 'Since my mother's last visit, anyway. She'd had a call from Gerald just before she came. Trying to scrounge money, of course.'

Olivia sighed. 'All right. I do believe you've been thinking about it. But I don't believe you've been thinking about me. Surely you must have . . .' She hesitated. 'Women friends. You're what, thirty-seven –?'

'Thirty-eight.'

'OK, thirty-eight. You can't have been celibate since Sylvia.'

'No. I was celibate *with* Sylvia,' he replied. 'Honourably waiting for a wedding night that never came to pass. And yes, I have enjoyed one or two somewhat more satisfactory interludes since then. But I took care that they didn't last long. I'd no wish to raise hopes I had no intention of fulfilling.'

He sounded very cold and calculating. With that attitude, it wasn't surprising he had no one to turn to now that his requirements had changed.

'So I'm all that's available,' she said bitterly.

'No. I've considered a couple of other candidates,' Simon drawled. 'My mother favours Althea Carrington-Coates.'

'Althea *who*?'

'Carrington-Coates. To please Mother, I've taken her out a few times. But Althea doesn't like the country, is frightened of the Ripper, and suspects I'm a cross between Bluebeard and Captain Bligh. So you see, you're the *best* that's available.'

Was he *trying* to make her hit him? 'Thank you,' she said. 'I hope you don't expect me to take that as a compliment.'

'*I* wouldn't,' he admitted. 'But as far as I'm concerned you can take it any way you like. Now – do you suppose you could give me an answer?'

Just like that. He honestly meant it. As if he was asking her to hire on as his housekeeper. 'It's not that simple,' she said.

'I think it is. You say yes, we pick a date, I call my mother and the vicar, and within a month the dastardly deed is done. How do you feel about Paris for a honeymoon? Or perhaps New York?'

Olivia didn't want to feel any way about a honeymoon. The thought was altogether too erotic and disturbing, especially with Simon standing less than a foot away from her so that she was breathing in the faint musky scent of his body.

'I don't know,' she said again. 'Simon, this is absurd.'

'No. It isn't. I am never absurd. It is a carefully considered and well-thought-out plan of action which ought to benefit us both. As I told you, I spend a lot of time in town, so we needn't be much in each other's way.'

'What you mean by that,' said Olivia, 'is that I needn't be much in your way.'

'Correct.' He nodded approvingly. 'You catch on fast, Olivia. Another reason why I think you'll suit me nicely.'

'And what if I don't think you'll suit me?'

'Ah, but I will. You want me to convince you?'

Olivia didn't trust that provocative, heavy-lidded look. She glanced over her shoulder, seeking a way of escape. But there was no escape, except into the blackness of the night. A soft breeze stroked her skin through the open window and it felt like fingers of fire on her bare arm. When she realized the fingers were Simon's, she turned back to face the room.

'No,' she whispered. 'No, I don't need convincing. I need time to think.'

He nodded. 'I thought you would. That's another thing I like about you. You're not impetuous.'

'I used to be,' said Olivia, her gaze riveted on the fingers stroking up her arm.

'Yes.' He sounded unsurprised. 'But life has taught you the benefits of caution. Hasn't it? You can have until tomorrow evening.'

'What?' She looked up, startled.

'You can have until tomorrow evening to make up your mind.'

'Oh. Yes. All right.' It was long enough. If she didn't know her mind by then she never would.

'In the meantime,' Simon said, 'maybe this will set the wheels in motion.'

Olivia started to say 'What?' again. But she didn't get to finish before Simon's arms closed around her waist, and his mouth came down hard over hers.

Just before their lips touched, she caught the white gleam of teeth in the lamplight.

She made no attempt to resist him. Not this time. She couldn't. Her blood was steaming, her body felt as if it were set to boil. So she put her hands on Simon's shoulders and clung to him, feeling the hard muscles contract beneath his shirt. Soon, as he pulled her closer, she felt something else – something that told her his need was as devastating as her own. Then, almost immediately, and even as he continued to explore the welcoming warmth of her mouth with a studied expertise that left her gasping, she sensed that he had in some way withdrawn. When she uttered a soft moan of acceptance, he let her go.

'There,' he said. 'Perhaps that will help you make up your mind.'

'Oh!' Olivia cried, once she had recovered her breath sufficiently to speak. 'How could you? Do you honestly think one kiss from Your Arrogance is all it will take to have me panting to marry you? Because if you do –?'

'I don't,' Simon said promptly. 'Shall I try again?'

'No!' She tried to step around him, but he caught her wrist. 'No, Simon. It will take a lot more than kisses to get me to the altar. And will you please let go of my arm?'

'In a minute. There's something I want to set straight before I take you home.'

'What's that?' Olivia, trying to sound indifferent, knew that in fact she sounded breathless and uncertain.

'That I know it will take more than kisses. And that I aim to provide a lot more. Think about that when you're making up your mind.' His eyes met hers with a lazy, unmistakable innuendo, and Olivia was furious to feel herself blushing.

'Conceited jerk,' she muttered, unable to hold his gaze and glaring at a portrait of a pretty, bright-eyed child on the white wall.

Simon's lips quirked, and he took her chin in his fingers and turned her gently to face him. 'I'm not, you know. It's just that you're irresistibly beautiful when you glare at me like that, and the temptation to provoke you is sometimes overwhelming. Believe me, it was never my intention to offend you.'

'No,' said Olivia. 'I know. Your intention was to get me started on a litter.'

'I wouldn't quite put it that way,' Simon said drily. 'But if your kittens are anything like you, my little cat . . .' He didn't finish the sentence, but dropped her wrist and gestured at the door.

'Yes?' said Olivia, not moving. 'Go on? If my kittens are anything like me . . .?'

'I'll have to trim a lot of claws.' Simon was suddenly brisk again. 'Now, as Cousins is undoubtedly asleep in front of his television, I'll leave him to his dreams and drive you home.'

Business concluded, thought Olivia. One dinner out, one proposal, now off you go, Olivia, and hurry up and make up your mind. She wondered if Simon had always been this outrageous.

They were silent on the drive back to Mrs Critchley's. After Simon's bombshell of a proposal, there didn't seem much left to say.

That night Olivia lay in her alcove staring sleeplessly into space. After a time, as Jamie snored softly in the bedroom, she realized that she hadn't turned off the light. Reaching for the switch, she pressed it and lay very still in the darkness. It was hot so close to the roof, and if she moved it would only be hotter.

Was there any reason even to *think* about Simon's offer?

Jamie murmured something in his sleep, reminding Olivia that there was at least one very good reason. If she married Simon, her son's future would be assured.

Jamie liked Simon. He had said so. And sometimes, when Simon made her laugh, she even liked him herself. But he also frightened her in a way. He was so contained and self-assured, so certain of his place in the world . . .

Not the point, Olivia, she reminded herself. It was his place in the world that would ensure Jamie's future security. And Simon wasn't repulsive. Quite the opposite. She sighed, and dragged a corner of the sheet through her fingers. That, of course, was the whole trouble. That was what scared her the most.

What if she found herself coming to care for Simon? He would never care for her in any but the most superficial – and purely physical – sense. He had been brutally honest about that. But for her, the physical side of marriage went with loving. And if she allowed herself to love him . . .

No. What was she thinking of? That couldn't happen. She wasn't going to lose any part of her heart to a man ever again. Because she had learned the hard way that survival depended on staying in control and depending on herself and no one else.

So why was she hesitating? Restlessly, Olivia pushed the sheet down to her waist and allowed her mind to linger briefly on the memory of Simon's kiss – the kiss that she recognized as part of the reason for her reluctance to consider his proposal. Yet she wasn't sure why that was so. It made little sense. Surely the fact that Simon was physically attractive was a plus . . .

For the next three hours, she lay fidgeting with the sheet, snapping on the light to check the time, snapping it off again, fiddling with her hair and trying desperately to pretend she wasn't remotely tempted to accept Simon's proposal.

At around half-past three, when her resistance was at its lowest, she stopped fighting her instincts and made up her mind.

If Jamie was not too upset by the plan, she would, God help her, accept Simon's offer of marriage. And all the consequences that came with it.

An owl hooted softly in the night, and Olivia lay on her side and tried, without success, to conquer the twin demons of fear and excitement that made her heart race at the very thought of being married to Simon. She turned on her other side. It didn't help.

She spent the remainder of the night lying in hot discomfort on her back.

In the morning she asked Jamie how he would feel about having Simon for a father.

Jamie said, 'Cosmic!'

In the afternoon, just five minutes after Olivia and Jamie had returned from buying groceries, Simon arrived at the door. He looked cool and casual in a light blue shirt and grey trousers.

Olivia's eyelids felt heavy after her sleepless night and busy morning. Now it seemed all hopes of catching an hour or two's rest before the evening were about to be summarily dashed.

When Simon raised his eyebrows and said, 'Well?' her reply was tart.

'It's still afternoon. You said evening. But since you're here, yes. All right. If you still want me, I'll marry you.'

'No,' said Simon, draping himself in the doorway. 'Let's take that again from the beginning.'

'What are you talking about?' Olivia felt her patience begin to snap. But her eyelids no longer felt heavy.

'I will knock on your door again,' explained Simon, as if he were talking to a child. 'You will open it without scowling and say, "Good afternoon, Simon, how nice to see you." Then I'll ask you if you've come to a decision, and you will say, "Yes, Simon, I have. I'll be honoured to accept your proposal." After that I will put my arms around you and we'll seal the bargain in the time-honoured way.'

Olivia gaped at him, not sure whether she wanted to laugh or tell him to take a jump in his private lake. But she supposed he was right in a way. Her response to his offer *had* been less than gracious. And he did look delectable lounging coolly in her doorway with a small, inscrutable smile on his full lips.

She nodded. 'All right. Shut the door, then.'

If Simon was surprised by her easy acquiescence he didn't show it. Instead he stepped out on to the landing, clicked the door shut, then rapped his knuckles smartly on the solid white panels.

Olivia fixed a smile on her face, turned the handle and stepped back.

'Good afternoon, Olivia,' said Simon in a deep, subtly provoking drawl. 'Do you have an answer for me?' His eyes were half-closed as he allowed his gaze to skim over her pinkly flushed body in a black and white sundress.

Olivia felt her skin begin to tingle. 'Yes,' she said, struggling to keep her voice steady. 'How nice to see you, Simon. I'll be honoured to accept your proposal.' Her lip began to quiver, and she couldn't altogether suppress a smile.

'Much better,' said Simon. 'Now on to Phase Two.'

Before Olivia could tell him Phase Two wouldn't be necessary, she found herself clasped firmly against his chest. Then his lips were on hers and he was kissing her with an explicit thoroughness that drove all thought of resistance from her mind. Soon she was conscious of nothing beyond the warmth of Simon's lips, and the hard strength of a body that seemed built to meld deliciously with hers. As his tongue searched the soft interior of her mouth, drawing sweetness from her willing response, she felt as if she had come to a magic place where Simon was the source of all enchantment. And she stood on tiptoe to twist her arms around his neck and draw him closer.

'Mum? Mum, do you know where . . . oh.' Jamie's childish voice paused, then went on matter-of-factly, 'I was looking for my T-shirt with the bulldog on it.'

Olivia disentangled herself from Simon's embrace so quickly she almost fell over. How could she have forgotten that Jamie was in the bedroom changing his clothes? She must have been even more exhausted than she'd thought. 'Your T-shirt's in the laundry,' she gasped. 'Jamie, I have something to tell you –'

'Yeah,' said Jamie. 'I know. You *are* going to marry Mr Sebastian. Aren't you? You said you might. And Dave said I'd know for sure if you started doing that kissy stuff. And you did.' The last words were more reproachful than accusing.

'You're right, Jamie.' Simon lowered himself on to his heels in front of the boy and took the narrow shoulders in his hands. 'Your mother and I *are* getting married. How do you feel about that?'

'That means you'll be my Dad, doesn't it?' said Jamie, looking solemn.

'Mmm. It does in a way. Is that all right with you?'

'Would we get to live in your big house? With Ripper?'

'With Ripper and Annie and Mrs Leigh. And my horses. They live in the stables.'

'Can I ride them?'

'When you're old enough. For now you'll have to settle for a pony.'

'A pony? Of my own?'

Olivia, seeing both incredulous hope and the fear of disappointment on her child's face, had to turn away so he wouldn't see her tears. Not that he was looking at her. He was looking at Simon as if he'd just offered him the moon. She saw the dawning of adoration in Jamie's eyes.

'Yes, of course of your own.' Simon pulled Jamie in between his knees. 'What do you think we should call him?'

Jamie screwed his face into its thoughtful shape. 'Tumbleweed,' he said after a moment. 'Like in cowboy films.'

Simon chuckled. 'The perfect choice. Nothing wrong with your imagination, is there, Jamie?'

'Course not,' said Jamie. He frowned suddenly. 'Will I have to call you Dad?'

Simon, noting the slightly mutinous slant to the child's mouth, said, 'No. You had a dad. He was special, wasn't he? You can call me Simon if you like.'

'Not Mr Sebastian? Or Sir?'

'Heaven forbid. And not Uncle Simon either.'

Jamie nodded. 'OK.'

Simon had just started to rise to his feet when Jamie added doubtfully, 'If you're not my real dad, does that mean I won't get to stay at your big house after I'm grown up?'

Olivia blinked. Jamie had a better grasp of the niceties of inheritance laws than she had thought. Someone in the village must have been talking.

Simon smiled at him. 'If you want to stay at Sherraby, then of course –'

'No,' Olivia interrupted sharply. 'He means, will the manor be his? Jamie, it –'

Simon put up a hand to silence her. 'Jamie,' he said, placing an arm round the boy's shoulders, 'I can't hand the manor over to you, however much I may want to. But it will always be your home. For as long as you want it to be. And when you grow up I'll help you to become anything you're willing to work for –'

'Good,' said Jamie. 'I want to be a spy like you.' His face lit up suddenly. 'Hey, it'll be cosmic having a spy for a dad –'

'Jamie,' Olivia groaned. 'I told you –'

'Don't worry,' Simon said. 'Jamie and I will have a quiet talk some time. About how spies have to keep secrets. And not say things that might spoil an important operation. But right now . . .' This time he did rise to his feet, 'Right now, Jamie, I think your mother needs a rest. She looks as though someone put her through a mangle at work – I mean she looks hot and tired,' he added hastily, seeing the quick flash of alarm on Jamie's face. 'So why don't you and I go back to the manor and take the Ripper out for a walk? Keep his mind off tomorrow's post. Then your mother can catch up on her sleep before we pick her up for dinner. OK with you?'

Jamie nodded happily and said, 'Cosmic.'

Olivia smiled gratefully at Simon. He really could be nice when he wanted to be. Look how he had handled Jamie. And he had noticed how tired she was and found a way to ensure her some peace. He was nice in other ways too . . .

Stop it, Olivia, she chided herself before she could take the thought further. You are going to marry the man. You are *not* going to start liking him. Fleetingly, she wondered if she ought to change her mind – tell Simon that he would have to find someone else to marry him after all. Then she caught sight of Jamie's face. He was gazing up at Simon with a light in his eyes that she knew she couldn't bear to extinguish.

Jamie had accepted Simon as a substitute for Dan almost too easily. And yet she couldn't deprive of him of this chance to lead a life free of worries about money – and with a mother who would be home when he needed her, at least until he was old enough to be left on his own.

When she noticed that Simon was regarding her with raised eyebrows and a quizzical smile, she said quickly, 'Thank you. That's thoughtful of you. I just need a couple of hours' sleep.'

Simon nodded. 'We'll be back to collect you for dinner. I told Mrs Leigh there'd be three of us.'

'You couldn't have known that. I hadn't given you an answer.' Olivia was puzzled and little indignant.

'Yes, you had,' Simon replied enigmatically. 'Come on, Jamie. The Ripper awaits us.' He held out his hand and Jamie took it. When Simon saw that Olivia was frowning, he bent forward and kissed her lightly on the cheek. 'Smile,' he ordered. 'Frowning causes wrinkles, and I refuse to have my wife turn into a prune before she's forty.'

Olivia tried to maintain the frown on principle, but it didn't work and she found herself smiling instead.

CHAPTER 6

'Zack!' Emma's accusing voice greeted him the moment he stepped into the hall. 'Zack, where have you *been*? Why didn't you call? You've been gone almost three days. Simon said not to worry, but I thought something dire must have happened to you –'

Zack shrugged off a small backpack and dropped it at his feet. Inwardly, he groaned. All he wanted to do at this moment was close his eyes and sleep the clock around. One of Emma's dramas was the last thing he needed at eight o'clock on a hot Long Island morning – especially after three nights spent in a stuffy warehouse putting a stop to the after-hours activities of employees with more avarice than brain.

'Why?' he asked, wondering if she was wearing anything under the skimpy white T-shirt that barely reached the top of her thighs. 'Why should you think that? My arrangement with your parents was that I could use this house as a base, not a check-in point. Didn't Harvey explain?'

'I didn't ask him,' Emma admitted. 'But you did check in. You let us know you wouldn't be home for dinner Tuesday night.'

'My mistake,' Zack muttered.

The truth of the matter was that he had been passing a deli displaying a window full of salads, and the salads had reminded him of the meal he'd shared with Emma. He had phoned on the off-chance that she might take it into her head to start preparing food for him again – food he knew he wouldn't be there to eat. He hadn't thought to phone again, having other, more pressing matters on his mind.

'Mistake?' Emma repeated in a small voice.

Zack was halfway across the hall before the wounded look in her eyes fully registered. Immediately guilt socked him in the stomach.

'Don't look at me like that,' he growled, half turning towards her.

'You don't want me here, do you?' she said.

Hell! Emma was what Morag would have called a 'load on the organization'. But he couldn't stand it when she forced him to be blunt with her.

No, of course he didn't want her here. In that damned useless T-shirt she was altogether too much of a distraction. And even if she hadn't been Emma Colfax, he was on a job. He hadn't time to indulge his libido. Oh, it was tempting, he had to admit that. Deliberately he averted his eyes from the smooth length of her glorious bare legs. God, was it tempting! Emma, with her scantily clothed figure and hopeful pixie smile, had grown into a knockout of a woman. She had been lethal enough as a teenager – so much so that in desperation he had turned to Samantha as an antidote. But eight years was a long time for a man to hold out against the lures cast so brazenly, and with such sweet peristence, by this giddy little butterfly with the body of woman, the morals of one of the scrawny cats that had haunted the alley behind the house in Aberdeen, and the single-mindedness of a mosquito after blood.

His blood.

Trying not to scowl too ferociously, Zack bent to pick up the backpack. Simon, and almost everyone else, seemed to find Emma's obsession amusing. He didn't.

She was still looking at him with that hurt-little-girl expression. He didn't even think it was calculated.

'No,' he said, frustration roughening his speech. 'I don't want you here. I don't want anyone here except Harvey. I came to work, Emma, not to play games.' When she went on gazing at him with reproachful, green-tinted eyes, he shook his head and said irritably, 'I'm sorry. It's not personal. I'm not objecting specifically to you.' He was, but there was no need to say so.

'That's good,' Emma said. 'Because I happen to live here.' She turned her back on him and headed for the kitchen.

Zack sighed. His hand was already curled around the banister when her low, injured voice reached him. 'I suppose you don't want breakfast,' he heard her say.

Breakfast? All he wanted was sleep. But if eating breakfast with her would keep Emma happy and out of his hair, it might be worth putting sleep off for another hour.

'Yes,' he said with forced enthusiasm. 'Yes, if you're offering, I would like some breakfast. Thank you.'

Her salads hadn't been too bad. Maybe she knew how to fry eggs.

'Fifteen minutes,' Emma said. 'If Harvey will let me at the stove.'

Harvey was no fool. Suppressing a yawn, Zack went to wash away the evidence of a sleepless but profitable night.

When he went downstairs fifteen minutes later, no enticing aroma of coffee greeted him in the hall, no smell of frying eggs or buttered toast. He approached the kitchen with a wariness that was more or less habitual. There *was* a kind of burnt, woolly smell – like fried socks.

He pushed the door cautiously open – and froze to the blue and white tiles.

Emma, enveloped in one of Harvey's butcher aprons and very little else, was standing on the kitchen table holding a long-handled mop in one hand. She was waving it at what looked like a patch of raw sewage on the ceiling.

'Emma?' Zack said. 'What are you doing?'

Emma swayed slightly on her perch. 'Washing the ceiling,' she replied, in an odd, breathless voice. 'Or trying to.'

'Why?' He moved to the edge of the table and stared up at her. 'Last time I looked it was clean.'

'Last time you looked, Mr Kent,' a voice said from behind them, 'Miss Emma hadn't tried to make no pancakes. Miss Emma, I told you, didn't I? Told you –'

'I was trying to toss them,' Emma said, lowering the mop and lurching sideways. 'But they got burnt and stuck to the pan. Then all four of them unstuck at once and went splat on the ceiling.'

Zack glanced at the heavy, black frying pan with its lining of unappetising black crumbs. 'You didn't put enough oil in,' he said.

'Thanks for telling me.'

Harvey cleared his throat. 'Better leave it, Miss Emma. Better leave it. You'll break your pretty neck, you will, standing up there.'

Emma lurched again. 'No. No, I won't, Harvey. But thank you for caring.'

Zack wondered if that was a dig at his own lack of sympathy. 'Going out, Harvey?' he asked, seeing that the old man was carrying a jacket.

'If you and Miss Emma don't mind. My sister, the one in Manhattan, she isn't well.' He shook his grizzled head. 'Not well at all. Needs an operation. An –'

'Oh, I am sorry. Of course we'll be all right,' Emma said, gripping the mop so tightly that her knuckles turned white. 'You must stay as long as you need to, Harvey. Of course you must. Don't even think of rushing back.'

Harvey mumbled something that sounded like 'Hurmph,' several times, and shuffled out through the door.

'Poor Harvey,' said Emma, 'He does look worried.'

'Yes. Do you plan to spend the day up there?' Zack asked.

Emma gave the sewage a half-hearted swipe. 'No. I can't reach it properly. I suppose Harvey's right. It'll just have to stay there.' She dropped the mop and held out her arms. 'Help me down, please.'

Zack stared at the striped apron covering her thighs, took a deep breath and placed his hands on her waist.

'Mmm,' said Emma, and slipped off the table into his arms.

Zack flexed his fingers, and his palms slid over the smooth curve of her hips. She was so soft, so much a woman in spite of her up-and-down figure. She smelled like a woman too. Like – what was that scent his sister Jean wore to dances? Some sort of flower. Not violets. Emma was no violet. A snapdragon maybe. Definitely not a wallflower . . .

Cut it out, Kent. Zack forced his brain back to reality. This was impossible. Ridiculous. He couldn't . . .

'Emma,' he said, in a voice that even to his ears sounded cracked, 'Emma, for God's sake . . .' He started to pull away, but her hands were on his chest and she was smiling at him – the brightest, sweetest, most beguiling smile he had ever seen.

When she reached up and began to stroke his cheek, he was lost.

Her lips, those lips he had sampled only once, and then with the deliberate intention of teaching her a lesson, were less than an inch from his own. He closed his eyes as her woman-scent drifted all around him, washing away all memory of the reason for restraint. Then he was kissing her, and her mouth was as soft and yielding as the rest of her. She tasted of mint tea and honey. And he wanted more, wanted to drink until his thirst was quenched, then refill the glass and start again . . .

No! She touched the buckle on his belt and sanity returned. What was he thinking of? This was Emma. He couldn't – *wouldn't* touch her. Not that way. He wasn't afraid of trouble, had known plenty of it in his life. But Emma, however tempting, was one load of trouble he must do without.

If not for himself, then for her.

With a groan that was wrenched from some part of his being he hadn't known existed, Zack tore his mouth away from hers and staggered back. He could feel the sweat running down his back, dampening his shirt.

'I'm sorry,' he said, when his breath was restored enough to speak. 'I had no right to do that. Not with you.'

'You don't have to be sorry, Zack. I liked it.' She gave him her deadly sweet smile and reached to take his hand.

He snatched it away. 'Listen,' he said, 'I made a mistake. There was no excuse for it and I've said I'm sorry.' He gulped another long draught of air. 'Now – it's been a long night, so if it's all the same to you, I'm going to bed.'

If only she wouldn't look at him like that, so small and stricken in the sunlight streaming through the white-framed windows.

'Goodnight,' he said unthinkingly, and left the room without looking back.

A man's voice came to Emma through the mists of a dream in which she was standing on a rocky beach watching a small boat disappear into the distance to the strains of a harmonica playing the *Skye Boat Song*. A solitary figure stood in the boat, his dark hair blowing about his shoulders in the wind. The figure turned and held out his hand, but just as Emma was about to follow him into the waves, he said bluntly, 'That's a grisly mess you made of the kitchen ceiling. Are you not going to stir yourself to do anything about it?'

Emma jumped and opened her eyes. The dream faded into the purple warmth of a summer evening.

What time was it? A shadow fell across the *chaise-longue* where she had been reclining on the sundeck wrapped in gloom. She must have fallen asleep. Glancing at her watch, she saw that it was nearly six o'clock.

Zack, dressed in denim shorts and a khaki short-sleeved shirt that he hadn't taken the trouble to button, was standing over her with his hands on his hips.

Emma rubbed her knuckles over her eyes and sat up. Was he hungry? Was that what this was all about? Obviously he had investigated the kitchen.

'I'm not going to do anything about it,' she said, when it dawned on her he was waiting for an answer. 'Harvey said to leave it. The staff will see to it once they get back.'

Zack dropped into one of the Cape Cod chairs and hooked an ankle on his knee. Emma knew at once that she had said the wrong thing. He was looking at her as if she'd said, 'The slaves will see to it.'

'They *are* paid,' she told him. 'Very well, as a matter of fact.'

'Which doesn't mean they have nothing better to do than run around cleaning up your messes.' Zack's dark gaze rested on her as if he didn't like her very much.

'No, of course it doesn't. But I can't reach the ceiling. Dammit, Zack, I *tried*.'

'So how do you expect the staff to manage?' He placed a faintly jeering emphasis on the word 'staff'.

Emma winced. 'Someone will get a ladder.' When he went on looking at her with dark-eyed disapproval, she explained resentfully, 'I get dizzy on ladders. I don't know why.'

'It's convenient, I suppose,' Zack said.

'*No*. It's not at all convenient.' Why was he so determined to think the worst of her? She swung her legs to the deck and stood up. 'It must be nice not to know what it's feels like to have – flaws. I suppose *you've* never been afraid of anything.'

She didn't wait for him to answer, but flounced off into the kitchen and started opening and closing cupboard doors. When slamming them didn't relieve her ill-humour, she opened the fridge door and slammed that too. Glass jars rattled ominously, and something clattered off a shelf.

'Does it help?' Zack asked from behind her.

'Does what help?'

'Slamming things. It's what I used to do as a child. Until I broke the lock on our front door once, and Morag put a stop to my nonsense.'

'Is that a threat?'

'No. Just an observation.'

Emma slammed the door to the oven. She was about to tell him what he could do with his observations when she realized he was no longer in the room.

All the fury leaked out of her, and she collapsed on to the nearest kitchen chair. After a while she put her arms on the table and laid her head down.

It was hopeless. In Zack's eyes she was, and always would be, a spoiled, silly child who couldn't do anything right. She might as well give up and go back to Greece and Ari – if he'd have her. Or accept that boring London banker's thinly veiled offer of bed and breakfast. What did it matter? Zack wouldn't care. She should just forget him and and get on with her life. Somehow, somewhere, with someone. Or maybe alone.

In the distance a ship's horn sounded, reminding Emma that there was nothing to be gained by wallowing in self-pity. She lifted her head. Before she got on with anything though, there was something she had to prove – to Zack or to herself. She wasn't sure which, and it didn't matter. Because if he thought she wouldn't fight back after he had virtually accused her of manufacturing vertigo to save herself trouble . . . well, he couldn't be more wrong.

He wanted the kitchen ceiling cleaned? Right. She would clean it.

Throwing back her shoulders, Emma marched out to the tool shed behind the house.

By the time she emerged into the sunlight again, she had tripped over a lawnmower, a rusted gerbil cage, two plastic buckets and a rake without tines. But she had what she wanted.

'I'll show you, Zack Kent,' she muttered. 'Just you wait.'

* * *

Zack was leaning on the railing of the sundeck staring out over the Sound when he heard the clanking noise. It was as if someone was dragging something heavy and metallic across concrete. What the devil was Emma up to now? He heard a door bang, the noises ceased and he switched his gaze to a profusion of yellow pansies lined up in boxes along the rail.

He hadn't been fair to her, he knew. First he had demanded to know if she planned to stay perched on the table all day. Then, when she had dropped obligingly into his arms, he had kissed her and explained it away as a mistake. Which it had been, but only in one sense. Not content with that, he had accused her of leaving the cleaning of the ceiling to others – whose job it was to clean ceilings.

Zack laid his hands flat on the railing. There had always been something about Emma that brought out the worst in him. She could get under his skin as no one else had ever been able to do. It wasn't that he begrudged her her pampered childhood, or even that he envied or resented her parents' wealth as once he might have done. He was wealthy himself now, hard as it often was to believe.

No, what bothered him was Emma's rock-solid conviction that if there was something she wanted she ought to get it. Preferably at once. He, who came from a very different background, would never be able to cope with that about her. And she would never be able to see why.

If only she wouldn't keep looking at him as if he had stolen a precious toy from a child. The toy, in this case, being himself. And if only he didn't want her so badly it had become a permanent ache in his gut.

How the hell was he going to get through these next few weeks in her house?

Zack slammed his fist savagely on to the railing, causing one box of pansies to slide dangerously close to the edge. He swore and dived to catch it before it fell.

Afterwards he wasn't sure how many minutes had passed before he heard the crash. It was followed by silence. Dead silence. He waited, half-expecting further crashes, followed by attention-getting screams. But there was nothing. Only the restless sound of the sea washing the rocks.

With a grunt of exasperation, and more out of habit than concern, he went back into the house to investigate the cause of the disturbance.

Still dead silence. Not a whisper of movement to tell him where the sound had originated. Right. Start with the obvious. When last seen, Emma had been sulking in the kitchen.

At first, as he stood in the doorway looking round, he noticed nothing more startling than an old metal ladder slanted at an odd angle against one of the chairs. But when he directed his glance downwards, for a few seconds he had to put out a hand out to steady himself against the doorframe.

The next instant he was across the floor and kneeling beside the slight figure crumpled on the tiles next to the table.

'Emma!' He put a hand beneath her breast to feel her heart. 'Emma, in the name of God! What have you done? He pressed his fingers into the soft cloth of her T-shirt.

Emma opened her eyes, then closed them again at once. This had to be too good to be true.

Zack was kneeling over her with his hand on her heart. His long hair had fallen across his face, but not before she had seen his eyes. Wild eyes, black with an emotion that looked a lot like fear.

But Zack was never afraid. Cautiously, not daring to hope, she raised her eyelids.

'I fell,' she said.

With a peculiar detachment, she watched every muscle in his body expand, as the fear – if it had been fear – was replaced by a slow-burning anger. He pulled his hand away as if all at once he couldn't bear to touch her. The place where it had lain felt cold.

'You *fell*,' Zack said through his teeth.

'Yes.' Emma put a hand to her head and found a tender spot just above her temple. 'I think I hit the table.' She wriggled her shoulders on the hard tiles. 'I feel a bit bruised, but that's all.'

'Brruised,' Zack said, all at once sounding very Aberdeen. 'You feel brruised? I'm glad to hear it. Because it's surely what you deserve.'

He'd said that to her once before. Emma, who was feeling vulnerable as well as bruised, pushed herself up so that her back was against the leg of the table. 'Why should you care?' she asked. 'I was only doing what you wanted.'

'What *I* wanted! Damn and blast it, don't blame your idiocy on me, woman. Just because I regularly get the urge to murder you, it doesn't mean I expect you to do the job yourself. You . . .' Emma watched, bemused, as it dawned on him what he was saying. He snapped his mouth shut in mid-sentence.

'I thought I'd save you the trouble,' she said.

'No, you didn't. You didn't think at all.'

Emma stopped feeling detached. She was tired of Zack's harping on her lack of thought, tired of his near-permanent disparagement – tired of wasting her energies on a man who probably had no idea what it meant to be in love. A man who hadn't been able to make his marriage work. No wonder he was single again – not to mention terminally bad-tempered.

'If that's the case,' she said, grabbing the edge of the table and pulling herself to her feet, 'you won't be surprised if I keep *on* not thinking. Especially about you. Now, if you don't mind, I'd like to finish cleaning the ceiling.'

She righted the ladder and attempted to drag it back into place.

Behind her Zack made a noise that sounded like a bagpipe deflating. Then he caught her by the shoulders and swung her around. She flinched when he touched a bruise, but he didn't seem to notice.

'You're not doing anything of the sort,' he said. 'What the hell does it take to teach you common sense?'

Emma stuck out what there was of her jaw. 'You said I got dizzy on ladders because it was convenient. And since you're always right, I don't see what the problem is. Let me go now, please.'

'I will not let you go, you absurd, ridiculous woman. Not if you think you're climbing that ladder again.'

Emma looked him in the eye and didn't answer.

'All right,' he said. 'All right. So I was wrong. Does that satisfy you?'

No, Emma thought. It doesn't satisfy me. What would satisfy me would be for you to slide those big hands off my shoulders and down my back and . . . She swallowed, and said aloud, 'No. No, it doesn't.'

'You want me to apologize.' It was a statement rather than a question.

'If you like.'

'Very well, I apologize. For casting doubt on the usefulness of your brain and for suggesting your dizziness was faked. Will that do?'

His hands still gripped her shoulders, and he was standing so close to her that she could feel his breath fanning her forehead. Her very own glowering Celt. Except he wasn't hers. But he *had* been worried when he'd thought she was hurt – and there was a look in his eyes she hadn't seen there before.

It was now or never.

'No,' she said. 'It won't do. Take me to bed, Zack.'

'What?' The change in his expression was instant. Controlled exasperation one moment, shock and incredulity the next. 'Emma, you don't know what you're saying. I suppose instant gratification and hopping from one bed to the next may be the way it's done in your world. But I was brought up to have respect for a woman's body.' Without seeming aware that he was doing it, he shook her. 'Not that women like you make it easy –'

'That's all right, then.' Emma, devastated, was beyond dignity, beyond even the semblance of rational thought. All she knew was that she wanted to hurt Zack as his words were hurting her. 'Since you don't respect me, you needn't pretend to play the gentleman you're not. Or is that just an excuse? What happened with Samantha, Zack? Couldn't you even play the *man*? Is that why she left you?'

Zack's fingers dug into her shoulderblades. 'So help me,' he said, thrusting his jaw out to meet hers, 'so help me, if you weren't my partner's cousin –'

'What would you do?' she taunted. 'Smack me on the bottom and wash my mouth out with soap? Why don't you try it?'

She pulled away, putting her hands on her hips and challenging him to retaliate. But instead he let out his breath, his wiry body relaxing until only the narrow-eyed glitter of his eyes betrayed that he was on the verge of explosion.

'Don't tempt me,' he said. 'Don't tempt me. As you said yourself, Madam Emma, I've never been a gentleman.'

Emma took a step backwards and ended up with her back against the table. Help! Now look where her bravado had got her! She'd pushed him too far. He looked positively menacing as he closed the gap between their bodies – as well as gloriously, savagely sexy. She gasped as his hands gripped her arms.

And in that moment everything changed.

Without meaning to, Emma let out a quick, half-frightened moan. Zack heard it. His eyes widened, and he went unnaturally still. She gazed at him, holding her breath, waiting.

'Emma.' His voice was a dry rasp from the back of his throat. 'Emma, don't look at me that way. You know I'd never hurt you.'

She smiled then, but not entirely with relief. Of course he wouldn't hurt her. How could she ever have thought he might?

'Yes, I know,' she said. 'I've always known.'

'Hmm. No doubt.' Zack shook his head in slow motion, as if he couldn't think what to do next.

Emma, never much good at waiting when she didn't have to, raised her arms and wrapped them around his neck.

'You start by kissing me,' she said.

Zack let out his breath. 'I *know* what to do, lass,' he growled.

And he did.

It was night when Emma woke up. She could see the stars through the uncurtained windows of her bedroom. Beside her, unbelievably, lay Zack. Zack, who had shown her what all those years of formless yearning had been about. She wanted to laugh, to sing, to throw her arms around him and experience the wonder he had shown her all over again, for the sixth – or was it the tenth time that night. But Zack was sleeping. He needed to sleep.

For now she would have to be content. No need to disturb him.

She turned on her side and examined the dark sweep of his eyelashes in the moonlight. Zack. Beautiful, tough, complicated Zack. The man she had wanted forever. The man who had carried her with him to places that, until tonight, she had thought were fantasies like *Shangri-La* or *Brigadoon*.

He had told her he knew what to do. And oh, he *had* known. She had seen *An Officer and a Gentleman* as well as *Gone With the Wind*, but she hadn't imagined the day would ever come when she would find herself being picked up, carried upstairs, and made love to with such breathtaking abandon. But that was exactly what had happened. And when at last, sated, they had fallen asleep in each other's arms, she had known that all the years of waiting had been worth it.

Emma lay for a long time watching him sleep, and dreaming of a lifetime of nights spent like this one.

It was nearly nine o'clock when Zack woke up. 'Good morning,' she said, smiling at him, and putting a hand under the sheet to touch him where he couldn't fail to be aroused.

He turned his head, but his eyes when they met hers were sombre, inscrutable, shattering her mood of euphoria.

'It is not a good morning,' he growled, removing her hand and placing it on top of the covers. 'Why didn't you tell me?'

'Tell you what?' Emma was genuinely bewildered.

'That you – that I was the first. I was, wasn't I?'

'Oh, Zack. Of course you were. Don't tell me you thought – oh.' She put a hand to her mouth, remembering what he had said last night. Something about 'women like you', and 'instant gratification'.

'You meant it, then.' She crushed the sheet into a ball between her fingers. 'You really believed I was – that sort of woman.'

'What else *could* I think?' he asked bitterly. 'You've waltzed from one man to another ever since the day you left school. You went to Greece with Ari Andrakis. Of course I thought you were that sort of woman. The kind my sister Morag would not approve of.'

'Oh.' Emma buried her face in the pillow so that when she spoke her voice came out muffled. 'Zack, I didn't stay with any of those men long enough to love them. Don't you understand? I was looking for a man just like you. But there isn't anyone like you.'

'For which you may be grateful.' His tone was gruff, but the edge of bitterness was gone.

'I am grateful.' She removed her nose from the pillow, hesitated, then said in a rush, 'Zack, I didn't mean it when I said you weren't a gentleman . . .'

'Or even a man,' Zack said drily. 'I don't suppose you did. All the same you were right. I'm no gentleman when it comes to you, Emma, even though I would give you back what you gave me if I could.' He met the hope in her eyes with a look that made her cringe. 'I'm not going to make an honest woman of you.'

'Oh.' Beneath her fingers the sheet felt damp and cold. Her dreams of endless happiness with Zack crumbled even as she struggled to hold on to them, drifting to dust in the sunbeam shining through the skylight above the bed.

'It doesn't matter,' she said, salvaging her pride.

What a naïve fool she had been. Last night had meant no more to Zack than a temporary release of sexual tension. Or a way of paying her back for suggesting he was not a man in every sense of that loaded word. It wasn't like Zack to be vindictive, but if that *had* been his intention – well, then, his revenge had succeeded, probably beyond his wildest dreams.

'Doesn't it?' he said. 'Matter?'

'No. Of course not. Why should it?'

'No reason.' He linked his arms behind his head, not looking at her. 'No doubt now that you've had your way with me, you're ready to move on to greener pastures.'

Emma propped herself up on her elbow and gazed down at him. His blank face told her nothing.

'No,' she said. 'I like the pastures the colour they are. But you don't have to marry me.'

Zack started to smile, then seemed to change his mind. He curved a hand round the back of her neck. 'You still don't see, do you? Emma, last night – it should not have happened. But you goaded me and I wanted you, and it did. I'm sorry. I should have known better. I *did* know better.'

'You mean now that you've had me you don't want me any more?' She wished her voice didn't sound so thin and beseeching.

Zack rubbed his thumb gently over her nape. 'No, I don't mean that. I want you very much, wee Emma. But I'm not going to have you again. We're wrong for each other. I grew up having to fight for every penny I earned. Sometimes we didn't have enough to eat. And although Morag loved us all, very often she was too damn tired to show it. For you it was different. It's not your fault, but you've always had everything. Love, food, admiration –'

'Not everything,' Emma interrupted him. 'And anyway, what difference does it make? You're not in need now. Nobody would ever guess you hadn't always –'

'Been a gentleman,' Zack finished for her.

'No! That's *not* what I was going to say.'

'Maybe not, but it's what you meant. Emma, I'm a gloomy, suspicious fellow at heart. You're all laughter and light and fun. If we married I'd only make you miserable. Much better to end it now, before you start regretting last night. You can do better than me, lass.' He touched a finger to her nose.

'I don't want better than you.' Emma whispered. 'Just because you made a mistake with Samantha –'

'Samantha has nothing to do with it,' Zack snapped.

Oh. He was angry again. She'd made a mistake reminding him of his marriage. Not that it mattered much. Pleading wasn't going to make him change his mind. He didn't love her, would never love her. So maybe it *was* best to end it now, while she still had the remnants of dignity . . .

Oh, but she couldn't. Couldn't let it end like this. Not now, not when she had only just tasted the unbearable sweetness of Zack's passion . . .

Closing her eyes so he wouldn't see her tears, Emma slung a leg across his thighs, shifted herself on top of him, and stamped her lips hard against his mouth.

Zack put his hands on her shoulders to lift her up. 'No,' he said. 'No –'

'Please. Please, Zack. Just once more.'

'No.'

She reached down and put her hand between his legs. He groaned and pushed her on to her side, holding her fast against his arousal.

'Little witch,' he murmured against her mouth. 'You know what you do to me, don't you?' His fingers trailed a path of fire down her spine.

But when his hand slid between her thighs, and his tongue began to move in maddening little circles around her nipple, Emma was aware only of what he did to her. She moaned, and curled her fists in his thick hair, squirming as he turned her on her back, away from the release she so violently craved. Zack laughed, and only when she thought she would die of wanting him did he at last lift himself above her and give her the gift her body was crying out for. Slowly, so slowly that she groaned in frustration, he lowered his hips until he was inside her. Frantic, she bit his lower lip. His teeth found a place in the soft skin of her neck. Then his hands stroked down her thighs, holding her so she couldn't move.

'Zack!' she cried, and he laughed again and released her, easing himself deeply inside her until every pleasure-point in her body exploded with a radiance that was as much pain as rapture.

It was everything and more than she remembered.

Minutes passed. She lay beneath him, spent. Surely Zack wouldn't, *couldn't* mean to make her leave him now. Not after this. Not when together they had learned what loving meant.

She was still lost in the glowing aftermath of that loving when, without a word, Zack rolled off her and on to his back.

As Emma whimpered a protest and tried to curl herself into his side, the phone rang.

She jumped. The world couldn't intrude on them now. It couldn't. But by the time she had disentangled herself from the bedclothes, Zack had already lifted the receiver. Just before he put it to his ear she heard a man's voice saying, 'Emma? Is Zack there?'

'Indeed he is,' Zack said. 'Hello, Simon.'

Emma watched his expression change from the instant alertness that came to him so naturally, to stone-faced disbelief. 'You are *what*?' he said. '*When*? Who? Oh. I see. September. Yes, of course that's all right. Yes, yes, we'll be there.'

There was a pause and then he said, 'Emma? Yes, she is.' This was followed by a clipped, 'No. Definitely not.' He listened for a while longer, and said, 'Hmm. Good. All right,' several times more before he hung up.

'What was that all about?' Emma asked. 'It was Simon, wasn't it?'

'It was.' Zack's back was to her. 'He's getting married. I'm to be his best man. His bride, whoever she is, will be phoning later. Apparently she wants you for a bridesmaid. And Simon has booked us both on a flight to Gatwick the week after next. I said we'd be on it.'

'Just like that?' Emma said.

'Just like that.'

Emma started to reach for him, but at once he rolled to the edge of the bed and sat up. He hadn't looked at her once since the phone call.

She lay still, gazing at his naked back. 'We forgot to eat last night,' she muttered, knowing the comment was irrelevant, but too bemused to think of anything more useful to say.

Zack laughed. At least she thought it was a laugh. 'No, we didn't,' he said. 'We made a mistake and changed the menu. We'll know better another time, won't we?'

CHAPTER 7

Olivia stood at the back of the small stone church with the steeple, trying to pretend she wasn't afraid. But she had to hold her arms, sheathed in cool white silk, tightly against her sides to keep herself from shaking. Was it too late to escape? She looked at all the smart hats and smart backs seated in the pews. What was she, Olivia Naismith, doing in St Mary's Parish Church, this sacred place where the Sherraby brides had been married for longer than anyone could remember? Behind the altar an ornate canopied memorial to a former squire and his lady stood as an inescapable reminder that she didn't belong.

She too must have had ancestors, but nobody knew, or cared, who they had been.

'Mum!' A penetrating whisper from the front of the church startled her out of her panic-stricken trance. 'You're supposed to come in.'

The congregation murmured amused agreement, and Olivia knew that escape was no longer an option.

Straightening her white hat with the red ribbon, she glanced enquiringly at the man standing stolidly beside her. Alistair Cameron, her mother-in-law-to-be's new husband, had volunteered to give her away. He was a quiet little man who reminded her of a squat Sherlock Holmes. She had taken to him at once because he was kind, and understanding of her nervousness.

Alistair smiled and tucked her hand under his elbow. 'Shall we?' he asked, as the organ music soared to the roof, and the occupants of the pews shifted to get a better view.

Olivia nodded and looked over her shoulder at Emma. She had asked Simon's cousin to be her bridesmaid, not only because she had liked her at once, but because her friend Sidonie was on her own honeymoon. Her sister Ellen had been forced to decline Simon's offer to pay her fare to England because she was expecting the birth of her second child any day, and the friends Olivia had made with Dan had long since drifted away.

Emma's gaze was pinned wistfully on Zack, but when she saw Olivia looking at her she grinned and gave a thumbs-up sign.

Olivia squared her shoulders, accepting her fate. She had made her decision. Now she would have to go through with it and pledge herself, for better or for whatever, to the tall stranger standing at the altar.

As she walked down the aisle beside Alistair, she shivered. It was cold in the church despite the brightness outside. It had been cold the day she had married Dan, too. All the warmth and laughter, and the grief, had come later. But it wasn't cold that made her shiver today.

Drawing closer to Simon, she saw that the sunlight filtering through the stained glass windows had cast a bronzed glow over his face as he waited unsmilingly beside Zack. Both men, in their different ways, were imposing figures in their morning coats, yet it wasn't Zack's encouraging smile that gave her strength. It was the reassuring touch of Simon's hand when, briefly, he took her cold fingers in his as she came up beside him after the endless walk down the aisle.

Behind them, Jamie whispered to Annie Coote, 'When are they going to start getting *married*.'

Olivia heard Emma stifle a chuckle, and when she looked up at Simon she saw that he too was suppressing a grin.

The rest of the ceremony passed in a kind of dream. Afterwards the only thing Olivia remembered clearly was Simon's strong voice saying, 'I will.' The words rang out as if he truly meant them.

Olivia meant it too when she promised, in a much softer voice than his, to take Simon Charles Sebastian for better or for worse. He had smiled at her then, an encouraging, almost conspiratorial smile that for a while had made her stop doubting her own common sense and begin to believe this unlikely marriage stood a chance.

The reception was held in the manor gardens immediately following the service. A marquee had been set up on the lawn with tables of food and champagne, but it was too warm to stay huddled under canvas once the toasts and the photographs were over.

Olivia was certain the scent of new-mown grass mingled with sweet peas, honeysuckle and roses would remain with her for the rest of her life.

She was standing beside her new husband, shaking hands and smiling dutifully at a succession of well-wishers with sweaty palms, when Simon's mother, tall and long-nosed, swept up to them and drew her aside.

'Your son is a fine boy, Olivia. A credit to you,' Celia Cameron pronounced in a voice that instantly turned heads.

'I'm not a credit,' said Jamie, emerging from the marquee where he had been surreptitiously picking icing off the wedding cake. 'I'm a cowboy. Simon says so.'

'Of course you are.' Celia smiled absently and patted his head.

Jamie scowled, waited until his mother wasn't watching, and went back to dismantling the cake.

Olivia noticed that her mother-in-law's gaze was directed pointedly at her figure – but not, as she had thought at first, at the simple but glamorous white silk dress with the red trim that she had chosen to be married in. Celia's attention was entirely centred on the flatness of her daughter-in-law's stomach.

'Not yet,' Olivia said, shaking her head and smiling. 'But soon, I hope.'

Celia raised her eyebrows and laughed. 'Oh. Simon told me you would suit him far better than Althea Carrington-Coates – and do you know, I believe he may be right. You and I are going to get along splendidly, my dear.'

Olivia thought so too, a fact which vaguely surprised her. She had expected Simon's relatives to be an intimidating lot, especially as the only person at the wedding who would truly be there because of her was Jamie. Her sister's regretful refusal had been a great disappointment. But she had come to know Simon's family and friends fairly well in the weeks preceding the wedding, and had discovered that, after all, they were human. In particular, Simon's friend and partner, Zack, who boasted even less ancestry than she did.

'We weren't born on different planets,' Simon had once pointed out tersely, when he found her skulking nervously at the back of the hall during a family gathering. 'Stop underestimating yourself. It doesn't suit you.'

Olivia decided he was right, and after that she kept her chin up and her smile prominently in place when confronted by people who, in her other life, would never have known she existed.

Behind them a cork popped cheerfully, and as Celia marched off to confer with Mrs Leigh, Simon extracted himself from the embrace of an enthusiastic honorary aunt and came to stand beside his wife.

'Holding up all right?' he asked, taking her hand and drawing her into the marquee where a crowd of hot and overdressed guests were doggedly swilling champagne.

Olivia nodded.

He smiled approvingly. 'Good. Because I think we'd better cut the cake while there's still some icing left on it.'

Olivia followed the direction of his eyes. A grimacing Jamie was standing near the cake while Annie, muttering, dabbed briskly at a sticky white smear around his mouth.

'Oh, dear,' said Olivia. 'I am sorry.'

'Don't worry. The damage isn't that bad. And it's Annie who'll have to cope if he's sick. You and I will be enjoying our honeymoon.'

The gleam in his eye was so suggestive that when, shortly afterwards, they cut the cake to the accompaniment of polite applause from the assembled guests – and an excited war-whoop from Jamie – Olivia's stomach started to tango the moment he put his hand over hers.

After that Simon barely left her side. She felt his protective eye on her each time she was introduced to a new face, as if she were a rare jewel he was reluctant to let out of his sight.

Olivia, amused by his possessiveness and deciding she rather liked being a jewel, felt as if she had walked into a dream.

The dream ended abruptly halfway through the afternoon.

Simon had just taken her arm to steer her away from a lascivious honorary uncle when a flaming red sports car swept up the driveway in a shower of gravel, and screeched to a halt beside the rose-bed. Moments later an unlikely figure in goggles and a helmet erupted on to the terrace.

'Gerald. Damn,' Simon muttered. 'I was beginning to hope he wouldn't turn up.'

Gerald was definitely no dream. More of a black-clad nightmare, Olivia decided, when Simon, looking stern and disapproving, led her over to his cousin and introduced her as if he were introducing Lady to the Tramp.

'Charming,' said Gerald, flashing a mouthful of teeth. 'Sorry I'm late. Couldn't tear myself out of bed, if you know what I mean.'

From the look on Simon's face, Oliva gathered he knew exactly what his cousin meant – and was not amused.

Gerald cocked his head in a manner she supposed was intended to be engaging. 'So you decided to take the plunge, cousin,' he said. 'Pretty hot water too, from the looks of her.'

Simon's jaw hardened, and Olivia knew she would have to think fast if they were to avoid a most unseemly and unfestive scene. At the same time, she felt a certain sympathy for the flamboyant Gerald. He must be at least fifteen years younger than Simon, and until today his chances of inheriting Sherraby had been good. He couldn't be expected to feel much joy at the news that his hoped-for inheritance was likely to slide from his grasp.

When Simon took a threatening step forward, Olivia extended the tips of her white-gloved fingers and said in her haughtiest voice, 'Delighted. So glad you were able to come, Gerald. Yes, the water *is* a little warm today, I expect?'

Gerald's flashy smile slipped a little as he took the proffered hand and mumbled incoherent civilities. A second or two later he gave Simon a malevolent look and swaggered off in search of champagne.

Simon brushed a hand across his mouth. 'Not the way I would have handled my charming cousin,' he murmured. 'But nonetheless well done. What a pity I'm not a duke. You'd make a splendid duchess, my dear.'

Olivia felt an absurd glow of pride. Simon was amused, but she sensed that, in spite of his slightly pompous phraseology, for once he wasn't teasing. He really was pleased with the way she had handled his cousin.

Emma, looking ethereal in pale green chiffon, came hurrying up to them just then and asked with a breeziness that deceived no one, 'Have you seen Zack?'

'Yes,' said Simon. 'He was my best man.'

Emma frowned. 'There's no need to be sarcastic.'

Simon shook his head at her. 'There's a difference between sarcasm and teasing. What's the matter, sourpuss?'

Emma's shoulders slumped. 'Sorry. It's not your fault.'

Simon's rugged features softened. 'I didn't suppose it was. Zack's in the house, as far as I know. I think he's reached his limit of sociability.'

'What limit?' Emma scoffed. 'He's hardly spoken two words to me since the morning you phoned to say you were getting married.'

'You flew home together,' Simon pointed out mildly.

'Yes, and he spent the whole trip pretending to be asleep. He was worse than Ari.'

Olivia, quietly observing the two cousins, saw Simon's eyes narrow. 'New York wasn't a success, then? Your plan didn't come off?'

'How do you know what I planned?'

'My dear Emma, I've known you since before you were born. The ability to hide your feelings has never been one of your strengths.'

'Oh, Simon.' Emma's face crumpled at once, proving his point. 'Sometimes I'm not sure I have any strengths. Zack certainly doesn't think so.'

'What does that mean?' he demanded.

Emma turned away and kicked at the grass exactly the way Jamie did when he didn't want to tell the truth but couldn't think of a better alternative. 'My plan did come off,' she mumbled.

'What did you say?' Simon too must have been reminded of Jamie, because he spoke in the kind of voice that, when he used it on her son, meant he expected an answer.

'I said my plan did come off. Sort of. We did – well, you know. It just didn't work out, that's all.' She went on kicking.

'Oh,' Simon said grimly. 'I see.'

'No, you don't . . .' Emma broke off because Simon was already striding towards the house. She stared worriedly after him. 'Olivia, he wouldn't . . . I mean you don't think he'd *say* anything to Zack. Do you? He looked so – funny.'

'I don't know,' Olivia admitted honestly. 'You know him better than I do. He's very fond of you, you know. He wouldn't want anyone to hurt you.' She took in the stricken expression on Emma's face, and asked gently, 'Would it matter so much if Simon did speak to Zack?'

'Yes,' Emma said. 'Zack's so private. He'd hate Simon knowing that we – that we . . .'

'I understand,' said Olivia. 'You don't have to say it.'

'I think I want to. We – made love. And it was wonderful. Then Zack said it was all over. But we made love again, and I thought . . . anyway Simon phoned, and after that Zack went back to saying there wasn't any more to be said, and that one day I'd be grateful to him.'

'Mmm,' Olivia murmured sympathetically. 'Men have a habit of saying that when they don't want to do what we want them to do.'

'I know. And after that he wouldn't come near me. Sometimes I think I hate him, Olivia. At least I would if I didn't love him so much.'

'I know what you mean.'

'Do you? Yes, of course you do. Oh, I am sorry.' Emma pulled a tissue out of her handbag and blew her nose. 'I didn't mean to rain on your wedding . . .'

Seeing that her bridesmaid looked ready to disintegrate, Olivia put an arm around her shoulders and said bracingly, 'You haven't rained on it. And I'm sure Simon won't say a word. Now come and have some champagne before my son tries to feed it to the Ripper.'

'Would he?' asked Emma, distracted.

'Jamie? Probably, if he manages to give Annie the slip. Would the Ripper drink it?'

'Probably. If Gerald hasn't already polished it all off.'

They were both laughing by the time they reached the marquee, where Gerald was indeed doing his best to drink the champagne off the menu.

Jamie was under the table helping the Ripper search for crumbs.

Simon, as he had expected, found Zack in the room the family always referred to as the library, although nowadays it boasted only one glass-fronted bookcase and was mainly dedicated to the watching of television. The leather chairs and reading lamps so beloved of the ancestors had long since been replaced by comfortable wing-backs and sofas. Yet on a warm day the smell of polish and old books still lingered.

Zack always chose this room over the larger and more formal sitting room when he wanted somewhere quiet to brood. Probably, Simon guessed, because along with a passion for privacy, his impoverished childhood had instilled in him an instinctive discomfort with underused space. No one had ever said his partner was an uncomplicated man.

Zack had thrown off his jacket and was lying on a brown tweed sofa with his eyes closed.

'What's the idea?' Simon asked, closing the door with a click. 'There's a wedding going on out there. Mine, as a matter of fact.'

Zack opened an eye. 'I know.'

Simon moved into the room and flung himself into the nearest wingback. 'Emma?' he asked in a clipped voice. It wasn't really a question, and Zack didn't bother to answer.

'Are you going to marry her?' Simon refused to be ignored.

'No.'

'I think you should.'

Zack opened the other eye. 'Why? Got wedding-bells on the brain, have you? They say misery likes company.'

Simon conquered an urge to grab his friend by the throat. 'What happened in New York?' he asked stiffly.

'None of your business.'

'It is my business if it concerns Emma. You'll remember that I'm the one who arranged for you to stay in her parents' house.'

'And did you also arrange for her to be there? She's a big girl, Si. Old enough to make her own decisions.'

Simon remembered he had said much the same thing to himself at one point in regard to Zack. He took his time about answering. 'No,' he said finally. 'I didn't arrange it. But nor did I attempt to stop her going. And she may be old enough, but I still don't want to see her hurt.'

'Would it surprise you to know I don't either? That's why I'm not going to marry her.'

Simon frowned. 'Then you had no right to –'

Zack sat up abruptly, his feet landing on the floor with a thud. 'And you've no right to tell me what I have, or haven't, a right to do. This is exactly what I was afraid of.'

'What was?' Simon's smile was crooked and not very warm. 'I've never known you to be afraid of anything. Certainly not a skinny bit of a girl.'

'Emma's not skinny, she's . . .' Zack broke off. 'Never mind. What I'm saying is that I don't want any – entanglement with your cousin to interfere with our partnership. You've always looked out for her, Si, even when there wasn't a bloody thing you could do to keep her out of trouble . . .'

'Did you say *entanglement*?' Simon asked, ignoring the rest of his friend's speech.

Zack shrugged. 'Stop playing the heavy father. She's not your daughter.'

Simon grinned, but without much conviction. 'No. Thank God. If she were, I have a feeling I'd be obliged to have you horsewhipped.'

'I'd like to see you try.'

'I wouldn't.' Simon rose to his feet and stood frowning down at his friend. 'She's hurting, Zack. You know how she gets. All brittle and giggly and infuriating . . . and then she goes off and does something stupid. Like Ari Andrakis. Or that banker fellow she was going on about last night.'

'What's wrong with the banker fellow?'

'He's twice her age and engaged in a messy divorce.'

'My divorce wasn't that hygienic.'

'No. But you, at least, are fond of her.'

'What makes you think that?'

Simon knew he had to leave before he lost his temper, which could cause Zack's predictions about the partnership to come true.

'I've known you for over ten years,' he said from the open doorway. 'We've worked together. And both of us are conditioned to be observant.' He started to close the door. 'Now, I have a wedding to get back to. Emma's looking for you. Shall I tell her you're here?'

He waited with his back to the room. For several seconds there was only a telling silence. Then, as the grandfather clock in the corner began to chime the hour, Zack muttered as if the words were being dragged from his mouth, 'If you like.'

Simon said, 'Right,' and slammed the door so hard the panels shuddered.

Zack stared at the vibrating woodwork.

'All very well for you, Si,' he muttered. 'You've found a woman who's perfectly agreeable to being used as a convenience.'

There had never been anything convenient about Emma, who would likely as not up and run off with another Ari the moment she thought she had him in the bag. Or with that damned banker. And even if she didn't, what chance did the two of them have of making a marriage work? They had nothing in common.

Except bed.

He tipped his head against the back of the sofa. Bed was a different matter. If he could just *keep* her there, refuse to let her get up . . .

His lips parted in a slow smile as the fantasy began to take hold.

Emma, small teeth bared in a sexy grin, lying naked and squirming on his . . .

Don't be a fool, Kent, Zack brought himself up short. You've already made a dog's dinner of one marriage, and you know damn well there's more to matrimony than bed. Children, for instance. He had a sudden vision of Emma holding a baby, and swallowed, trying to shift an unexpected swelling in his throat.

'What are you thinking about?' Emma's voice brought his head up with a start.

She was standing in the open doorway. In her filmy green dress, and with a garland of wildflowers in her hair, she looked as fragile and insubstantial as a wood-sprite. But in his mind he was still seeing her as she had been that night on Long Island. There had been nothing insubstantial about her then. She had been very much there, in body as well as in spirit. And her bright eyes had shone with desire. For him.

'I was thinking,' he said, 'that I'd like to take you to bed with me and keep you there. For good.'

'Oh.' She didn't sound particularly ecstatic.

'You don't like the idea?'

'Not really.'

He ought to feel relieved. What he actually felt was an illogical urge to shake her. 'Easy come, easy go, is it?' he said. 'Back to Ari now that you've learned what to do?'

When he saw the look in her eyes, as if she were a puppy he had stepped on, Zack wanted to kick himself.

'I told you that's all finished,' Emma said, twisting her fingers in the folds of her dress. 'Not that it ever started.'

Zack nodded and held out his hand. 'I'm sorry. I didn't mean it. Come here.'

She stared at him with her limpid, sad-puppy eyes – they were turquoise today – and for a few seconds he thought she would refuse. Then, but with obvious reluctance, she moved towards him. Her subtle, wood-sprite fragrance teased him as she drifted across the room.

Zack took her hand and pulled her onto his knee. 'I surrender,' he said quickly, before he could change his mind. 'You win. Marry me, then.'

Hell! What demon had let those fatal words out of his mouth? Zack waited, half-expecting Emma to fall on his neck and burst into tears of gratitude. But with heartbreaking dignity, she stood up and said, 'No. Thank you. It's good of you, but I know you don't want to. Was it Simon's idea?'

She'd turned him down. Emma Colfax, after eight years spent pursuing him, had actually turned him down.

'Good of me!' Zack exploded. '*Good* of me? No, it was *not* Simon's idea. Don't you think I can make up my own mind about a matter like marrying?'

'Yes, of course you can.' Emma spoke soothingly, in the kind of voice Morag had used on her baby brother to calm him down when he threw a tantrum. It had irritated him beyond belief then, and it irritated him no less coming from Emma.

'So are you going to marry me?' He was aware that it wasn't done to snarl at a girl when you asked for her hand in marriage. But he was having one devil of a job keeping his voice down – and his hands off Emma's slim body poised warily just out of his reach. She had felt so light, so right there on his knee, as if it was where she belonged . . .

'No,' she said, with a composure that failed to deceive him. 'Thank you, but I'm not. You said yourself it wouldn't work.'

'Why?' Zack swallowed exasperation and an improbable desire to tell her to stop being an idiot and do what she was told. 'In New York you were all for it.'

'Yes. But I didn't understand. Now I do.'

'And what do you understand?' He gripped an arm of the sofa in one hand and attempted to pulverize a gold tweed cushion with the other. So help him, if she went on looking at him like that – so sad, so beautiful, and so damned obstinate – he would begin to understand some of those incomprehensible acts of violence he read about all too often in the papers.

'I understand you're trying to be kind,' she said, pleating another fold in her dress. 'And that Simon has said you ought to do the right thing. But you don't have to worry. I'm not going to accept. So you can go on being dour and bad-tempered and alone. I promise not to bother you any more.' She turned and walked sedately towards the door.

'Emma!' Zack shouted after her. 'Woman! Where the devil do you think you're going?'

Emma went on walking, and when he leaped up to follow her, she shut the door in his face.

He listened to her footsteps receding down the passageway, then picked up his jacket and shrugged it on before going after her. Outside the door, the scent of her still hung in the air.

He was halfway across the hall before common sense took over. What did he think he was doing? He didn't want to marry Emma. And if he didn't want to marry her, had proposed to her almost by mistake, this hollowness in his gut must have come from drinking too much champagne.

He frowned and stopped to adjust his collar. That was all very well. But if it was only a matter of champagne, why did he feel as if he'd lost something? Some vital part of himself? Dammit, he'd been trying to discourage Emma from chasing him for years. Not because he didn't want her, but because that kind of wanting had nothing to do with permanence and marriage.

He had never wanted Emma for keeps.

Or had he? Was he the biggest fool ever to come out of Scotland?

Zack glared at the sneering visage of a Sebastian ancestor staring down from his vantage point on the wall. 'What do you know, you old goat?' he snapped. '*You* haven't just proposed to a woman you don't want to marry and been turned down.'

The ancestor went on sneering. Zack swung a fist at the wall, bruising the knuckles of his right hand, and slouched back out to join the revellers in the garden.

On his way across the grass he tripped over a hose and paused to look at it longingly. If only he could turn it on the lot of them.

Himself included.

Emma awoke with a start from a deep, dreamless sleep. She blinked as the sun struck her eyes.

'Mmph,' she mumbled. 'What the . . .?'

'It's me,' Jamie's cheerful voice penetrated the lazy moment of waking. 'Mrs Leigh said I could bring you a cuppa.'

'Oh. Thank you.' She struggled on to her back, and saw, blearily, that the flowered curtains had been pulled back, exposing her small, circular bedroom to the ruthless light of day. Beside the bed, the blurred figure of Jamie stood clutching a pale blue cup and saucer at an alarming angle.

Emma reached for her glasses and put them on. 'You'd better put that down,' she said, indicating the mahogany table beside the bed. 'What time is it?'

'Ten o'clock, I think.' Jamie slopped milky tea into the saucer as he laid the cup down. 'Mrs Leigh said you might want to be getting up before Mr Kent goes back to London. But you don't, do you?'

'Don't what?' Emma wasn't at her brightest after the excitement, strain, and in the end the despair of yesterday's wedding – which had been followed by long hours spent lying on her back staring dismally at the moon.

'Don't want to see Mr Kent,' Jamie explained. 'He's awfully grumpy. He said I couldn't play my drum in the house. And he yelled at Rip for putting toothmarks in *The Times*.'

'He doesn't mean to be grumpy.' Instinctively Emma sprang to Zack's defence. 'That's just the way he is.'

'All the time?' Jamie was scandalized.

'No, not all the time. Just sometimes. Especially when I happen to be around.'

'Like Chrissy's Dad? He's always mad when *I'm* around.'

Emma smiled and sat up to drink the tea. 'Yes, something like that. But Zack's not mad at *you*, Jamie. When is he going back to London?'

Jamie shrugged. 'I don't know. Mrs Leigh said soon.'

Oh. Of course. After yesterday, Zack would be anxious to get away as soon as possible. He had only stayed on because he'd said he would and Annie had already been to the trouble of making up his room.

After their meeting in the library Zack had done his best to avoid her, until she had begun to feel like an unpleasant smell. It had been the same on Long Island once he'd decreed the end of their all-too-brief affair. She had scarcely seen him the whole time he'd been there.

Emma took another bracing sip of tea. Was he afraid that if he hung around she would change her mind and accept him after all? If he was, he needn't worry. She knew he had never meant to propose, didn't really want to marry her. He had only, belatedly, behaved like the gentleman he said he wasn't because Simon had told him he ought to.

Zack hadn't succeeded in avoiding her completely, though. Emma, remembering, dropped the cup into its saucer with a clink.

Late in the afternoon, all the guests except one had assembled in front of the house to wave the newly married couple off on their honeymoon. Caught in the midst of a hail of confetti and rice, Zack and Emma had found themselves pushed together.

As exuberant guests had jostled all around them, Zack put a steadying hand on her shoulder. When she'd looked up, startled and tremblingly aware of him, he had surprised her by remarking, 'Would you believe those two actually look happy together?' His voice was so heavy with gloom it might have made her laugh if she hadn't wanted so badly to cry.

'Yes,' Emma agreed. 'I suppose they do.' Privately, she thought Simon looked more satisfied than happy, and Olivia seemed *too* frantically bright – as if she was balanced precariously on that fine line between laughter and tears.

'At least they're under no illusions,' Zack said, carefully avoiding her eye.

'No. No, they're not. Neither am I any more.'

'Emma . . .' He caught her arm as she made to move off. 'Don't you dare.'

'Dare what?'

'Don't walk away on me again.'

'Why not?' she said, bristling. 'There's nothing I . . .' She broke off as Celia Cameron, long nose pointed due north, floated up to them like a minesweeper bent on scooping up trouble.

'What a shame your mother and father couldn't be with us today, Emma,' she said. 'So disappointing.'

'Yes,' Emma agreed. 'They did hope to come, but Dad's still in Japan and Mom wouldn't come without him.'

'Ah, well. Never mind, my dear. We're delighted *you* had no pressing engagements elsewhere.'

'Give her time,' muttered Zack.

Smiling fixedly, and digging her pink-painted nails into her palms, Emma turned her back on him and took half a dozen steps towards the house. She couldn't, *wouldn't* allow Zack to goad her into losing her temper on Simon's wedding day. It was bad enough that Gerald, having siphoned up too much champagne, was lurking behind a rose bush being sick.

But before she could make good her escape, Celia's penetrating voice called after her, 'Emma! Emma, you mustn't leave now. Olivia is going to throw her bouquet.'

Reluctantly Emma turned around.

A sea of hands rose in front of her. She stared at them blankly. When the bunch of white roses and red carnations flew straight towards her, she made no attempt to catch it until an instinct for self-preservation drove her to lift a hand to protect her face.

She tried to smile and look pleased that she'd captured the prize, but when she bent her head to smell the roses their scent had already faded, and the vibrant colour of the carnations had misted into a uniform pink.

She didn't realize the mist was in her eyes until after the bride and groom had driven off with Cousins in the Rolls. No one was watching her, so she took the opportunity to retire to the seclusion of her room.

By the time she went downstairs again, Celia, with the help of Mrs Leigh and the caterers, had eliminated most of the signs of revelry, and Sherraby was once again the peaceful country house she called home.

The peace turned out to be deceptive.

Emma, certain Zack would be brooding in the library, made her way to the drawing room in search of Celia. But there was no one there. She was about to leave again when she heard what sounded like a soft burp. At the same time her nose was assaulted by the smell of something rancid and alcoholic. Glancing around the room, she detected a dark shape draped across a sofa beneath the windows. Zack? She moved cautiously forward to investigate. Immediately the shape began to snore.

Not Zack, but Gerald, sleeping off the effects of the champagne.

As Emma turned to tiptoe out again, a hand caught at her thigh and hung on, pinching her through the folds of her dress.

'Let go, Gerald,' she snapped. 'I'm not one of your shady ladies.'

'My ladies aren't shady,' Gerald mumbled, his voice still thickened with sleep and too much champagne. 'They're not nesh – necessarily ladies either.' He hiccuped. 'Doesn't matter as long as they're rich. Like you. How about standing me a loan, Em?'

'Get one from one of your lady friends.'

'Tried. No good. You're my lasht hope.'

The door to the drawing room creaked sharply. Emma spun round as Gerald switched his hand to her other thigh.

Zack was standing in the doorway, motionless, still in his wedding clothes. But to Emma's eyes in that moment, he was Man the Hunter – primitive blood-lust cloaked in the trappings of civility. And Gerald was the prey. She drew a shocked breath. Yet there was something about that unbridled masculinity that excited her, made her long to hurl herself across the room and into his arms.

She did take a single step forward, but Gerald's hand was still gripping her thigh.

'Let go,' she whispered, her gaze riveted on Zack. 'Gerald, for God's sake let go.'

'What about my loan?' Gerald mumbled.

'The only loan you'll be getting will be the loan of my fist if you don't let go of her this second.' Zack's tone was almost conversational, but no one in the room was deceived.

Gerald let go.

'Now get out,' Zack ordered. When Gerald made no attempt to move, he added, 'I don't mean tomorrow.'

'You don't own this house,' Gerald muttered, unwisely.

Zack took a step forward. 'Don't I? Maybe not, but I come from a long line of fighting Scots on my mother's side. And where I grew up, no one's heard of the Queensberry rules.'

'OK, OK.' Gerald slid off the sofa and held up his hands. 'I wash leaving anyway. Emma's not my type.' He sidled past Zack, and from the safety of the hallway jeered, 'But I bet you're in for a pretty warm night if her rep-reputation's anything to go by.' He hiccuped.

Zack's response, delivered in the expressive but incomprehensible language of his native Scotland, made Emma put her hands over her ears. But as he started after Gerald, she caught his arm.

'Let him go,' she said. 'Please. It doesn't matter. *He* doesn't matter. No one pays attention to Gerald.'

She watched, heart in mouth, as Zack's skin changed from a dark, furious bronze to a kind of brick. He shook her arm off and glowered at her, hesitating, as they listened to Gerald's footsteps beating a strategic retreat across the hall.

'Please,' Emma repeated, because his body was still vibrating with rage.

Zack let out his breath. 'Did you not hear what he said about you?'

'Of course I heard. You're not always polite about me either.'

Zack looked at her as if she were mad. 'That's different,' he said.

'I don't see why.'

'Don't you?' He shook his head slowly. 'Then you're more of a wee idiot than I thought. But as the scumbag's your cousin, I won't do anything to spoil his pretty face. Unless you want me to.'

'Thank you,' Emma said with feeling. She didn't think she could stand the thought of a round of fisticuffs just now.

Zack sighed, and to her astonishment she caught the beginnings of a smile. 'It's been a while since I smashed up a nose,' he said regretfully. 'Are you sure you don't want me to? I wouldn't mind keeping my hand in. And the recipient would surely be deserving.'

Emma laughed, not because she was in any mood to laugh, but because she couldn't help herself. 'I'm quite sure. Zack . . .?'

'What is it now?'

'Nothing. I just wouldn't want you to think . . . I mean, when I said I wouldn't marry you, it wasn't that –'

Zack stopped her by placing two gently convincing fingers across her lips. 'I don't care why you refused me. It's enough that you did.' He removed the fingers, leaned forward, and gave her a lingering kiss on the lips.

Before she had recovered from the shock, he was gone.

Somewhere outside, the Ripper barked. Emma stood still, staring into the empty hallway. Zack had moved fast. He had said goodbye in his own way and didn't mean her to catch up with him. Was he afraid that if he allowed her speak she would change her mind and accept the proposal he hadn't meant to make?

The Ripper barked again. Emma dashed the back of her hand across her eyes and went into the kitchen in search of the familiar comfort of tea and Mrs Leigh.

Pushing back the memories, Emma made herself look around her bedroom. Oh, yes. Morning had come again – and Jamie was perched like a small, companionable sparrow on the edge of her bed.

It was time to begin a new chapter of her life.

'Do you *like* Mr Kent?' Jamie asked, frowning at her.

'Yes.' Emma smiled at his evident disbelief. 'I'm afraid I do.'

'Oh.' Jamie shook his head. 'I don't get it.'

'Don't you?' Emma didn't feel like explaining. Anyway she wasn't sure she could.

'He says he likes you too,' Jamie confided. 'But that was before he told me to go away. Simon hardly ever tells me to go away.'

'Simon is your stepfather.'

'Yes. I'm glad Mr Kent isn't.'

'I expect he is too,' Emma said drily.

Jamie put his head on one side. 'Do you think so?'

'Mmm,' said Emma. 'I do. Listen, Jamie, I think I'd better get up. It's getting late, and –'

'You *do* want to see Mr Kent.' It was an accusation, she was sure.

'Yes, perhaps I do.' She put the cup and saucer back on the bedside table.

Jamie made a face, but he said, 'OK, then, I'll go. But first can I watch you put your eyes in?'

Emma was glad she wasn't still drinking tea. 'If you like,' she agreed. Funny how even when life seemed at its bleakest, someone, or something, always seemed to come along to make her laugh. Lately it had quite often been Jamie.

She climbed out of bed, glad she was wearing her high-necked nightgown with the ruffle, and went into the attached bathroom to 'put her eyes in'. This she accomplished with a speed and skill born of long practice. After supervising the operation with a fascination that never seemed to wane, Jamie skipped off to find the Ripper, and Emma was left to enjoy her bath in peace.

As the warm water lapped around her, and she breathed in the fresh, piny scent of the soap that always reminded her of Zack making music in the woods, Emma decided Jamie was right. However much it hurt, she did want to see Zack before he left, even if it was only to say goodbye. Her way this time. She didn't like untidy endings.

Twenty minutes later, dressed in white trousers and a kingfisher-blue blouse, Emma gave her hair a final quick comb and marched downstairs to the dining room.

The moment she opened the door, she began to wish she'd stayed in her room. If only Mrs Leigh wouldn't insist on serving breakfast in this long, narrow coffin of a room with its dark furniture and faded tapestry walls. It always seemed such a serious place to start the day – especially when it was occupied by Zack in one of his strong, silent moods. No wonder Celia always breakfasted in her room.

'Good morning,' Emma said to the newspaper with the toothmarks that Zack was holding up in front of his face.

'Good morning,' the paper replied repressively.

'Nice day.'

'Is it?'

Emma sat down, reached across the table, and pulled the paper down. 'Yes, it is. Jamie says you're leaving soon.'

'Jamie's right. Some of us have work to do.'

'On Sunday? And what do you mean, *some* of us have work to do.'

Zack lifted the paper again, obscuring the disapproving line of his lips. 'I mean I have to earn a living.'

'And I don't?' Emma helped herself to eggs from a covered silver dish.

A cup of coffee disappeared behind the paper. 'To the best of my knowledge you never have.'

'That's not true. *Fashion Fair* buys most of my articles. And I have sold to other magazines.'

'Yes? And do you live on the proceeds?'

'No. But I could.'

'Good.' The coffee cup reappeared, the paper rustled aggressively, and a page was firmly folded over.

'Have I offended you?' Emma asked in desperation after five minutes had passed without further communication. Her eggs felt like wet sponge in her stomach.

'Not at all.' At last the paper came down, and Zack's eyes met hers squarely and without warmth. 'What do you want from me, Emma? Another proposal? The chance to turn me down again? You won't get it.'

What *did* she want from him? Respect? That was laughable. No, she wanted him to love her enough to want to spend the rest of his life at her side. But that seemed to be the one thing he couldn't, or wouldn't, do.

'I don't want anything from you, Zack,' she said finally. 'But can't we at least stay friends?'

'Friends? I think not. Friends keep their hands to themselves. I doubt if I'd be able to do that.' His voice was as dry as fall leaves. But – Emma's heart gave a hop. He still wanted her, then, even though he was making a joke of it.

'Perhaps if we gave ourselves time . . .' she suggested.

'Time? Emma, we've had time. I wasn't joking when I said it wouldn't work. You were right to turn me down.' He smiled, an odd, twisted sort of smile that made her want to cry. 'I'd like to finish my paper now, if you don't mind.'

He picked it up and began to read.

Emma stared at a headline about the latest political scandal, the letters dancing up and down in front of her eyes. If she stuck her egg-stained fork through his damned paper just – there . . .

No. The fork fell from her fingers with a clatter. No, Zack had said all he wanted to say. There was no reason for her to confirm his opinion that she was a spoiled, self-absorbed child.

Emma laid her napkin carefully beside her plate and stood up.

Zack didn't stir.

She sighed, waited a few more seconds just in case, then left the room.

She wasn't sure, but just as she closed the door, she thought she heard a sound like paper being crushed, and something that might have been a fist hitting the table.

Annie Coote was in the hall. Emma gave her an over-bright, 'Good morning,' and hurried up to her room.

'Zack,' she groaned, flinging open the door of her wardrobe. 'Zack, why can't you see . . .?' Her gaze fell on the green bridesmaid's dress.

What was it Simon had once said about Olivia? That he admired her capacity to get on with what needed doing without a lot of fuss and complaining. He had called it respect, though, not love . . .

After all, respect was a start. Maybe she could never make Zack love her. But she too could get on with things without complaining. If she had to.

Thoughtfully she tugged the green dress off its hanger and laid it over the back of a chair. Then she dragged a suitcase out of the cupboard and thumped it on to the bed.

She hadn't planned to leave until tomorrow. But, as she had heard Olivia say to Jamie when he balked at picking up his toys, there was no point in putting things off. The job would still remain to be done.

She opened a drawer and began throwing clothes into the suitcase. Olivia was wise in so many ways. She deserved to be happy with Simon. Yet she seemed – apart from him somewhow. And yesterday her smile had been too bright.

Emma folded the green dress haphazardly as she stared through the window at the wind-rippled lake. Sherraby had been such a happy place once. One day, when it was happy again, she would come back.

Half an hour later she left the house.

She didn't see the man standing at the dining room window, watching her. Nor did she see him squash *The Times* into the shape of a missile and hurl it on to the floor.

CHAPTER 8

'Olivia.' Simon's voice, deep and hypnotic, held an underlying note of command. 'Olivia, come here.'

Reluctantly, Olivia removed her gaze from the crowds milling about the Champs-Elysées, and turned to face her husband. He was sitting on the edge of the big double bed with his legs apart and his hands resting lightly on his thighs. In an expensively tailored grey suit, he looked effortlessly elegant and at the same time unconsciously seductive. Olivia ran her tongue across her lips.

They hadn't spoken much during the flight to Paris. Olivia had been tired, wary, still not entirely convinced she hadn't lost her senses, and uncomfortably aware of Simon's long legs stretched casually beside hers and occasionally brushing up against her thigh. He had seemed content with her silence, although sometimes he had turned to look at her with a speculative, disturbingly enigmatic smile.

Olivia, her confidence at an unusually low ebb after the long, endlessly eventful day, wondered if he was thinking how different it would have been if he had made this journey with the mysterious Sylvia.

If Sylvia was on his mind, it certainly wasn't apparent once they arrived at the magnificent old hotel on the Champs-Elysées and were shown to a luxuriously appointed suite on the third floor. The bathroom alone, with its marble tub and washbasin with gold taps, made Olivia's eyebrows shoot up. The golden eagles looming over the headboard of the bed would have made her giggle if she hadn't been so nervous – because at last, and for the first time since their wedding, she and Simon were completely alone.

With an air of purpose, Simon settled himself on the intimidatingly large double bed and hauled Olivia on to his knee.

Immediately she stiffened, and Simon muttered something under his breath and let her go. Confused, embarrassed, not sure how to handle this situation which found her married to a man she had known for less than two months, Olivia jumped up – and spent the next ten minutes with her knuckles pressed to the window-sill while she gazed silently at the activity below.

A young man on a bicycle weaved his way through the traffic, and she fastened on him as if he could somehow help her to escape from this trap of her own making.

'Olivia.' Simon's demanding voice brought her back to the reality of the present.

She forced herself not to look away again. He lifted a finger and beckoned. 'I said come here,' he repeated.

Olivia gulped. 'Do you think Zack will marry Emma?' she asked.

'I have no idea. And at this particular moment I don't much care.'

'Oh. She's terribly in love with him.'

'And you, I gather, are not terribly in love with me.'

'I – what's that got to do with it?' She fidgeted with the cord on the cream velvet curtains. 'I think she slept with him, Simon.'

'I've no doubt she did. I also think it would be a good thing if she married Zack, who just might be able to manage her. But as the matter is out of my control, and out of yours, do you think you could see your way clear to –?'

'I was just thinking,' Olivia interrupted him hastily. 'She looked so unhappy. Even when she caught my bouquet. And Zack was prowling around as though he was on the lookout for someone to murder.'

'Zack often looks like that. And if you don't stop prevaricating this minute, *I'll* know exactly who to murder.' He beckoned again. 'Olivia, for the third time, come here.'

Because there was no escape, and because she didn't know what else to do, Olivia at last found the courage to do as he said.

Simon reached up to take her hand, and her knee brushed up against his thigh. At once she sank down beside him and shifted sideways so that there was a good ten inches of rose-quilted bedspread between her leg and Simon's smart grey trousers.

She watched him remove his jacket and tie, toss them on to a chair and lean back on his elbows. 'I'm not going to storm the barricades,' he said. 'But don't you think it's a little late for second thoughts?'

Olivia picked at a quilted rose. 'I know you're not going to storm me. If you'd meant to do that you would have done it. But – Simon, everything's happened in such a rush. We've talked, but I still know very little about you . . .'

'Such as? There are certain things, Olivia, that, by their very nature, you never will know.' His low voice was unexpectedly harsh.

Olivia stopped trying to mutilate the rose and made herself look him in the eye. 'Have you ever killed anyone?'

'Yes.'

Just like that. As if it were all in a day's work. But he didn't surprise her. She had sensed a darkness in Simon that could only have come from his past. 'I think I knew that,' she said slowly. 'And you can't, or won't, tell me how or why?'

'No.' His face was unrevealing as a rock.

She nodded. 'And Zack? Has he killed too?'

'Possibly. I don't think so. But we weren't always assigned to the same job.'

'I see. What does it feel like? To kill a man?'

'Relief. It feels like relief. That it's his life instead of your own.' He didn't sound harsh any more. Just starkly truthful. Olivia, believing she ought to be shocked, was disconcerted to feel a stirring of sympathy. She knew instinctively that Simon had never wanted to kill.

'Was that the choice? Your life or his?'

This time she detected just the faintest flicker of emotion. 'Yes.' He pushed himself upright. 'Olivia, if that makes you uncomfortable –'

'No. No, it doesn't really. At least, it does, but that's not why . . .' She stopped. His smile had become shockingly cynical, and she edged a little further away. She didn't think she wanted to talk about Simon's past after all.

When he continued to look at her with that odd, unnerving smile, she said suddenly, 'Simon – I've only ever been with one man –'

The smile vanished. 'I know. Your husband. A most commendable devotion. One that I must heartily approve, since *I* am now your husband.'

'Yes, but it's been different for you. You said there were others besides Sylvia . . .'

Why did his eyes always take on that glassy look at the slightest mention of his Sylvia?

'One or two others,' he agreed. 'But if that's my cue to launch into a detailed account of my love-life, you can forget it. There's been no one I took seriously since Sylvia. With whom, as I told you, I never shared an intimate relationship – if that makes a difference.'

'It doesn't. Not really.' She wound a lock of her hair around her thumb. 'What happened between you and Sylvia?'

Maybe if she knew about that, it might help her to understand Simon. Understanding Simon was suddenly desperately important.

He shrugged and sat up, then moved away from her to settle his shoulders against the headboard. 'Nothing much. We met up at Oxford and fell in love.' His lips turned down – in contempt for such youthful foolishness, she supposed. 'We were going to get married. But in those early years my work took up most of my time. Often I couldn't tell her where I was or when I'd be back. When I failed to turn up for social engagements she didn't understand, or care, that my absence was unavoidable. I, of course, was convinced I was helping to build a better world.'

'And now? Do you still think you were building a better world?'

He shrugged. 'Let's say I don't have the illusions I had then.'

Olivia nodded. 'And Sylvia . . .?'

'Sylvia didn't want a young idealist with a penchant for risking his neck. She wanted a sensible country gentleman like Martin. I don't think she realized that wasn't on the cards. Not then anyway, even if I'd been willing to settle down. Which I admit I wasn't. I knew where my talents lay, and I meant to use them in the way they'd be most useful.' His eyes darkened, and Olivia wondered if that long-ago disenchantment was still a source of bitterness and pain.

'Sylvia required a man who would turn up on demand,' he continued in a dry, flat voice. 'I wasn't that man. So in the end she found someone else. I suppose I can't blame her entirely. Later, I found out she'd been meeting my replacement for six months. I could, and did, blame her for that. And for other things.' He gave Olivia a look that might have been a warning, swung his legs to the floor and stood up. 'Sylvia taught me a valuable lesson.'

He wasn't telling her the whole story. She knew he wasn't. But she would get no satisfaction from pressing the matter. Simon was a very experienced clam.

When he continued to stand over her with his hands thrust into his pockets and his mouth flattened into a ruler-straight line, Olivia gulped and said, ''Yes? What lesson was that?' She was fairly sure she already knew the answer.

'Not to let foolish fantasies of everlasting love get the better of ordinary common sense. It's a lesson I haven't forgotten. And it's why I think you and I ought to suit each other well once you've overcome your maidenly misgivings – which, in the circumstances, come as something of a surprise.' He added the last words with a welcome relaxing of the tension around his mouth.

'The circumstances being my seven years of marriage, I suppose.' Olivia found herself furiously resenting what she recognized as a gibe.

'Mmm.' Simon pushed his hands deeper into his pockets. 'More or less.'

Olivia's heart sank. He sounded so matter-of-fact, so passionless. She had no difficulty accepting that Simon didn't believe in love; in the long run that should help to keep the waters of their unusual marriage flowing smoothly. But passion – that, surely, was something they could share. Not just as a means of creating future Sebastians, but as a means of communication, of pleasure given and received. As once, long ago, she had shared that special rapture with Dan.

But Dan was dead. And now she was married to this complex, enigmatic man who one moment exuded a very intimate and charismatic charm, and the next displayed about as much charm as a shark on the point of wrapping up the deal that would ensure his next meal. The deal, in this case, being Jamie's security in exchange for her body in Simon's bed. The bed that she herself had made. And that now she must lie in.

Briefly, she imagined Jamie as he must be now, fast asleep in his room at Sherraby Manor, his long eyelashes sweeping innocently over the childish curve of his cheek while Annie, sleeping next door, kept a fond ear open for trouble.

Olivia smiled wistfully. She missed her small son already. More than she would have believed possible . . .

Above her, Simon moved suddenly, and she became aware of the subtle scent of his body, of the irresistible pull of his masculinity – and of the reason why she was here with him in this Paris hotel room that exuded old-fashioned luxury from the white and gold walls, to the eagles on the headboard, to the marble fittings in the bathroom.

Dashing a hand across her eyes, Olivia stumbled awkwardly to her feet. 'All right,' she said, beginning to unfasten her red travelling jacket. 'Let's get on with it, then.'

'What?' Simon's eyes narrowed and he stepped back. 'Oh, I see. No sense putting off the inevitable. Is that it?'

He wasn't pleased. She could tell. Still, it was what he wanted, wasn't it? She went on unbuttoning.

'Don't be ridiculous.' Simon's arm shot out and he caught her hand just as it reached the last button. 'They don't sacrifice virgins in France any longer. I'm not at all sure they ever did. And in any event, I'm afraid you wouldn't qualify.'

Olivia gasped, tried not to look as if she were a trout gasping for air, and failed miserably. After that she was astonished to find herself struggling not to laugh. And with the urge to laugh came an urgent awareness of the warmth of Simon's hand over hers, of the firm texture of his skin and of the intoxicating tremors spiralling up her arm.

'I suppose I wouldn't,' she managed to choke. 'Qualify, I mean.' She looked up in time to encounter the sardonic blue beam of his eye. 'Simon, I thought you *wanted* –'

'I do. But there's no hurry. I didn't plan to drag you into my bed the moment I got you behind closed doors. I think I can manage to control my raging lust a while longer.'

He was teasing her, but there was a certain hard edge to his mockery, and Olivia, already on edge herself, felt flustered and even more ill at ease. 'I'm pleased to hear it,' she said primly.

Simon's smile was annoyingly condescending. 'I had thought of kissing you,' he admitted. 'After that I meant to have a shower, change my clothes and take you out for a rather late dinner. Is that such a terrifying prospect?'

It wasn't. Suddenly Olivia felt like a fool. 'I'm sorry,' she said. 'I thought you wanted to start on the litter right away.'

He drew in his breath sharply. 'What I'd like to do at this moment has nothing to do with reproduction,' he assured her, strumming his fingers on his thigh. 'But unfortunately, I don't think it's legal.'

'Would that worry you?'

'Not much. Don't push your luck.' Abruptly he put his hands on her waist, spun her around and gave her a push in the direction of the bathroom. 'Go on. Get cleaned up. Then we're going out to eat.'

Olivia didn't say, And after that? But she thought it.

'No,' said Simon, as usual reading her mind. 'Not until you're ready. What do you take me for, Olivia?'

What she actually took him for was an extraordinarily sexy and compelling man who also just happened to be her husband.

'For better or for worse – and for Jamie,' she replied, covering her confusion with flippancy. 'That's what I took you for, Simon.'

As she closed the door of the bathroom she heard him call after her, 'Keep it up, Mrs Sebastian, and it will give me great pleasure to make sure you start with the worse.'

Olivia grinned. She hadn't missed the amusement mixed with frustration in his voice. Maybe this evening wasn't going to be so awful after all.

In the event, it was almost magical. They ate in the sort of dining room Olivia had heard of but never expected to visit. The service was discreet and impeccable, the food a delight to the eye and deliciously French, and the atmosphere one of warmth and relaxation – the perfect refuge after the strains of a day during which emotions had run continually on high.

Simon, seated across from her in a dark and beautifully cut suit, seemed to realize that she needed time to adjust to her new estate, and he kept his natural magnetism turned low. They spoke of the flight from London, what they would do in Paris, of the fatal attraction of opposites as demonstrated by Emma and Zack, and of Jamie and their plans for his future.

Olivia felt a warm thrill of pride when Simon mentioned casually that he thought she'd done a good job of raising Jamie.

Later, they walked along the Champs-Elysées and admired the floodlit magnificence of the Arc de Triomphe. When Olivia caught her breath and said, 'Wow,' Simon laughed and took her hand in his. He didn't speak, and eventually he didn't need to. Her hand felt right in his. She felt right walking proudly beside him.

When they got back to the hotel it seemed quite natural that she should turn to him with a smile, say, 'Thank you. That was a lovely evening,' and lift up her face for his kiss.

When it came, at first it was gentle. Then, Simon's tongue began to probe deeper and she felt the faint clash of teeth. When she put her hands on his shoulders to draw him closer, he wrapped an arm around her waist and lifted her up until she was supported against his chest. She discovered her feet had left the floor and gave a little cry that was part surprise, part anticipation, and part sheer unabashed desire. Hearing her cry, Simon let her go, and she fell back on to the bed.

Olivia lay still, her new red dress pushed up and twisted around her hips. She watched as Simon, without taking his eyes from her, slowly removed his jacket and tie and tossed them over a rose velvet chair. She could see that his breath was coming faster than usual but otherwise he gave no sign that the sight of the wisps of white silk covering her thighs were having any effect on him at all.

After a while Olivia couldn't stand it. She had always wanted this man, even as she had fought to convince herself she shouldn't. And he looked achingly desirable standing there with his legs apart and the hint of a frown between the thick brows that were so much darker than his hair.

She held up her arms and whispered, 'Simon, I don't feel maidenly any more.'

He didn't move.

'Simon?' she repeated, and heard a note that was almost panic in her voice.

He shook his head, ran a hand through his waving brown hair, and said, 'Olivia. My beautiful, convenient Olivia.' It could have been an accusation. But it was said with the ghost of a smile and she knew the words weren't intended to wound.

She laughed, a low, triumphant laugh, the laugh of a woman who was about to get her man. He had called her beautiful. He wanted her as much as she wanted him. And he was unfastening the buckle of his belt. She watched as his shirt followed the jacket and the tie.

Then he was stretched out beside her, his hand curving over her thigh, sliding with delicious suggestion beneath the white silk. She gasped as he touched that warm and intimate part of her that no man besides Dan had ever touched. And when his fingers began a slow, excruciating exploration, she heard herself crying out, 'Please, oh, yes, please . . .'

But it wasn't Dan she was thinking of now. Not any longer. Maybe never again with the same sense of loss. Because Simon had become the centre of her world.

'Please what?' he teased, continuing to move his thumb in a lazy, erotic motion that drove her wild with the need and longing for more of him. For all of him.

'Please don't, I mean please do . . . Simon . . .' She groaned, unable to articulate her hunger. Then his lips found hers and she tasted the sweetness of wine as he began to lay a trail of kisses along her jaw, down her neck and over her shoulders until he came to the straining peaks of her breasts. 'Simon . . .' Her voice sank to a low, pleading whisper.

And Simon said, 'Olivia. Beautiful Olivia,' as he peeled off her dress and his trousers.

'Now,' she groaned. 'Now, Simon.'

Simon laughed and rolled her on top of him, and when their eyes met she saw that his were as glazed with passion as her own.

He stroked his palms lightly over the roundness of her bottom, eased her legs apart and slowly lifted her hips. Then gently, ever so gently, he lowered her until she was all around him – until, at last, she was filled with the glory that was Simon.

And in a little while Olivia's world exploded as Simon gave her the gift she hadn't known how to ask for.

When at last the world resumed its place in the heavens, and ecstasy became the warm sanctuary of lying at peace in Simon's arms, Olivia turned to him with glistening eyes and said, 'I thought I knew . . . But I didn't. I didn't know it could ever feel like that.'

Simon ran his fingers through her hair, smiled pensively, and murmured as if he were talking to himself, '"Rich the treasure; Sweet the pleasure." Sweet Olivia.'

Olivia made no sound. She couldn't. She was frozen with horror.

At first her limbs wouldn't move. It was as if, with that careless bit of verse, Simon had swept away the wonder they had shared and replaced all her bright joy with shards of broken glass.

The words he had spoken so softly were the words Dan had spoken on their wedding night.

Dan had been partial to the words of Dryden, written over three hundred years ago, and it hadn't mattered to him that the poet had been extolling the pleasures of wine rather than those of the flesh. It hadn't mattered to her then either.

But the coincidence was too great to be pure chance. And there was only one possible way Simon could have come up with the very words Dan had spoken, nearly eight years earlier, on that other, very different wedding night.

He had to have read her diary.

Still soft and melting with love, Olivia felt her body go rigid in Simon's arms. When his fingers brushed against her ear she shrank back and turned her head into the pillow.

'Olivia?' he said. 'Olivia, what is it?'

'You lied to me.' Her voice came out cold and detached as chipped ice.

'What the hell are you talking about?' he snapped. 'I didn't steal your virtue by stealth. And to the best of my knowledge, I haven't uttered one word to you tonight that wasn't true.'

'Do you know what you just said to me?' she asked dully. 'The verse you quoted?'

'Of course I . . . hell!' Simon threw himself on to his back. After a while he said, 'I must be slipping. In the old days, no matter what the situation, I'd never have betrayed a source of information.'

'Is that all my private thoughts are to you? A source of information?' Olivia flung an arm across her face, willing herself not to cry.

Simon drew a deep, frustrated breath. 'All right,' he said. 'I read your diary. I'm sorry. It wasn't intentional, and I didn't meant to invade your privacy. But old habits die hard, and when I found myself in possession of a mysterious red book, it was a foregone conclusion that I'd investigate.' He put a hand on her shoulder. 'Olivia, you wrote nothing in that diary that need embarrass you.'

'Why did you lie to me?' she asked, as if he hadn't spoken.

'It seemed the right thing to do at the time. The kindest thing.'

'Reading my diary seemed kind?'

'Not *reading* it, no.'

Vaguely, in the midst of a stunning sense of betrayal and isolation, Olivia was aware that Simon was trying to suppress his exasperation. She listened, without really believing, as he went on. 'I had no idea the damned diary was yours. I hadn't met you. The Ripper found it and dumped it on the manor steps. I picked it up thinking it had come with the morning post. By the time I realized that what I was reading had never been intended for my eyes, I'd finished it – and, if it's any consolation, been considerably impressed by the writer's loyalty to a man who didn't seem to deserve it.'

'Dan was my husband.'

'What am I supposed to say to that?'

He was on the verge of losing his temper. Simon Sebastian, who had read her diary and told her he hadn't, didn't even grasp what he had done.

'I can accept why you read it,' she said. 'I can't accept that you lied.'

Feeling his fingers touch her cheek, Olivia wriggled to the edge of the bed. Simon moved his hand back to her shoulder.

'Olivia,' he said, 'if you could have seen your face when you asked me if I'd read that red invitation to trouble, you wouldn't question why I told you I hadn't.'

'That's an evasion.'

'Is it? Fine. Let me put it another way. You looked terrified. Any man with eyes in his head could see that it was important to you to know that I hadn't read what you'd written. It made no difference to me, but it wasn't hard to tell that it made one hell of a difference to you. So, yes. I lied. Because it seemed kindest, and because, if I thought about it at all, I assumed that any future encounters between us would be confined to the occasional "Good morning" on the street. Besides, to be honest – *this* time,' he added pointedly, 'I doubt if I did think about it. I saw big, anxious eyes gazing up at me and reacted instinctively – as I've been trained to do, by the way – by telling you what you wanted to hear.' He paused, and when Olivia felt his breath brush her cheek, for a moment she thought he meant to kiss her.

She stiffened. But he must have thought better of it, because after a few seconds he said crisply, 'Olivia, If I'd known you would ever be more to me than just a passing stranger, naturally I'd have told you the truth.'

'Naturally? And if you had, we never *would* have become more than passing strangers.' She folded the top of the sheet, crushing it into a rag.

'Olivia, for heaven's sake. I'm beginning not to find this amusing.'

She heard the frustration in his voice and didn't care. 'I'm not a comedy act,' she said coldly. 'I'm your wife. The one you married to ensure your posterity.'

Simon took a deep breath. 'I'm glad you mentioned that. Because I don't believe in secrets – or lies – between us any more than you do. But as my life has depended on it on occasion, I've got in the habit of keeping my own counsel. Which is why, as far as I was concerned, I had read your sainted diary and forgotten it. You have it back, and that had better be the end of the matter.'

'It was the end of the matter until you quoted John Dryden,' Olivia said bleakly. 'You didn't forget that, did you?'

'Apparently not.' Abruptly Simon pulled her over onto her back, and she saw that he was propped on one elbow glowering down into her face. 'Olivia, I am not going to grovel. I'm sorry you're upset, but I've told you there was nothing in that diary to be ashamed of. Does it really matter that I've read it?'

'Dan used to lie to me,' she replied obliquely. 'Never in the beginning. But later, when he didn't want me to think he was still drinking. I always knew, though.'

'Olivia, I have lied to you precisely once. I don't mean to do it again, nor do I expect you to lie to me. So can we please get over this as quickly as possible and get back to where we were?'

'Where we were? But we weren't anywhere, were we? Except in this bed satisfying a temporary lust.' She hadn't known her voice could sound so bitter.

'That may be so in your case,' Simon replied harshly. 'But my lust is anything but temporary.' He put a hand on her stomach as if to stake a claim.

'Stop it,' she said. 'That isn't going to work any more.'

'Right,' he snapped. 'Then perhaps you'll let me know once you've decided to get over your pique and start behaving like the sensible woman I think you are. In the meantime, I propose to get some sleep.'

He turned his back on her and within minutes, to her bitter chagrin and disbelief, he was asleep.

Olivia stared at a sliver of moonlight on the wall. She kept very still. Behind her, Simon's breathing was steady and rhythmic. But between the six inches separating their bodies gaped a chasm so wide she doubted it would ever be bridged. Yet he was sleeping soundly, as if nothing important had happened.

Oh, she understood how he had come to read her diary. She even understood, in a way, that he had failed to tell her the truth only because he wanted to spare her feelings. Dan too had lied to spare her feelings. But in sparing hers he had also spared his own.

It wasn't like that with Simon. She knew enough of him now to him now to realized that he possessed a core of strength that would never allow him to spare himself momentary embarrassment at someone else's expense.

But it changed nothing.

At the root of her problem, at the very centre of the ache that filled her being, was the unbearable knowledge that Simon had seen into her soul. He knew her hopes, her dreams, her illusions, all the mindless follies and regrets – the mistakes she had made, the hurts unintentionally inflicted. And he knew everything there was to know about her unquestioning, disastrous devotion to the man who had been her first, and last, love. He had even journeyed with her through the disintegration of her marriage. That was the worst part. That there was nothing about her he didn't know.

Except how she felt about him.

He would never know that, because she doubted if she would ever know herself.

A breeze ruffled the curtains over the window, causing the moonlight to flicker on the wall. Olivia made herself close her eyes. How, oh, how could she live through all the years that lay ahead knowing that she would always be totally exposed, totally vulnerable, to a man who had married her for convenience. A man whose intimate knowledge left no part of her she could truly call her own.

Simon said she had written nothing she need be ashamed of. That was true. And she wasn't ashamed –

just naked before a man who had no right to see her so unclothed. He was her husband, of course. But not in any real sense of the word. They had been drawn together by nothing more than expedience, desire, and Simon's need to produce a child of his own loins.

If only he had told her the truth that day in the woods . . .

Simon stirred in his sleep, rolled over and draped an arm across her chest. Olivia didn't move. She dared not.

Close to five in the morning she fell into a restless, unsatisfying sleep. Hours later, when the sun was on the wane, she woke up feeling like a discarded and unsavory dishrag.

For a moment she didn't know where she was. Then she saw the white and gold walls – and remembered.

Last night. Paris. Eagles on the headboard. Cream velvet curtains – and Simon, making love with her so beautifully. Then Simon quoting the words that had shattered the fragile beginnings of a dream. A dream that even then had been formless, and that now would never take shape.

Olivia turned her head. There was no one in the bed beside her. Glancing at the watch she hadn't bothered to take off, she saw that it was already two o'clock. No wonder Simon was up. She listened for sounds from the bathroom, but there were none.

Had he gone out, then? Without waking her? Or – no. No, of course he hadn't left her for good. He had read her diary, and he was angry that she couldn't shrug and forgive him. But he wouldn't leave her alone in a strange land . . .

The door banged and Simon strode into the room with a newspaper tucked under his arm. He was dressed casually in jeans and a black shirt, and he looked so appealing that just for a moment Olivia forgot he had stripped her soul naked, and lifted her arms to him. Then she remembered, and allowed them to drop.

A corner of Simon's mouth slanted downwards. 'Still sulking, I see,' he said.

Sulking? Was that all he thought this was? A fit of childish pique over nothing?

'No,' she said. 'I don't sulk. But of course you know that. Along with everything else there is to know.'

'Right,' he agreed, ignoring the barb. 'I *thought* I knew that. So tell me what we have to do to put a stop to it.' He came up beside the bed and stood looking down at her as if he wanted very much to take her by the scruff of the neck and shake her.

If only it were that simple.

'We can't put a stop to it,' she said. 'What's done is done.'

'I see. I assume that means we're back on the damned diary. I can't unread it, Olivia, or believe me, I would. So how else do you expect me to make amends?'

Amends? He didn't understand. How could he? No one had ever seen into *his* soul. 'You can't make amends,' she told him. 'It's too late.'

'Too late to undo the vows we made? Too late to undo what happened between us last night?' He slapped his paper against his thigh. 'You know, I'm not sure I want to untie those particular bonds. Yet. Do you?'

On this warm September afternoon his eyes, blue and bright as a winter's morning, delivered a challenge that stirred her blood and made her want to do things that she, sensible Olivia Naismith, had never so much as dreamed of until last night. But that was in the past. She couldn't allow herself to dream such dreams again.

There could be no going back. She had married Simon Sebastian for better or for worse. The fact that now it would all be for worse made no difference. She had made a bargain; she would stick to it. There was still Jamie to think of, and even if there hadn't been it wasn't in her nature to break faith.

'No,' she said, forcing herself to meet those commanding blue eyes. 'I don't want to untie – anything.' Except their mockery of a marriage. But she couldn't say that.

'Good. Then you'd better get up. Housekeeping wants to get at the room.' He turned away and, flinging himself into a chair, folded back the paper and began to read.

So he counted the ability to read French among his accomplishments. Why was he always so – so damned *competent*?

Olivia lay still, staring at the flat white expanse of the ceiling. Why hadn't she had the brains to see what being married to Simon would actually involve? That she was likely to spend her days alternately craving his magnificent body, and wishing she had never set eyes on him.

If only he hadn't read her diary . . .

'Olivia. I said you'd better get up.' Simon's voice broke roughly into her thoughts, making her jump.

She noted vaguely that he sounded far more angry than the mere fact of her still being in bed would seem to warrant. But she decided she'd better get up.

Ten minutes later she came out of the bathroom already dressed in jeans and a black blouse.

Simon raised his eyebrows. 'You could have dressed in the bedroom,' he drawled. 'In the circumstances I wasn't planning to look. Too hard on the libido.' He ran a brisk eye over her choice of clothes and slowly laid down his paper. 'On the other hand, they say imitation is the sincerest form of flattery. Was it deliberate?'

'Was what . . .?' Oh. All at once she saw why he was smiling that malicious little smile. In her haste to get dressed, by some kind of horrendous Freudian aberration, she had chosen to put on clothes almost identical to the ones her husband was wearing.

'No,' she managed to choke. 'It wasn't deliberate. Shall I change?'

'What, and miss the chance to show the world what a devoted couple we are? Certainly not. Besides, it's time you had breakfast.'

'Breakfast? But it's after two.'

'And you just got up. Come on.' He tossed the paper on to the marble-topped table and stood up. 'Time to let the maid do her job. No doubt she'd prefer to get home before midnight.'

That was something she liked about Simon, Olivia thought wistfully as she allowed him to lead her from the room. He might be Lord of the Manor, but he was considerate of people like maids. If only . . .

Ah, no. She dragged her thoughts back from that futility. There was no point in dwelling on 'if onlys'.

They managed to find coffee and croissants at a bustling pavement café, and when they were finished Simon told Olivia he had hired a limousine to show her around Paris.

'A limousine?' she exclaimed. 'Did you say a limousine?'

'Mmm. You surely weren't expecting to take the Métro?' His voice was dry, derisive. 'I thought you married me for my money, Mrs Sebastian.'

'Oh!' gasped Olivia, 'Oh, how could . . .?' She stopped. The truth was she *had* married him for his money. Or for what his money could do for Jamie. But did he really think she was the kind of woman who cared about the trappings of wealth? He must know . . . Yes, of course he knew. He knew everything. Which meant he was merely paying her back for being unable to laugh off the fact that a stranger who had never claimed to love her had read her diary.

'A limo will be fine,' she said coolly. 'Unless you feel like slumming. In which case perhaps we could take a bus.' There. That should take the wind out of his sails.

She didn't think it had, though, because as he helped her into the limo she was almost sure she saw the ghost of a smile lift his lips.

Paris was even more magical and lovely than she had imagined. But as they drove through the historic streets, admiring the grandeur of buildings both venerable and new, and the sheer inventive genius of the Eiffel Tower, Olivia couldn't help wishing that the chasm between her and Simon had never opened, that he had continued to keep his knowledge to himself . . .

No. No, that would have been worse, surely? She might, given a chance, have come to care for him as a wife cared for her husband. And then one day, when it was too late, she would have found out it was all a charade. It was better this way. Now all she need do was somehow keep her part of the contract they had made. As Simon, of course, would keep his.

Later, as they strolled across one of the bridges spanning the Seine, Olivia couldn't stop herself exclaiming in delight at the loveliness of Paris, the most beautiful city in the world. But when Simon reached for her hand, without meaning to she snatched it away.

His jaw stiffened, but he said nothing and he was careful not to touch her again until they got back to the hotel and he took her arm to help her off the lift.

By the time they returned to their room it was after midnight and time for bed.

Olivia yawned ostentatiously. Perhaps if Simon thought she was tired, he would be willing to put off the inevitable. But as the yawn stretched beyond the realms of believability, he narrowed his eyes and placed his index finger deliberately in between her lips.

Olivia choked and clamped her mouth shut. When he made no attempt to remove the finger, she bit it.

His eyes flickered briefly, but beyond that his face remained impassive. 'If you don't remove your pearly whites from my flesh immediately, I'll break them,' he said, in a tone that sounded a lot more reasonable than his words.

Olivia opened her mouth. 'You wouldn't,' she gasped.

'Probably not,' he admitted, examining his chewed finger. 'But it got your teeth out of my skin.'

'I haven't hurt you, surely? I couldn't have.'

Simon held up the finger. 'No, but you drew blood. Are you a closet vampire, Olivia?'

Olivia stepped closer. There was indeed a drop of blood on his skin. 'I'm sorry,' she said grudgingly. 'I'll fetch a plaster.'

'Don't be ridiculous. It's hardly a mortal wound.'

Was he laughing at her? She raised her eyes doubtfully. No, he wasn't laughing. There was irritation in the set of his mouth, but not amusement.

'It was an instinctive reaction,' she explained defensively. 'I didn't mean to hurt you.'

'Better make it up to me, then.'

Olivia swallowed. It was more of an order than a suggestion, one with a clear undertone of sensuality. 'How?' she asked, taking an instinctive step backwards.

'You know how.' The words slid over her like warm silk. And the message they contained was unmistakable.

He was telling her to fulfil the bargain she had made on the day she married him.

It wouldn't be difficult, surely? As Simon leaned towards her she could feel his breath fanning her cheek, see the dusting of silky hair where the top buttons of his shirt had come undone – and the scent of him was the scent of her desire.

She had no choice but to do as he wanted.

Drawing a quick breath, she reached out to unfasten the remaining buttons of his shirt, hesitating for only a moment before slipping her arms around the solid maleness of a torso that was all hard muscle and taut skin.

'That's better,' said Simon. He let her stand there for few seconds while she wondered what was coming next. Then he lifted her up and carried her to the bed, laying her on it with a gentleness that surprised her. After that he stood looking down at her with a slight frown between his brows, as if she were a racehorse he had bought that had turned out not to be quite the winner he had hoped.

After a while he sat down beside her and began, in a curiously businesslike way, to undress her.

It wasn't as it had been the night before. Then she had felt that Simon was sharing himself with her, taking pleasure in giving her pleasure, perhaps even caring a little. Now he seemed to be proceeding briskly and efficiently with something that needed to be done. He wouldn't hurt her, she knew. But there was no joy in what he was about.

Simon Sebastian was getting on with the business of producing an heir.

Olivia didn't try to stop him, but the desire she had experienced faded. It was her own doing, of course. Simon was responding to the message she had sent him.

The clear message that she too would do what she had to do, give what had to be given – but nothing more.

Simon would always respond to her messages, because Simon could read her like a book. Or a diary.

He shifted her up the bed so that her head was resting on the pillow, and began to peel off her jeans with practised efficiency. Olivia closed her eyes and lay still.

After a while she felt a tear slide from under her lashes and trickle damply down her cheek.

Simon swore. His line in profanity was as succinct and efficient as his skill in peeling off her clothes. 'Is it such a terrible penance?' he demanded.

She shook her head. 'No. It's all right.'

He swore again, but after that there was silence. It was only when a faint breeze from the window stroked her bare skin and made her shiver that Olivia made herself open her eyes.

Simon, shirtless but still with his jeans on, stood with his back to her staring out into the night. His waving hair gleamed like dull silver in the moonlight.

'Simon?' she whispered. 'Simon, what are you doing? Come back to bed.'

'What for?' he asked, so harshly that she winced.

'I thought –'

'Yes, I know what you thought. You thought all you had to do to fill your part of the bargain was to lie there like a sacrificial lamb and allow me to take my pleasure.' He threw his head back, and she watched the silvered hair brush across his neck. 'I suppose I thought that would do too. It turns out I was wrong.'

Olivia shivered again and climbed quickly in between the sheets. 'Just tell me what you want me to do and I'll do my best,' she said, trying to inject some warmth into her voice but knowing it sounded thin and unconvincing.

Simon swung round. 'Olivia . . .' He paused then started again. 'Olivia, I realize it may seem that way to you, but I didn't buy you. I married you.'

'Yes,' she said. 'I know.' And she did know. She knew that Simon wanted what they had had last night before she found out he'd read her diary. Deep down she wanted that too. But it wasn't possible. Not any more. Simon had deceived her for all the right reasons. But she couldn't lightly hand him that small part of herself he didn't have already. She needed that part to call her own. Besides, there was a small matter of trust.

'I know you married me, Simon,' she repeated. 'That's why I said I'd do my best.'

The sound that came from his throat was like no sound she had ever heard before. It wasn't a roar, nor even a growl. But it most effectively expressed frustration, exasperation and a probable urge to smash glass.

Olivia wriggled further underneath the sheet.

It seemed as though hours had passed by the time Simon relinquished his post by the window. When he did, moving across the room with sinuous grace, he removed everything but his shorts and climbed silently into the bed beside her. He didn't touch her, didn't even say goodnight, but turned pointedly on his side and went to sleep.

Like a big, sleek tiger, she thought resentfully. How could he possibly fall asleep so easily after . . . well, after nothing. Her lips twisted. Of course he had probably learned to sleep at the drop of a hat in the days when he'd had to snatch rest when he could.

It occurred to Olivia then that it was a talent she had better learn to cultivate herself if she meant to stay married to Simon. Which she did. Whatever happened, she would have to find some way to make this marriage work.

But as each day passed, Olivia saw the likelihood of their marriage working become ever more remote.

They did all the things honeymooners were supposed to do. Simon escorted her to intimate and romantic restaurants where delicious food was accompanied by candlelight and wine and soft music. He ordered the limousine again and took her to places in the sun where they walked through fairytale gardens beside the Seine – and when she asked to see Versailles he managed not to look as though he'd seen the famous palace of the Bourbon kings a dozen times before. He even bought her roses and took her on a moonlight cruise on the river – and through it all he was studiously polite and completely distant. He answered her questions, pointed out beauty spots and discussed the weather and the architecture of Paris.

But he gave her nothing of himself.

In the end Olivia knew less of Simon than she had known on the day she married him. And that had been little enough.

Only once did the civilized façade crack, when, in her confusion and unhappiness, Olivia started across a wide boulevard without looking where she was going and was almost run over by a bus.

Simon hauled her back with an oath, and when she turned to confront him, expecting to see mild irritation, she surprised a look of fury that was out of all proportion to what she'd done. As she gazed up at him, stunned, he closed both hands around her cheeks and said in a voice that made her think of crushed gravel, 'Olivia, don't ever do that again.'

When she assured him she didn't intend to, for just a moment his features relaxed, and she caught a glimpse of the assured, maddeningly charming man she had met that first day in the glade in Sherraby woods.

Then the reserved and formally correct bridegroom returned and Olivia went back to smiling with equal formality and thanking him dutifully for his every sterile attention.

Each night when they returned to the hotel, Simon took a fistful of papers out of his briefcase and worked into the small hours of the morning. Olivia, lonely, confused and convinced she must fulfil their agreement, asked him to come to bed. When he didn't, she bought three sexy new nightgowns and did everything she could think of to lure him from his monastic isolation.

It wasn't that she wanted him, she kept telling herself. But she had promised him an heir, and until that promise was kept she wouldn't feel she had played fair by the man who had given her his name, a permanent roof, and a security she had never known before.

On the last night of their honeymoon, when she asked him point-blank why he wouldn't make love to her, he told her he wasn't an altar and he was damned if he wanted her sacrificial blood on his hands.

'But you said it was an advantage,' she protested.

'What was?' He laid down his pen and leaned back.'

'That I wouldn't fall in love with you. You said –'

'I know what I said. And there's a difference between not being in love and behaving like a nice, obliging iceberg. Icebergs are hard on a man's ego. They tend to impede his performance.'

'Oh. I didn't mean –'

'I know you didn't mean. But there it is. You're very lovely, Olivia. Unfortunately I've never found much satisfaction in trying to melt ice before I start up a fire. End of story.'

And end of marriage? No. She couldn't allow that. And how dared he call her an iceberg? Olivia swung her legs out of bed and walked towards him, her red see-through nightgown flowing around her legs like moonlit fire.

'You mean you're not hot enough?' she taunted, tossing her hair back and sliding the thin straps seductively down her arms.

Simon's nostrils flared. 'You know better than that, Olivia,' he said softly. When she was almost upon him his eyes went peculiarly blank and he murmured with a small, malignant smile, 'Very well. For England and Sebastians, then,' seconds before he put his hands on her hips and pulled her between his legs.

CHAPTER 9

'You two look like a wet Wednesday in purgatory,' Diane remarked, insinuating her nose round the door of Simon's office. 'Lost our biggest account, have we, Mr Sebastian? Or is it that cousin of yours again?'

'Cousin?' Simon removed his feet from his desk and sat up. 'You mean Gerald?'

'No, the other one. Emma. If it was Gerald, you'd say, "Get a job," and hang up the phone.'

Diane, Simon reflected wryly, had become considerably bolder and less mousy since she'd acquired herself a boyfriend last month. Too bad marrying Olivia hadn't caused a similar improvement in his own disposition. Instead marriage had, if anything, had the opposite effect. Lately he had caught himself becoming almost as taciturn and introspective as Zack.

'Diane,' he said, 'don't you have anything to do?'

Diane rolled her eyes at Zack, who was sprawled in his shirt-sleeves on one of the soft swivel chairs Simon had installed for the comfort of clients. 'I've got at least as much to do as he has,' she said pertly, and closed the door with a snap.

'We ought to get rid of her,' Zack grunted.

'Why? She does the job. And she puts up with your Celtic brooding and my Anglo-Saxon arrogance.'

'I suppose so. But she's been too damn full of sauce this last month.'

'You have something against sauce?'

Zack's grin was reluctant. 'Not necessarily. I do have something against taking bloody cheek from a secretary who used to keep her mouth shut and get on with the job.'

Simon shrugged. 'Diane's not hard to deal with.' He flipped on his computer and, without looking at his partner, asked, 'Heard from Emma lately?'

'No. Why should I? She's probably hooked up with that banker. Or some other panting young stud.'

'No, she isn't. She has her own flat in Greenwich Village or somewhere like that, and she's hooked up with a charity that raises funds for – I think she calls them "underprivileged" children. In other words, kids whose parents, if they have parents, earn no money, have little education and precious little to look forward to.'

Zack stopped sprawling and sat up. 'You mean Emma has moved out of Oakshades?'

'Mmm. Uncle Matthew and Aunt Margaret are not pleased.'

'A bit of independence won't hurt her.' Zack sank back into the chair and crossed his legs.

'I don't think it's her independence that worries them. It's the job she's doing.'

'Job? Emma?' Zack pushed back a length of hair that had fallen across his face. 'You don't mean this charity? That'll just be her way of killing time.'

'Apparently it's more than that. She masterminds appeals calculated to wring sizeable contributions out of conservative corporate accounts. But in order to do that she says she has to see for herself what the children she's trying to help are up against.' Simon made several keystrokes and punched up a set of figures, waiting for Zack to react – which he had no doubt his partner would in his own good time.

'What the hell does that mean?' Zack rose to the bait almost at once.

'I believe it means she goes into areas where – well, where my aunt and uncle didn't bring their little girl up to be seen.'

'Is that so?'

'Mmm.' Simon pretended to concentrate on the figures. In the outer office Diane was humming 'Yellow Rose of Texas' over and over. Her new boyfriend came from Texas. Simon opened his mouth intending to shout at her to change the tune, but Zack spoke first.

'What sort of areas?' he asked.

Ah. Hooked him. 'Unsavoury ones. She's ended up in Emergency twice. Or so I've been told.'

'Emerrgency?' The R's rolled sharply off Zack's tongue. 'What the hell was she doing in Emerrgency?'

'Getting patched up after putting herself in the way of a drunk who was attacking his wife and five-year-old son. That was the first time.'

The lines around Zack's mouth looked as though they had been scored with a carving knife. 'And the second time?'

'Some joker tried to rape her. The police turned up and put a stop to it.'

Zack stood up.

'Going back to work?' Simon asked, affecting absorption in the numbers on his screen.

'No. I'm going to give Diane something to do.'

'Thank God. I'm getting tired of that damned Yellow Rose.'

Zack didn't laugh. 'She won't be singing for a while. She'll be getting me on the next direct flight to New York.'

Simon allowed himself to look up. Zack's features were as uncommunicative as ever, but his body was coiled as taut as waxed rope. Good. He didn't envy Emma, or anyone else who tried to get in his old friend's way over the course of the next twenty-four hours – but Zack was the only one who might be able to persuade his idiotic cousin with the newly developed social conscience to stop trying to get herself maimed or murdered.

'Have a good journey,' he said to Zack's back, and went on studying his screen.

The 'Yellow Rose' sputtered to a halt. Into the silence that followed, Simon heard Zack's voice rapping out instructions. He didn't catch Diane's muttered response, but it was impossible to miss the indignant tap of her fingers on the phone dial.

Satisfied with his day's work, Simon flipped off the computer and lifted his feet back on to the desk.

Mission accomplished. If anyone could sort out Emma, it would be Zack. He had always believed that, even when he'd judged his young cousin's obsession to be hopeless.

He was no longer so sure about its being hopeless, and when his distraught aunt and uncle had appealed to him for help, his immediate instinct had been to dispatch Zack Kent to the rescue. But *ordering* his partner to New York, or even suggesting he ought to go, would have been about as much use as ordering a tank. The subtle approach always worked best.

Except with Olivia.

Simon swiped a hand across his face, his sense of accomplishment dimming. No approach seemed to work with his lawfully wedded wife.

It wasn't that he wanted her to fall grovelling at his feet, or even that he expected her to love him. But dammit, how could he spend the rest of his life married to a woman who thought of him as no better than a liar and a fraud? Who offered up her body as some kind of payment of a debt? Oh, he could bring that body to life any time he wanted to; he'd already proved that. And at one time he'd thought bringing it to life now and again would be enough. But he had since discovered there was very little satisfaction in making love to a dutiful automaton. Not that she hadn't responded to him quite acceptably the one time he had taken her purely out of a sense of family obligation. But he hadn't enjoyed it much, and he didn't think she had either.

After that he hadn't been able to bring himself to touch her.

'Serves you right for marrying in haste, my friend,' he growled at his reflection in the screen. 'For thinking of a trim bottom and a pair of soulful eyes as some kind of basis for a marriage.'

A voice in the outer office snapped a gruff, 'Thanks,' a door slammed, and a minute later Diane's nose reappeared.

'Talking to ourselves now, are we? Ought to watch that, Mr Sebastian.'

When Simon said that if anyone ought to watch anything it was her, and that, by the way, he didn't like yellow roses, Diane only laughed and said she pitied his poor wife.

Olivia was frowning as she climbed the manor's broad staircase and made her way along the gallery to her room.

'For England and Sebastians,' Simon had dared to say to her.

Her lips tightened, and automatically her mind began to replay the scene that had taken place in that bedroom in Paris eight weeks ago on the very last night of their honeymoon.

She forced herself to turn the replay off.

'Sebastians be damned,' she muttered, pushing open a door and glancing vaguely around her sunny yellow and cream room with its flowered curtains and yellow-quilted bed. Her eyes lit on the door to Simon's adjoining bedroom, which had reamined firmly closed ever since their return from Paris.

'Especially be damned to *Simon* Sebastian,' she added, twisting the belt on her red shirtwaist dress.

Not that this ridiculous mess was entirely Simon's fault. She knew it was her inability to live lightly with the knowledge that he'd read her diary that had become the real fly in the ointment of what might have been a satisfactory, if purely pragmatic, marriage.

Instinctively her gaze strayed from the closed door between their rooms to the comfortable bed with its primrose-yellow cover – and she thought of the much larger bed she had shared with her husband in Paris. Only it hadn't been a bed they had shared on that last memorable night. It had been a rose-coloured carpet.

England and Sebastians indeed! She remembered how she had tried to squirm out of Simon's grasp when he had said that. And how her squirming had resulted in his hands sliding over her hips and lower back in a way that made her gasp with a need that had nothing to do with any desire to escape, and a great deal to do with a very different, more immediate desire.

She had leaned forward then and kissed him hungrily on the mouth. And he had kissed her back and pulled her on to his knees. Then somehow they had no longer been on the chair but on the floor, and her nightgown had become a flame-coloured heap beneath the table.

There had been no holding back this time, no sudden change of plan, and once again Olivia had experienced that explosive, shattering release that she had known with no other man – a release that left her limp, sated and glowing with some strange new emotion she couldn't name.

At first she had been sure Simon felt the same.

But almost at once he had picked himself up, helped her to her feet and said, 'So the iceberg suffered a thaw. Does this mean you've had a change of heart?'

His tone was so nonchalant, so detached, that Olivia's scarcely formed hope that they might find a way to make their marriage succeed on at least one level shrivelled as if it had never existed.

In the end, all she could think of to say was, 'No. My heart was never involved.'

Simon nodded. 'Good. In that case let's hope we've done the job.'

Done the job? It was several seconds before she realized what he meant. Then it hit her.

Simon hoped he had succeeded in getting her with child. As if he were talking about a successful vaccination. She supposed she ought not to mind his attitude, considering he had never pretended to want much from her beyond that. But she did mind. Quite dreadfully. It made her feel like a sow acquired at the market for the express purpose of breeding healthy piglets.

Olivia lowered her eyes, inexplicably crushed by an indifference she knew she had brought on herself. When Simon made no move to touch her again she crept away from him and slipped quietly back into their bed.

Eventually she fell asleep. But when, or if, Simon joined her, she never knew, because by the time she opened her eyes on a grey and misty September morning, he was already up and dressed and snapping the locks shut on their luggage.

Since their return to the manor, Olivia had seen little of her husband. He spent most of his time at his flat in London, returning home only at weekends – and when he was home, he seemed purposely to avoid her. Often he buried himself in his study, saying he'd brought important work home from the office. And when he wasn't working, or pretending to work, he took long rides on Cactus – to see to his tenants, he said. She had met most of the tenants now, and knew that they generally saw to themselves.

At mealtimes, which couldn't be avoided without offending Mrs Leigh, Simon was scrupulously courteous to Olivia, and kindly but firm with Jamie.

She was amazed to see how naturally Jamie responded to his stepfather – and she didn't think his co-operation was entirely due to the advent of Tumbleweed, the promised pony, who had arrived two weeks earlier in time for Jamie's birthday.

A quick whirring of wings drew her eyes to the window. A flock of starlings dotted the morning sky, heading for the shelter of the woods. Olivia drifted across the room to watch them pass. When they became no more than points of light on the horizon, she lowered her gaze to the meadows.

Somewhere out there, in a field still green and fresh from last night's rain, Simon was teaching Jamie to ride.

Her husband had returned home late the night before, and vanished with Jamie as soon as she came down for breakfast. He always found time for Jamie. Lucky Jamie.

That thought brought her up short. She definitely didn't resent the time Simon spent with her son, was relieved and happy that Jamie finally had a man to look up to . . .

So why couldn't she look up to Simon too? And why was she feeling so neglected and out of sorts? If she wanted Simon's attention, no doubt all she had to do was let him know it. Then he would do whatever he felt was his duty in order to maintain his part of the agreement they had made.

The problem, of course, was that she wasn't sure if she wanted his attention on those terms. Why spend more time than she had to with a man she desired but could never be totally at ease with . . .?

That was as far as Olivia's musings took her, because just as she leaned forward to catch a first glimpse of Simon and Jamie returning from their ride, a smart knock sounded on her door.

'Mrs Sebastian,' Annie called from the hall. 'Mr Downer's here to see you.'

Mr Downer? Chrissy's father? What on earth could he want? Olivia had a disturbing presentiment of trouble. Although Chrissy had been over to play with Jamie once or twice, she certainly wasn't here now. And Harold Downer still regarded Jamie and his mother with suspicion. Her marriage to Simon hadn't changed anything there.

'I'll be right down,' she told Annie, pulling on a heavy black cardigan. It was November now, and all of a sudden she felt cold.

Harold Downer was waiting in the drawing room. Olivia found him sitting on the edge of one of the Hepplewhite chairs scowling at a bust of a particularly fierce-looking Sebastian. Harold's beard jutted aggressively and both fists were planted squarely on his knees.

'Good morning,' said Olivia, hoping she sounded

suitably at ease in her new role of Lady of Sherraby. 'How nice of you to call.'

The scowl deepened, and Harold's Adam's apple began to work up and down. 'Not a social call,' he muttered. 'Got something to say.'

'Yes?' Olivia raised her eyebrows. 'Is there a problem? With Chrissy?' She sat down on the sofa and crossed her legs.

Harold fidgeted in his chair. 'Not Chrissy who's the problem. It's your boy. Chrissy says he stole the composition she was doing on caterpillars. For her teacher. It was supposed to be handed in yesterday.' He cleared his throat. 'Chrissy's a clever girl, Mrs Sebastian. She's never late with her work. That's why when she said she'd lost it, I knew right off something wasn't right.' He nodded as if he'd proved a point.

Olivia blinked. '*Jamie* stole her work? Mr Downer, I don't think –'

'My girl's not a liar, Mrs Sebastian. Lived in Sherraby all her life, she has.' Chrissy's father nodded again, as if length of residence settled the matter.

Olivia began to get the picture. Jamie was an interloper, and therefore entirely likely to go around stealing little girls' homework.

'I'm sure Chrissy isn't lying,' she said briskly. 'But perhaps she made a mistake –'

Harold Downer played his trump card. 'No mistake. Your Jamie admitted it.'

'Oh.' Olivia recrossed her legs. It wasn't at all like Jamie to steal, but you never knew with children. And he had just been through the third upheaval of his young life in just over a year. First his father's death, then the move to Sherraby, and now his mother's remarriage. It might have affected his behaviour – although he *seemed* remarkably well-adjusted . . .

'I'll talk to Jamie, of course,' Olivia said. 'But I really don't think – he's only a little boy, Mr Downer.'

'Big enough to cause trouble,' Harold growled.

'Yes, well – as I said, I'll speak to him. He should be home soon. And of course if he is responsible, naturally we'll make sure he explains to Chrissy's teacher –'

'Not good enough. Boy needs a damn good spanking.' Harold's beard quivered with righteous indignation.

As Olivia searched for a response that wouldn't antagonize him further, a movement at the corner of her eye made her glance in the direction of the door.

Simon, his legs braced and still in his riding clothes, stood there with a hand on Jamie's shoulder. She wondered how long they had been there.

Her husband was a formidable figure at any time, and although he didn't look exactly threatening at this moment, Olivia recognized the slight flaring of his nostrils as a sign that Simon Sebastian was not amused.

Jamie, as the only boy in the room who might be a candidate for the recommended spanking, looked frankly scared.

'Good morning,' said Simon, smiling coolly at Harold. He turned to Olivia. 'Trouble, my dear?'

If Olivia hadn't been so worried, she would have laughed at this deliberate demonstration of aristocratic family solidarity – which she knew very well was intended to throw Harold off balance.

Unfortunately, Harold was too busy glaring at Jamie to take it in.

'What d'you mean by it, boy?' he demanded, rising to his feet and bending down so that he and Jamie were standing almost nose to nose.

Jamie started to shake.

'If you don't mind . . .' Simon leaned down and calmly scooped his stepson into his arms. 'Now, Mr Downer. What can I do for you?'

Olivia guessed Simon had overheard Harold's story already, but was making him repeat it in order to give Jamie time to get his fear under control.

'I see,' Simon said, when Harold had voiced his complaint for the second time. 'What do you have to say, Jamie? You didn't steal Chrissy's work, did you?'

'Yes, I did,' mumbled Jamie, burying his face in Simon's shoulder. Then he added with a gulp. '*Are* you going to spank me?'

'I doubt it,' said Simon, settling the anxious boy more comfortably in his arms. 'Now how about you tell me the truth.'

'The truth is he stole my daughter's composition. On caterpillars,' Harold added, as though that made it worse. He tilted his beard at Simon, who merely raised his eyebrows. 'Chrissy said so.'

'I'm sure she did,' said Simon, sounding bored. 'Jamie, why did you tell Chrissy to say you stole her work?'

Jamie lifted his head, and Olivia saw that his lip had started to quiver. She had to grip the arm of the sofa, hard, to prevent herself from leaping up to pull him into her arms. But she knew that would be a mistake. Simon was handling the situation more than efficiently without her intervention.

'I didn't –' Jamie began.

'Jamie.' There was a warning note in Simon's voice now, and after a moment Jamie gulped and tried again.

'Well, I *sort* of told her,' he admitted.

'Yes? And what did you sort of tell her?'

'That – that she'd better tell her dad I did it because her dad doesn't like me much and he'd believe it and I didn't want – didn't want . . .' The words came out in a rush and then trailed off.

'Didn't want the Ripper to be blamed? Is that it?'

Jamie rubbed a knuckle into his right eye. 'I heard – heard you say next time you caught Rip eating the post you were going to – to put him in a shepherd's pie. And he didn't *mean* to eat Chrissy's homework, really he didn't, but she was swinging it round her head and he thought she wanted to play tug-o-war and – and –'

'Jamie.' Simon put his hand gently on the back of the blond head. 'I didn't know you heard me say that to Rip. About the shepherd's pie. If I had known, I would have explained. It was just a joke, Jamie. A joke between the Ripper and me. We understand each other, you see. And now that Mr Cousins has put up a basket to catch the letters, you don't have to worry about Rip. Now . . .' he paused and turned to face a frowning Harold Downer '. . .my wife will explain things to Chrissy's teacher . . .' He smiled blandly at Olivia. 'Won't you, my dear?'

Olivia nodded. Chrissy's teacher was the least of her worries at this moment.

'And as Chrissy is such a good pupil, I'm sure there won't be a problem,' he went on. 'In the meantime, as Chrissy and Jamie seem to have become such good friends, perhaps we can make amends for your trouble by having Chrissy to stay with us for a few days . . .'

Again he glanced Olivia's way, and again she nodded.

'I'm sure you and Mrs Downer would appreciate some time to yourselves,' Simon finished firmly, and as if there were no more to be said.

Olivia tried not to giggle. Simon's one raised eyebrow practically dared Harold not to agree. She watched the transparent little man weigh the desire to maintain his grudge towards newcomers against the prospect of a few days' peace and the chance to brag that his daughter was staying at the manor.

Peace and self-esteem won out.

'Well, I suppose that would be all right,' he agreed reluctantly. 'If you're sure it wasn't the boy . . .' He shook his head. 'Still can't believe my Chrissy would've lied to me.' Harold wasn't going to give up without firing a last salvo.

'She didn't want to,' Jamie said quickly. 'It was all my idea, Mr Downer. And Chrissy likes Rip a lot.'

'Humph. Well, now.' Harold made a supreme effort and managed a half-hearted smile. 'We'll forget it, then.'

'And can Chrissy still play with me?' Jamie asked, not leaving anything to chance.

'Humph,' Harold grunted again. 'Fond of my Chrissy, are you?'

'Oh, yes,' said Jamie. ''Course, she isn't a boy, but –'

'That's settled, then,' Simon interrupted. He turned to Harold. 'I don't think we need take up any more of your time.'

Before Harold had a chance to close his mouth, Simon was showing him politely to the door.

Olivia slumped against the back of the sofa and let out a long, heartfelt sigh.

When Simon came back into the drawing room, she looked up at him with a rueful little smile. 'You did that so well,' she said. 'I was wondering what on earth I ought to say to him, and . . .' She paused as another thought came to her. 'How did you know the Ripper was the guilty party?'

'Experience,' drawled Simon. 'And a certain familiarity with his eating habits. Incidentally, you weren't doing so badly with Downer yourself. Did I ever tell you you have the instincts of a born duchess?'

'Yes, once. On our wedding day.' Olivia dug her nails hard into her palms and sank on to the arm of a handy wingback chair.

'Hmm.' Simon frowned, then demanded abruptly, 'Where's Jamie?'

'Gone to find his partner in crime.'

'Rip?' Simon shook his head. 'He'll be hiding out under the toolshed. He always smells trouble in time to make himself scarce.'

His eyes were smiling at her. Olivia was annoyed to feel a lump in her throat. 'You're good with Jamie,' she muttered, turning her head away so he wouldn't see the moisture on her cheek. 'Better than Dan was. Not that I ever allowed Jamie to see his father's bad side.'

'I know. You did well.'

His tone was reserved now, and Olivia remembered that he had known from the beginning exactly what kind of father Dan had been.

She made herself look around, and encountered a formidable length of leg in well-cut riding breeches propped casually on the rung of a chair. Raising her eyes hastily, she said, 'I did my best. Simon . . .?'

'Mmm?' He straightened, shrugged off his coat and slung it over his shoulder. 'What is it?'

He was about to leave. She knew he was. But she had to say something to keep him in the room. She wasn't sure why, but she had to. For a little while there, when they had been united in dealing with Harold Downer, she'd had a feeling there was still a chance . . .

A chance for what, Olivia? she jeered. That you'll get Simon back in your bed? A man you never liked and now can never wholly trust – who can use his knowledge of you in any way he chooses?

Simon began to move towards the door. And all at once none of it mattered. She *had* to find a way to reach him.

She said the first thing that came into her head.

'Simon, I . . . You're kind to Jamie, and I . . . well, I don't have a lot to do now that I'm not working. Mrs Leigh does the cooking, and there's Annie and her helpers to keep the house clean. When Jamie's older I expect I'll go back to accounting, but in the meantime – isn't there something I can do? For you, I mean?'

'There's a chance you will, I suppose.' His reply was laconic, and his eyes weren't smiling any more.

'A chance? What . . .? Oh, that I might be pregnant.' Her heart plummeted. She didn't think she was pregnant. 'Yes, but I wasn't talking about that.'

'Then what were you talking about?'

He was obviously impatient to be gone, and offhand she couldn't think of a reply. She just knew she didn't want to go on forever living with a man – at weekends only – who knew everything about her and yet shut her out completely. Or had she shut him out? What, in fact, did she really want from Simon?

Olivia bit her lip. When it started to hurt, inspiration struck, and she said quickly, 'I could – well, perhaps I could, um – help you with the business side of your work. I can do accounts. And I was a secretary before I became an accountant.'

Simon's narrowed eyes flicked over her appraisingly, as if it had never occurred to him that she might possess a brain as well as a body. She felt herself flush.

Damn him. Why had she been fool enough to give him yet another opportunity to remind her that he had only married her because he needed an heir?

But to her surprise, after a brief pause, Simon jerked his head at the door and said, 'All right. Come with me.'

When she hesitated, put off by his peremptory tone and ill-concealed impatience, he muttered something under his breath and, seizing her wrist, hustled her down the corridor so fast that she had to run to keep up.

Simon's study overlooked the lake through the green trellis of the ancient vine which he had once told her produced quite palatable wine. As she stared through the greenery, Olivia was struck anew by the extraordinary change in her circumstances. From dreary terraced housing and an attic to all this. If Simon had truly been a prince, she might have begun to believe she was Cinderella . . .

'Olivia. You said you wanted something to do. Stop daydreaming.' Simon's brisk voice jerked her out of her fantasy.

She nodded coolly. 'Sorry. What would you like me to do?' She glanced round the panelled room with its floor-to-ceiling bookshelves, modern computer workstation and an incongruous wooden filing cabinet that looked as though it had seen better days. It was the only object that lent a touch of warmth to what in every other way was a functional but characterless room.

'Here.' Simon took a file folder from the middle of a neat stack of papers on his desk. 'You're a good speller. You can check this for spelling and punctuation. The spell-check on this computer seems to have a mind of its own.'

Olivia took it from him. 'What is it?' she asked.

'A report I'm writing for a government department.'

'Oh. Isn't it secret?'

'No,' said Simon with a resigned and annoyingly condescending smile. 'Not all government reports are top secret. In fact most of them are exceedingly dull. This one involves someone I had reason to keep an eye on in the old days. He's in custody now. It's not top priority, but I'd like it finished before Christmas.'

He was patronizing her again. 'Yes, I see,' she said acidly. 'Are you sure you trust me with it?'

'Why shouldn't I? You're my wife.'

Yes, she supposed she was, but . . .

'But that's no reason to trust you?' he suggested, accurately divining the direction of her thoughts. 'I disagree. Trust is an essential in a marriage like ours.'

A marriage like ours? He hadn't said 'one based purely on convenience', but she could tell that was what he meant – not least from his obvious impatience to have her gone.

'Simon,' she said impulsively, 'I wish –'

'Yes?' Simon sighed and lowered himself onto a corner of his desk, folding his arms as if he were dealing with a difficult employee. 'What do you wish?'

When she didn't answer because she couldn't think of anything to say, he lifted his eyebrows and began to swing an elegant leg gently back and forth. Olivia didn't move, and after a while he nodded at the folder in her arms and said, 'You can take it with you.'

He was dismissing her. Just like that. And she wasn't ready to go. There was too much left unsaid between them. And yet, when it came right down to it, what *could* she say? That he looked so hypnotically desirable, even sitting there all casual and dismissive, that she wanted to drop his report and fly into his arms?

But what good would that do? It wouldn't change anything. Because however much she wanted him, she couldn't give herself wholeheartedly to a man who had married her under false pretences. Dan, at least, had been honest and open when he'd asked her to marry him.

She was already at the door when she felt Simon's hand on her shoulder.

'Wait a minute,' he said. 'There's something I want to find out.'

Olivia waited. She couldn't have moved if she'd tried. Her feet were pinned to the floor by the seductive shaft of his touch. Spears of fire seared through her abdomen, making her gasp, and all she could think of was that the man behind her was the centre of the flame. When he put both hands on her shoulders and drew her backwards, the flame turned molten and she sagged against him.

'Ah,' said Simon. 'I thought so. That answers one part of my question.'

'Wh-what?' stuttered Olivia, who was beyond comprehension, beyond anything but her need for this man.

'It wasn't purely duty that led you to seduce me that night.'

It had been in a way, although duty had had precious little to do with it in the end. 'Not entirely,' she admitted, struggling hopelessly not to betray what he was doing to her.

'Well, well,' murmured Simon. 'Duty and lust. One dull, the other frequently sordid. A combination to be avoided, don't you think? Unless, of course, it's accompanied by trust.'

His words had a dampening effect. Olivia discovered she could move after all. 'You don't ask for much, do you?' she said bitterly.

'I don't think so.' He slid his hands down her arms, then stroked them slowly, and with excruciating sensuality, over her hips.

Olivia moaned and clasped the manuscript folder tightly to her breast. Simon went on stroking. When she could stand it no longer, she turned in his arms and looked up at him with a kind of desperation.

Just what she expected to see she didn't know. Certainly not the absence of emotion, the chill untouchability that met her gaze. It was a look that filled her with a sense of loss so deep it went beyond tears, beyond words, beyond any grief she had ever experienced. Yet how could she be grieving over the loss of a love she had never had?

What was happening to her? What had happened to this marriage that should have been so convenient for all concerned? It wasn't working for Simon. At least she didn't think so. And it certainly wasn't working for her.

But it was working for Jamie.

Olivia closed her eyes to blot out the cryptic mask that had become her husband's face. Could she go on like this, fighting doubt and confusion and loneliness for the sake of her curly-headed son? She had done so with Dan and survived.

But this was different.

After a few seconds, she made herself look at Simon again.

The planes of his strong face stood out harshly against the bright morning light, and there were deep lines etched around his eyes that she was certain hadn't been there a month ago. His nose seemed longer too, more aquiline, making him seem older than his years. He was looking at her as if he didn't really see her. Yet he continued to inflict agonizing torture with his hands as he moved them expertly over her hips and rear, stroking, caressing, cradling, so that she wanted to scream at him to take her right here, on the desk if necessary, before she went out of her mind.

And he was doing it on purpose to torment her. She could tell from the thin curl of his lips.

'Why, Simon?' she whispered. 'Why are you doing this to me?'

'Why not?' he replied. 'I'm rather enjoying it. Aren't you?'

He knew she was, in a tortured sort of way. But what was he trying to prove by making her admit it? What did she want him to prove?

'How could I enjoy it?' she asked hotly. 'I'm no masochist. Simon, I thought you didn't want –'

'Oh, I want,' he said softly. 'What man wouldn't? Unfortunately I seem not to want to play stallion to your mare. For all you have a sexy little tail.'

Olivia groaned as his fingers drummed a meaningful tattoo on the part of her in question. When the fingers moved to her inner thigh, she could bear it no longer and tore herself out of his arms.

'This isn't going to work, is it?' she gasped, leaning against the door and struggling to catch her breath.

'What isn't?'

'Us. This marriage –'

'Oh, I don't know. What do you suggest we do to spice it up?'

So nonchalant, so mockingly unconcerned. Olivia conquered an urge to scratch his face. 'It's too late,' she said coldly. 'I realize we made a vow that day in the church, and that I promised . . .'

'You promised to have and to hold. From this day forward,' Simon said. 'Do you expect me to absolve you from that promise?'

A painful band was tightening inexorably around Olivia's chest. Absolution was what she wanted, wasn't it? And yet . . .

'Would you?' she asked. 'Absolve me?'

'I didn't say that.'

'No. But if you did, I . . .' She pushed a shaky hand through a lock of thick hair that had fallen in front of her eyes. If he did, what then? 'Simon, what is it you expect of me?' she asked. 'We've only been married two months, but . . .' Her voice broke unexpectedly. 'I lasted seven years with Dan. If he'd lived I would have lasted a lifetime.'

Through the exasperating mist that had formed in front of her eyes, she thought she detected the first real emotion she had seen on Simon's face since they walked into his study. But she couldn't tell what it meant. It was more of a shadow than anything, just the barest flicker of a muscle. Then once again he had his features under control.

Olivia didn't wait to see more. She knew that if she tried to speak she would fall apart. So, still clasping Simon's report, she turned on her heel and stumbled from the room.

Behind her she thought she heard him call, 'Olivia, come back here. I haven't finished.'

But she had. Ignoring him, she hurried into the garden to fill her lungs with air.

CHAPTER 10

Rain. Cold, persistent, wet and coming straight down. New York as no one ever reported it. Not summer hot, or winter freezing. Just wet and endlessly depressing. Zack paid the taxi driver, turned up the collar of his coat and made for the protection of the awning that shielded the entrance to Emma's apartment block.

She didn't live in Greenwich Village. Simon had it wrong. Her Manhattan apartment overlooked Central Park – and it bore no resemblance whatsoever to the artistically squalid lodgings Zack had envisioned.

When Simon had told him Emma had taken up work in areas of the city that those who had a choice did their best to avoid, he had imagined her sharing some seedy one-room dump with a busy crew of resident bugs. But seedy one-room dumps didn't support uniformed doormen or lifts – Emma would call them elevators – with polished brass fittings and shiny white doors.

Zack pushed the button for the seventeenth floor and waited to be wafted smoothly skywards.

A young girl with long blonde hair got on before the lift took off. She kept glancing at him nervously, as if she expected him to assault her between floors. He had to resist the unworthy temptation to bare his teeth at her and growl. Being regarded as a potential hazard just because he happened to be male was a fact of modern life that often got him down. Not that he could blame the girl, he supposed. Some terrible crimes were committed in this city – or any big city, for that matter.

Which was why he was here.

From the moment Simon had told him about Emma's two trips to Emergency, Zack's single clear thought had been that he had to put a stop to her nonsense before she got herself killed. He didn't much care how he did it, nor did he wait to figure out why it mattered to him to the exclusion of every other demand upon his time.

The blonde scuttled off at the tenth floor, and Zack continued his upward journey alone.

Emma, who had been informed by the doorman that a Mr Kent was on his way up, was waiting for him in the hall. She was wearing jeans and a baggy grey sweater that made her small frame look thin and undernourished. There was a faint grey bruise on her left cheek.

Zack dropped his hold-all on to the carpet. Emma glanced at it, then raised her eyes fleetingly to his face.

He made himself remain calm. She was nervous. He

could tell from the way she kept pulling at her sweater. If he gave way to the explosion that was threatening to blast off the top of his head, he would frighten her and get nowhere.

'Hi,' Emma said, extending her hand in an awkwardly formal gesture. 'It's nice of you to call. Will you come in?'

Zack ignored the proffered hand and kissed her cheek. Emma flinched, looked down at the floor and waved at the open door behind her.

Not the reception he had expected. Zack opened his mouth, closed it, and picked up his hold-all. Once inside, out of habit he immediately began to file away impressions.

Bright, original and airy. Like Emma. Big, soft sofas in turquoise leather, a medium-sized television, glass-topped tables on an almost-white carpet. Pale walls, and a few undistinguished but colourful pastels. Through an arched opening to the left he glimpsed a compact white and grey kitchen. Zack placed his hold-all beside the door. A pleasant enough room. Yet something about it disturbed him. After a while he realized it was the lack of anything personal or permanent. Not a sweater, a magazine, a book, or even a vase disturbed the clean, flat surfaces of Emma's furniture.

'Very nice,' he said, pushing his hands into the pockets of his trousers. 'I expected to find you nestled among the cockroaches.'

'I've seen my share of those,' she replied. 'But I see no reason to live with them.'

'No. Neither do I. But when I heard what you'd been up to lately, and where, it did cross my mind that you might not know where to stop.'

'Why shouldn't I?' Emma covered her irritation well, but he knew her too well to be fooled. 'I do get paid for my work,' she pointed out when he didn't bother to answer. 'Not a princely amount, but enough to hold the line on the cockroaches.'

Zack nodded. 'I see. So you spend your days being hauled off to Emergency, and your evenings behind uniformed security? Is that it?' He spoke quietly, without inflection, determined not to betray to her too soon that the sight of that bruise on her cheek had made him want to break furniture and punch holes in her blameless white walls.

Emma must have conquered her nervousness, he decided. Her smile was now perfectly composed. 'Not exactly,' she replied. 'I usually spend my days gathering material for my appeals. Sometimes my evenings too. Would you like to sit down?'

Zack scowled at her, unable to maintain his façade of tolerant unconcern, and took a seat on the nearest turquoise sofa.

'Why did you come?' Emma asked, pulling at the neck of her sweater.

He considered tossing off some lame excuse for his presence in the city. But he preferred to tell the truth when he could. 'Simon told me you've been trying to get yourself killed,' he said. 'I came to see for myself if it was true.'

'Oh. And what if it was?'

'That depends. If necessary, I'll make it my business to see you take a slower route to heaven.'

'Nice of you to care.' She moved behind him so he couldn't see her face. 'As it happens, Simon told you wrong.'

'I'm glad to hear it. Does that mean you've given up going to such places?'

'Places?' Her tone was light, as though he was talking of a trip to the circus or the zoo.

'You know very well what I mean. The kinds of places where trouble is a way of life. As I've no doubt you have found out for yourself.' Zack shifted round to face her. She was hovering in the archway to the kitchen looking like a skinny grey mouse defending her nest from the ugly black cat.

'No,' she said. 'I haven't given up going where I'm useful. You're the one who always accused me of being spoiled. So why should you object to my finding out how the – the *unspoiled* live?'

Zack stood up. A slow-burning heat that had nothing to do with lust was blazing to life deep inside him. In a moment he would be unable to control it. This was Emma. *His* Emma. She had no idea what she'd got herself into. It was pure luck that she had survived as long as she had with no worse damage than a bruise and a few scratches. But if she was planning to acquire any more of them, she was *not* going to be able to lay them at his door.

'I do object, very strongly, to your getting yourself killed,' he said. 'Or worse.'

'Worse?' Emma's eyebrows went up. 'Are you talking about a "fate worse than death".'

Zack began to feel as he imagined a bull must feel in the bullring when goaded by the picador's lance. 'I'm talking about *you*, dammit. The streets of New York are no place for butterflies, Emma. You may think it's a game, or clever, to play at social crusading. But you won't be laughing when you wake up some morning in the morgue.'

'No,' Emma agreed, backing into the kitchen as he took a menacing step forward. She gave him a brittle smile. 'I don't suppose I will. But I won't feel anything then, will I?'

Although she was doing her best not to show it, Zack guessed she was on the verge of tears. He thought of that other creature who called himself a man, touching her, bruising her delicate skin – and for a moment he thought his blood vessels would burst.

Emma blinked rapidly, and her pert little face with the turned-up nose was suddenly so unbearably dear to him that he had to stop himself from closing the space between them, grabbing her by the shoulders and shaking her until she promised him faithfully that never again would she risk her pretty neck.

It wasn't much of a neck. Thin. He could probably circle it with one hand . . .

Only the sadness in her enormous eyes – grey, not green this evening – stopped him from laying a hand on her. What was he doing, standing here indulging in thoughts of pointless violence when all he wanted to do was hold Emma in his arms and keep her safe?

He put his hands in his pockets to guard against temptation. It wasn't going to be easy to protect Emma from herself. She was brave, as well as obstinate and just plain headstrong. He remembered how, before she had even learned to swim, she had thrown herself into the lake at Sherraby to rescue a cat she thought was drowning. He had been there to pull her out that time. But short of kidnapping her and shipping her back to England in a crate, he wasn't sure how he was going to effect a rescue this time.

But he meant to do it, whether she was willing to be rescued or not.

'Emma,' he said reasonably, but without much hope she would listen, 'I don't want you to carry on with that job. It's too dangerous. You can raise money just as well from an office.'

Emma turned to pick up a kettle. 'I do that too. Would you like some coffee?' She glanced at her watch. 'Or would you prefer something to eat?'

Zack took a deep breath. 'I've eaten, but I would like coffee. And I would prefer that you begin to face facts.'

'Such as?' Emma filled the kettle.

'Such as the fact that there's a bruise on your cheek and a cut across the knuckles on your right hand.'

'Those are nothing. You should have seen the ones on the rest of me. They've healed up nicely now, though.'

Zack could take it no longer.

'Emma,' he roared, ramming his closed fists into his pockets to prevent them from doing any damage. 'Put down that kettle at once and look at me.'

Emma obligingly put down the kettle. But when she turned to face him her expression was one of such deliberate artlessness that he had to struggle to keep his hands to himself.

'All right,' he said. 'All right, then. That's enough. You will promise me, on everything you hold sacred, that from now on you will work in an office or not at all?'

'I thought you wanted me to work,' Emma replied, patting a hand at her perfectly tidy hair.

'I did. I do. But I was never talking about the kind of work that could put your life in danger.'

'*You* did that kind of work for years. For all I know, you still do.'

'In case you hadn't noticed,' Zack ground out without pausing to think of the effect his words might have on her, 'I'm a man.'

Far below them, a cacophony of car horns blasted through the regular drone of traffic. 'I had noticed,'

Emma said, and backed herself up against the sink. 'What's your point, Zack?'

Zack gave up trying to make sense, either to himself or to her. 'My point,' he shouted, 'is that I won't have it. Either you agree to take a safe, reasonable job like other women, or –'

'Or what, Zack?' Emma's voice was quiet now, but with a sharpness to it that should have given him warning.

'Or I'll see to it that you do.'

Somewhere at the back of his mind, as he watched her chin come up, and her fingers curl around the sink behind her, he was aware that he was taking the wrong approach – the approach most likely to make her dig her heels in and do exactly the opposite of what he wanted her to do.

But he couldn't seem to stop himself behaving like a Victorian father. Hell, he *felt* like a Victorian father. It was the bruise that had done it. Which meant that until he could come up with an alternative plan, there was only one thing left for him to do.

'What are you plotting?' Emma asked, gripping her fingers more firmly around the edge of the sink.

Zack smiled grimly. She knew him almost as well as he knew her.

'Nothing,' he said. 'Do you have any plans for this evening?'

Emma blinked at him. 'Just some TV and then early to bed.'

He nodded. 'Good. That will suit me fine.'

'Suit *you*?' She eyed him suspiciously. 'Zack, where do you plan to stay the night?'

'Right here.' He took off his jacket. 'That sofa by the door looks quite comfortable.'

'No! You can't.' Her yelp of alarm was almost flattering.

'I can. I am.'

'But why? We – you can't . . .'

'No. I don't mean to. I said I was sleeping on the sofa.'

Emma's shoulders sagged noticeably. 'Zack, what are you up to? We agreed we weren't suited to each other. Why should you *care* what I do? And why – why do you want to stay?'

He smiled. He could afford to now. She was asking questions instead of telling him where to go. With Emma, that was always a good sign.

'I'm up to catching up on my beauty sleep,' he said. 'That's why I want to stay. As for why I care what you do – I suppose it's a habit. I also refuse to take the blame for your lack of common sense and common responsibility.'

Emma bit her lip. 'I'm not irresponsible, Zack. I know exactly what I'm doing. And for heaven's sake, even if I didn't – why should you be to blame?'

'Because I suspect that if I hadn't accused you of being spoiled – which you are, by the way, but it's not a crime – you wouldn't have gone off like Don Quixote on the lookout for windmills and tried to prove to me that you're no more pampered than the rest of us.'

To his surprise, instead of indignantly denying it, Emma only gazed at him with her huge eyes and turned her head to the wall.

Zack immediately felt like a heel. But there was no point letting her off the hook. 'It's true, isn't it?' he said.

Emma nodded. 'Yes. But that doesn't change anything. I'm not giving up my work just to salve your conscience.'

'I'm not asking you to give it up. I'm asking you not to be a damn fool about it. You're not a social worker, woman, you're a journalist. A publicist, if you like. And you can't tell me there's any reason for you to go on getting in the way of those who *do* know what they're doing, making them drop everything to pick up the pieces when you get yourself into trouble, just so you can raise funds for kids who are a hell of a lot more capable of surviving in that environment than you are. I know. I used to be one of them.'

Emma stared at him, not speaking, twisting her fingers together at her waist.

When her eyes began to swim, and a single tear trickled down her cheek, Zack gave a groan of defeat and pulled her into his arms.

He didn't kiss her, just held her, and Emma dropped her head on to his shoulder and let him stroke her hair. She didn't move, didn't seem to be crying, but when she finally lifted her face the material of his shirt was soaking wet.

'Now then,' he said, tilting her chin up with one finger. 'You go and wash your face, then we'll both have that coffee you offered.'

'And after that?'

He smiled crookedly. 'After that we'll talk. And after *that* I hope to get some sleep.'

Emma nodded. 'OK,' she said, and walked away as meekly as the lamb he knew she wasn't.

Zack, watching her straight back and bowed head, had to conquer an urge to go after her and tell her he hadn't meant a word of it.

He *hadn't* been fair to her, he knew. Emma was, on the whole, inclined to be obliging. If he had tried a different tack instead of throwing his male weight around, she might have agreed to listen to reason. But he had lost his temper, and now she would find it hard to back down. He knew his Emma of old. Bless her generous, loyal, hopelessly contrary heart. The heart that, until that day when he had finally agreed to accept it, had always belonged to him and no one else.

Swearing softly, Zack picked up the abandoned kettle. He knew now what he had to do. There was only one sure way to save Emma from herself – a way that a few weeks ago he would have rejected out of hand.

Not any more.

He smiled with a certain cynical self-mockery and put the kettle on to boil.

Emma leaned over the bathroom sink, wondering if she was going to be sick.

She wasn't sure when her stomach had started to rebel. Perhaps at the moment when Zack stepped out of the elevator and the sight of his beloved face had been so painful that she'd had to look away. Or perhaps it had happened when he'd held her head against his shoulder and allowed her to saturate his shirt. The only thing she was certain of was that her insides currently felt like curdled sponge. She had that feeling a lot around Zack – and it had nothing to do with what she'd eaten. Poached eggs on spinach followed by ice-cream were hardly likely to bring on indigestion.

If she hadn't known better, Emma might have begun to wonder if she was pregnant. But she was as regular as fish on Fridays had been at school. Not that there could be the smallest chance that she was having Zack's child. *She* hadn't cared about precautions, but he had, and he had made sure his point of view prevailed.

Emma soaked a pale pink facecloth in cold water, ran it over her face and eventually found the courage to look in the mirror.

'Ugh!' she moaned, and held the facecloth over her eyes.

Why was she thinking this way? Did she actually want to have Zack's child? He had been so gentle back there in the kitchen. Yet he wasn't a particularly gentle man. His upbringing hadn't encouraged softness. Even so, she just knew he would make a wonderful father . . .

'Stop it, Emma.' She spoke out loud to make sure the words sank in. 'You turned him down because he proposed to you out of duty. You surely don't think he'll propose to you again? For a different, more flattering reason.'

No, she didn't think that. It was only Zack's conscience that had brought him back to her now. His opinion of her hadn't changed. He said the work she was doing was foolish, yet the only reason he wanted her to give it up was so that *he* wouldn't feel responsible if something happened to her. As, she had to admit, on two occasions it had.

Emma gave the tap a vicious twist. Maybe Zack was right. Maybe she would be more useful in an office. Not that it made any difference. She had no intention of giving up her work to suit him.

She dried her face without looking in the mirror again, and marched into the kitchen with a bright smile plastered to her lips.

Zack was seated at the white wooden table with his arms crossed. His dark head rested against the wall. A carafe of aromatic coffee was being kept warm on the stove, and he had poured out two steaming cups and set them on the table.

Emma, feeling better at once, gave an appreciative sniff as she sat down. 'Good. I'm glad you made yourself at home.'

'Home?' Zack waved at the bright, bare living room. 'Home? Emma, are you sure you're not on the run?'

'What do you mean?'

'This flat. It's empty. As if you're preparing for a moonlight flit.'

'Oh. No, it's not that. I just – well, I haven't felt able to put down roots.'

How could she tell him that *he* was the chief reason for her reluctance to settle? A great restlessness had come over her since that morning in the dining room at Sherraby – a sense that permanence and security were for other people.

Of course Zack misunderstood. 'You mean you may decide to move back in with your parents? Simon tells me they'll welcome your return to the nest.'

Was that a gibe? Emma wondered. Was he suggesting she wasn't up to standing on her own feet for more than a month or two?

'No,' she said. 'I mean I'm not sure what I want to do with my life in the long run. Or even where I want to do it. So there's no point in acquiring a lot of clutter.'

'I suppose not.' Zack uncrossed his arms and leaned across the table. He had pushed up his shirt-sleeves, and Emma found she couldn't take her eyes off his tanned, muscular forearms. Tough-looking arms with tough skin and strong, sinuous veins. Not the arms of a man in the habit of spending much time in an office.

'What did you want to talk about?' she asked.

'You. Emma, you can't keep on driving us all crazy the way you have been –'

'I suppose by "us all" you mean yourself.'

'Among others.'

'If you and the *others* would mind your own business, there wouldn't be a problem, would there?'

'I think there would. You're behaving like a child, Emma.'

Oh, so they were back to that again. Round and round in a never-ending circle. Emma, grow up and get a job. Emma, do as you're told, like a good girl. Emma, get a job. But not that job. Don't act like a child . . .

Emma could feel the heat surging up into her face. Angry, resentful heat that turned her skin an ugly shade of red. Unable to keep still a moment longer, she pushed her chair back and made to leap up. But her knee caught the edge of the table, rattling her coffee cup in its saucer before toppling it on to its side.

Zack didn't move fast enough to avoid the stream of hot coffee that cascaded over his trousers before it hit the floor.

'Hey!' he yelled, knocking over his chair as he too sprang to his feet. 'Watch what you're doing, for Christ's sake.'

Emma stared at the wet stain spreading across his thigh. 'You're not – are you burned?' she asked.

'Only second degree. Don't let it bother you.'

Emma moved swiftly to the sink. 'Take them off. You have to put cold water on burns.'

'What?'

Something in his voice gave her pause. He didn't sound angry any more. Reluctantly, she made herself face him.

His dark eyes were gleaming at her with something that might have been amusement – although it could just as easily have been malice. And he was grinning. Actually grinning. 'You do it,' he said, hitching a hip on the corner of the table.

'What, take your trousers off?' Emma couldn't believe her ears. Was he serious? It wasn't like Zack to make suggestive jokes.

'Why not? Then you can minister most tenderly to my wounds.'

'What if I rub salt in them?' she asked.

'I won't let you. Shall we get on with it?'

Emma shook her head, not sure whether to laugh or run away. 'No. I'll leave you to get on with it yourself. Give me a shout when you're through and I'll come and clean up the mess.'

Without giving Zack time to object, she hurried back to the bathroom and locked the door.

Pressing her ear firmly against the wall, she waited for his shout of indignation. It didn't come. She went to the sink and washed her hands, working up a thick, lemon-scented lather. Still no sound from the kitchen. When her watch told her ten minutes had passed, she opened the door and slipped cautiously back into the living room.

At first she didn't see Zack. But as she passed one of the turquoise sofas it occurred to her that something was out of place. She stopped, glanced behind her, and saw that the something was Zack.

He was stretched out on the sofa wearing a pair of black silk boxer shorts and nothing else. There was a faint pink stain on his left thigh, and his eyes were closed.

Emma moistened her lips and tiptoed across the carpet to stand beside him.

Zack. The man she loved. The man who, with some emotion born of chemistry and adolescent passion, had come to be her reason for being. But her passion was no longer adolescent. It had grown into something strong and lasting that she was going to have to learn to live without.

She swallowed, trying to shift the aching obstruction in her throat, and her eyes strayed to the pale pink burn on Zack's thigh. That was her fault. But he had fallen asleep, so it couldn't be hurting him too much. She went to the linen closet, selected a baby-blue blanket and laid it gently over his nearly naked form. It was a shame to cover that tough, hard body. But she couldn't let him get cold.

Zack smiled in his sleep. He looked so vulnerable without the protective mask he habitually wore to hide his thoughts.

Surrendering to impulse, Emma bent over to drop a quick kiss on his forehead.

Not quick enough. She lingered just a few seconds too long, inhaling the remembered scent of his body and basking in the sweet warmth of his breath. Then, as she straightened reluctantly, an arm shot out and grabbed her around the waist. In the next instant her feet left the floor, and before she had time to protest, she found herself sprawled on top of Zack with her mouth only inches above his. His free hand clasped the back of her neck.

Emma gasped. Then his lips were on hers – or hers were on his, she wasn't sure how it came about – and she forgot that she was supposed to resist him, forgot everything but that she needed him, hungered for him, as much as he hungered for her.

After a while, but only gradually, some semblance of sanity returned. Emma tried to speak, tried to tell him he was supposed to be asleep. But he wasn't asleep, and in the space of a few seconds she had forgotten what it was she wanted to say.

Zack slid his hands expertly over her hips and thighs, and in a manoeuvre so swift she didn't know or care how it came about, he had her jeans peeled off and tossed on to the floor. The grey sweater followed.

'Better,' murmured Zack. 'Much better.'

Emma thought so too, especially when her bra and panties joined the heap of discarded clothing on the carpet.

'Now yours,' she whispered, pushing the blue blanket out of the way and moving her hand to his waist.

Black silk slid between her fingers, sending sensuous signals up her arm. But she wasn't as practised as Zack, and in the end he laughed and did the job himself.

'Don't worry,' he whispered. 'You'll learn, wee Emma. You'll learn.'

During the next hour Emma did learn, more than she had believed there was to know, about Zack's body, and about her own.

When it was over, and they lay side by side on the turquoise sofa, too sated for speech and too intimately aware to think of sleep, Emma slowly floated down from the clouds.

What had happened to her this last hour? What had it all been about? One minute Zack had been telling her to take his trousers off and minister to his wounds; ten minutes later he was taking hers off – and making love to her most beautifully. If this was his idea of revenge, then she was beginning to understand why revenge was called sweet.

She gazed bemusedly at the flat shape of his ear, thinking how perfectly it lay against his head. Then Zack reached down to pick up the blanket and the movement stirred her from her trance.

'Why?' she asked as he tucked it around her. 'Why, Zack? That was – that was fantastic. But it will only make it harder to do without.'

Zack's hand was resting on her bottom. He patted it lazily. 'Yes, but you see I have absolutely no intention of doing without.'

'But you said –'

'No, *you* said. That you weren't going to marry me. But that, my Emma, is exactly where you were wrong. You are going to marry me. It's the only way I can think of to keep you in my bed and out of trouble. So tomorrow you can hand in your notice.' He patted her again. 'What do you have to say to that?'

Oh, dear lord. Emma pressed her cheek against his chest. If she'd been standing, her heart would have taken a nosedive to her feet.

'No,' she whispered. 'No, Zack. That's – I can't. *We* can't.'

'And why not?' He didn't sound particularly put out.

'Because I won't give up my job to relieve your conscience. And because I can't marry a man who only wants me out of a feeling of obligation.'

'I see.' Zack disentangled his limbs from hers and sat up. 'And what makes you think I only want you out of a feeling of obligation? Is that what you think we just had? Obligation? The dictionary calls it something else.'

Emma rested her head on the soft leather arm of the sofa, too numb to think beyond the moment. Whatever Zack said, the inescapable, unbearable truth was that sooner or later she was going to lose him.

'The dictionary calls it lust,' she said dully.

'And very nice too. Lust is not an obligation, wee Emma.'

'No,' she agreed. 'It isn't love either.'

'Ah.' He stroked her leg through the blanket. 'Love. So that's it. I should have known.'

She waited for him to say more, but he didn't. He went on stroking her and gazing into space darkly, as if he could see something she couldn't.

'Yes,' she said. 'That's it. That and my job.'

He nodded. 'Of course. It would be.' He stopped stroking abruptly and stood up. She watched, blinking, as he pulled on his shorts and went to stand by the window.

Emma pushed herself up, dragging the blue blanket around her shoulders. Zack had his back to her and appeared to be watching the rain. It showed no signs of letting up. When he didn't speak, she broke the silence by saying the first thing that came into her head.

'It's raining very hard. And the leaves are falling. I suppose it will be winter soon.'

'Yes. Emma . . .?' He paused, then moved quickly across the room with a silence and agility that reminded her forcibly of how he made his living.

'What is it?' she asked, disturbed by the look in his eyes.

'Emma, I am not marrying you out of duty –'

'You're not marrying me at all.'

He made a gesture of impatience. 'But nor can I promise you I love you. I thought I loved Samantha, though looking back on it, I'm not sure I did. All I can tell you for certain is that when I heard what you were doing over here –'

'You came to interfere.'

Zack frowned. 'No. I came to stop you. Because I couldn't bear the idea of your soft little body lying bleeding in some gutter. Or . . .' He turned away so that only the hard edge of his profile was towards her. 'Or of some drunken lout trying to . . .' He broke off, and Emma finished for him.

'To rape me,' she said quietly.

'Exactly.' He took a deep breath, and she watched the skin pull tight around his jawline. 'Is that what you call love? If it is, well then, maybe I do love you.'

'If you loved me, you wouldn't try to make me do what *you* want. You'd understand that my job is important to me.'

It wasn't *that* important. Why couldn't she just give in and say yes?

'That is exactly what I would do,' he told her. 'If I loved you. It is also what I would do if I didn't love you. Now – are you going to see sense, or do I have to drag you to the altar kicking and screaming? A fine spectacle that would be, wouldn't it?'

'What?' To her chagrin, a giggle burst out of her. She couldn't seem to stop it. Zack really meant it. He honestly thought he could get her to marry him by sheer brute force.

'That's right,' he said. 'Laugh. It suits you. Well?'

Emma stared at him. If only she could accept his ultimatum, agree to do exactly as he wanted. But she dared not. If she let him dictate to her now, he would expect to go on ruling her life forever. And yet if she turned him down . . . No, she couldn't do that either. Because if she did, there would be no forever. Not for them.

'I don't know,' she whispered, clutching the blue blanket around her neck.

'Good,' Zack said. 'That's settled, then.' He looked at his watch. 'It's too late to call our families, so we may as well carry on where we left off.'

'But . . .' Emma began. 'I didn't say –'

'No,' agreed Zack. 'I did. Now, let's get that blanket off you and make it official.'

Tomorrow, Emma thought vaguely, as Zack whipped the blanket off and lifted her legs on to the sofa. Tomorrow, I'll make him understand . . .

Then she forgot about tomorrow and gave herself up to the excruciating pleasure of today.

In the morning, when she woke up, the rain had stopped and Zack had already left the apartment.

A note on the kitchen table said her cupboard was bare and he had gone to fetch bagels and eggs. A postscript added that she needn't hurry, as he had already phoned her office to let them know she was leaving New York to get married, and so wouldn't be able to work for them any longer.

Emma threw the note on the floor and stamped on it with both feet before she tossed it into the trash can.

Then she went to pick up the phone.

CHAPTER 11

Olivia gazed at the TV screen and tried to pretend she cared about the tribulations of the ageing comedienne with the raucous voice whose TV daughter had just joined a hairless rock group.

Jamie was in bed, Simon was in London, and she was bored, restless and lonely. There must be something more interesting to watch. She pressed the channel-changer, and the image of a gracious country house came on screen. Olivia made a face. She had a gracious country house of her own, for all the good it did her.

Would it have made a difference if she had paid attention to Simon last weekend when he'd shouted at her to come back as she fled down the hall clasping his report to her bosom like a shield? He had said he wasn't finished talking. But she wasn't a little girl any more, hadn't obeyed the voice of authority for years. So she had ignored him and headed instinctively down the passage to the kitchen, knowing that if Simon chose to follow her, he wouldn't make a scene in front of Mrs Leigh.

Thank heaven for Mrs Leigh. The whippet-sharp little cook had become the closest thing she had to a friend in the vicinity of Sherraby, and she had been badly in need of friendly company that day.

'Dear me,' she had said, closing the big oven door and looking around as Olivia flopped down at the scrubbed wooden table to gaze despairingly into a large bowl of trifle. 'You look as white as if you'd seen a ghost, Mrs Simon.' Her keen eyes narrowed. 'Nothing wrong with that trifle, is there?'

'No, it smells wonderful.' Olivia took a long, calming breath and wrinkled her nose in tactful appreciation. She'd come to the right place. Only Mrs Leigh would suggest it was possible to be haunted by a trifle. 'It's just that I seem to feel a bit queasy,' she explained.

It was part of the truth at any rate.

When Mrs Leigh's gaze automatically flew to her waistline, Olivia, who was getting used to Sherraby's well-meant concentration on her figure, shook her head and said, 'No, it's not that –'

'Hmm. Must be Mr Simon, then. Isn't he treating you right? I noticed he don't spend much time with you.'

'He's been busy,' Olivia said loyally.

'Busy! I know his kind of busy.' Mrs Leigh dismissed Simon's busyness with a toss of her head. 'It was the same thing with that Miss Sylvia, mind you. Now *there* was a strange one.'

'Sylvia? Was she strange? Simon doesn't talk about her much.'

'Well he wouldn't, would he? You being his new wife, an' all.'

'No, I suppose not.' She waited, hopefully, for Mrs Leigh to expand on Sylvia's strangeness. But she didn't, and Olivia was left wondering. Had Sylvia had a breakdown or something? Was that why Simon's eyes had a tendency to go all shuttered whenever his ex-fiancée's name came up in conversation?

So many enigmas, so many unanswered questions . . .

'Mind you,' Mrs Leigh was saying, 'I doubt Mr Simon meant to be unkind to Miss Sylvia. He's all right, is Mr Simon. Spite of the awful things he used to do.'

'Awful things?' Olivia asked weakly.

'*You* know.' Mrs Leigh waved a flour-covered hand. 'All that spying and playing about with guns. People could've got hurt. Not right, it wasn't.'

She spoke as if Simon's former occupation had been, not a dangerous quest for information crucial to the safety of the realm, but a game indulged in by naughty little boys.

Olivia felt her spirits begin to lift. Mrs Leigh was always a tonic.

'Simon doesn't do those things any more,' she pointed out, picking up a spoon and helping herself absently to trifle.

'I should hope not. He's a married man now.' Mrs Leigh removed the spoon from Olivia's hand and replaced it with a clean one and a clean glass dish.

'Sorry,' Olivia said, feeling like a child caught with her finger in the pudding. 'Mrs Leigh – you're fond of Simon, aren't you?'

'They don't come much better'n him. You ought to know that, Mrs Simon.'

'Yes. Yes, of course I do,' Olivia agreed quickly. Was she as transparent as all that? Were her doubts and confusion plain on her face for all to see? Much as she enjoyed Mrs Leigh's company, she had no great wish to discuss her marriage with the cook. She had a feeling Simon wouldn't like it much either.

'I'd better – um – go and find Jamie,' she said, standing up and knocking her chair sideways. 'He's outside playing with the Ripper, so I expect he'll need cleaning up before he has his lunch.'

'Humph. That Ripper's a bad influence,' muttered Mrs Leigh. 'No sense telling Mr Simon that, though. Too soft-hearted by a mile, he is.'

Soft-hearted? Olivia was shaking her head as she made her way out into the gardens. Simon? Well, yes, she supposed he could be when it happened to suit him. But lately he'd been about as soft as a granite rock where she was concerned.

When that disquieting voice in her head murmured that Simon had a reason for his indifference, she replied to it with silent irritation. Dammit, she hadn't invaded *his* privacy and then pretended she hadn't. And she had never refused him her bed. What did he expect from her? Total acceptance of his right to do anything he wanted – read anything he wanted, whether it belonged to him or not?

Well, he wasn't going to get it. Total acceptance could only come with love, and she would never love him the way she had once loved Dan – any more than he would ever love her.

But could she make this new marriage, to a very different, much stronger, more forceful and disciplined man than Dan had ever been, hold together as somehow her first marriage had held? She wasn't a quitter. But in a way she was tired. Tired of pretending things were normal when they weren't. And she had no doubt Simon would continue to freeze her out as long as she was unable to give him the unquestioning acceptance he practically demanded.

For all he had no right to demand it.

Overhead, a bird began to sing, and, as Olivia's eyes focused on the thin branches of the lime trees etched against the pearl-tinted sky, it occurred to her, for perhaps the first time, that she very much wanted to trust and accept Simon – and she resented him enormously for making that impossible.

If only there hadn't been Jamie to consider . . .

As if on cue, her thoughts were interrupted by a shout. A second later Jamie and the Ripper came hurtling out of the bushes and almost knocked her down. After that Olivia hadn't time to think of Simon, because the next half-hour was spent removing accumulated mud and leaves from boy and dog, and convincing Jamie that he couldn't go to the table disguised as compost.

By the time they sat down to eat, Jamie was sulky, Olivia weary and subdued, and Simon as impersonally charming and arctic as only he could be. It was as if the scene in his study had never happened.

But somehow the meal was endured, and afterwards Simon said he was going back to his study to finish up some work. Jamie and Olivia went out to play a brisk game of croquet on the lawn.

On Monday, early, Simon had gone back to London.

And there, of course, he would stay until the weekend.

Olivia stared glumly at the house on the TV. Were its residents as separated from each other in mind and body as she was from her husband? With a shrug, she flicked the set off and went upstairs to read herself to sleep.

'Emma! What are you doing here?' Olivia's spirits lifted at once when she walked into the dining room the following morning and found a welcome visitor seated at the table.

'Reading about euthanasia,' Emma replied.

Olivia choked into her fist. 'What a way to kick-start the day. Have you seen Jamie? He wasn't in his room.'

She wanted very much to know what had brought Simon's cousin to Sherraby again but, as always, her first concern was for her son.

Emma put down her paper. 'Yes. He ate three of those revolting, smelly kippers you people are so fond of, then Annie took him to school.'

'Already?'

'He said they were having an early morning rehearsal for the Christmas play.'

'Oh. Yes, of course they are.' How could she have forgotten? This estrangement from Simon must be getting to her. Or else she was becoming so used to Annie's competent help that she had come to depend on it.

'Jamie's playing a Wise Man,' she explained to Emma.

'Yes. That's what he told me.' Emma's reply was non-committal.

Olivia smiled. 'I know what you're thinking: that whoever was in charge of casting must be off her head.'

Emma smiled back, but it was a wan smile, as if she might be close to tears. 'I did wonder.'

'So did I. But his teacher assures me that so far he has neither set the manger on fire nor organized a Shepherds' Revolt.' Olivia pulled out a chair and began to help herself to breakfast. 'So I'm keeping my fingers crossed. Emma, what *are* you doing here? Not that I'm not pleased to see you.'

'I'm not sure. Running away, I think. Mom and Dad are off on their travels again, and I've always used Sherraby as a bolt-hole.' She took a triangle of toast from the toast rack, thought better of it, and put it back.

'But I thought you had a flat of your own now,' Olivia objected. 'You can't be running away from yourself.'

'I gave up the apartment. There didn't seem much excuse for keeping it on when I no longer have a job.'

'Oh.' Olivia received a distinct message that she'd better tread warily. 'Did you – um – quit?'

'Not exactly.' Emma stabbed a fried tomato with her fork. 'Zack quit for me. He called up the office and told them I was moving to England.'

'He did that?' Olivia poured herself coffee when she'd meant to pour tea. 'And are you? Moving to England?'

'Oh, Olivia.' Emma stopped attacking the tomato and started on an egg. 'I don't know what I'm doing. I feel so – so lost.'

'I know the feeling.'

'Do you?' Emma looked up. 'Yes, I guess you *have* been through some pretty rough times, haven't you?'

Olivia didn't bother to explain that the rough times were by no means confined to the past. She could see that her friend, desperate for help with her own problems, was in no state to solve anyone else's. 'Do you want to talk about it?' she asked.

'I don't know. I suppose so.' Emma folded the paper to a column on life-threatening tropical diseases.

'Something happened between you and Zack, didn't it?' Olivia prompted.

'Yes. You could say something happened. Specifically, he came to New York, told me to quit my job, and announced that he was going to marry me. Just like that.'

'And did you accept?'

Emma shook her head. 'No. How could I? He doesn't think he loves me but he expects to run my life.'

'I suppose that's a start,' Olivia observed drily.

'But it isn't. He spent the night, and when I woke up in the morning he'd already gone out. He left me a note saying he'd told the Foundation I wouldn't be working for them any longer.'

'Oh, dear. What did you do?'

'I phoned the office and told them it was all a mistake. But they said my contract had run out anyway, and they'd decided not to renew it. According to them, my appeals have been so effective that all they'll need to do for the next few months is keep on using them – with a few minor changes perhaps. They also said I'd become a – a liability. So Zack was right all along,' she finished tragically.

Olivia guessed that Zack's rightness was the unkindest cut of all.

'Well, then,' she said cautiously. 'Doesn't that mean you can marry him? You could get a job over here.'

'Only if His Bossiness approved of it,' Emma said bitterly.

'You can't altogether blame him. You *were* attacked twice. Don't you think any man who loved you would find that hard to take?'

'I suppose so.' Emma picked up her fork and mashed a defenceless fried potato. 'But I don't think he does love me. He just feels responsible for me. And bossy.'

'That doesn't sound much like Zack. Of course, I don't know him as well as you do . . .'

'You're taking his side,' Emma accused.

'No, I'm not. I'm trying to see both sides. What did he say when he came back? Did he apologize?'

'No. He said, "What did I tell you?"'

How like a man, Olivia thought resignedly. If Zack had only had the brains to say he was sorry, and that he'd handed in her notice because he loved her, Emma would probably have tumbled straight into his arms – which, she strongly suspected, was where both of them wanted her to be. She had seen the way Zack looked at Emma. It wasn't just a matter of bed.

A long time ago, Dan had looked at her in just that way.

She buttered a slice of toast, and asked neutrally, 'What did you do then?'

'I told him he was a bastard and walked out. But – oh, Olivia . . .' Emma laid down the fork and lifted a hand to her mouth. Her eyes, turquoise this morning, brimmed with what looked improbably like merriment. 'The trouble was, when I got as far as Fifth Avenue, I realized I'd walked out of my own apartment. So I went back to tell Zack to walk out.'

Olivia tried, unsuccessfully, to suppress a giggle. But when Emma lowered her hand, she was relieved to see that she was laughing too.

'Oh, Emma,' Olivia gasped, several hysterical minutes later as the two of them dried their eyes on Sherraby's monogrammed napkins. 'I really don't think you ought to worry. I don't believe anything will ever keep you down for long.'

'Except Zack,' Emma said, sobering. 'And I don't mean that the way it sounds,' she added severely, as Olivia's lips started to twitch.

Olivia pulled herself together and nodded sympathetically. 'Did he walk out when you told him to?' she asked.

'No. He'd already gone. I haven't seen him since.'

'Do you know where he is?'

'Back in London, I suppose.'

'Hmm.' Olivia eyed her narrowly. 'Is that why you're here?'

'No. Of course not. He's impossible.' Emma spoke with such vehemence that Olivia was tempted to start quoting Shakespeare on the subject of protesting too much. Instead, when the hall clock chimed, she stood up and said she had to see Mrs Leigh about dinner.

She didn't have to see Mrs Leigh, who had her own very definite ideas about dinner. But Emma had taken up the paper again, and was absorbed in the story of a woman who had murdered her lover with a flowerpot.

Olivia went up to her bedroom, and for a minute or so stood staring thoughtfully at the meadow grasses rippling in the wind. Then she picked up the phone beside her bed and began to dial.

'Good morning. Sebastian and Kent.' Diane's voice was tart, as if she resented the interruption.

'Good morning. Is Mr Sebastian there. This is Mrs Sebastian.' It still felt strange to say that.

'Yes, he is. Just a moment.' Olivia thought she heard the receptionist mutter, 'Unfortunately,' under her breath.

After a brief pause, Simon came on the line.

'Yes? What can I do for you, Olivia?'

Cool and polite, as always. Olivia sighed. 'Emma's here,' she said.

'Is she? In that case your week won't be dull.'

'No, but that's not why I phoned. Is Zack there?'

'Not at the moment.'

'But he'll be back?'

'I certainly hope so. Olivia –'

'Wait.' Olivia held up her hand, though she knew he couldn't see it. 'I was thinking – she seems terribly confused and unhappy. Is Zack – confused too?'

'If by that you mean is he glowering more than usual, and making life difficult for Diane, yes. He is. But then so am I, so she tells me.'

'Oh. Poor Diane. Simon . . .?'

'Yes? Olivia, did you call for a reason, or –?'

'Of course I did. I wouldn't call just to waste your time. Simon, do you think Zack's in love with Emma?'

'Probably. But I don't think you'll get him to admit it. He's had first-hand experience of the kind of havoc being in love can wreak.'

Oh, dear. His tone was terribly scornful and bitter. Through the window, Olivia watched Cactus and Tumbleweed trot up to the fence in the far meadow. How sweet and peaceful they looked.

'I see. All the same, would you tell Zack Emma's here, please?' She did her best to sound brisk and uninvolved. 'He may want to know.'

'All right. If you like. I'll see you at the weekend, then. Everything going smoothly? No more confrontations with Harold Downer?'

'No. Everything's fine.'

'Good. Goodbye, then.'

'Goodbye.'

Simon hung up the phone. Hell. Why was it that just the sound of Olivia's voice could make him want to smash things? No wonder Diane complained about his temper. He glared at the creeping plant his receptionist had brought in two weeks ago to cheer him up. The blasted thing was slowly taking over his credenza.

Dammit, he had married Olivia to solve a problem, not to create one. He had wanted a wife who would suit him in bed, who wouldn't make demands, and who would shortly present him with an heir. And in all but the last, he had to admit Olivia had fulfilled those expectations. She had professed herself willing to share his bed; her only demand had been for something to do to fill her time, and he could hardly claim it was her fault that no heir was on the way.

So why, whenever he saw her or spoke to her, was he overcome with the most juvenile and inexcusable desire to . . . all right, he might as well admit it. He wanted to hurt her. Not physically, that wasn't his way. But somehow to pay her back for making such a mountain out of that damned useless diary.

Not that he'd been kind to her these past weeks. Civil, yes. But not kind. And when he had kissed her last weekend, not to give pleasure but to punish, she had looked so crushed, so desperate, that he had instantly been racked with remorse. So he had called after her, wanting in some way to make amends . . .

But she had run away from him, refused to listen.

Simon clenched his teeth. The truth of the matter was that he didn't know what to do about Olivia. If it was only a matter of taking her to bed – well, she wouldn't refuse him. Her innate sense of fairness wouldn't let her. The trouble was, there was a lot more to his dilemma than bed.

Growling a few choice words he didn't normally utter within earshot of Diane, Simon stood up, turned around, and quite deliberately banged his head three times, slowly, against the wall.

'I shouldn't do that, if I were you.'

Simon swung round to see Zack draped in the doorway wearing a small, malignant grin.

'It's bad for business,' his partner continued. 'Clients get suspicious about holes in the wall.'

'Damn you,' Simon said, more amiably than he felt.

Zack shrugged. 'If you say so. Is it personal, or something I should know about?'

'Personal. By the way, Olivia called. She says to tell you Emma's at Sherraby.'

'Ah.' Zack settled his shoulders more comfortably against the door-jamb.

For the first time since his partner had returned from the States, Simon thought he detected a certain lessening of tension – as if a long-awaited package had finally arrived.

'How long is she staying?' Zack asked.

'I've no idea.'

'Right.' Zack abandoned his air of detachment as if he were tossing off a cloak. 'Diane!' he shouted. 'Cancel my appointments for tomorrow. I have business to see to in Lincolnshire.'

'*Mr* Kent,' Diane shouted back. 'You can't just leave. Not again!'

'Yes, I can,' Zack yelled cheerfully. To Simon, he added in a lower voice, 'See you at the weekend, Si?'

'I expect so – if you're planning to avail yourself of my hospitality. Not that I can remember inviting you.'

Zack ignored him and swung out the door whistling 'Hark the Herald Angels Sing,' in a tuneless C flat.

Simon sat down heavily behind his desk. Zack never whistled. Which meant that, if he wasn't mistaken, he could look forward to a more than usually disrupted weekend.

'Diane,' he called. 'Come here.'

When Diane appeared in the doorway, he said, 'Remind me never to mention my cousin Emma around this office. It has an unsettling effect on my partner.'

'You're telling me,' said Diane. 'He's cancelled all his appointments. Why doesn't he get it over with and marry her? Not that marriage looks to have done *you* a lot of good.'

'Thank you, Diane,' said Simon. 'I see your powers of observation are as sharp as ever. However, if you value your job I'd suggest you make an effort to keep your damned observations to yourself.' He picked up a rubber band and a paper clip and snapped it at Diane's creeping plant.

'You missed,' said Diane, and flounced back to her desk.

* * *

Emma lay in her familiar bed at Sherraby listening to the wind howling around the eaves. In just a few weeks it would be Christmas. It didn't feel like Christmas – perhaps because by then she wouldn't be here. She would be back on Long Island with her parents and a million miles away from Zack Kent.

She moved her head restlessly. This was hopeless. Whatever had made her think she could sleep? She hadn't slept the night through in weeks. Maybe if she tried lying on her stomach . . . No, that was no good either. Grumbling under her breath, Emma threw back the covers and swung her legs to the floor.

Brr. She'd forgotten about the British attitude to central heating. Simon said his parents had installed it years ago, but he could have fooled her. She stood up and reached for a robe, then, contrarily, felt a sudden compelling need for fresh, cold air. Knowing it made no sense, but unable to stop herself, she walked across to the window and flung it open.

Wind swirled into the room, flapping the curtains, knocking over a silver bud vase, and blowing a stack of postcards all over the floor. With a gasp, Emma pulled the window shut and went to pick them up.

Was she going crazy? What had made her open that window in the first place? And had she really heard what she thought she'd heard above the howling uproar outside?

It wasn't until the last postcard had been picked up that she finally acknowledged the message that had come to her during those brief moments when the wind had carried its song into her room.

Hurrying now, and without further thought, she threw off her robe and nightgown and donned warm trousers, a heavy grey sweater and the blue parka she had brought with her from the States. Then she went downstairs, across the silent hallway and on into the cloakroom. Switching on the light, she discovered boots in every conceivable shape and size lined up on the scuffed wooden floor. She grabbed the first pair that looked as though they might fit, tugged them on, and half ran, half walked down the passage leading to the kitchen and the back door.

To her surprise, the wind had died down by the time she let herself outside, and the air felt crisp but not cold. She paused to listen.

Yes, there it was. Her very own song of the night.

Her heart beating fast, every nerve in her body quivering with life, Emma hurried across the fields towards the woods.

Long before she got there, she knew what, and who, she would find.

Zack was seated on the same mossy stump where she had come upon him all those years before. But this time the tune he was playing was 'Greensleeves'.

'*Alas, my love, you do me wrong to cast me off discourteously* . . .' The haunting words swam into Emma's mind as she came to a stop in the shadows.

There wasn't much of a moon, and Zack's face was only a pale blur in the darkness.

'*When I have loved you so long . . .*'

But he hadn't loved her. And she hadn't cast him off. Had she? No, she had gone back to the apartment only to find him gone.

But you meant to cast him off, she reminded herself. He beat you to it, that's all.

'Zack?' she said. 'Zack, what are you doing? Why are you here? It's the middle of the night.'

'. . . *And who but my Lady Greensleeves*?'

Zack finished the tune and put his harmonica back in his pocket. 'I wanted to see if you would come,' he said, as if his answer made perfect sense.

'But I might not have heard you.'

'I knew you would.'

There didn't seem much to say to that except, 'You were right. I'm here.'

'Yes.' He held out his hand. 'Come, then.'

Emma moved towards him as if he were a magnet and she a pin, and when she was close enough he took her wrist and pulled her between his knees. 'Well, wee Emma,' he said. 'Have you forgiven me?'

'Forgiven you?'

'For depriving you of that most unsuitable job.'

'Oh. Yes.' She swallowed. The heat from his thighs was warming her blood. 'I would have lost it anyway. They said I was becoming a liability.'

'Good. And did you miss me?'

'You know I did,' she whispered, touching a tentative hand to his hair.

'I don't know anything. Except that you walked out on me in a terrible huff.'

'I came back. But you'd already gone.'

Zack put his hands up under her parka and cupped his hands over her rear. 'I knew you needed time to calm down. To decide what you really wanted –'

'But you knew what I wanted. You've known from the very first day.'

'You were only sixteen that first day. People change. And it was entirely possible you were one of those females who glory in the chase but lose interest once they've captured the – for want of another word, the prize. At least that's the way I saw it.'

'But how *could* you think that? It wasn't true.'

'Wasn't it? I did offer to marry you. Eventually. And you refused me.'

An owl hooted, and something soft brushed across Emma's face. 'I had to,' she said. 'You must see that.'

'No, I don't see that. I don't go around proposing to people unless I mean it. I'm not your revolting cousin Gerald.' He moved his hands up higher.

Emma shivered, but not with the cold.

'Oh, I knew you *meant* it,' she said. 'But I wasn't sure *why*. I'm still not sure.'

'Aren't you? Well, I can't hold that against you. I wasn't sure myself until the morning you walked out on me – and I was faced with the dreadful prospect of spending the rest of my life with no wee Emma around to drive me mad.'

Oh, if only she could see his face. It was so damned *dark*. 'What do you mean?' she whispered. She couldn't have raised her voice to save her life.

'I mean that when you refused me the first time, I thought it was probably for the best. The second time was different. I didn't believe you. So I took you to bed.'

'A very underhand move,' Emma murmured.

'Underhand?' She saw the flash of his teeth in the darkness as a hand slid in between her legs.

Emma gasped. 'Don't,' she pleaded.

Zack laughed, but the hand stayed where it was. 'Why? Don't you like it?'

'You know I do. Zack, please, I can't think . . .'

'I don't want you to think. I want you to say, "Yes, Zack, I will marry you." Then we can celebrate in the usual way.'

'Why?' Emma moaned, scrambling off his knee and stepping backwards. 'Zack, *why* do you want me to marry you?'

'Why do you think, you ridiculous woman?' His voice thickened and his accent became broader. 'I love you, damn it. I expect I always have.'

'Oh, Zack.' As joy and an incredible relief filled her heart, Emma leaned over and took his face in her hands. 'Are you sure?'

'As sure as I've ever been of anything in my life.'

'Then – yes. Oh, yes, yes, *yes*. I'll marry you, Zack Kent. For better, for worse and forever.'

Zack gave the kind of whoop she associated with Highland chieftains going into battle, and thumped her back down on his knee.

After a while, when he had finished kissing her, he lifted her gently and laid her on a bed of dead leaves and moss. There was a stone somewhere under her left shoulder, and something sharp pierced her leg. It didn't matter. She held out her arms, and in a moment Zack's dark shape had covered hers.

Just before she lost all sense of the world around her, she smelled the familiar earthy scent of his skin.

A long time later, when the vows of the heart had been sealed most beautifully in the flesh, Zack pulled Emma to her feet and began to button up her clothes.

'Well, now,' he said. 'That's settled.'

Emma put her arms around his waist and laughed up at him. 'Yes,' she said. 'That's one way of putting it. Zack . . .?'

'Yes. What is it?'

'Why did you wait all these weeks to come back to me?'

'Because you needed time. Time to make up your mind what you wanted. I handled things very badly in New York. You needed to get over that too.'

'You were disgustingly bossy,' Emma said.

'Yes. I know. But you must understand – I'm not going to change.' He fastened the last button and zipped her parka up to her neck. 'Not if you're thinking of taking up any more jobs like that last one.'

If he had said that a few hours ago, Emma reflected, she would have gone into orbit. But now, knowing he loved her, it didn't matter. Olivia had been right about that. Love did make the difference.

'I'll probably do the same kind of work,' she said pensively. 'I like it. But I don't think I'll need to do on-site research.'

'No,' Zack said. 'You won't.'

Emma heard the note of finality in his voice and smiled. If Zack Kent thought he was going to run her life, married to him or not, he couldn't be more mistaken. But she kind of looked forward to the pleasure of teaching him that.

'What would you have done if I hadn't come to England?' she asked.

'Probably gone back to the States to collect you. But I knew you would come if you cared.' He turned her on to the path. 'It's been a long wait. Diane will be glad to see the end of it as well. I'm told I've not been a pleasure to have around the office.'

Emma laughed. 'I can believe that. Because I've been waiting too. Through eight long years – and Samantha.'

'Ah. Samantha. You drove me to her, you know. I foolishly thought she would protect me from your wiles.' His arm tightened possessively on her waist.

Emma laughed and laid her head on his shoulder,

secure at last in the safety of his love. 'I'm the one in need of protection,' she told him. 'Do you realize there are pine needles stuck into my backside?'

'And a very good place for them too,' Zack said smugly.

'Bastard.' Emma spoke without conviction. Pine needles were a small price to pay for what she had with Zack.

They were out of the woods now and halfway across the fields. Ahead of them the sloping roofs of Sherraby gleamed like tarnished silver in the pale light of the waning moon.

As they approached the back door, it opened and the Ripper dashed out. Behind him, silhouetted against the light, stood Olivia wearing a scarlet robe. Her hand flew to her mouth. But as they drew closer, and her gaze lit on the pine needles and remnants of moss, she shook her head and started to laugh.

'Oh, Emma,' she gasped. 'Oh, Emma. Congratulations. You look like a pair of hedgehogs. Didn't I say nothing could keep you down?'

'Yes,' said Emma. 'You did. But I said, "Except Zack." And he did.'

The three of them were chuckling uncontrollably as they went into the house, and the Ripper took advantage of their inattention to slip into Mrs Leigh's pantry and eat a roll of waxed paper, a packet of tea and two currant buns.

CHAPTER 12

Simon came home late on Friday night. Olivia was in bed, but she heard the Ripper's squeals of delight, followed by the sound of a door closing and drawers being opened and shut. Then the faint creak of springs as Simon climbed into the ancestral four-poster.

After that Olivia lay awake remembering how firm and warm his body had felt sprawled beside hers, how soft his breath on her cheek. If the wall weren't there, she could touch him . . .

This was hopeless. Quite hopeless. Sighing, she gave up trying to sleep and sat up. She switched on her bedside lamp and picked up the P.D. James mystery she had been reading for over two weeks. It was taking her longer than usual because her mind wouldn't concentrate on the problems faced by Adam Dalgleish and his latest list of suspects. She had too many problems of her own. No, that wasn't true. She had one problem. And his name was Simon Sebastian.

If only she could be half as happy with Simon as Emma was with Zack . . .

The two of them had left Sherraby for London the day before. There had been so much unused electricity sparking impatiently between them that Olivia had laughingly told them to be careful not to set the bed on fire.

'What bed?' Zack scoffed. 'We'll be doing all right if we make it through the door of my flat.'

'Hmm.' Olivia watched him wrestle Emma's five suitcases and his hold-all into the small luggage space of his late model Porsche. 'I'll have to remember to keep an eye on the headlines. I can see it all now. "Indecent Exposure in Hallway of Exclusive London Flats. Riot on Lift as Tenants Stampede for Best View." '

'Fool,' Emma said amiably. She bounced on to the seat beside Zack and slammed the door.

Olivia, returning Emma's frantic waves as the car sped down the driveway, brushed a tear from her eye and blew her nose. They were so sure of their new found love, and of each other. She remembered, vaguely, what it felt like to be so hopelessly, happily in love. Of course she and Simon would never feel like that. But, oh, if only they could be friends . . .

Simon's bedsprings creaked insistently, and Olivia laid down her book and gave up. Maybe tomorrow she would care enough to finish it.

But tomorrow, when she went downstairs, Simon had already left the house with Jamie, and Olivia discovered she was too tired to care much about anything. When they didn't return for lunch, she hung around the kitchen for a while, helping to load the dishes and getting in Mrs Leigh's way until the long-suffering cook said, 'Get on with you now, Mrs Simon,' and chased her out.

Eventually Olivia drifted back to bed.

Two hours later, after a fitful sleep, she was standing in front of her washbasin splashing cold water over a face that seemed to have grown longer and paler overnight, when she heard a childish shriek from the bottom of the stairs.

'Rip!' Jamie screamed. 'Rip, come back. That's *my* plane. You can't have it. Hey! Gimme that . . .'

Olivia dried her face hastily, tugged on trousers and a red sweater, and sped in the direction of the commotion. When she reached the hallway she heard the scritch-scratch of canine paws on wooden flooring and caught just a glimpse of the tail of an animated painbrush with something in its mouth disappearing rapidly down a corridor with a still shrieking Jamie in hot pursuit.

Olivia hurried after the noise, and was just in time to see the Ripper, followed by Jamie, hurtle through the door of Simon's study.

Oh, dear. Simon wasn't going to be pleased at this invasion of his domain. But Jamie was *her* son. She couldn't just sneak away and leave her husband to deal with the problem. Whatever it was.

She advanced cautiously through the door in the wake of the two noisy miscreants.

The first thing to register was Simon's absence. He wasn't at his desk. Olivia closed her eyes in relief. The second, that his orderly study was no longer orderly. Papers were scattered across his desk, the filing cabinet was open, several folders had been knocked to the floor and the wastepaper basket lay on its side with its contents spread over the rug.

'Jamie!' Olivia gasped. 'Did you do this?'

'No.' Jamie pointed at Rip, who was lying on his back in a corner beneath the window chewing pensively on a yellowing sheet of paper. 'Rip did. I think he was cross 'cos he couldn't eat the post. He jumped right into that – that drawer . . .' He pointed at the filing cabinet. 'And then on to Simon's desk. It's a cosmic mess, isn't it?'

Cosmic wasn't what Olivia would have called it. And she had yet to meet a dog who could open a filing cabinet. She pointed this out to Jamie.

'Oh,' said Jamie. 'Rip didn't do *that.* Simon did. I saw him. He was clearing out old stuff he didn't need. But when he got to this one part he stopped and said he'd finish it later because he was going for a ride. I wanted to go with him, but he said, "not this time".' Jamie looked aggrieved.

'That doesn't explain what you and Rip are doing in Simon's study – apart from turning it into a shambles,' Olivia said sternly.

'Is a shambles the same as a mess?' asked Jamie with interest.

'Yes.' Olivia gritted her teeth. 'Jamie, what is this all about? This is *Simon's* study –'

'I know, but he gave me some paper to make airplanes. An' Rip stole it, so I chased him and he ran in here and started jumping on everything. Like he was Batdog. It was –'

'I know,' sighed Olivia. 'It was cosmic.' She began taking a mental inventory of the devastation, and was trying to decide whether she ought to make an effort to tidy it up herself or leave Simon to put everything back where it belonged, when she heard a crunching sound from the corner by the window.

'What's Rip eating now?' she asked. 'I hope it's not something important.'

'No,' said Jamie with a shrug. 'I thought it was my plane, but it wasn't.'

Ominous. Olivia went over to the Ripper and removed the ball of chewed paper from his mouth. When she smoothed it out, she saw that it seemed to be a page from some kind of report.

'Where did he get this?' she asked.

'Don't know.' Jamie wasn't interested. 'Come on, Rip. Mrs Leigh said she was making biscuits. Chocolate ones. 'Spect they'll be ready by now.'

The Ripper thumped his tail, cast a reproachful look at Olivia, and padded after Jamie in pursuit of food.

Olivia spread the tattered page on Simon's desk.

Perhaps it wasn't important. The print was a little faint, but that might be because she had left her reading glasses upstairs. Or perhaps it was an early draft of the government report Simon was still working on at odd moments. The one he had asked her to check.

She started to read. It wasn't the report, but – Olivia rubbed her eyes and started again.

No. No, it couldn't be. She didn't see well without her glasses, but surely there had to be some mistake. She lifted the paper off the desk and held it up so that it was closer to the light.

There was no mistake.

The report was about a Miss Sylvia Leander who was bringing a paternity suit on behalf of Simone Leander, aged two.

Olivia went on reading, unaware of her surroundings, unaware of anything now except the shocking words in front of her and the terrible pounding in her head.

It wasn't a report she was reading at all, but part of a letter. From a firm of solicitors, informing one Simon Sebastian that Sylvia Leander would be willing to accept a lump payment in return for keeping the case out of court.

At that point the page came to an end, breaking off in the middle of a sentence.

Olivia stared down at the crumpled paper. The grainy type seemed to dance in front of her eyes.

She glanced numbly at the top of the page, and saw the number two followed by a date.

The letter was almost nine years old.

She shut her eyes, but nothing changed so she opened them again. The words were the same, brutal in their simplicity.

Eleven years ago Sylvia had given birth to Simon's child. Nearly three years later she had asked him for support.

But – but only a few weeks ago Simon had married *her*, Olivia, because he wanted a legitimate heir. She pressed a hand to her throbbing head. Why, then, had he not married Sylvia all those years ago? Sylvia, with whom he swore he'd never shared a bed? Another lie? It had to be. The pain in her head spread to her chest. She drew a long draught of air into her lungs.

Why? Why had Simon not told her the truth? She had always known he was holding something back. But it made no sense. There was nothing in Sherraby's entailment to stipulate that Simon's heir had to be a male. Unless . . .

She swallowed. Her mouth felt as if it were filled with sand, and the pain in her chest was getting worse.

Unless, of course, Simone was *not* Simon's daughter. But the courts had been involved. Sylvia wouldn't have sued unless she had a case. Would she?

Outside the window, cold drizzle fell relentlessly over the vine, obscuring Olivia's view of the gardens. She shivered, and wrapped her arms tightly around her chest. What was she doing here, reading something so obviously not intended for her eyes?

Mindlessly, barely aware of what she was doing, she folded the paper in half, pressed it with her thumb, then opened it again.

How could he? How could Simon, her husband, have fathered a child, and then tried to escape all responsibility?

Were all men like that? Even Simon? Certainly Dan had let her down, disappointed her – but she had hoped and believed Simon would be different. He *should* have been different.

As Olivia sat glaring without really seeing it at the fatal page, she heard Jamie's excited laugh coming from somewhere down the hall. Jamie. Her son. The child she had married Simon to protect. She gripped her hands around her elbows and began to shake, as hopeless desolation turned into a blinding, all-consuming rage.

How dared Simon hide the truth from her, his lawfully wedded wife? How dared he add his personal brand to the scars already scored into her heart?

It wasn't until she realized she was, quite literally, grinding her teeth that Olivia unclasped her arms to slam both fists down hard on Simon's green blotter. A stapler and a jar of paper clips joined the rest of the debris on the floor.

The noise of the crash muffled the sound of the door opening behind her.

'So, Olivia. Reading my correspondence?' a deep voice enquired. 'A classic case of the pot accusing the kettle, don't you think?'

Olivia stiffened. She hadn't heard him come in, but she would have felt Simon's presence even if he hadn't spoken in that terse, biting voice that only served to raise her hackles further. And perhaps it *was* a case of the pot accusing the kettle. She couldn't seem to care.

Olivia swivelled the chair slowly around.

Simon was standing in the middle of the floor with his head lowered and his arms hanging loosely at his sides. Olivia guessed that the condition of his study was only just starting to register.

She watched as initial shock was followed almost immediately by disbelief, and then an anger that showed itself in the quick narrowing of his eyes.

'Olivia,' he said, with a casualness that didn't deceive her for a second, 'What do you think you're doing in *my* study looking as frustrated as the Ripper balked of the morning post – and surrounded by what looks like the aftermath of a stampede of raging turkeys?'

Incredibly, Olivia felt her indignation recede, and she had to conquer an impulse to burst into hysterical laughter. Simon often had that effect. But she mustn't laugh. If she did she would only start to cry. She *had* to hold on to anger. It was her only defence against a pain she didn't even begin to understand. All she knew was that the sight of Simon, standing there all mocking and sarcastic, was like a hot needle plunged into her heart.

She reached behind her for the incriminating page, and Simon frowned. He *was* right about the pot and the kettle. Which was strange, because all at once it didn't seem to matter any more that he'd read her diary. It did matter that he hadn't told her about his child. If the letter told the truth.

'Simon,' she said, 'Is it true?'

'Is what true?' He didn't even blink.

'That you have a daughter.' She tried to control the quaver in a voice that didn't sound remotely like her own.

Simon didn't reply – and she couldn't maintain her anger after all. Not when he looked at her as if she were something unpleasant the Ripper had dug up in the the woods and brought home to lay at his master's feet. It was a look that killed anger, turned it to despair. Because behind it there was something else, something raw and frightening that made her want to hide her face.

'Do *you* think it's true?' Simon asked at last. He buried his hands in his pockets.

'What? How can I tell? Simon . . .' Olivia broke off. Couldn't he be straight with her even now?

He shrugged. 'You don't usually have trouble making up your mind. But if you had to search for that letter, was it necessary to turn my study into a cross between a tip and one of the Ripper's archeological digs.'

'Oh!' cried Olivia. 'How could you? Surely you don't think I –'

'I don't know what to think. Unless this is your warped idea of revenge for imagined wrongs.' He turned, very deliberately, and shut the door. 'Although I admit that does seem out of character.'

'Does it? Then perhaps you don't know me as well as you'd like to think. At the moment the idea of throwing things has a lot of appeal.' She met the challenge in his eye with a furious challenge of her own.

Instead of answering, Simon sauntered across to the window and hitched his hip on the sill.

'Olivia,' he said, 'if you don't have a good explanation for all this . . .' He gestured at the devastated study, 'So help me, you're going to wish you had.'

Olivia eyed him warily. He was strumming his fingers on his thigh. And she knew it wasn't the mess in his study that was responsible for the friction that crackled between them like faulty wiring. Yet no matter what he said, she wasn't physically afraid of Simon. She never would be.

'I hope you're not threatening me,' she said.

'So do I.' He shifted his hip to a more stable position. 'Perhaps you'd care to start by telling me what this is all about.' He waved at the mess on the floor. 'If there was something you needed, you had only to ask.'

'Oh! But I wasn't . . .' She stopped. There hadn't been anything she needed. But a while back she had asked him a question. A critical question, which he hadn't answered.

All at once the impact of the letter hit her with redoubled force.

Sylvia. Simone. The demand for money.

'Yes?' Simon's harsh voice broke into her thoughts. 'You were saying?'

Olivia closed her eyes so she needn't look at him sitting there all hard and commanding – as if *she* were the one who had committed the unforgivable crime.

'I didn't do this to your study,' she said, with a steadiness that surprised her. 'It was the Ripper. But that's not what's important at the moment. What matters is why you didn't tell me about Simone –'

'I'll be the judge of what matters,' he interrupted.

'What?' Olivia paused, seeking the right words to tell him what she thought of such inexcusable arrogance. But as she hesitated, their eyes met, and she saw that there was more than arrogance in the austere line of Simons's lips. His rigidly squared jaw betrayed a barely contained tension that she guessed went far deeper than exasperation at what had happened to his study. Something was missing, some critical piece of a puzzle she would have to solve if ever she hoped to understand her husband.

Rain pelted against the window at Simon's back, and Olivia heard the faint chiming of the clock in the hall. It was getting late. Night would soon be upon them. She tried again.

'Simon, don't shut me out. Please. Tell me the truth. *Is* Simone your daughter?'

There was no doubt she had touched him. This time he didn't turn the question back on her. She heard the indrawn rasp of his breath, saw the white lines deepen around his mouth and his fingers flex and tighten into fists. Was he angry? Or was he fighting, as he so often did, to hide from her the true nature of his feelings.

'Simon?' Unthinkingly, wanting somehow to ease pressures she felt but only dimly understood, Olivia held out her hand. She had asked him for the truth. God knew, she had a right to it. But in this moment all that mattered was to breach the wall he had built to keep her out.

He didn't take her outstretched hand. Instead he stood up and turned his back on her. 'I have never shut you out, Olivia. Now you tell me. *Is* that little girl my daughter?'

When she didn't answer at once, he swung round again, so fast that Olivia sprang to her feet, instinctively seeking to defend herself.

'I don't know,' she said, grasping the back of the chair and glancing at the door. 'I suppose, if you won't answer me, she must be.'

Simon sat back on the window-sill. 'There you have it, then,' he drawled, removing a length of bristly brown hair from his sleeve.

'Simon! Please, if you tell me she isn't yours, I'll believe you.'

Simon said nothing.

Olivia tightened her grip on the chair.

If only she could take him by the shoulders and shake him. How she hated that derisive curl on his lips, that taunting blue glitter in his eyes. Why couldn't he look at her as he had done when they first met, with laughter, teasing provocation, and . . .?

She staggered. Why was the room spinning around her like a ferris wheel gone mad? Why did she feel as if her knees had turned to water just because Simon wouldn't laugh with her any more?

There had to be something else, some emotion more lasting than laughter . . .

Oh. No. It couldn't be. She stared at her husband in frozen consternation. She had only married him for Jamie's sake . . .

Hadn't she?

When his features began to blur, Olivia forced herself to look away, and after a while her anguished gaze came to rest on a picture above the filing cabinet. It was of a big man with eyes just like Simon's. An ancestor probably. He had his hand on the shoulder of a seated woman holding a baby. All three of them had the contented smiles of a family secure in their world and with each other. If only she and Simon . . .

It hit her then, like a comet falling out of the sky.

She was in love with Simon. Had been almost from the beginning.

And it had taken this disastrous confrontation to make her see it.

Slowly, without thought, she sank down at the desk again and dropped her head in her hands.

That was why she had accepted his outrageous proposal, why his deception over the diary had hurt so much. It wouldn't have mattered if he'd loved her. As she loved him. Oh, how could she ever have thought otherwise?

Olivia lifted her head. Simon, with the grey sky as background, was a sculpture in bronze against the window. A sculpture with burning blue eyes that were pinned on her with a look she couldn't fathom. Olivia put her hands on the desk and staggered to her feet.

'Simon,' she whispered, 'it's all right. You needn't tell me anything unless you want to. But please –'

'You're right,' he said. 'I needn't tell you anything.' He folded his arms as Olivia moved towards him.

When she was close enough, she reached up to touch his face.

He caught her wrists and held them at her sides. 'No,' he said. 'You're a charming distraction, my dear. But I can do without that kind of distraction just now. Olivia, it's time you and I had a serious talk.'

'About what?' she asked, beseeching him with her eyes. He looked so stern and unapproachable that she didn't think talking would be possible. Tomorrow maybe. But not now.

Simon said, 'About how we're going to arrange our lives so that neither of us is unduly inconvenienced.'

Dear heaven! What did he mean? Was he talking about ending their marriage? Now, when she knew she loved him?

But Simon had never wanted love. He despised – what had he called it? Stardust and dreams.

She took a deep breath. If she didn't fight for her dreams now, dust was all they would be.

'Simon,' she began, 'I . . .'

She couldn't say it. Couldn't say, 'I love you,' to a man who was looking at her as if she were no more to him than a mistake he had made in a moment of inattention – one he would have to rectify as soon as it was practical.

'I trust you,' she murmured in the end.

It wasn't what she'd meant to say. But it was the truth. She would always trust Simon. She knew that now, as surely as she knew that it was raining and that he had not rejected his own child.

She tried to break free of his grip, wanting to hold him, wanting in some way to convey to him the depth of her love and trust. But he wouldn't let her go. Instead he took her by the elbow, turned her around, and urged her politely but firmly towards the door.

'No,' he said, pulling it open. 'You don't trust me. You never have. Although I've no doubt you find it convenient to be my wife.' He put her firmly out into the corridor. 'We'll postpone our talk, shall we, until both of us feel calmer?'

Olivia gazed up at him as her dream world splintered around her. He couldn't mean it. He couldn't just dismiss her like that. 'That's not true,' she cried. 'I don't find it convenient. But it's more than that. Much more . . .

'No doubt,' Simon said – and closed the door in her face.

It was solid oak with a brass doorknob. Behind it Simon was as inaccessible to her as the stars.

Shock mingled with pain as she leaned against it. And along with the pain came anger. It was anger that in the end gave her the strength to move.

Her headache was getting worse. Putting both hands over her face, Olivia stumbled along the corridor, for the moment intent only on reaching the sanctuary of her room.

She didn't get far. As she entered the hall, she smelled the fresh scent of sandalwood aftershave. An instant later her face slammed up against something cool, smooth and immovable. She started back, opened her eyes wide, and saw that she had connected with a black leather jacket.

She had last seen that particular jacket on the day of her wedding, when it had been accompanied by a motorcycle and occupied by . . .

'Gerald!' Olivia gasped. 'I'm sorry. I didn't . . .' She stopped, as it occurred to her in a dreamlike way that she was apologizing to a black leather jacket, albeit a familiar one, that had no business in the manor's main hall.

'You didn't see me,' the jacket finished for her. 'I'm not surprised, the way you came charging out of there. What's the panic? Ripper mistake you for the afternoon post? Or has Simon turned homicidal at last?'

Olivia caught her breath, and looked up to meet a pair of gleaming, Casanova-type eyes with long, seductively drooping lashes. Not a face easily forgotten.

'Gerald,' she groaned. 'What are you doing here?' She seemed to say that a lot to Simon's cousins.

'Visiting my beloved cousin, of course.' Gerald's reply came with a grin calculated to charm. 'Is he at home.'

'Yes,' said Olivia, who had never been charmed by overworked grins, and just wanted to get away as quickly as she could. 'Yes, he's home. He's in his study.'

'Good.' Gerald did something with his eyes that she supposed was meant to be sexy. But he made no effort to move away.

Olivia started to edge past him. 'Simon's in his study,' she repeated.

Gerald caught her arm. 'Oh, but I'd much rather talk to you,' he announced with a leer.

Olivia didn't see why, and said so.

Gerald got busy with his eyebrows. 'You're much prettier than Simon, for one thing. And I'd like to get to know you. My pious cousin isn't the easiest man to live with, is he? I'll bet you could use a friend to talk to. Someone who really wants to understand you.' He gave her a smile that was all silk and sympathy.

The only effect it had on Olivia was to make her feel nauseous. She was already dizzy from her encounter with Simon.

She put a hand behind her back to brace herself against a wall that wasn't there. When she stumbled, Gerald promptly – too promptly – encircled her waist with both black leather arms.

Olivia closed her eyes, and at once the hall and the ancestors stopped spinning like out-of-control tops. 'I have all the friends I want,' she said stiffly. 'And Simon is *not* hard to live with.' He wasn't, either. He was polite, considerate – and unbearably remote. But she couldn't claim he was hard to live with.

'Ah,' exclaimed Gerald. 'There speaks the loyal little wife. You don't know much about him yet, do you?'

No. No, she didn't. She had found that out with a vengeance only today. But it didn't matter. She loved Simon, and even though he had flatly rejected her, she couldn't, *wouldn't* talk about her husband to this leather-clad playboy who seemed hell-bent on stirring up trouble.

'I knew him well enough to marry him. Surely that's all that counts?' she said. 'And you can let go of me now, if you don't mind. I'm quite capable of standing on my own feet.'

'It should be all that counts,' Gerald said cryptically. He ignored her request to let her go.

'What are you trying to suggest?' Olivia spoke frostily. She had never dealt well with innuendoes and mischief-making hints.

Gerald nodded at the door of the small cloakroom off the hall. 'Let's talk in there – where we won't be disturbed.' He gave her a double dose of the smile.

'No,' she said, now acutely and unpleasantly conscious of his octopus-like grip. 'I am not going to hide my head in a pile of coats and dirty boots while you tell me lies about my husband. Now please let go of me.'

Gerald's eyes narrowed. 'Well, well. Such a *very* devoted little wife. Don't tell me you're in love with my honourable relation?'

'That's none of your . . .' She stopped. The hall had started spinning again. What was the matter with her? There was no reason why anything Gerald had to say should make her faint. Only Victorian misses with tightly laced stays were supposed to do that.

'Ah,' Gerald said, when she didn't finish her sentence. 'So you *do* love my cousin. But even love can't be blind to his faults. Didn't he ever tell you about Sylvia?'

She hated the soft sneer in his voice, hated the way that, just for a moment, she actually needed the support of his clutching arms. But she managed to lift her chin and say quite calmly, 'Yes, of course he did.'

Gerald smiled again. She blinked, as it came to her that his lips were only inches from her own.

'Well,' he said, 'in that case you know he's no saint. So why should *you* try to be one?'

Olivia gaped at him. She was still gaping when it dawned on her that, with incredible presumption and obvious intent, his lips were advancing on her mouth. Once again she was overcome with nausea. But as she fought to control her heaving stomach, her traitorous body went limp in his arms.

Behind them the air seemed to move. Olivia felt it sweep across her back. A second later an icily composed voice said, 'What a touching *tableau*. I suppose I could suggest it be continued in private where there'd be less chance of entertaining passing staff. But I'm not going to. Gerald, take your paws off my wife. Olivia, perhaps you'd care to wait for me in the library.'

Gerald released her abruptly, and Olivia recovered her senses and swung around. Strangely, the feeling of nausea lessened as soon as she saw Simon, who, with a face like scarred granite, jerked his head at the door of the library.

'No,' she said. 'Simon, it's not what you think.'

'You have no idea what I think.' Simon's gaze was riveted on Gerald. 'Go on. I'll be with you in a minute.'

Oliva stared at his tight-lipped profile and swallowed a gulp. But she made no effort to follow his direction. Briefly she considered trying to force him to listen. But Simon wasn't an easy man to force. And she could see he was in no mood to pay attention to the wife he had just ejected from his study and immediately afterwards found drooping in another man's arms.

But surely even Simon couldn't think . . .

Her thoughts skidded to a halt. Simon had said it first. She had no idea what he might think. And just at this moment she didn't care.

Without another word to either man, she spun on her heel and ran down the passage to the kitchen. Mrs Leigh would be resting in her room now, Jamie in the playroom with Annie. But at least the kitchen would be warm. She felt a great need for warmth.

Behind her, as she stumbled along the uneven floor, she heard Gerald laugh and say, 'Just a little bit of fun, Si. No harm intended.'

She didn't hear what Simon said.

Olivia came to a halt beside the kitchen table, wondering why the big, comfortable room was all of a sudden unfamiliar. The smell of chocolate biscuits hung in the air, and something was bubbling in the oven. She felt lost, giddy, as if she had been scooped up and dumped on another planet.

Bewildered, she stood in the centre of the floor and stared at the scrubbed red countertops. Everything was so clean, so organized. Unlike the chaos in her mind.

Simon hadn't come after her. Was he busy dealing with Gerald? Or had he decided he didn't care enough?

Haltingly, Olivia crossed the room. There was an old black mac hanging on a peg beside the door. She took it down and put in on.

The sky was pewter-grey now, the rain relentless. But the air outside would be clear, the wind bracing. Perhaps, out there in the cold she would get her thoughts into some kind of order. Perhaps, away from the manor and her husband, she would be capable of deciding what to do. For Jamie, for herself – and for Simon.

Simon *couldn't* think that she and Gerald . . .?

Olivia lifted her chin. He could think what he liked. *She* knew the truth. And if he could believe that of her, he'd believe anything. Which meant . . . She took a deep, painful breath. Which meant that whatever might once have been between them was over. For good.

Slowly, as if it weighed a ton, she dragged the hood of the black mac up and over her head and stepped out into a swirling grey curtain of rain.

Wind hit her in the face, making her blink. She drew a long breath of wet, cold air and forced herself to walk on, down the path, through the swaying lime trees to the gates at the end of the driveway, then along the road. When she reached the first bend, she paused.

The fields, more hazy-grey now than green, stretched ahead of her to the edge of the woods. On an impulse born out of pain and the memory of a brighter, happier day, she climbed the fence. The black mac flapped crazily in the wind as she made her way up towards the trees.

It was dark in the woods despite the fact that most of the evergreens were bare. The soft ground was carpeted with pine needles and leaves, and it wasn't as wet as it had been in the open fields. Olivia shivered violently and her stomach gave an unwelcome lurch as she came to the glade where she had first set eyes on Simon.

It looked different.

What was she doing here? Was she mad? The moss was soggy now, not soft like velvet. And the sky was growing dark. Soon night would fall.

No tall man with a small dog would appear today to change her life forever. Besides, it was already changed. Irrevocably.

Emma had once told her that when she was a child she had believed the Sherraby Woods were magic woods. And perhaps they had been for her. But there was no magic here tonight. Only the coming darkness and the biting chill of endless rain.

Olivia shook her head, brushed a strand of damp hair off her cheek and turned around. Running could solve nothing. She must return to the manor, face Simon, and do whatever needed to be done. At whatever cost.

Olivia closed her eyes, rejecting the momentary solace of tears. She knew what Simon would want done – had known from the moment he turned her out of his study back there in a world where the wind wasn't freezing on her face and the rain was only in her mind.

She came to the edge of the woods, but now she couldn't see clearly. In front of her the white bark of a birch tree shimmered and turned black. She staggered, and her foot in its flat black shoe caught on a tree root. She put out her hand to catch a branch, but it seemed to move, and she encountered only air.

With a cry that was lost on the wind, she fell on her face in a mixture of mud and wet leaves.

Her last thought before she lost consciousness was that if she didn't get up and get herself out of here before she died of exposure, she might never see Simon, or Jamie, again.

Jamie, her little blond boy, was impatiently waiting for Christmas. She couldn't, *wouldn't* spoil it for him. Which left her no choice. She must get up. She had to get out of these damp woods before she became a part of them.

Closing her hand around a tuft of sodden grass, Olivia tried to shift herself on to her knees . . .

When she came to, a small dog with a tail like a brown paintbrush was worriedly licking at her face.

Simon, his mouth grimly set, closed the heavy door on Gerald's sullen face and turned back into the hall.

That hadn't taken long, once he'd resisted the impulse to go after his wife and haul her summarily back to face the music.

Gerald had been resentful and indignant to find himself standing on the steps of the manor with his cousin's hand twisted in the collar of his jacket. But it had been a simple enough matter to convince him that no portion of the manor's funds was going towards the payment of his latest gambling debts. He had shown no inclination to stay on after that.

Simon dusted off his hands and went in pursuit of Olivia, last seen heading for the kitchen.

'Olivia,' he snapped, shoving open the door, 'I believe I told you –'

He stopped. Olivia wasn't there. Neither was Mrs Leigh, although delectable smells from the oven gave tantalizing hints of gastronomic delights to come.

All right, then. So much the better. He could use some time to cool down. In more ways than one.

Simon was on the point of returning to his study when he heard a familiar scratching at the back door.

The Ripper, of course, anxious to escape from the rain. Simon let him in, along with a gale-force gust of wind.

'Got yourself soaked, did you, boy?' He bent down to scratch the dog's ear, then straightened as Rip pulled away from him to dart back to the door.

'Don't be an idiot,' Simon said. 'It's pouring out there.'

The Ripper barked, turned in a circle, and made another dash for the door. When his master didn't respond, he gave a little growl and took Simon's trouser leg in his mouth.

'What the hell?' Simon exclaimed, as Rip gave the cloth a little tug.

Rip tugged again.

Simon frowned down at him. 'I'm beginning to get a message,' he muttered. 'You want me to follow you? Outside?'

The Ripper let go, barked, and hurried back towards the door.

'Olivia?' Simon asked. 'Is that what you're telling me? She's out there?'

Rip whirled round three times and barked again.

Simon listened to the rain beating at the windows, and bent down to pat the Ripper's damp head. 'Right,' he said absently. 'Good dog.'

Could she be out there? Was it possible . . .?

Rip growled, and he made up his mind.

Seconds later he was in the cloakroom reaching for a waterproof jacket. It wasn't until he was halfway back across the hall that he paused again.

What if Olivia was merely skulking in her room? Perhaps all Rip wanted was a walk.

In the rain? Not likely. And Olivia wasn't a skulker. All the same he'd better make sure . . .

Damn. Simon grabbed the banister and tore up the stairs three steps at a time.

His wife's bedroom, which he entered without knocking, was as neat, uncluttered and maddeningly feminine as its owner. And it was empty.

'OK, Rip,' he said to the anxious dog scuttling at his heels, 'You win. Let's go.'

He couldn't risk pausing to search further. Nor could he afford to let himself imagine what might have happened out there in the worst damn night they'd had this winter. Happened to Olivia. His wife. Simon inhaled deeply, and shut her bedroom door behind him with a snap.

Two minutes later, after shoving a torch into his pocket, he was following an agitated Ripper out into the storm.

He had no trouble keeping up with the little dog as Rip ran across the fields towards the trees, doubling back every now and then to make sure his master was following. But after a while Simon began to be convinced he was on a wild-goose chase. Or a tame dog chase, he thought without humour.

Why on earth would Olivia, obstinate, practical, sensible mother-of-one, who knew exactly on which side her bread was buttered, go wandering in the woods on an evening like this? Surely she, of all people, would have the sense to be scared? Or was he deluding himself?

He had read her damn diary, but that didn't necessarily mean he knew her.

Simon scowled into the darkness. If he did find her out here, and if she wasn't scared already, she would be by the time he was through with her. Of all the senseless, idiotic things to do . . .

No. Wait a moment. He shook back the wet hair plastered to his forehead. What was he thinking of? Olivia wasn't the fool in this insane drama. He was, for taking Rip's antics to heart.

His jaw clenched as a blast of rain hit him in the face. The Ripper yelped and disappeared into the woods.

Simon shrugged and strode after him.

He had only taken a few steps when his foot connected with something lying on the path. A dead branch, probably? He shone his torch at the ground. And saw that the dark bulk crouched at his feet was neither dead nor a branch.

It was a live body with a white, muddy face and pain-filled eyes.

'Olivia?' he said. 'Olivia? Dear God! What the devil have you done to yourself?'

'I think I've broken my ankle,' she replied.

To his utter disbelief, she was smiling.

CHAPTER 13

Strong hands were smoothing the tangled hair back from her forehead. Olivia gave a small sigh of recognition. Simon. He had come for her. It was too dark to see much beyond the dim light thrown by his torch, but she would have known him even if he hadn't said a word. Only he had ever touched her with just that blend of gentleness and knowledge. When his arms went around her and he lifted her up against his chest, even the throbbing in her ankle became bearable.

'Simon,' she whispered. 'You found me. I tried to get up, but I couldn't. I must have passed out . . .'

'You have only yourself to blame for that,' Simon said. He swung round and, with a smug Ripper trotting at his feet, bore her in grim silence down the path.

Once clear of the trees, he pulled her hood up and turned her face towards his chest. But it wasn't until they reached the top field that he shifted her weight again and asked in a deceptively conversational voice,

'What the hell did you think you were doing coming out here on your own? Didn't you notice there's a storm going on?'

'I wanted to clear my head.'

'*Clear* it?' Simon exploded. 'If you ask me, you lost it. Olivia, how could you be such an idiot?' He bent his head to examine her face, then added roughly, 'What are you smiling at? That wasn't a compliment.'

Olivia heard his frustration and angry concern, felt the hard pressure of his chest against her ribcage, and the reassuring strength of his arms. 'I can't seem to stop,' she said simply.

Simon shook his hair out of his eyes, and a fine spray fell across her cheek, adding to the relentless assault of the rain. But she went on smiling.

'You are out of your mind,' he snapped. 'About as out of it as I was to marry you.'

'No,' said Olivia. But she didn't want to smile any more. 'Neither of us is out of our mind. And I think I know why you married me.'

'Do you? Well, it's more than I do.' Simon came to the fence at the bottom of the field, tipped her across his shoulder and climbed over it.

As he settled her back into his arms, a flash of lightning slashed the darkness ahead of them and they heard the first faint rumble of thunder in the air.

At once all Olivia's doubts came crashing back.

She had thought, in that moment when Simon had found her huddled on the ground, that the blast of shocked compassion in his voice had meant he loved her after all. That was why she had smiled at him with such joy. Why, briefly, she had dared to dream of a true and enduring bond growing between them, instead of this farce of a marriage they had now.

But Simon had spoken so roughly, with such brusque impatience, that she wasn't sure of anything any more.

'Perhaps I'm mistaken,' she said, in a voice so low he didn't hear it.

When she ventured a look at him again, he was frowning. She supposed she couldn't blame him for being angry. This was no night for walking in the woods by moonlight – especially as there wasn't a moon.

'Simon,' she whispered into the rain-slicked smoothness of his jacket. 'I'm sorry I caused you so much trouble –'

'We'll discuss it later,' he said. Ominously. 'After the doctor's had a chance to look you over.'

'I don't need a doctor.' Olivia's protest was more in response to his tone than to what he'd actually said. If she had broken her ankle, of course she would have to see a doctor.

'Don't be an imbecile.' Simon's reply was justifiably curt.

Olivia subsided against the comforting hardness of his chest. For the moment, silence seemed the better part of conversation. And she had been through too much today to muster much of an argument.

Ten minutes later she was lying on her familiar yellow bed and Simon was briskly unbuttoning her blouse.

'There's no need –' she began.

'There is. And don't worry, I'm not about to ravish you.' The muscles around his mouth tightened. 'For one thing, I don't think you're up to it. For another, as I've mentioned before, I like my women warm and welcoming. At the moment you're neither.'

Olivia longed to tell him it wasn't true. But for the moment it was. She was frozen. And her leg hurt too badly for her to welcome even Simon's touch. She winced as he eased her jeans down over her hips, gasped when they reached her ankles, and gave a groan of relief when they finally hit the floor.

'Panties next,' said Simon, his hands going to her waist.

'No! You can't –'

'They're wet. Like the rest of you. Come on.' She gasped again as he slipped the panties down, and this time it wasn't entirely a gasp of pain.

'Now then. Nightgown,' Simon snapped. 'Where is it?'

'In the top drawer, but –'

'Right.' He rose abruptly, yanked open the drawer and pulled out the red negligee she had worn on their honeymoon. She thought she heard him swear before he shoved it back and replaced it with a demure white cotton number. 'Here, this will do. No need to give Dr Marfleet palpitations.'

That startled a giggle out of her, but Simon scowled so ferociously as he slid the nightgown over her head that she stifled it at once. Since he was obviously more than a little out of temper, she nodded primly and didn't argue when, a few seconds later, he said he was off to organize some tea.

Olivia looked at her watch and saw that it was long past tea-time. Jamie must have been wondering where she'd got to.

'Jamie?' she said, the moment Simon reappeared bearing a tray set with china teapot, two delicate blue cups and a plate of Mrs Leigh's chocolate biscuits. 'Is he–?

'He's fine. Stuffed full of biscuits and playing snap with Annie. She says he's won every hand.'

'That's because she lets him. Annie spoils him.'

'Won't hurt him. He'll find out life's not all about winning soon enough.'

He sounded exceptionally grim. Olivia considered asking him if he was speaking personally, but before she had a chance to say anything there was a knock on the door, and Dr Marfleet bustled in.

'Got your call on my car phone,' explained the cherubic little doctor who always reminded Olivia of an elf. 'Came right over. Now then, Mrs Sebastian, what's all this about an ankle?'

'I think I broke it,' said Olivia, who was continually amazed at how quickly people seemed to respond to the manor's needs. No doctor had ever rushed to her side like this when she'd been plain Olivia Naismith.

Simon, muttered something that sounded like, 'Her own damn fault,' and went to glare out of the window at the storm.

Dr Marfleet glanced at him shrewdly but said nothing as he began a practised examination of his patient.

In the end it turned out the ankle was only sprained.

'Not badly,' the doctor assured her. 'But now that I'm here, I may as well give the rest of you a quick check-up.'

'Oh, there's no need –' Olivia began.

'I think there is,' the doctor said – and he proceeded to poke and prod and listen while Olivia stared balefully at the ceiling and Simon continued his inspection of the weather.

When he was through, Dr Marfleet put his head on one side and asked briskly, 'Any other symptoms, Mrs Sebastian?'

'Symptoms?' Olivia echoed. 'No, I –'

'She fainted,' Simon said from the window.

'Yes, but that was because I hit my head when I fell.'

Dr Marfleet examined her head. 'No bruises,' he said. 'First time it's happened? Any nausea, dizziness . . .'

'Well, I . . .' Come to think of it, she had felt dizzy a couple of times, and today, when Gerald had turned up, she'd felt positively sick. 'I suppose I haven't been feeling quite myself,' she admitted grudgingly.

'Aha. Thought so. We'll run some tests to be sure. But if I'm not mistaken, there's another little Sebastian on the way.' He beamed at Olivia, who blinked at him and turned instinctively to Simon.

His back was rigid as a blackboard. Olivia and Dr Marfleet, waiting for his reaction, watched as he swung slowly round to face the room.

Olivia's heart sank like a rock. There was no joy in his eye, and his features were a mask from which all expression had been ruthlessly eliminated.

'Simon?' she said, afraid to express her elation in the face of his lack of response. 'Dr Marfleet says –'

'I heard what Dr Marfleet said. Thank you, Doctor. We both appreciate your help.' He smiled at the mystified little man, who had already risen to his feet, flicked only the barest glance at Olivia, and escorted the doctor courteously from the room.

Olivia leaned back against the pillows and closed her eyes.

Simon had barely looked at her. He hadn't even seemed pleased that she was soon to bear his child. Yet that was the reason he had married her. And today, when he had found her in the woods, she could have sworn his furious concern was based on more than a feeling of responsibility for her welfare.

Had she been totally mistaken, then? She ran the back of her hand across her forehead. It was damp, although she didn't feel overheated. Didn't Simon care for her at all? Did he regret his marriage in spite of the fact that it was now almost certain to give him exactly what he had told her he wanted – an heir to the Sebastian estates?

She turned on her side and stared, dry-eyed, at the reflection of the light in the windows. Would her life with Simon always be like this, a pale reflection of what might have been?

As if in answer, the wind howled through the chimneys, and a cascade of rain beat against the glass. Olivia thought of Emma, safe and warm in the arms of her mate. When *her* turn came to announce the start of a new life, it was certain Zack wouldn't say, 'Thank you, Doctor,' and leave the room.

Simon returned a few minutes later, and found Olivia lying very still in the bed gazing stonily up at the ceiling. Her face was as white as the pillowcase supporting her head. 'Olivia, what is it?' he said. 'Are you still cold?'

She nodded. Yes, she was cold. All the way through to her heart.

Simon sat down on the edge of the bed and poured a cup of the now tepid tea.

'Drink,' he ordered, putting an arm behind her shoulders to hold her up.

Olivia drank dutifully. The tea did have a warming effect. When she'd finished, Simon laid the cup down, removed his arm, and pulled the yellow quilt up to her neck.

'Now,' he said. 'We talk.'

Olivia twisted to look at him. He had just been told he was to be a father. But he sounded so brisk and businesslike. As if – as if it *was* just a matter of business. Or as if she was about to add a new horse to his stables.

She lowered her eyes. Perhaps that was all their child meant to him. The satisfactory conclusion of a deal. What did she really know of her husband's heart?

When she found herself unable to think of a thing to say, he said, 'Well?'

'Well?' she repeated. 'Simon, I don't understand . . .'

He sighed, and gave her a smile so aloof that a shiver of apprehension trembled down her spine. 'It appears you've fulfilled your half of the bargain,' he observed.

'Bargain? Is that what you call our baby? A bargain?' How could he? How dared he? Olivia raised her hand to strike back, not caring where she hit, wanting only to hurt Simon any way she could. To hurt him as he was hurting her. But before her blow could find a mark, he had risen to his feet. When she struck out at whatever part of him she could reach, he bent down and seized both her wrists.

Olivia opened her mouth to shout at him to let her go – but just for an instant, before he turned away, she saw something in his face that gave her pause.

It was as if a rock had briefly cracked open to expose seams and facets normally invisible. There was strength there, certainly. The strength which he had always drawn on in order to keep his feelings to himself. But along with the strength she saw pain, doubt – and the profound cynicism that had driven him to marry a woman he didn't love.

'Simon,' she said, meeting his clouded gaze with a look that was both demanding and pleading. 'Tell me the truth. Is there any chance at all for our marriage?'

Hearing the calmer note in her voice, Simon released her. But instead of lowering himself back on to the bed he went to lean against the door. It was almost a minute before he answered her, and then it was only to say obliquely, 'We're going to be parents, Olivia.'

'Is that so bad?' she asked, her joy and hope crushed by an awful foreboding. She held out a hand, willing him back to her side.

He stared at it as if it held a dagger.

'No,' he said, all gravel and steel now. 'It's not so bad. I want this child. I believe you'll be a good mother. But I'm too old for games, Olivia. Too old to believe in youthful illusions any longer. I don't know what you expect of me, but I know I expect you to fulfil your role as agreed. I won't put up with cheating or –'

'Simon,' she said, wishing her ankle were strong enough to stand on so that she could get up and wipe that line of dictatorial arrogance from his mouth, 'I have never, and I will never cheat on you, but if you think – oh.' Her hand went to her mouth. The flash of blue fire in his eyes was so daunting that she expected to feel it scorch her skin. 'Simon. Surely you *don't* think –'

'Think what?' he drawled, all cold and mocking again. 'That you have designs on my indigent cousin Gerald? Bad choice, my dear.' Very deliberately, he unfastened a cuff of his white shirt and began to roll up his sleeve.

'Simon! How dare . . .?' With an effort, she choked back the rest of her indignant retort. Anger would, after all, accomplish nothing. She made herself carry on in a level voice, 'You don't really believe that, do you?'

'No,' he admitted. 'The thought did cross my mind when I saw you in his arms. But I thought it unlikely. Or should I say I credited you with more taste?'

How could he? How could he stand there, all remote and sexy and sarcastic, and even suggest the *possibility* . . .?

'Simon,' she said through her teeth. 'You may not have chosen to notice it, but I am your wife.'

'Yes,' said Simon. 'That's what I told Gerald. Before I showed him the door.'

Was there just the faintest trace of humour in his voice? Olivia frowned, confused and unsure of herself again. And even more unsure of Simon. 'I still don't understand,' she said finally.

'Don't you?' There was a heartbreaking emptiness in his eyes now, a kind of baffled frustration that, contrarily in view of the way he was behaving, made her want to cry. It also made her want to take him in her arms.

'Simon,' she said. 'If it's not Gerald, then what is it? I'm sorry, desperately sorry, that I read your letter, especially after – after –' She couldn't go on.

He finished the thought for her. 'After suggesting I was a combination of Peeping Tom and Machiavelli for reading your diary before I even knew who you were.'

Olivia winced. 'Yes. More or less,' she agreed.

'Mmm.' He unfastened the other cuff. 'Tell me – would you have told me you'd read that letter if I hadn't caught you at it?'

Olivia lowered her eyelids, folded a crease in her nightgown, then smoothed it out again. 'I don't know. I knew you hadn't meant me to see it. But – yes, sooner or later I would have had to ask.' She hesitated. There was something that needed to be said, something she could no longer escape. 'Simon, I was wrong. I'm sorry. I should have trusted you – trusted you not to use your knowledge of my diary to hurt me.'

He made a gesture that could have been negation and said, 'Why? I wasn't at all sure I trusted you when I found you reading my private papers.'

He sounded so harsh and uncaring that Olivia automatically drew back against the pillows. Her ankle was throbbing unbearably, making her bite her lip to keep from screaming at the pain. And at Simon, who seemed as far away from her as ever.

'How could you trust me?' she asked, in a strangled voice. 'I'd already proved that I didn't trust you.'

'Yes. That *is* what it's all about, isn't it,' he agreed. 'Trust. And since neither one of us seems able to trust the other, what do you suppose the future holds for our child?'

Olivia swallowed and started to form an answer. But before she could get a word out, before she even knew what she meant to say, the rain renewed its assault on the window with shattering force, and in the same instant the room was flooded with dazzling orange light.

She gasped as the brightness, glowing and electric, illuminated every corner, turning the yellow walls to gold and throwing Simon's bronzed head into fiery relief against the door.

The brightness was followed by a crack of thunder. But in the moment before it faded, as if she had been granted a vision, Olivia found the words she needed to save her marriage.

'Simon,' she said quietly. 'I love you. And although it's taken me far too long to see it, I swear to you I'd trust you with my life.'

Would he believe her? Would he care, even if he did? His eyes were filled with such bleak and deep-seated scepticism that she was terribly afraid her declaration had come too late.

'I love you, Simon,' she repeated. 'I think I always have. But I didn't know, couldn't believe . . . You see, after Dan, I didn't think I'd ever . . .' She stopped, unable to go on.

How could she explain to the stone-faced man lounging against the door how she had been so sure she would never love again that she hadn't recognized love when it came – not even when it hit her over the head and knocked her down?

Nor had she recognized that along with love must come trust.

As she lay there, struggling to find the right words, Olivia saw Simon pass a hand across his eyes. When he lowered it, his face wasn't closed any more. It was alive with a wild, almost savage elation. 'Olivia,' he said, 'so help me, I ought to murder you for the hell you've put me through. Is this another game, or do you mean it?'

'Yes,' she said. 'Yes, of course I do. It was never a game.'

His lips parted then, in the widest, whitest, most magnetically seductive grin she had ever seen. 'In that case, sweetheart,' he said, 'if you hadn't sprained your ankle, you wouldn't be sitting there much longer looking as soft and misleadingly innocent as a kitten. You'd be flat on your back making it up to me for all the nights I haven't been able to sleep for wanting you. Wanting you so damned badly it tore at my guts –'

Olivia, breathless and not quite able to believe he meant it, laughed brokenly and held out her arms. 'But you could have had me,' she groaned. 'I wasn't sleeping either. I wouldn't have turned you away.'

Simon smiled crookedly and, taking his time about it, moved across the room to fold her in his arms. 'I know,' he said. 'I always knew you would do what you thought I'd paid you for. But after that night in Paris I found I couldn't accept your – sacrifice. I discovered it wasn't enough. I think that was when it first began to dawn on me that I might be wrong about stardust and dreams.'

Olivia curled her hands in his hair, still afraid to believe, yet revelling in his closeness, in the glorious male scent of him and in the certain hope that somehow, incomprehensibly, everything was going to be all right.

Simon loved her. It was all that mattered, whether or not she understood.

'It was no sacrifice,' she said. 'And why wasn't it enough? It should have been. You told me that was what you wanted.'

'Yes. And you tried so hard to see I got it. In that sinfully seductive red negligee.' He smiled reminiscently. 'But I found out that night that I was caught in a trap of my own making. I'd married you because I thought you were safe, that you would give me what I wanted without expecting me to give you more than security and a roof for yourself and your son. Unfortunately it didn't work out that way.' He stroked his hand slowly down her spine. 'You won my heart right along with the roof. And how could I make love to you without betraying how I felt? Without leaving myself wholly vulnerable to a woman who would love me only out of duty? Who, because I had read her diary, seemed to think I was only about one step removed from a snake?'

Olivia wriggled guiltily. Simon dropped a hand over her hip. 'It seemed to me,' he went on, 'that the only way I could save my sanity was by keeping you at a distance and hoping that, by some miracle, you had already managed to conceive.' He pulled the quilt down and moved his hand to her stomach. 'Which you have, my darling. Thank you. Thank you, my darling wife. I don't know what else to say.'

His eyes were filled with such tender gratitude that Olivia didn't know whether she wanted to laugh or cry.

She did neither. Instead she rubbed her cheek lovingly against the roughness of his five o'clock shadow, thinking that never in her life had she been so at peace – with herself, and with the man she had so surprisingly come to love.

'And I *am* going to have your baby,' she said dreamily. 'Simon, do you think Jamie will be pleased? We could tell him at Christmas. As a kind of extra present.'

'I think,' said Simon, 'that Jamie would much prefer a guinea pig. Or a space station. Or anything that whistles, shrieks or makes noise. But yes, if we're careful how we break it to him, he'll be pleased.'

'Babies make noise,' said Olivia. But she knew Simon was right. He understood her son as only another male could. Oh, she *was* glad she'd had the sense to marry him, in spite of all her doubts and reservations.

'Just think,' she murmured, lifting her face up to his, 'if it hadn't been for my reading that letter, and you looking so – so *haunted* and then throwing me out so that I ran into Gerald, I might never have gone outside and fallen down in the storm. And you would never have come to find me and –'

'Olivia.' Simon placed two fingers across her lips. 'Shut up.'

Olivia shut. And as Simon turned her face up to kiss her breathless, once again the room was flooded with orange light.

'That's better,' Simon said when the job was completed to his satisfaction. 'How's your ankle?'

'I can't even feel it,' she said.

'Good. And now it's my turn to talk.'

'What about? Our baby?'

He shook his head. 'Soon. Olivia – I know you said you trusted me. But are you sure?'

'Of course.' She spoke without hesitation. 'Why would I say I did if it wasn't true?'

Simon pulled her head against his shoulder and splayed his fingers in her hair. 'We haven't always been honest with each other, sweetheart.'

Olivia frowned. 'No. You didn't believe I was being

honest back there in your study. Did you? When I said I trusted you just before you threw me out?'

'No.' His voice deepened. 'No, I didn't. I thought you were protecting your convenient role as Lady of the Manor. That you thought I was quite capable of deceiving you about Simone, of refusing to take responsibility for my own child, but that you would put up with me for the sake of that convenience. Which didn't do much for my ego. Or my temper. I confess, if I hadn't thrown you out in that moment I'd very likely have done you worse damage.'

'Oh, Simon. You wouldn't. And I didn't really believe you had deserted your own child. Not in my heart. But you wouldn't come right out and deny it –'

'Pride.' A corner of his lip slanted wryly. 'Sebastians have always had more than their share of – which is it? The fourth Deadly Sin? I thought you ought to know without my telling you. When you didn't – and how could you? – I was flaming angry. So I threw you to the wolves – or wolf, as it turned out. In the guise of my charming cousin Gerald.'

Olivia giggled. 'I don't want your cousin Gerald, Simon. I only want you.'

'So I should hope. And I promise you you'll have me from now on.' He put his knuckles under her chin and tipped her head back. 'Olivia, don't you even want an explanation?'

'Explanation?'

'About Sylvia. And Simone.'

'Oh, that. No, not really. Funny, it doesn't seem to matter any more.' She laughed disbelievingly and shook her head. 'Is *that* what love does to the brain?'

'No,' Simon said. 'I think that's what trust does to the brain. But I want to tell you anyway.'

'Not if it causes you pain,' Olivia said quickly. She thought of the look on Simon's face when she'd confronted him with her knowledge of his letter. 'I don't want to hurt you, Simon. Not ever again.'

'It doesn't cause me pain,' he said, smoothing away the small frown between her brows. 'It hasn't for some time.'

'I'm glad.'

He dropped a kiss on to her forehead. 'Of course I should have told you in the beginning. But it was over, I've spent most of my life learning to keep my mouth shut – and it happened a long time ago. Sylvia hasn't had the power to haunt me for years. But you have.'

'*I* have?'

'Oh, yes. Seeing you suspect me of the worst, knowing there was less chance for the two of us than ever was – a nightmare. In the end it was easier to lose my temper with you than deal with that.'

'You did a good job of it,' Olivia remarked.

'Of losing my temper? I did, didn't I?'

She was about to tell him that was nothing to be smug about when another crack of thunder rattled the room. It was further away now.

When the reverberations had rumbled into silence, Simon put his hands on her shoulders and said, 'That letter from Sylvia's solicitors came at me out of the blue over three years after we'd parted. I thought she had married her new boyfriend, but it turned out they were never married. He walked out on her soon after she had the baby and she had a pretty rough time of it for a while. That's why she came to me. I'd been crazy about her. For all she knew, I still was.' His smile was cynical. 'So she called me and said the baby was mine. Sylvia was no fool. She'd already given Simone the female version of my name – as some kind of insurance against the future, I suppose.'

'But you told me –'

'I know. I told you I'd never slept with her. Technically that wasn't quite true. I did spend a night with her once. She said she wanted to wait for marriage, and I was young enough, and besotted enough, to respect that. But she had a key to my flat, and one night she woke me up and practically fell into my bed. I thought she was a gift from the gods.'

Olivia nodded. She could well imagine that a lusty and youthful Simon wouldn't have paused to question such a gift.

His answering smile was wry, less cynical. 'But the gods were playing a joke on me,' he said. 'Sylvia was drunk. Dead drunk. I found out later she'd been out with her boyfriend. Suffice it to say, nothing happened. But Sylvia didn't choose to believe that when she came to in the morning and found herself in my bed. She was furious with me. Mostly, I think, because I'd seen her at her worst. And that, of course, was the end of our engagement.' He planted a kiss on Olivia's nose. 'I expect, deep down, I knew it was a lucky escape, that I was well out of it, but that wasn't the way I saw it at the time. Later, when Sylvia found herself in dire financial straits, I must have seemed a likely Golden Goose.'

'But Simone wasn't yours. So of course you refused to help her.' Olivia nodded understandingly.

'Simone certainly wasn't mine. But as a matter of record I did help Sylvia. On three separate occasions.' His blue gaze hardened, settled on the wall above her head. 'But when it dawned on me that I was expected to become a permanent source of income for a child I'd never seen, I told Sylvia to look for an alternative bank.'

'So she hired lawyers?' Olivia found it hard to believe.

'That's what they called themselves, yes.'

How bleak and derisive he sounded. 'So what happened,' Olivia asked.

'Oh, after the case had been dragged back and forth through the courts for some time, with nothing decided, Sylvia up and married one of her lawyers. They dropped the suit eventually when blood tests proved I couldn't be the father. And that put an end to the matter.' Simon picked up her hand and ran his thumb absently over her palm. She could see that his mind was still turned inward on the past. 'The odd thing was, I would have liked that little girl to be my own.'

'Oh, Simon.' Olivia found herself sniffing back tears. 'I can see why you didn't want to talk about it. Of course you wanted to forget.'

'I suppose I did.' He lifted her hand to his cheek. 'But it isn't in my nature to throw out legal papers. So I've kept them all these years just in case. I should have known that sooner or later the Ripper was bound to expose all. He always does.' He tried to suppress a grin and failed. 'I'm sorry, sweetheart.'

Olivia returned his grin with a softer, more seductive version.

The tail end of the thunderstorm grumbled away into the distance.

'Speaking of the Ripper,' she said, 'where is he?'

'Under your bed, I expect.' Simon tipped his head to one side. 'Ah, yes. I believe I do hear the familiar sound of crunching paper. I suppose you didn't happen to leave any useful bills lying about?'

'No,' said Olivia. 'Just the report you asked me to check. I finished it a week – oh! Simon!' She tried to leap up as a contented burp wafted up from under the bed.

Simon caught her arms and held her down.

'Don't even think it,' he said. 'I won't have you breaking your ankle in earnest.'

'But . . .'

'It's all right. I have several more copies on disk. Besides, I rather think we owe the Ripper a treat. If it hadn't been for him, you'd still be lying out there in the mud. And although mud can be quite fetching on the right face, I don't want to see it on the face I expect to see on my pillow in the morning.' He put a hand on her thigh and began to stroke it.

Olivia gave him a shove and told him to him to behave. But instead of behaving, Simon stretched himself out beside her on the yellow quilt.

'It's not morning,' she said hastily. 'Mrs Leigh will be serving dinner any minute.'

'So she will,' Simon agreed. 'Ankle still all right?'

'Yes, it's fine, but –'

'Good. Then to hell with dinner.' He reached up, put an arm around her waist and pulled her over on top of him. 'We've a lot of missed opportunities to make up for, Mrs Sebastian.' He gave her an anticipatory pat on the rear. 'Merry Christmas, sweetheart. It's time to get down to some serious business.'

When Mrs Leigh rang the dinner bell fifteen minutes later, and only Jamie appeared, she turned to Annie and said with approval, 'Better put it back in the oven. If you ask me, the honeymoon's just getting started. And about time too.'

Upstairs, beneath an unusually active bed, the Ripper was inclined to agree. Page ten had been consumed without interference, and page eleven awaited his disposal. He heaved a satisfied sigh, rested his head on his paws and added the gentle sound of canine snoring to the curious noises going on above his head.

EPILOGUE

The bells of St Mary's Church pealed across the countryside in joyful proclamation of the marriage of the latest in a long line of Sherraby brides. Not that Emma Colfax actually belonged to Sherraby but, as Simon's cousin, she had long ago been taken to the villagers' hearts.

It had been Emma's decision to celebrate the marriage at St Mary's in April, the month of daffodils and blossoms, because it was the church where so many of her ancestors had made their vows. And Sherraby was where she had met Zack.

For his part, Zack had been relieved. Morag would have said it was a disgraceful waste of money for all of them to fly to New York – even though the money was her brother's and he had more than enough of it to spare.

As he waited beside Simon at the altar with his hands locked firmly behind his back, he twisted to exchange a quick smile with Morag, standing tall and straight among his three brothers and five sisters in the front pew. It was the first time he had ever seen her in a hat – and pretty gloves that were neither practical nor warm. Of course she and the rest of the family would never admit that they were puffed with pride because their little brother was marrying an heiress from America who was the cousin of a Sebastian of Sherraby – but it was evident in the square set of Morag's shoulders, the cocky tilt of Catriona's chin and the way his brother, Iain, was lifting his eyebrows at Emma's old schoolfriend from the States.

Zack no longer paid attention to Emma's connections and prospects himself. They weren't important, because he had his own prospects. What *was* important was that he was about to pledge his hand in marriage to the woman he loved above all others.

When he had married Samantha it had been a hasty affair in front of a registrar, a mistake he had later sworn never to repeat. At that time he had seen marriage as a trap, one he didn't plan to fall into again.

Yet here he was, waiting to marry Emma Colfax, not in front of a registrar, it was true, but in front of the vicar and congregation of St Mary's.

The organ music changed from slow and soothing to the familiar chords announcing the approach of the bride. The muscles in Zack's shoulders tensed. He turned sideways – and saw the sprite who had haunted his dreams for eight years walking serenely down the aisle on the arm of her father. Her smile was so radiant he had to look away.

How sweet and desirable she looked, his pixie-faced Emma with the changeable eyes. They were green again today. He was surprised and touched to see that she was wearing only a plain white linen dress with a wreath of cherry blossoms wound into her hair. She, who could have chosen satins and silks or cloth of gold, had opted for what she knew he would like. A simple frock, and a quiet ceremony among family and friends . . .

'That's my mum!' A boyish voice jolted Zack from his fond contemplation of his bride as the wedding party neared the front of the church. 'She's going to have a baby. But not today.'

The congregation rustled and murmured its amusement. Annie Coote and Mrs Leigh said, 'Shh!' and someone who sounded like Simon's cousin Gerald growled quietly, but not quietly enough, 'Let's hope you're wrong on both counts, kid.'

Zack suppressed a grin as, briefly, his gaze shifted to the woman preceding Emma down the aisle.

Olivia, resplendent in red, appeared to have doubled in size since the last time he had seen her. Yet motherhood suited her. She looked tranquil, happy, and her gaze sought Simon's with a message of such tender affection that Zack immediately turned to look at Emma.

Was it possible she felt that way about him?

Their eyes met, and the organ music came to a sudden stop. Yes. It was possible. His answer was in the translucent glow that lit her face from within.

As Zack took his bride's small hand in his he thought his heart would very likely burst with the love he bore her.

How lucky he was that the love she had borne him for so many years had only been strengthened by his refusal to accept it.

'Wilt thou, Zachary Mark, have this Woman to thy wedded wife . . .'

Zack started, and turned guiltily to face the vicar. He, Zachary Mark Kent, was in the process of being married to Emma Marie Colfax. And he had been so lost in contemplation of his beloved that he hadn't noticed the service was up and running.

'. . . so long as ye both shall live?'

'I will,' Zack said. He might have lost his place in the service, but he knew the answer to that question.

'Wilt thou, Emma Marie, have this Man . . .'

'I will.' Emma's solemn response rang with sincerity.

Thank heaven she had agreed without argument to the words of the traditional marriage service. He had been afraid she would want some cooked-up modern vows complete with poetry composed by the groom. It was a good thing she hadn't. His lips quirked. Composition, especially of the poetic variety, had never been one of his talents.

'. . . and live together in holy love until your lives' end. Amen.'

Zack raised his head. In holy love. With Emma. It was over.

Except for the hymn singing, the signing of the register and the congratulations, it was over. For better or for worse, he was married to Emma Marie – Kent.

'You may now kiss the bride.'

At last. Needing no further invitation, Zack wrapped his arms around Emma and kissed her soundly on the mouth. He went on kissing her until the vicar cleared his throat, twice, and said, 'You may now *stop* kissing the bride, Mr Kent.'

Behind them, the congregation tittered. Except Morag, who exclaimed reprovingly, 'Zachary Mark!'

Taking his time about it, Zack released Emma from his arms and, holding her hand in his, followed the vicar into the vestry behind the alter. Simon and Olivia brought up the rear.

Zack glanced around without much interest. Brooms and cleaning supplies fought for space with the vicar's second-best vestments, a wicker chair and a pock-marked table bearing an important-looking leather-bound book that smelled of must. The marriage register, no doubt.

'Good luck, old friend.' Simon clapped him on the shoulder.

'Do you think I'm going to need it, then?' Zack asked.

'Mmm. Along with an extra helping of patience.'

Emma bristled, and punched her cousin on the arm. 'I like that! I'm the one who's going to need the patience if I'm going to cope with your bossy partner here.'

'I doubt it. From the look in your husband's eye, I'd say all you're going to need for the next while will be your birthday suit.' Simon flashed her an inflammatory grin.

Emma laughed and relaxed. 'I can live with that.'

'For a while, maybe,' Olivia put in, smiling. 'But just wait till you're in my condition. I swear to you, it's not a pretty sight.'

'I think it is,' said Simon, placing a proprietorial hand on his wife's bulging stomach.

'*When* did you say you're due?' Emma asked, eyeing the bulge with suspicion.

'Not for another month,' Olivia said glumly.

The vicar went into another paroxysm of throat-clearing, and the four of them got down to the solemn business of signing the register. As soon as the deed was done, Zack took Emma's arm, and said, 'Right. The whole line will now advance.'

Quickly suppressing their chuckles, and avoiding the vicar's repressive eye, they marched back into the church to the murmured approval of an expectant congregation. Seconds later the murmur was augmented by Jamie's voice, shrill with agitation, shrieking, 'Rip! Rip, I told you you had to stay *outside*. You weren't *invited*.'

The organist abandoned his efforts in a crash of groaning chords, and the wedding party came to a halt at the top of the steps leading down to the chancel.

A commotion was going on in the left pew second from the front. At one end Dr and Mrs Marfleet, both in smart suits, were edging into the side aisle. At the other end Jamie, seated between Annie and Simon's mother, was attempting to persuade a small brown and white dog with a length of rope trailing from its collar that it couldn't climb on to his knee and eat a hymn book.

Simon took in the situation at a glance, murmured, 'Excuse me,' to Olivia, and strode down the steps to scoop the Ripper up under one arm. Moments later, as the organ started up again, and the bride and groom completed their triumphant march down the aisle, he resumed his place beside his wife.

'I told Jamie the Ripper couldn't come,' she whispered. 'I don't see –'

'Chrissy,' Simon said tersely. 'I detect the hand of an accomplice in this.'

'Oh. Yes, I . . . Oh, dear . . .' Olivia winced.

Simon hoisted a squirming Ripper more securely beneath his arm. 'Don't worry. No damage done. The happy couple have other things on their minds. Besides . . .' He grinned. 'This must be the first time in the history of St Mary's that a dog has featured as an honoured guest at a Sherraby wedding.'

'And the last, I should think.' Olivia sounded unusually breathless.

'I wouldn't count on it. Jamie may be married here one day.'

Simon's grin broadened at the shocked expression on his wife's face. The prospect of Jamie, grown up and responsible, was evidently too much for her to grasp.

'Simon,' she said. 'I think . . .'

Something in her tone made him look at her more closely. That wasn't shock twisting her features into a grimace. It was pain.

'Olivia? What is it?' he asked sharply.

'I think I'm . . .' She staggered, and he grabbed her around her non-existent waist and pulled her out of the path of the crowd of guests streaming down the aisle behind them.

'What is it?' Simon repeated.

'I think I'm . . .' she put a hand to her stomach '. . . having the baby.'

'You can't be –'

'Oh, yes, I can,' Olivia groaned. 'Believe me, I've been here before.'

Fear, greater than any he had known in his days as a paid risk-taker, clutched Simon's heart in a paralytic grip. She wasn't due for a month. Something was wrong. No. No, it couldn't be, *mustn't* be . . . Because if anything happened to Olivia . . .

Stop it, Sebastian. Snap out of it. Simon forced the movement back into his limbs. Nothing's going to happen to her unless you stand here like a chunk of rock while she gives birth to your child right here on the back pew.

'It's all right,' he heard himself saying. 'It's all right, sweetheart. I'll take care of you.' Without allowing himself further time to think, he put the Ripper down, and lifted Olivia – all twenty stone of her? – against his chest. Then he swept her through the door, down the stone steps and onto the grass where the wedding guests were standing about in groups awaiting their turn to congratulate Zack and Emma.

'Mum!' Jamie came running up to them. 'Mum –'

'Find Dr Marfleet, Jamie,' Simon interrupted. 'Your mother is about to have a baby.'

'Oh,' Jamie said. 'Does that mean she won't have time to be cross about Rip.'

'Very probably. Jamie, I said –'

'I know. Get Dr Marfleet. OK. He's over there by the cherry tree, I think.' Jamie waved cheerily and trotted off across the grass. 'It's all right. My mum's just having a baby,' he shouted to Chrissy, who was standing by the fence. 'She won't have time to be mad.'

Vaguely, Simon was aware of heads turning in his direction, of Olivia's pain-stretched face gazing up at him with a trust he wasn't sure he deserved. Then Dr Marfleet was at his side, and Zack, and . . . Good God! even Gerald was helping him load Olivia on to the back seat of a large grey car.

It wasn't his car, but it didn't matter. Simon got in beside his wife and took her hand. As the door closed, his mother's voice said bracingly, 'Now, then. No need to look like a cod in parsley sauce, Simon. She's a perfectly healthy young woman.'

Simon knew Celia was right, but it didn't help. The drive to the manor seemed to take forever.

'Hospital,' Simon said as they pulled up outside the front door. 'Shouldn't she be –'

'She'll be all right,' Dr Marfleet assured him with crisp confidence. 'We'll call an ambulance if we need one, but just now we don't have time to waste.'

Simon closed his eyes. No time to waste? Did that mean . . .?

'Olivia,' he murmured. 'Olivia, don't . . .' He had been going to say, 'Don't die.' But he mustn't let her think of dying. Not now, when they'd had so little time together . . .

He felt her slip her hand into his. 'I won't,' she whispered. 'I'm going to have our baby now, Simon.'

And she did, only moments after they got her into the house.

Hours later it came to Simon that in all the confusion and dread he hadn't once thought about the survival of the baby whose hoped-for conception had been the reason for his marriage.

His fear had been all for Olivia. His beloved wife.

* * *

Olivia opened her eyes. It was an effort, because she wanted to go on sleeping. Yet her tiredness was a comfortable tiredness, peaceful and deeply contented. She was lying on her side, and the evening sun was streaming gold through the window. Gradually, as its rays began to warm her cheek, she absorbed the knowledge that something was different. She put a hand to her stomach. It was no longer quite such an overblown beach ball – and there was an old-fashioned wooden cradle beside the old-fashioned four-poster she shared with Simon.

Simon. Where was he? She reached a hand behind her, but he wasn't there.

'Olivia?' His voice came from somewhere above her, low, amused, infinitely dear. 'Olivia, I'm here.'

She wriggled on to her back. He was standing at the side of the bed holding a small white bundle in his arms. What was Simon doing with a baby?

'Olivia?' he said again.

Then she remembered.

The church, Jamie, the Ripper, the drive back to the manor with someone blasting away on a horn. Then being carried upstairs to the bed where generations of Sebastians had been born. After that everything had become more or less a blur. There had been confusion, pain, Simon's unnaturally white face – and Dr Marfleet doing efficient things with surgical gloves. It had all ended when something squalling pink and naked had been laid on her stomach, and the squalling had instantly ceased.

Someone, Dr Marfleet probably, had said, 'It's a girl.' Soon after that she had fallen asleep – but only to dream of Simon, who was standing beneath a canopy of trees laughing, and saying, 'Didn't Emma tell you there was magic in the Sherraby Woods?'

'The baby?' she said, pushing the dream memory away. 'Simon, is she . . .?'

'She's beautiful. Thank you, my darling.' He bent down and laid the tiny sleeping bundle beside her on the bed. Olivia gazed reverently at downy bronze hair and a puckered face that made her think of a walnut with lips.

Simon was right. She was amazingly beautiful.

Olivia held out her thumb, and the walnut grasped it in her fingers. Such small fingers. Like a doll's. She'd forgotten how small . . .

'Hello, little Ellen,' she whispered, awstruck, just as she had been at Jamie's birth by the miraculous perfection of her child.

Some time ago she and Simon had agreed that a boy would be called Martin after Simon's brother, and a girl after Olivia's sister, Ellen. Now, as she looked up at Simon almost shyly, she said, 'You're not – you don't mind, do you, that the heir of Sherraby isn't a boy?'

Simon shook his head, and if he hadn't spoken, his eyes would have answered for him. 'I would only mind if the heir of Sherraby were called Gerald,' he assured her solemnly. His lips parted in a smile. 'By the way, you should have seen my freeloading cousin's face when he thought you were about to give birth right there in front of him in the churchyard. He even helped me load you into the car.'

Olivia put a hand over her face. 'Oh, dear. Don't remind me. I didn't mean to spoil Zack and Emma's wedding . . .'

'You didn't. Zack said it was the perfect conclusion to the ceremony. He's become positively human since settling things with Emma. And *she* said she was sure Ellen's birth was a sign that she and Zack were destined to be blessed with a large family. Zack turned a bit green at that point.'

Olivia laughed. 'He'll feel differently when it happens. But what about the reception? Did –'

'It went ahead as scheduled. Swimmingly, in fact. Aunt Margaret started the floods. Then my mother joined in –'

'Your mother? She was crying?'

'Yes, believe it or not. That set Annie off, and pretty soon half the guests, including Gerald, were sniffing away too. It was a resounding success. Especially when –'

The rest of what Simon had been about to say was cut off by a tentative knock on the door.

'Come in,' he called.

Olivia turned her head in time to see Emma,

wearing a suit the colour of fresh lemon, bound into the room towing Zack behind her.

'Where is she? Oh! Oh, she's beautiful,' Emma cried, ignoring Olivia and gazing in rapt admiration at baby Ellen. 'She looks just like you, Simon.'

'I'm not sure I take that as a compliment,' Simon observed. But they could all tell from the proud beam in his eye that he didn't meant it.

'We're leaving for Florida in a few minutes,' Zack explained. 'Just came to say goodbye, and pay our respects to the newest Sebastian. We'll be back in time for her christening, of course.'

'I'm glad to hear it,' said Simon. 'I had horrible visions of running the office without a partner for the next year while you two spent all your time in the States working on the next generation of Kents.'

'It's a thought,' Zack said, grinning and giving Emma a proprietorial pat on her behind.

'One you can forget,' Simon said severely.

Zack glanced at his watch. 'Come on, Emma. We'll miss our flight.' He looped his arm around her waist, dropped a kiss on her nose, and drew her away from the bed.

'I never thought I'd see old Zack behaving like half of a pair of lovesick turtle-doves,' Simon commented, as the newlyweds waved goodbye from the door. 'I'm not sure it suits him.'

Olivia laughed. 'Of course it does. And you're a fine one to talk. Oh, Simon, I *am* so glad they found each other.'

'So am I.' Simon sat on the edge of the bed and draped his arm around her shoulders. 'But not nearly as glad as I am that I found you.'

In a little while he laid the baby gently in the old family cradle. Ellen stretched her arms and gave a little gurgle, but she didn't wake.

Olivia, certain that her heart was about to explode with love and pride, smiled up at Simon and held out her arms.

Jamie, sticking his head into the room several minutes later, turned to the Ripper and said disgustedly, 'The baby's still sleeping, Rip. I s'pose that's what girl babies do. And Mum and Simon are kissing. *Again.*' He thought for a moment, then bent to pat the Ripper's furry head. 'When I grow up I'm going to be a spy. Being married must be awful *boring*.'

Hearing him, Simon and Olivia pulled hastily apart. 'Do you find marriage boring, my love?' Simon asked.

Olivia shook her head. 'If it is,' she replied, 'I hope you're going to go on boring me for at least a hundred years.'

Jamie said, 'Yuck!' and went off with the Ripper to track down Mrs Leigh and chocolate biscuits.

THE EXCITING NEW NAME IN WOMEN'S FICTION!

PLEASE HELP ME TO HELP YOU!

Dear ***Scarlet*** Reader,

As Editor of ***Scarlet*** Books I want to make sure that the books I offer you every month are up to the high standards ***Scarlet*** readers expect. And to do that I need to know a little more about you and your reading likes and dislikes. So please spare a few minutes to fill in the short questionnaire on the following pages and send it to me. I'll send *you* a surprise gift as a thank you!*

Looking forward to hearing from you,

Sally Cooper

Editor-in-Chief, ***Scarlet***

*Offer applies only in the UK, only one offer per household.

Note: further offers which might be of interest may be sent to you by other, carefully selected, companies. If you do not want to receive them, please write to Robinson Publishing Ltd, 7 Kensington Church Court, London W8 4SP, UK.

QUESTIONNAIRE

Please tick the appropriate boxes to indicate your answers

1 Where did you get this Scarlet title?
Bought in supermarket ☐
Bought at my local bookstore ☐ Bought at chain bookstore ☐
Bought at book exchange or used bookstore ☐
Borrowed from a friend ☐
Other (please indicate) ____________________

2 Did you enjoy reading it?
A lot ☐ A little ☐ Not at all ☐

3 What did you particularly like about this book?
Believable characters ☐ Easy to read ☐
Good value for money ☐ Enjoyable locations ☐
Interesting story ☐ Modern setting ☐
Other ____________________

4 What did you particularly dislike about this book?
____

5 Would you buy another Scarlet book?
Yes ☐ No ☐

6 What other kinds of book do you enjoy reading?
Horror ☐ Puzzle books ☐ Historical fiction ☐
General fiction ☐ Crime/Detective ☐ Cookery ☐
Other (please indicate) ____________________

7 Which magazines do you enjoy reading?
1. ____________________
2. ____________________
3. ____________________

And now a little about you –

8 How old are you?
Under 25 ☐ 25–34 ☐ 35–44 ☐
45–54 ☐ 55–64 ☐ over 65 ☐

cont.

9 What is your marital status?

Single ☐ Married/living with partner ☐

Widowed ☐ Separated/divorced ☐

10 What is your current occupation?

Employed full-time ☐ Employed part-time ☐

Student ☐ Housewife full-time ☐

Unemployed ☐ Retired ☐

11 Do you have children? If so, how many and how old are they?

____

____

12 What is your annual household income?

under $15,000	☐	or	£10,000	☐
$15–25,000	☐	or	£10–20,000	☐
$25–35,000	☐	or	£20–30,000	☐
$35–50,000	☐	or	£30–40,000	☐
over $50,000	☐	or	£40,000	☐

Miss/Mrs/Ms ________________________

Address ____________________________

____

____

Thank you for completing this questionnaire. Now tear it out – put it in an envelope and send it before 30 July, 1997, to:

Sally Cooper, Editor-in-Chief

USA/Can. address
SCARLET c/o London Bridge
85 River Rock Drive
Suite 202
Buffalo
NY 14207
USA

UK address/No stamp required
SCARLET
FREEPOST LON 3335
LONDON W8 4BR
Please use block capitals for address

SHBRI/1/97